Katie, Bar the Door

Katie, Bar the Door

A NOVEL BY
RUTH HULL CHATLIEN

BOOKS BY RUTH HULL CHATLIEN

Katie, Bar the Door

Blood Moon: A Captive's Tale

The Ambitious Madame Bonaparte
AMIKA PRESS

Modern American Indian Leaders
MASON CREST PUBLISHERS

First Edition ISBN 13: 978-1-937484-93-4

AMIKA PRESS
466 Central AVE #23 Northfield IL 60093 847 920 8084
info@amikapress.com Available for purchase on amikapress.com

Edited by Jay Amberg. Cover photography by Dimitris Vetsikas and Demaerre. Author photography by Richard Mack. Book designed and typeset by Sarah Koz. Body in Garth Graphic, designed by Constance Blanchard & Renee LeWinter in 1979 from John Matt in the 1960s; digitized by Monotype in 1990. Titles in Poetica, designed by Robert Slimbach in 1992. Ornaments in Type Embellishments, designed by Colin Brignall & Michael Gills in 1993. Thanks to Nathan Matteson.

In memory of my brother Keith (1947–2020), who was the inspiration for Joe.

Katie, Bar the Door

(colloquial expression):
Take precautions;
trouble is coming.

Ritchie turned onto Washington Street and drove until we caught sight of a skinny copper-green cupola poking above treetops. Slowing the van, he braked in front of the county courthouse, a red-brick building with a huge portico and the cupola rising above it. My armpits broke out in a sweat. I felt as though I were being driven to a sentencing, not my wedding. My breathing grew fast and shallow, and I pressed a hand on my breastbone.

A horn behind us blared. Ritchie raised his hand, gave the driver the finger, then drove to the corner, and turned right. He found a parking lot in the block behind the courthouse and parked there. From this side, the building looked functional and less impressive.

Ritchie switched off the ignition and sat motionless. Wondering if he was as scared of marriage as I was, I decided to plead, *Let's go home.* Before I could, he said, "You wait here."

"What?" I turned toward him. He was staring at the building across the street and refusing to look at me. "Don't I have to come in too?"

Ritchie rubbed his chin. Usually, he was a good-looking guy with wavy mid-brown hair, dark liquid eyes, and a slightly pudgy face that tended toward an Elvis pout. That morning, however, his eyes were bloodshot from drinking too much beer the night before, and his lower face was covered with stubble. His features settled into a mulish expression that I'd seen him wear all our lives—ever since we were children playing together in his father's sun-dappled apple grove or wading in the creek at the back of my yard.

"I got to find out how much it costs, stuff like that." He shot me a sideways glance. "Maybe we should find a motel so we can clean up, come back tomorrow."

He was right that we didn't look like a bridal couple, both of us still wearing the clothes we'd run away in the day before. Instead of spending the night in a motel, he'd parked in a rest area and we slept in the back of the van. That is, once he'd gotten around to letting me sleep. Knowing exactly what lay ahead of me if I agreed to the motel suggestion, I balked. "You promised we'd get married today."

Ritchie gripped and ungripped the steering wheel. "Sure. If everything goes OK." He took the keys, climbed down from the van, and started toward the courthouse. Halting, he turned back, opened the driver's door, and leaned inside. "Look, Katie—"

"What?" I snapped.

His face shuttered. "Forget it." Shoving his hands in his pockets, he slouched across the parking lot, looking for all the world like a guy who would spend his life sweeping floors. *You're making a mistake,* a panicked voice within me screeched. *I don't care if you slept with him, you don't deserve to be tied to him forever.*

My right hand gripped the passenger door handle, and I peered through the side windows to see if there was anywhere I could run to ask for help—but all the buildings within sight looked anonymous and unwelcoming.

Anyway, where would I go? Even if I got to a phone and reached my mother, I wasn't sure she'd take me back. She had forbidden my relationship with Ritchie over a year ago after she caught us necking and told me that, in God's eyes, I was as guilty as if I'd slept with him. Defying her low opinion of me, I had clung stubbornly to my virginity until we ran away, surrendering it then only because of the promise that I'd be Mrs. Richard Pelletier in the morning—and because Ritchie's rage at being asked to wait one more day was too menacing to defy. Now that the deed was done, according to the stringent doctrines of my mother and my church, my only chance to redeem myself was to marry the partner of my lust.

Checking my watch, I saw that it was a little after 1:00. Ritchie came out of the building and paused near one of the plain columns in front of the glass doors. He lit a cigarette and then trudged toward the van.

He didn't even glance at me as he pulled himself into the driver's seat and started the ignition. "We can't get married. You're too young."

"But you said that in Kentucky—"

"I know what I said. Paul was wrong."

The panicky feeling came back as I exclaimed, "What are we going to do?"

Ritchie gave me a backhanded slap that sent me crashing into the window. "Shut up! How do you expect me to think with you bitching in my ear?"

Pain radiated through my skull. I inched as far away from him as possible, shifted my jaw to make sure it wasn't broken, and willed myself not to cry.

Ritchie took a deep drag on his cigarette and tossed it out the window. He shifted into reverse. "I got to get something to eat."

The café was paneled in light pine and decorated with autographed photos of country music stars. A blackboard listed fifteen kinds of "ho-made" pie, and a jukebox played Tammy Wynette.

I stared at my plate, which held a slab of meat loaf, a mound of mashed potatoes, and a spoonful of overcooked peas. The sight roiled my stomach, so I put down my fork and sipped water.

Ritchie gestured to the waitress. "Give me another pork chop sandwich and a refill on the Coke. And a slice of that pecan pie."

"Sure thing." The waitress, a thin, brassy blonde in a salmon uniform, frowned at my untouched plate. "How 'bout you, hon? Everything OK?"

"Fine."

As the waitress walked away, Ritchie belched and stretched his legs under the table until they touched mine. He opened a matchbook and used the cover to pick at his teeth. "Wonder how long it'll take to drive to California."

I stared at him. Did he think if he ignored the problem I'd forget about it? If so, he had another think coming, as Grandma would say. "We should find a public library first."

"What the hell for?"

"To find out where we can get married."

Ritchie leaned across the table. After two days in that dark blue T-shirt, he stank. "There ain't no place."

"You don't know that. We have to check."

"I know." With an air of finality, he sat back and took out a cigarette.

Looking at his face, dark with unshaved whiskers, I felt a rush of hatred. "Yesterday you swore we could get married. Or was that a lie?"

"If you're calling me a liar, I'm going to have to learn you a lesson."

"Is hitting the only way you can win an argument?" I fell silent as the waitress brought Ritchie's food. Once she left us, I asked, "How'd you find this out anyway?"

After biting into the sandwich, Ritchie wiped his mouth with a crumpled paper napkin. "The courthouse lady went in back to look it up."

"You weren't gone long enough."

He narrowed his eyes. "I swear to God, you call me a liar once more, I'm going to belt you."

The threat froze me; we were hundreds of miles from home, and I had no place to run if he turned on me. "I'm sorry. I'm just upset. We have to get married."

"So maybe we'll get married when you're eighteen."

In spite of my fear, I pushed back. "That's a year from now. Can you wait that long?"

"Huh?" He paused with his sandwich poised in the air. "What's that mean?"

I crossed my arms over my chest. "No wedding, no sex."

"Come on, Katie. That's not fair. You already did it once."

"Only because you promised we'd get married today."

"Shit." Ritchie leaned forward. "Listen, you ain't got nothing to save anymore. You're just like the rest of us now, baby."

He reached for my hand. The moment I felt his touch, a terrible certainty gripped me. "You never intended to get married, did you? You lied to get me to do it."

His eyes flashed. Squeezing my hand till it hurt, he said, "I told you. The guy at the courthouse looked it up for me."

I jerked free. "You said it was a woman."

"No, I didn't."

"Yes, you did. Don't you even care enough to keep your story straight?"

"Shit." He rubbed his mouth. Then he pulled his pie in front of him and began to eat it.

My stomach churned, and my scalp tingled as if jolted with electricity. "How could you do this? You said you loved me."

Ritchie spoke with a full mouth. "You been making me wait all these years. That ain't much like love."

"Then it's true. You really said it to trick me."

He shrugged. "You got this hang-up about sex, so I thought you should get it over with."

Horrified, I pushed back my chair. "I'm going to the washroom."

As I entered the bathroom, the powerful scent of pine disinfectant sickened me. I vomited into the nearest toilet, then rinsed out my mouth, and stared in the mirror. Except for bruising on my cheek, there was no sign of what I had been through. No one could look at me and see that I was damned.

Taking a deep breath, I returned to the dining room. Ritchie's chair was empty, and the waitress was piling our dishes in a beige plastic bin. "Here's the check, hon." She held it out to me. "Pay up front."

I took it and glanced around. "Where's my boyfriend?"

"He left."

"No!"

As I hiked up my purse strap and ran toward the door, the waitress shouted, "Hey, girl. You better pay!"

I jerked to a stop, returned to the cash register, and fumbled with my wallet. The cashier was so slow I wanted to scream. By the time I ran outside, I was almost hyperventilating. What I saw stopped my breathing altogether. The van was gone. Next to the space it had occupied was my suitcase, standing on the curb like a hitchhiker.

PART ONE

Daddy's Girl

JUNE 1965–
AUGUST 1979

"*Daddy,* guess what I found!"

Joe Thompson looked up from the concrete he was mixing in his dinged-up blue wheelbarrow and smiled across the back yard at his five-year-old daughter. "What?"

As Katie skipped toward him, her long black braid bounced against her back. "A feather." She stopped next to him and held it out for inspection. It was brown-black, probably from a robin.

"What're you going to do with it?"

"I don't know." Katie stared at her treasure with a face as solemn as a judge deciding on a sentence. As she pondered, she rubbed one dirty foot on top of the other. Then her face lit up. "I could find some more and make a fan."

"A fan? Of feathers?" Joe wiped sweat from his forehead with the back of his hand. Years ago, he'd gone to a state fair out west, where he saw Sally Rand perform her famous nude dance behind two huge, ever-shifting sweeps of ostrich plumes—not an image he wanted to associate with his little girl. "I don't think that will work."

"Yes, it will." She nodded for emphasis. "I saw it on TV. A lady went to a party in a long dress and carried a fan made out of white feathers."

"Oh." Joe cleared his throat, embarrassed by his assumption. "I see. But you'll need more than one."

"I know." Katie twirled the feather. "Can I go to the grove? Me and Ritchie most always find feathers there."

"No. You know you're not supposed to walk down the road by yourself. Look around our yard. I'll be done here in a few minutes, and then I'll help."

Joe and his wife owned a two-bedroom, ranch-style house in Moneka, a tiny hamlet of nine houses and a small grocery store ten miles east of Zebulun, Illinois, the county seat where they'd grown up. They lived on Sunset Road just north of the Pelletier farm, which bordered the main highway. The grove Katie referred to was more than a quarter mile away.

Sighing at the unreasonableness of grown-ups, Katie wandered away. Joe stirred the concrete one last time and scooped it into each of the holes he'd dug to anchor the legs of Katie's swing set, bought for her birthday last week. When he was done, he cleaned the wheelbarrow and washed his hands. Then he looked around for his daughter. She was nowhere to be seen.

Joe walked to the back edge of their lot and glanced down at the stone-littered shallow creek flowing there. No Katie. Then he headed to the front yard, where he found her sitting on the concrete stoop, holding her chin in her hand. "I couldn't find any."

He sat next to her. "That's OK. You can keep this one until you collect enough."

Katie scowled and used her big toe to rub out an anthill in the crack of the sidewalk. Joe covered his mouth to hide the grin at what he called her "Marietta look"—she could be as stubborn as her mother. He thought a moment and said, "I know what else we could use it for. I could be Robin Hood; he wore a cap with a feather in it."

She threw him a suspicious look. "Who's he?"

"He lived a long time ago in a country ruled by a bad king who wanted to make himself and his friends rich and didn't care if poor people starved."

Katie's blue-grey eyes widened. "What happened?"

"Well, Robin Hood was a nobleman." She drew her dark brows together, so Joe explained, "That means he ruled a piece of land that was a part of the kingdom. He was supposed to fight for the king, and the farmers on his land were supposed to obey him."

"Oh." Katie watched him carefully. "Was Robin a bad man too?"

"No, he wanted everyone to have enough money and enough food. But the king didn't like that idea. So Robin Hood became an outlaw and hid in the forest with a group of friends." Joe stopped abruptly as he realized that Marietta wouldn't like his telling Katie a story where a thief was the hero. "Um, so, whenever anyone came by who had robbed the poor, Robin Hood and his men took the stolen money to give back to the people it belonged to."

"Oh!" Katie breathed out the word in an ecstasy of satisfaction and extended her feather to him. "You can have this. Want me to get your hat?"

"No, I have to make a special one." Joe stood, walked the few steps to the garage door, pulled it up, and took a newspaper off the stack he stored against the inside wall. Extracting a single sheet, he folded it into a triangular hat with an upturned brim. "Imagine this is made out of green felt instead of paper." He poked in the feather so it stuck out at a jaunty angle over the back. Then he put the hat on and turned his head side to side. "What do you think?"

She squealed with laughter. "It's crooked!"

Joe squatted down. "Fix it."

As Katie adjusted his hat, she said, "Mommy says the sun makes your hair yellow."

"Blond," he said automatically. "Yeah, it gets lighter every summer."

Satisfied with the hat's position, she stepped back. "I want my hair to get yellow too."

"Katydid, the sun can't make black hair turn blond."

"Oh." Her lip quivered.

"Your hair is so pretty. Why do you want to change it?"

Her eyes glittered with unshed tears. "I don't know."

"Well, I like you the way you are." He pulled off the paper hat and handed it to her. "Why don't you put this on?"

Katie shook her head. "It's a boy's hat. Robin Hood is a boy."

Joe started to argue but then decided it would be safer to change the subject. "Let's go look at your swing." He reached for her hand.

As they walked to the back yard, he gazed down at her. Although Marietta pooh-poohed him, Joe was certain that Katie was going to be a beauty. She had inherited Marietta's white skin and black hair, and his own grey-blue eyes, straight nose, and high cheekbones. Her features were too stark to be considered pretty now, but she'd grow into them—and when she did, she would be a knockout.

For now, she was young enough to care more about toys than her appearance. When they rounded the corner of the house and Katie saw the swing set, erected on the far side of the yard between the patio and her mother's small vegetable patch, she ran ahead to stroke its gleaming green paint reverently. "Can I play on it?"

"Not till the concrete dries. Maybe tomorrow."

The light in her face dimmed, and she stared at the ground. Then she looked up and gave him her most coaxing smile. "Can I sit on it? I won't move."

Joe laughed. "Sure. I'll sit next to you."

As he lowered himself onto a swing, he congratulated himself for having finished another project. The place was finally starting to look the way he wanted. Last year, he'd poured a concrete patio along the back of the house, and later this summer, he planned to build a brick grill on its southeast corner. The weeping willow he'd planted by the creek their first spring here was now almost twenty feet tall, and the row of lilac bushes edging the north property line were mature enough to bloom in profusion. Marietta wanted a honeysuckle hedge on the opposite side of the yard, but Joe liked to stare across the gently rippling green sea of Pelletiers' soybean field, so he was putting that off for now.

Sometimes, he had to laugh at himself. Years ago, when he worked as an over-the-road truck driver—during the bad years after Marietta refused to marry an unbeliever like him—he scoffed at guys who settled down. But it had all worked out in the end. After four years apart, he swallowed his pride enough to come home and propose a second time, and Marietta climbed down off her Baptist high horse and admitted she'd never gotten over him. Lord knows, their marriage wasn't perfect, but they belonged together. Of that, Joe was certain.

Now they had this extraordinary child. Turning to Katie, he noticed her rocking her heels enough to move her swing in a shallow arc. He smiled at the slight rebellion; in that, she was all his. When Katie saw him watching, she put on the paper hat. "Tell me a story about Robin Hood."

"He was the greatest archer in all of England. An archer is someone who shoots a bow and arrow. One time—"

The back screen door creaked, and Joe turned to see Marietta step out onto the patio. She was short and, at thirty-one, curvier than she'd been in high school. Today she was wearing the red-checked dress he thought made her look Italian. As she came toward them, Joe let out a wolf whistle.

"Hush! Is the swing done? It's time to eat." Marietta frowned when she saw her daughter up close. "Look how dirty you are. Joe, you said you'd watch her."

"I did. She doesn't have any concrete on her, does she?"

"No, but..." Grimacing, Marietta pulled Katie to her feet and looked her up and down. She pulled off the hat and tossed it aside. "Go wash your face and hands. And use soap."

Joe caught Marietta's arm as she turned to follow Katie inside. "Not so fast. I deserve a kiss for a job well done." After glancing at the door to make sure Katie was out of sight, Marietta pecked his cheek.

Then Joe followed her across the patio, through the back door, up the four steps at the right, and into the kitchen. The room was furnished with light birch cabinets against aqua walls, gold-flecked white laminate countertops, and an aqua-and-white checkerboard linoleum floor.

"Guess what Katie asked me today."

"What?" Marietta crossed to the stove and turned the fire on under her hot salad dressing.

He leaned in the doorway. "She wanted to know if the sun would make her hair yellow like mine. Don't you think that's pretty smart?"

Marietta, who was sprinkling crisp bacon pieces on a salad of fresh leaf lettuce, froze and then dumped the whole bowl of bacon. "Katie, hurry up!"

Surprised by her sharp tone, Joe said, "What I mean is, she's try ing to reason things out. That seems pretty advanced for her age."

Marietta didn't answer. She poured the dressing on the lettuce and tossed it with jerky motions.

Shaking his head, Joe went into the living room to find his childhood copy of *Robin Hood* with the N.C. Wyeth illustrations. He carried it to Katie, who had taken her seat at the wooden kitchen table. Joe pushed away her place setting, set the book in its place, and opened it to the painting that showed Robin's first meeting with Maid Marian, a red-cheeked lass with long black hair. "Look, Katydid. That blond man is Robin Hood, and the lady with the dark hair is Maid Marian. Isn't she pretty?"

As Katie regarded the picture, her tongue touched her upper lip. Then she slid a glance toward her mother. Joe looked too and saw that Marietta was white with anger. "Let's put the book on the counter. I can read you some of it before bed."

After supper, when Joe returned from settling Katie in the bathtub, he found Marietta leaning over the sink. The water was running, but she wasn't washing dishes. "Mare, what is it?" he asked, hugging her from behind.

"Nothing." She remained rigid in his arms.

With an impatient sigh, he pulled away and poured himself a cup of coffee. "Don't give me that. You've been pissed off since before supper."

"I'm not angry." It was hard to tell over the sound of the running water, but Joe thought her voice sounded thick with tears.

"Then you're unhappy. What is it?"

Marietta turned off the water and scrubbed one of the flowered plates. "You think it's cute that Katie would rather look like you than me."

He pulled her around to face him. "Mare, it's not a contest."

Her dark eyes flashed. "Yes, it is. Maybe you don't do it on purpose, but you're the one she has fun with, and I make all the rules."

"Then lighten up. Stop expecting her to be so damn perfect."

She turned away to rinse the dishes.

"It's just a phase," Joe said. "Next month, she'll be clomping down the hall in your high heels."

When Marietta didn't reply, Joe shook his head. "I'll tell Katie to finish her bath."

Marietta poured herself some lemonade and sat at the kitchen table to take a break from cleaning. Katie was outside playing with seven-year-old Ritchie from down the road. A childish yell drifted through the back window, the sound distorted by the revolving blades of the fan.

The white eyelet curtains looked limp and dingy again. They needed to be washed so often in summer when the windows were kept open. Marietta thought that, maybe instead of laundering them, she'd run up a new set on the sewing machine. A turquoise-flowered print to go with the floral sprays on their plates. She wouldn't mind an extra pop of color in the room. When they signed the contract to have the house built, Joe had suggested they order turquoise appliances, but Marietta couldn't see paying extra for a trendy hue that they'd probably grow tired of long before the appliances broke down.

Using her apron to wipe sweat from her forehead, she wondered if they could afford to buy a small air conditioner on the installment plan. It would be nice to put one in their bedroom and get a decent night's sleep.

Or maybe, we could save our money and take a vacation. They'd never gone on a honeymoon. During high school, Joe used to spin stories about how he was going to take her away from Zebulun. They'd stroll over to Riverview Park, eating Dairy Queen ice cream cones and slapping at mosquitoes while Joe talked about the deserts and mountains and historical monuments he wanted to show her.

One evening, they were walking among fragrant roses in the park at twilight while Joe described the grand resort hotel that stood there in the 1800s. It had burned near the end of the century in what was rumored to be an act of arson committed by hooligans from a rival town. Nothing remained of the three-story wooden structure with its wide veranda and corner turrets, but the bandstand and formal rose garden had survived to become beloved Zebulun landmarks.

After their ice cream was gone, Joe and Marietta meandered to the river. He climbed onto a recently toppled tree, its roots wrenched from the ground, its crown submerged in the slow-moving water. Holding his arms out for balance, he walked the length of the trunk. "Know what I'm going to do? Come back with my old man's tools, saw this tree into planks, and build a raft. Then I'll kidnap you. We'll float down the Theakia till it joins the Illinois, then go down the Mississippi to the Gulf of Mexico."

Marietta laughed. "You've been reading too much Huck Finn."

Joe had run back along the trunk and jumped down beside her. "See what I mean? You'd never go if I didn't kidnap you."

Sipping lemonade in her kitchen now, Marietta thought, *We could go to New Orleans,* and smiled to think how happy the suggestion would make him.

The front door slammed, and she bit back the automatic urge to yell at Katie. Then Joe came through the kitchen doorway.

"You're early." She went over to kiss him, then drew back. He smelled like beer, and his jaw was set in a pugnacious expression. "You quit your job again."

After taking her glass of lemonade and gulping it down, he pulled out a chair and sat, his long legs sprawled in the middle of the floor, his scuffed work boots looking rough against her spotless pastel linoleum. He raked back his dark blond hair. "I told you Conover's been getting on my back."

Marietta shut her eyes and swallowed her bitter disappointment that the dream of a belated honeymoon was already out of reach. Her voice cracked as she said, "Joe, this makes six times since we've been married."

"Are you going to listen to me or not?"

Dropping into her chair, she crossed her arms and glared at him.

"He sent me into a stinking hot attic to fix an exhaust fan that's been busted for a week. I was up there two hours, sweating like a pig. When I came back down, I forgot to button my shirt before going into the plant, and he put me on report."

Grudgingly, Marietta felt her anger shift to Joe's boss. "I'm sorry. But couldn't you talk to Mr. McDonnell?"

"You kidding? If I went over Conover's head, he'd make my life hell."

As Marietta stared at Joe's defiant face, she saw he'd convinced himself he had no choice. He never saw a choice. He'd quit rather than put up with the petty indignities most people accepted as part of working life.

When they bought the house, he had promised he would keep a job—a promise he repeated five years ago when Katie was born and again the last time he quit. Marietta bit her lip. "What'll we do if we can't make the house payment?"

"Fuck, is that all you care about? Fine, I'll call Conover tomorrow and tell him my wife likes me to work in a hot box."

Marietta gave him the hard stare she used when Katie was being melodramatic. "I just don't see why every job turns out this way."

After returning her glare a moment, Joe glanced down and shrugged. "Too much of a maverick, I guess. Thought that's why you love me."

She leaned forward to touch his arm. "I do love you, Joe, but I don't want to lose our home. I think we can make one more payment, but then what?"

He grimaced. "If I have to, I'll go back to driving a truck. It's been nine years, but—"

"No!" Marietta gripped his hand. "I couldn't bear for you to go away again. I'd rather do anything else, even go to work myself. Promise me you won't do that."

He shook his head. "I won't promise. Not if it comes down to losing the house."

Marietta rose, walked away, and opened the cabinet next to the stove. Joe came up behind her. "If I did go, it wouldn't be forever. Only a week at a time."

Lifting up a stack of pots, Marietta pulled out the skillet underneath. "Go tell Katie to come in now."

The aroma of frying burgers and the sound of popping grease filled the kitchen by the time Katie came through the door that led to the basement and back entrance. Mud streaked her face, and her loose hair was a mass of tangles. "Kathleen Louise, what have you been doing?"

"Playing Robin Hood."

After turning off the burner, Marietta moved closer and found leaves snarled in Katie's hair. "Why did you undo your braid? It's a mess."

Katie's face grew stubborn. She shrugged.

"I ought to spank you with a hairbrush to teach you a lesson."

"Mare, that's enough!" Joe said as he came up the back steps.

Marietta turned on him. "That's easy for you to say. You're the one insists I keep her hair long, but I don't see you combing it out twice a day."

"I said that's enough." Pushing past her, Joe squatted before Katie. "I want a straight answer. Why did you unbraid your hair?"

She stalled a moment before saying, "We were playing Robin Hood, Daddy, and I was Maid Marian. I wanted to look like that picture."

Marietta saw him start. "You mean the one I showed you?"

Katie nodded, and Joe patted her arm. "Go wash your face and hands. And wait for me in the bathroom."

As she left, he stood and faced Marietta. "I'll comb out her hair."

"You do that."

Joe's chin jerked up. "Marietta, I'm only going to tell you this once. If you're mad at me, be mad at me. But don't ever take it out on her." He stalked from the room.

Marietta grabbed a stack of plates and slapped them on the table, grateful that they were Melmac so she could vent her anger without breaking one. Time was, Joe's first response had been to defend her. Now, he always sided with Katie.

Picking a stray piece of paper off the floor, she crumpled it and stared at her fist. If that hairbrush had been close to hand, she'd have swatted Katie with it. And then hated herself.

As though her very thoughts were weapons, she heard her daughter cry, "Ow!" Impelled by the urgent need to protect her child, Marietta rushed through the living room and down the hall to the bedrooms, stopping outside the open bathroom door at the end. Katie wailed again. "That hurts!"

Joe was tugging a comb through a snag near the crown of Katie's head.

"Let me," Marietta said and took the fine-toothed, rattail comb from his hand. "This is the wrong one. It pulls on her hair too much."

She reached into the drawer for her wide-toothed comb. Lifting the ends of Katie's hair, she combed out the bottom two inches. "You have to start down here. Otherwise, you push tangle onto tangle and make it worse."

Marietta turned Katie to face her. "I'm sorry I yelled at you in the kitchen, honey. I didn't mean it."

"That's OK," Katie mumbled.

Joe spoke up. "Don't you have something to tell your mother?"

Katie shot him a defiant look over Marietta's shoulder, then hung her head in response to a gesture Marietta couldn't see. "I'm sorry."

Lifting Katie's chin, Marietta observed her sullen expression. *What good does making her apologize do if she ends up resenting me?*

She turned Katie around again and continued to comb out the tangles. When they were gone, Marietta parted Katie's hair down the middle and suddenly thought of a compromise. "Joe, do you still have that copy of *Ivanhoe* you loaned me in high school?"

"Sure. Why?" He looked and saw Marietta swiftly plaiting Katie's hair into two braids instead of one. "Oh, yeah. I'll go get it."

Minutes later, he returned with another of his treasured classics. After finding the picture he wanted, a black-and-white illustration of a woman in medieval dress with two long braids, he showed it to Katie. "Look at this. Another book about Robin Hood, and this picture is a lady called Rowena. Would you like to wear your hair like hers?"

"Mommy won't let me."

"Yes, I will." Marietta held up a hand mirror. "See."

As Katie gazed at her reflection, her eyes grew wide.

"If I let you wear your hair like this, you have to leave the braids in. OK?"

Katie nodded eagerly.

Joe shut the book with a snap. "Good. Now that's settled, let's go eat."

"Yay!" Katie shouted and went skipping toward the kitchen.

Joe put his arm around Marietta. "You're brilliant, you know that?"

A *cricket* chirped outside my open bedroom window. At least, my five-year-old self hoped it was outside. It sounded awfully loud. What if the bug was in my room and jumped on my face with its raspy legs? Ritchie put a cricket down the back of my sunsuit once, and I hated the way it scratched my skin.

The memory made me shiver, and I wished it wasn't dark. A lamp stood on the nightstand, but Mom would yell at me if I fell asleep with it on. She always got upset when I wasted things—when I didn't eat all my food or left the water running as I brushed my teeth. I tried hard to remember not to throw good things away, but I didn't understand how anyone could waste light or that thing called electricity nobody could see.

When the chirping grew louder, I sat up and turned on the lamp. Next to it stood the Indian doll I had named Sacajawea after a story Daddy told me. I picked her up and stroked the red and blue beads on the fringe. More than anything, I wanted a dress like that. I lay down holding the doll and then remembered my mother's rule: "You can't sleep with your doll. You'll ruin it if you do."

Sighing, I put Sacajawea back in her place and wished for something else I could hug. I didn't have any other dolls because I thought most of them were dumb, and Mom wouldn't let me have stuffed animals because she said they got too dirty and couldn't be washed. The shelves on the wall next to the front window held books and a few plastic horses, but those were no fun to cuddle. Then I spotted my old daisy-flowered baby blanket on the back of the rocking chair by the window. I hurried over to grab it and, hugging the blanket to my chest, jumped back in bed just in case something was hiding underneath it.

As I wiggled around to get comfortable, I felt the urge to pee. Going to the bathroom meant walking alone into the black hallway, and

I didn't want to do that. Although I wouldn't have admitted it for anything in the world, I was afraid of the dark. I huddled under my sheet, squeezed my eyes shut, and tried to fall asleep. The burning sensation grew stronger.

Tossing my blanket aside, I crossed my room and stood in my bedroom doorway; the bathroom was to my left, and my parents' room was directly across the hall. I scooted into the bathroom and "took care of business" as Mom would say. When I came out, I noticed that up ahead, on the left, was the glow of a light. I thought I heard music.

That meant Daddy left the radio on. We'd been listening to country music after supper as he showed me his little toy soldier. "I'm going to paint hundreds of these and then build a model of Gettysburg. You remember, the fight your great-great-grandfather was in."

I'd nodded. "Great-great-grandpa Joe."

Now, I was sure music was playing in the kitchen. Mom was going to get really mad that we left the radio *and* light on. *I should sneak down there and turn them off.*

Holding my breath, I took three steps down the hallway and froze. I hurried back to my room and pushed the door all the way open so the glow from my small lamp would light part of the hall. Then I crept along close to the wall.

When I reached the end of the short hallway, I stared into the living room. About halfway along the left wall was the yellow rectangle of the kitchen doorway. Past it, I could see the edge of Great-grandpa's rolltop desk. Most of the rest of the living room was a mass of strange shadows, although I could make out the backs of the matching rose armchairs that faced the front picture window. Against the shade covering that window was a humped shaped that had to be the couch.

Standing this close to the kitchen, I definitely heard music playing. Then the floor creaked. Someone was in there! What if it was burglars, dressed in masks and knit caps, stealing Mom's silverware like on TV?

I glanced behind me to the closed door of my parents' bedroom. Maybe I should go get Daddy. But then he would find out I was afraid.

For a long time, I couldn't move. Finally, I bit my lip, held my breath, and took one step forward.

All I could hear was that song about the king of the road. Whoever was in the kitchen was keeping quiet. Maybe they were waiting by the doorway, ready to hit me with a skillet when I walked in the room. I wanted to go back to bed, but then I remembered Daddy's stories about brave people like Great-great-grandpa Joe. I took a step and breathed out slowly. Two more steps. I tried to stay in shadow as I stretched my neck to peek through the doorway.

My parents were in the kitchen. I was so surprised to see them there in the middle of the night, I couldn't say anything. Mom was wearing her pale blue nightie, the one with puffed sleeves and pink embroidered rosebuds. A new song started on the radio, sung by a woman with a loud, sad voice. Daddy put his arms around Mom, who rested her head on his bare chest. They were moving so slowly that it took me a moment to realize that they were dancing!

Sometimes when Daddy came home from work, he turned the radio on and asked me if I wanted to dance. He would pick me up, wait until I wrapped my legs around his waist, and then twirl me around the room. Mother always frowned at us like she thought dancing was bad.

The song on the radio ended, but my mother sang the last line again in a husky voice that was very different from the way she sang in the church choir. The words were something about being crazy for loving Daddy. Laughing, he bent down and kissed her. Then he moved his hands down her back and squeezed her butt. I'd never seen him do such a thing. My mother seemed to like it because she giggled and kissed him again.

Feeling hot and prickly, I sneaked back to my room. My throat felt like I'd swallowed too big a piece of something. Dancing wasn't bad after all—Mother just wanted to keep it to herself, something she got to do with Daddy and I didn't.

I climbed into bed and turned out the light. A little while later, my parents walked down the hall toward their bedroom. As they passed my door, my mother whispered, "Shhh. We'll wake her up."

Turning over, I pulled my pillow on top of my head so I couldn't hear.

Joe stood up and arched his back to stretch out muscles sore from bending over his model. A few minutes earlier, he'd heard footsteps upstairs, which signaled that Mare and Katie were back from church, so he was going to have to quit soon and go up for Sunday dinner. He'd been smelling the aroma of roasting pork for the last two hours.

The basement where he was working was a single large room with wood paneling and forest green linoleum. A washer and dryer stood against the wall that hid the staircase, and on the far wall was a grey metal workbench and a pea green couch over which hung framed photographs of Abraham Lincoln and a bearded Union soldier. In the center of the long room, sheets of plywood were nailed to trestles to form a fifteen-foot-square table on which he was constructing his model. Joe and Marietta had never used the basement for much except storage and laundry until he got the idea to replicate the skirmish that opened the three-day battle of Gettysburg.

All morning, he'd been using wooden slats and chicken wire to build the framework of a ridge of land. As he leaned forward to reshape a too-sharp undulation in the wire, he heard the quick staccato of his daughter running down the stairs.

"Hey, Katydid," he said when she rushed into the basement. He lifted her up and balanced her against his hip. "Come to tell me your memory verse?"

"Uh huh," she said, rubbing a paint stain on his white T-shirt. "In the beginning, God created the heavens and the earth."

"That's a long one!" Joe said, glad to find something positive to say. He didn't like it that the Sunday school teacher was making five-year-old children memorize the Bible like a rule book, but he had promised Marietta not to interfere with Katie's religious upbringing.

Katie grinned at his praise, and Joe kissed her forehead, delighted to see how proud she was of herself.

"Guess what?" he said. "I've been working on the ridge, and it's almost ready to plaster."

He set her on a stool near the model and watched her expectant smile disappear when she saw only bare wood and wire. "When will it be done?"

Joe laughed and tugged her braid, the single braid Katie had decided to go back to when she started kindergarten.

"This is just a frame." He pointed at the chicken wire. "I have to make a second, smaller ridge here. Then I have to cover both of them with cloth dipped in plaster of Paris, glue down green-dyed sawdust for grass, and use rock chips to build stone walls. And build a farmhouse and paint lots more soldiers and horses. You'll be old enough to help before I'm through."

She turned to stare at the twenty-five one-inch-high, painted soldiers lined up on a shelf. "I thought you were done with the little men."

"No, I need hundreds." Joe walked to his workbench, counted out a hundred nails into a shoebox top, and carried them back to her. "I need at least five times this many." Then he waved toward the table. "There will be several hundred Confederates sweeping down that ridge over there. And a smaller force of Union soldiers hunkered down over here."

Although Katie looked to where he gestured, she clearly couldn't picture the scene that Joe envisioned in his head. "That's a lot."

Joe patted her on the back. "It's bigger than you can imagine, honey. This is a tiny part of the battle. Someday, we're going to drive to Pennsylvania and visit the battleground so you can see how huge it all was. This was the turning point of the whole war. And your great-great-grandfather was part of it."

That brought the smile back to her face. "He was very brave, wasn't he, Daddy? Just like the knights in my storybooks."

"I suppose he was," Joe answered, amused by the comparison.

Marietta called them to dinner. Joe set his daughter down, and as they headed toward the stairs, Katie took his hand. "Someday I'm going to help. You promised."

Marietta waited outside Katie's door as Joe told their daughter a bedtime story: "The Twelfth Illinois Cavalry was commanded by Major General John Buford. Do you remember I told you what cavalry are?"

"Uh huh. They ride horses."

"That's right. Only sometimes, they had to get down and fight. When Buford ran into Confederates west of Gettysburg, he told his men to dismount and form a defensive line. Your great-great-grandpa was one of them."

Out in the hall, Marietta frowned at Joe's choice of subject.

"Early in the fighting, a bullet shattered his shinbone. He used to say it felt like a rocket exploded in his leg and sent pain shooting all the way up inside his teeth. But he didn't budge till Reynolds's men came to relieve him. A doctor had to cut off his lower leg, and he wore a wooden one for the rest of his life."

Bustling into the room, Marietta said, "Finished? It's getting late."

Joe grinned from where he sat on the edge of Katie's bed. "Yeah, that about wraps it up." He kissed Katie good-night.

Once he'd left, Marietta scrutinized Katie's face to see if the story had upset her. Marietta worried about her daughter; Katie wasn't like any other little girl she knew, not like herself at that age nor any of her younger sisters. After listening to Joe's story, the child wore a satisfied expression that was more disturbing to her mother than fear would have been. Marietta wanted to probe her feelings but didn't know how. Instead, she announced, "Time to say your prayers."

Katie said in sing-song, "Now I lay me down to sleep, I pray the Lord my soul to keep. If I should die before I wake, I pray the Lord my soul to take."

Marietta pulled the lavender chenille bedspread up to her daughter's chin and kissed her forehead. After another long look to make sure Katie wasn't upset, Marietta went to the kitchen where Joe sat sketching a farmhouse for his model. She sat down at the table, kitty-corner from him. "Do you think you should tell her war stories right before bed? What if she has nightmares?"

Joe's head jerked up. "She's heard that story lots of times."

"But it seems unnatural for a girl to enjoy hearing about bullet wounds."

Laying his pencil atop the drawing paper, Joe said, "All kids like grisly stuff. Besides, I tell her those stories to teach her history. She's real smart. I mean for her to have the education we both missed."

"That would be good," Marietta conceded. When she was in high school, she had wanted to study music at the Baptist college in Zebulun, so after she and Joe broke up, she worked as a grocery store clerk to earn money for tuition. Then her parents refused to pay for her favorite sister to attend college in Indiana, where her boyfriend from church camp was going. Marietta had sacrificed her own dream and used her savings to make Dee's dream possible.

"I don't mind you teaching Katie history," Marietta said. "But that story is so violent. And she's only five."

Joe pulled Marietta out of her chair and into his arms. "Don't look so glum. There's more to life than worrying about Katie. This winter, let's leave her with your folks and go down to Florida for a week, stay at my uncle's motel."

"It's not that easy."

"Sure, it is," he whispered in her ear. "All we have to do is go."

Marietta clung to him. Whenever they quarreled, she feared that Joe would pack up and hit the road as he had so many years before. Sometimes, she had the horrible suspicion that Katie was the only reason he stayed. "Florida's not important. All I ever wanted is to be with you."

He laughed. "You got me. That was an easy wish to fill."

Tightening her hold on him, Marietta tried to memorize how it felt to be in his arms—in case he ever left.

My Sunday school class was held in a room built of what my dad called cinder blocks painted mint green. It had a closet of art supplies, an easel to hold posters or the flannel graph board, and a blackboard with two rows of folding chairs facing it. At one side of the room was a child-sized brown folding table and chairs where we could do craft projects related to the theme of that week's Bible story.

I stared down the table at Butch Halteman, who was hogging the gold crayon. The box of crayons I had at home held sixteen colors, and I'd never seen a gold one. I longed to snatch it from Butch's hand, but I'd been told the virtues of sharing too many times to think I could get away with it. Instead, I bent back over the yellow construction paper crown I was making.

Earlier in class, Mrs. Loiseaux said that people who went to heaven would get to wear gold crowns. "Every time you obey God here on Earth, he adds another star to the crown you're going to receive."

I thought stars on a crown sounded stupid. Like the silver-spangled swim cap my aunt Colleen had. *My* crown was going to have jewels on it like the ones in my books. I drew lots of circles and colored them dark red and blue.

When Butch finished using the gold crayon, I seized it before anyone else could. I thought it would make my crown look like bright metal, but the color wouldn't go on smoothly. Every time I pressed down hard, the crayon left little clumps of wax that looked like boogers on the paper.

Frustrated, I hurled the crayon across the room. Instantly, Mrs. Loiseaux was beside me. She was a small woman with silver hair, purple-pink lipstick, and lines around her mouth and eyes that made me think of a dried-up apple. "We don't throw things in Sunday school."

"But it messed up my crown." I pointed so she could see.

"Don't be silly. It looks fine." Raising her voice, Mrs. Loiseaux said to the whole class, "Put your things away now. It's time for our memory verse."

Ignoring her, I scraped at the lumpy gold wax with my thumbnail.

"Katie, look this way, please."

I turned toward the blackboard where the verse was printed.

"Everybody, pay attention," Mrs. Loiseaux said. "Our verse today says, 'There is none righteous, no not one.' Now repeat it after me."

Everybody in class, including me, repeated the words. Then the teacher asked, "Does anyone know what this means?" Some of the students looked sideways at each other, but nobody dared answer. Mrs. Loiseaux went on in the bright teacher tone I had learned to distrust. "It means we're all bad. There isn't anything good in any of us."

Her gaze rested on me when she said that, so I glanced down at my crown. Mrs. Loiseaux couldn't mean me. I was a good girl. Daddy always said so.

The teacher's voice rose. "Even little children are full of sin. I'm sure you all try to be good boys and girls, but aren't there times you disobey your parents? It's because we're bad that Jesus had to die. He got punished instead of us."

At that, my stomach started to hurt. Maybe that's why Mom got so mad when I did something wrong. My mother knew just about everything in the Bible, and she probably thought it was my fault that Jesus got killed.

"Katie Thompson, stop daydreaming. It's your turn to say the verse."

My lips started to quiver, so I bit down hard. Then I whispered, "There is none righteous, no not one."

"Very good. Here's a star to paste on your crown."

When she handed me a gold star, I didn't stick it to the paper. Instead, I held it so long that my sweaty fingers rubbed all the glue away.

My stomach ache got worse during church. I always sat in one of the front pews with my mother's friend so Mom could be in the choir, and as I watched her dressed in her maroon choir robe, singing "The Old Rugged Cross," I worried about what she would say when I told her my memory verse. Would she be surprised? Or angry? Or—my heart leaped—maybe she would say that Mrs. Loiseaux was wrong. I squeezed my eyes shut and prayed, "Jesus, please don't let her be mad at me."

When Mother came out of the choir room after the service, having put away her robe and sheet music, I was sitting in our pew, hugging myself tightly.

"Are you all right?"

"My tummy hurts. Can I lay down on the back seat on the way home?"

"Of course." She put her hand on my forehead. "You don't feel hot. Maybe you ate something that didn't agree with you."

During the drive home, I closed my eyes and pretended to rest on the light-blue cloth seat, and Mom didn't talk to me. When we got to our house, I went to my room and threw myself on the bed. The tap, tap of my mother's footsteps came down the hall. She knocked on my door. "Change your dress."

Mad at myself for forgetting, I jumped up and undid my buttons. I hung the red plaid dress in the closet and straightened the white collar the way Mom always did.

The purple pedal pushers I wore yesterday lay across the arm of the rocking chair. I pulled them on. Glancing at the door, I picked up a purple-and-green striped top from the floor and put that on too. Then I returned a plastic horse to the shelf where it belonged. I was inching under the bed, looking for dirty socks, when Mom entered the room. "What are you doing?"

After crawling back out, I said, "Cleaning."

Instead of looking happy, she got worry lines on her forehead. "You don't have to do that when you're sick."

"I'm OK now."

"Did your Sunday school teacher tell you to clean your room?"

"No."

Mom hugged me. "Such a good girl."

A firecracker of happiness burst inside me. My mother said I was good, and she never lied. Humming a Sunday school song, I went to the living room, where Daddy sat reading the paper in one of the rose armchairs, and leaned on his arm. He smiled at me. "Come to tell me your memory verse?"

"N-no."

"Didn't you learn one today?" As he folded up the paper and tossed it on the blond wood coffee table, Mom walked into the room.

I looked from one parent to the other. "Um..."

Coming up behind Daddy, my mother laid a hand on his shoulder. "Talking about her verse?"

"I don't think she learned one this week," he answered, keeping his eyes on me. "Maybe it was too hard."

"It was not!"

Mother frowned. "Don't yell at your father. If you have something to say, say it nicely. What was your verse?"

Trapped, I stared at the beige carpet. "I...I don't like this one."

Daddy chuckled and tugged the end of my braid, which was hanging in the front over my shoulder. "That's OK."

"No, it's not." My mother came around the side of his chair to stand next to the coffee table so she could stare at me. "You can't just pick what parts of the Bible you like. It's all the word of God."

"Mare, leave it."

"No, I mean it. I want her to tell me the verse."

I lowered my head. My mother might be mad now, but she would get even angrier if she learned what my teacher said.

"Katie." Her tone conveyed that it was her last warning.

My eyes filled with tears, and I screwed up my face to keep from crying. If Mother would leave me alone, I'd be good from now on. *I would.*

"I'm waiting, young lady."

Feeling hot all over, I shouted, " 'There is none righteous, no not one!' Mrs. Loiseaux said I'm bad and I made Jesus die!"

"Jesus Christ!" Daddy jumped up from his chair. "What kind of shit is that to teach little kids?"

I cringed and hung my head. Because I was so angry at my mother, I'd forgotten my father was there. Now he knew how terrible I was.

"Joe, please. You promised not to interfere."

"I'm not going to let those bastards hurt her."

My mother sighed. "They haven't hurt her. She's got to learn it sometime."

"Look at her!" He gestured at me. "Don't tell me she's not hurt."

I had never heard Daddy sound so angry, and it was all my fault. He was standing—hands balled into fists—and glaring at my mother, who didn't look angry at all.

Mom crouched in front of me. "Honey, didn't your teacher tell you that everyone's bad? It's not just you."

I wasn't sure anymore, but I wanted to stop talking about it, so I said, "Yeah."

My mother stroked my cheek. "God loves you very much. That's why he died to save us and make us better. Understand?"

Her face was so full of hope that I couldn't bring myself to admit that I didn't understand. If Jesus fixed things, why did everyone say I was still bad?

"For Pete's sake!" Daddy swung me off the floor and held me close. "It's not true, Katie. You're not bad, you're good. Do you hear me? You're good."

I buried my face in his neck and didn't answer. Usually, I felt warm and safe when Daddy hugged me, but not today. For the first time in my life, I didn't believe him. He knew about history, war, and pioneers, but my mother was the one who knew about God. Mrs. Loiseaux must be right. I *was* bad.

I leaned back against an apple tree and kicked the trunk behind me with the heel of one of the hot pink Keds Daddy gave me for my eighth birthday.

The July afternoon felt as endless as one of our pastor's sermons. When Ritchie showed up after lunch asking me to play outside, I thought we would do something fun. Instead, as soon as we walked to the grove, he started throwing rocks up into the branches, trying to knock off some of the green fruit. His father would spank him silly if he caught Ritchie messing around with the apple crop, but I knew better than to say so.

"What do you want to do?" I asked for the fourth time.

"Nothing."

"We could play Green Beret." It was all he'd wanted to do for the last week, ever since he saw the John Wayne movie with his father and brother.

"Naw." He tossed a pebble from one hand to the other. His eyebrows lowered, and his brown eyes stared at me like I was his next target.

To play it safe, I wandered through the trees looking for something interesting. I knew why Ritchie was in a bad mood. His older brother had promised to take him fishing at the river, but then Paul changed his mind and went bike riding with friends. Paul did stuff like that all the time, but Ritchie continued to get his hopes up every time his brother said they'd do something. I thought Ritchie should know better now that he was ten.

Near the edge of the grove, a couple of branches had fallen to the ground. I picked one up and ran my hand along the bark. The branch was a little thicker than my thumb and reminded me of something, but it took a while to remember what. Last year, I begged my parents to get me a set of Lincoln Logs for Christmas. Daddy was reading me *Little House in the Big Woods,* and I wanted to build a cabin like the Ingalls family's home. My mom said I already had building blocks, and why couldn't I use those? I tried to explain why rectangles and squares painted red, blue, green, yellow, and orange could never look like a real log cabin, but she said I didn't need two kinds of building sets. No can of Lincoln Logs waited for me under the Christmas tree, but I did receive another book in the Little House series.

Now, looking at the branch in my hand, I wondered if I could make my own Lincoln Logs. Daddy would know how to chop them to the right length and cut notches near the ends so they could stack on top of each other. If I built a model cabin over the summer, I could take it to school to show my teacher in September.

When I turned to tell Ritchie my idea, he was yawning and stretching. "I'm going to go see if the Cubs game is on TV." He walked away.

Left alone, I prowled the grove, going up and down each row until I was sure I had found all the sticks that were the right thickness. Once I gathered them together, there were so many that the bundle would be difficult to carry home unless I took more than one trip. But I wasn't supposed to walk down the road by myself. My mother let me do it with Ritchie because he was two years older, which I thought was a silly rule. I was lots better than him at remembering to check for cars, but my mother had it in her head that older meant smarter or something.

After puzzling over what to do, I concluded that if I crossed the road carefully and then walked along its edge, my mother wouldn't be able see me because our windowless garage wall faced that direction. So I divided my sticks into three piles and began to transport them home.

On the last trip, as I walked out from under the shelter of the trees, a car turned onto Sunset Road. When I halted to let it pass, I saw from the light blue color and the funny red shape on the hubcaps that it was my father's Oldsmobile. Excited, I waved and yelled at him.

The oval brake lights went on, and he stopped a little ways beyond where I stood. By the time I reached the car, he had the passenger door open.

"Does your mother know you're down here?" he asked and moved his metal lunch box from the seat to the floor. "And what are you doing with all those sticks?"

"They're for a project," I said, hugging the bundle to my chest as I stood outside the car. "Mom knows Ritchie and I were in the grove." I tried to look truthful and hoped he wouldn't figure out that I'd already disobeyed the rule.

"All right. Put them in the back seat."

After making sure to shake off any dirt and dead leaves, I did as he said. When I climbed into the passenger side, Daddy reached for something on the dashboard. "I brought you a surprise."

It was a scarlet carnation with a stem that was about two inches long. Now that Daddy worked as a delivery driver for a florist, he often brought me blossoms that got knocked off arrangements. I turned down the rearview mirror and poked the carnation into my braid. It looked pretty in my black hair.

"Thank you!" Scooting across the bench seat, I kissed him and breathed in the mingled scent of aftershave and sweat that was his familiar end-of-the-day smell.

"Daddy, I got a really neat idea. But I need your help."

He yawned. "I'm beat tonight. We had a lot of deliveries today."

"We can do it Saturday."

"Do what Saturday? I have three wedding deliveries to make, so I'm not promising anything until I know what it is."

"I found a bunch of sticks, and I want you to help me cut them with notches and everything, so I can build a little log cabin."

"A log cabin?" He sounded surprised. "Why can't you want a doll house like other little girls?"

"I don't like dolls. Except for Sacajawea."

"I know." Gazing down the road, he said, "And your mother blames me."

Then he tugged my braid. "It's a neat idea, honey, but you're not old enough to work with the kind of tools that can do that."

"That's why I need your help. You know how, don't you?"

His forehead wrinkled, but then he shook his head. "I don't have the right equipment, and I'm afraid one of us will get hurt if we try to make those notches with a knife."

"Oh." I stared at my pink sneakers. "Then I can't make one."

Daddy laid a hand on my knee. "You know what? I think I remember seeing log cabins made out of popsicle sticks. Would you like to do that?"

Feeling a gleam of hope, I squinted and tried to imagine it. Popsicle sticks didn't look anything like logs, but at least they were bare wood. "I guess so. But...Mother says I can't eat more than one Popsicle at a time. How long will it take to save enough sticks?"

"I don't know, Katydid." Daddy rubbed his jaw. "I think I read in a magazine that you can buy craft sticks instead of saving them from popsicles. Tell you what. Tomorrow I'll stop by the hobby shop in town and see if they sell anything like that."

Climbing up on my knees, I clapped for joy.

He held up a hand. "Now wait a minute. I can't buy them if they cost too much. You understand that, don't you?"

I nodded vigorously.

"OK, then sit down like you're supposed to."

When I had my butt parked on the seat properly, Daddy shifted the car to drive and headed for home.

By the time I started third grade, I'd grown aware of the passage of time, measured by birthdays, holidays, and the milestones of each academic year. Each week also had its own rhythms. In the evenings and on weekends after my homework was done, I talked Daddy into letting me do projects. My new teacher, Mrs. Brown, had been impressed with my popsicle-stick log cabin. Now I dreamed of making a shoebox diorama of a prehistoric landscape complete with plastic dinosaurs I was saving my allowance to buy.

In mid-October, the first frost came, followed by a warm Indian summer. Scarlet and yellow leaves floated to the ground like confetti at a parade. Then the weather changed, bringing rain and gusts of wind that stripped the trees overnight.

Late one afternoon, I stared out my bedroom window at the road, then at my clock, then out the window again. Grey drizzle had fallen all afternoon. Now that I was in third grade, my father let me walk down to the corner to meet him in the evenings, but Mother wouldn't allow it when the weather was bad. Resting my cheek against the cool glass, I willed the rain to stop.

I couldn't wait to tell Daddy about school. Mrs. Brown had stapled brown wrapping paper completely across the back bulletin board and then outlined a forest scene: trees and fallen logs, cardinals and blue jays, squirrels and rabbits, foxes and raccoons. Every kid in class was going to paint part of the mural. I had already made up my mind to do the best painting job of anybody, and when Daddy saw it on parents' night, he would finally let me help with his model.

A thin gleam of golden light broke through the clouds in the west. Immediately, I ran from my bedroom. Before I even reached the kitchen, I called out, "It stopped raining. Can I go? Please?"

Mom looked up from her ironing. "What?"

"May I go meet Daddy?" I said, careful to ask the right way this time.

Using the point of her iron to press the neckband of my father's shirt, my mother shook her head. "It's too sloppy out, and it's bound to get dark early."

"Please. I didn't get to go yesterday. I promise to stay out of the mud."

After standing the iron on the board, Mom rubbed the bridge of her nose. "I don't see why it's so important. He gets home two minutes after he turns the corner." She gazed at my pleading face and sighed. "Oh, all right."

I left the house just before 5:30. Even though I had plenty of time, I ran down the road, making sure to skirt the puddles. When I reached the corner, I saw that my mother was right. It was darker out here than usual.

Just like Halloween. I shivered. Halloween was only nine days away, and my father was going to take me to buy a costume on Saturday.

Although the rain had stopped, the air felt damp. I stood on tiptoe to see the white tavern with its neon beer signs across the highway. Behind the tavern towered trees, dim now against the deep grey sky. I liked to imagine that the tavern was deserted—that a terrible murder happened there a long time ago, and no one had ever used it since.

Squeezing my arms, I thought, *I'll tell Daddy a story about the dead man who haunts the place and turns himself into a bat. And a bell rings at midnight when the ghost is hunting his killer.* I imagined how my father would pretend to be scared so I could hug him.

Craning my neck to look down the highway, I wondered why Daddy hadn't come yet. *I'll count cars,* I decided when I saw that all the oncoming automobiles had headlights on. *I bet he'll get here before I reach one hundred.*

Only the thinnest sliver of a moon rose in the sky, and the gloom deepened to full darkness. I had counted to 217 and was pacing with worry when a strange light-colored car turned onto the frontage road. As it rounded the corner and drove past me, I thought I saw a shape painted on the door but couldn't make out what it was. Then I resumed counting.

The air grew chilly. Eager as I was to see my father, I began to wish I'd stayed inside. I wasn't exactly scared of the dark anymore, but I didn't like being out in it alone. What if a monster was creeping up behind me out of Pelletiers' empty soybean field? Nobody would hear me if I screamed.

I thought about going home but quickly decided the walk would be even scarier than staying where I was. To get to my house, I would have to pass the grove. Anything could be hiding in the dark trees. A coyote or even bats.

Counting cars again, I noticed that there were a lot fewer than before. Then I heard a noise like footsteps on the road behind me.

My heart lurched. For a moment, I thought the ghost from my story had come to life—and I was a sitting duck, out on an open corner with no shelter nearby. Then I heard Mrs. Pelletier's voice: "Katie! Where are you, child?"

"Here." I stepped into the road, wondering what Ritchie's mom wanted.

As Mrs. Pelletier drew near, I saw her trying to button a too-small sweater across her large chest. "Your mother called. I'm to take you home."

"Why? I'm waiting for Daddy."

Mrs. Pelletier hesitated. "He's not coming home right now."

My anger flared. "I'm not a baby. I want to wait here." I stared down the frontage road, willing Daddy's car to appear.

With a heavy sigh, Mrs. Pelletier laid a hand on my shoulder. "Your mother said you have to come with me."

"No." Ducking from underneath her grasp, I ran a few steps down the road. "Daddy said I could wait for him."

"Sweetie..." Even in the blinding darkness, I could tell that Mrs. Pelletier was crying. Dread swooped down on me like one of my imagined bats.

"Where's my mother?" I screamed.

Mrs. Pelletier sniffed. "She's at home. She's all right. I shouldn't be the one to tell you, but...there's been an accident."

I had to ask, even though something inside warned me not to. "Daddy?"

Walking toward me, Mrs. Pelletier pulled me into a tight embrace. "I'm so sorry. Your daddy's...gone. He's gone to be with the angels."

When I woke up, a shaft of light angled through my bedroom window. I blinked. Something was wrong—it didn't feel like morning—but my brain was too fuzzy to figure out why. Rolling on my side, I tried to go back to sleep. The ticking of my bedside clock resounded in the silence. Why was the house so quiet? Fear churned in my stomach, and drowsiness fled.

When I sat up, everything went dark. My vision cleared, but I remained light-headed and my stomach felt icky. Frightened, I hugged myself and noticed I was wearing the black velvet dress Mother bought me for Daddy's funeral. The plush fabric was crushed and wrinkled.

Dimly, I recalled standing in the bathroom as Aunt Dee, my mother's favorite sister, set my hair so the ends would curl like her own long black hair. I touched my curls and found them tangled. "Mother!" When no one answered, I jumped out of bed and ran into the hall, where I collided with my aunt.

I backed away, terrified that I'd hurt her. Aunt Dee was pregnant, and according to family whispers, she'd already lost two babies. But Dee seemed fine as she asked, "Do you feel better?"

What does that mean? Ignoring the question, I said, "Where's Mother?"

Dee blinked; her dark eyes were red rimmed. "She's at the funeral."

"Why didn't she take me with?"

Taking a sick-sounding gulp of air, Dee braced herself against the wall. "Don't you remember? You..." She blinked again.

Watching her, I got the feeling that something creepy was going on.

"You didn't feel well," Dee finally said, "so I brought you home."

Bewildered, I shook my head. I hadn't gone anywhere.

"They'll be back from the cemetery soon. Let's see if we can clean you up."

Dee had steamed the wrinkles out of my dress and was brushing my hair in the bathroom when we heard the front door open, followed by a burst of conversation. I walked into the living room and halted by one of the rose armchairs. Across the room, Mom was talking to my father's parents, who sat stiffly on the pastel-striped sofa, quietly out of place amid the noisy throng of Mother's family. Grandpa Will was tall and thin like Daddy, but his face was stern instead of smiling. Grandma Rosemary was small and quiet. I liked her better than my other grandma, who was always in a bad mood.

Aunt Colleen, who had dark hair like Mom but was much skinnier, came through the front door, carrying a roasting pan with a large ham and calling over her shoulder, "Phil, I need the rest of that stuff right now." As she came toward the kitchen doorway, she saw me, frowned, and passed without a word.

Entering after Colleen, Grandma Brigitte carried a coconut cake. She was dressed all in black for the funeral, but she wore bright gold jewelry and dark red lipstick. When she saw me, she stopped short. "I hope you're proud of yourself, Kathleen."

"Mother," said my mom in a warning tone. As she approached us, Aunt Dee stepped up to her and whispered in her ear, causing my mother's eyes to grow wide and fix on me. She took my hand and led me into her pale blue bedroom.

As soon as the door was shut, I burst out, "Why didn't you take me to the funeral?"

"You really don't remember."

"Remember what?"

"Shhh." Mother glanced at the closed door. "What did Aunt Dee tell you?"

I stared at the floor, feeling guilty without knowing why. I decided I'd better not fight with my mother now that—now that Daddy wasn't here. "She said I was sick."

"I see."

The worry in her voice scared me. "Did I faint?"

"No. A doctor gave you a shot. Don't you remember?"

Frowning, I shook my head.

Mom pressed her lips together. I wanted her to hug me like she did when I was little, but she didn't. Instead, she stroked my hair. "Don't worry, honey. Everything's going to be all right."

Then she took my hand. "Come on. Let's get you something to eat."

The next morning, Marietta reached for the electric percolator, then snatched back her hand. Making coffee had been the first falling domino in a sequence of events that repeated itself each morning: start the coffee while Joe took his shower, call Katie, make lunches, and set the table while the other two dressed. Now Marietta never wanted to use that percolator again. It would be like sending a wake-up call to the dead.

I'll buy a jar of instant down at Jake's, she thought as she wound the cord around the coffeepot and put it in a bottom cabinet. The errand added itself to a list of chores she'd been compiling in her mind. She filled the stainless steel tea kettle, placed it on the stove, and went to get pen and paper from the rolltop desk in the living room. Sitting at the kitchen table, she started the list by writing, "Get coffee at Jake's store." The words looked frivolous compared to the more important things she needed to do.

First and foremost, there was the problem of Katie. Squeezing her eyes shut, Marietta whispered, "Joe, what do I do? She was always more your child than mine." Katie's flights of fancy and impractical projects baffled Marietta. Joe had understood their child so intuitively that she felt inadequate in comparison, especially now. It couldn't be normal for Katie to blot out the memory of the funeral—although just before the service started, she became so violently hysterical, they had to call someone in to sedate her. In comparison, amnesia might be a blessing.

The kettle whistled. Rising, Marietta poured boiling water over the tea bag in her cup and watched brown eddies color the water, just as Joe's death was staining every ounce of her life. Colleen's husband, Phil, was dealing with the insurance companies for her. Marietta remembered the day Joe had told her he was buying life insurance. She was still in the hospital after giving birth to Katie, and he marched into the room with a bouquet of crimson roses, a pink stuffed cat, and the policy for her to sign. "Got to plan ahead now I've got a daughter."

Finding relief in the hard-edged practicalities of money, Marietta began to jot numbers on her paper. In addition to Joe's policy, there would likely be a settlement from the other driver's insurance because he'd been drunk and run a stop sign.

Then Marietta listed expenses: the funeral, of course, and a new car—something smaller and cheaper than the Oldsmobile Super 88 Joe had bought—and for her own peace of mind, she intended to pay off the mortgage.

Drinking her tea black and bitter, Marietta stared at the numbers. If she were careful, several thousand dollars might be left after she paid for everything, money she could save. Marietta had already decided that once she had a car, she would look for a job. She wouldn't earn as much as Joe had, but even if she only equaled the wage she'd earned as a checkout girl when she was single, she could cover their monthly expenses.

Marietta gazed out the back window at the mist rising over the creek. By purchasing that insurance policy, Joe had made one of his dreams come true. He was going to send his daughter to college.

Monday after Katie went back to school, Marietta and her parents sorted through Joe's things, throwing some in the trash and packing the rest to give away. As Marietta cleaned out his dresser, Brigitte entered the bedroom with a glass of cola. She set it on the bare wood of the nightstand, went to the closet, and pulled out shirts so roughly that the metal hangers clanged.

A dull pain throbbed above Marietta's eyes. Crossing the room, she moved her mother's glass to the doily. She'd meant to wash Joe's shirts—sometimes he wore them once and hung them back in the closet—but she didn't have the energy to protest as her mother stuffed them in a carton. After Brigitte finished, she said, "I'll have your father carry this out to the car."

Alone, Marietta pulled out Joe's top dresser drawer and laid it on the blue-striped bedspread. The drawer was divided down the middle by a thin wooden partition, with papers on the right and junk on the left. Removing things one by one, Marietta found an old car key, a bottle cap for a defunct brand of root beer, and two dried up ball-point pens. In the corner was a lumpy pottery bowl, glazed green with a white chip on one edge. Scratched on the bottom was "JT, 1946." He'd been in seventh-grade art class when he made it, two years before they met. Next Marietta took out a pair of cuff links, embossed with American eagles, gold-colored but spotted with age. She also found a Mexican peso, an empty matchbook from a nightclub in California, and the blue velvet box from her wedding ring.

Oh, Joe. What's the point of all this? It was a puzzle without instructions on how to assemble the pieces. She threw away everything but the cuff links and green bowl, which she'd offer to Katie.

Then she sorted the papers, many of them Katie's drawings. Marietta gazed at one, done in crayon on light blue construction paper. The figure was that of a yellow-haired man dressed in green and brown, wearing a feathered cap and holding a bow. The drawing, labeled "Robin Hood," reminded her of all the stories Joe had told their daughter. Katie would miss that.

After a soft knock on the door, Marietta's father, Albert, entered. His once auburn hair had faded to pale ginger, and age spots dotted his face and hands amid the freckles. "Sorry to disturb you, Pumpkin," he said, reverting to his pet name for her. "Your mother and I been talking." He glanced back at Brigitte, who hovered in the door. "Wondering what to do about the war model."

In the hectic time since Joe's death, Marietta had forgotten the model. Now she pictured the green expanse of it, crisscrossed with roads and stone walls.

As Marietta hesitated, Brigitte pushed into the room. "You don't want that big thing cluttering up your basement. It'll just gather dust."

Marietta frowned. Joe had spent hundreds of hours on the model and for what? It was doomed to be an unfinished dream, just as he had been doomed to live an unfinished life. She looked to Albert. "I don't know. I don't think I can stand to look at it, knowing it will never be done the way he wanted."

"Maybe it's best to get rid of it." Albert rubbed the back of his neck. "You want me to keep the soldiers? I mean, for Katie?"

Brigitte let out a snort of disgust. "She's a girl."

"No, he's right," Marietta said, staring down at the picture of Robin Hood.

Marietta was chopping a green pepper for spaghetti sauce when the phone rang. "Hello?"

"Sissy, it's Cori." There was a pause. "I just heard the news. I'm so sorry."

"Mom said she wasn't able to reach you in time for the funeral."

"No. The pad where I'm crashing has no phone. You know how it is."

Not really, Marietta thought. Her youngest sister was a hippie, which Marietta blamed on Cori's haphazard upbringing. Their mother had been hoping for a boy to name after the brother who died in World War II, and when her sixth baby turned out to be a girl, Brigitte ignored her, leaving fourteen-year-old Marietta to raise her as best she could. Eventually, when Marietta got married, Cori felt she had no one, so she left home as soon as she turned eighteen.

"Are you still in San Francisco?" Marietta asked now.

"Yes, doing improv street theatre and selling tie-dye T-shirts."

Marietta set her knife down. "Can you make a living doing that?"

"Sissy, don't nag. I called to see how you're doing."

A lump formed in Marietta's throat. "I'm all right, but I worry about Katie. This has hit her hard."

"Of course, it has. She adored Joe. Is she crying a lot?"

"No, worse than that." Sitting down, Marietta told Cori what happened at the funeral.

"Maybe you should take her to a shrink."

Marietta's hand tightened on the phone. "I can't."

"Why not? Too expensive? I can send you some—"

"No, that's not it." Marietta rose, went to the pantry, and took out an onion. "I don't believe in psychology."

"What do you mean?"

"It's worldly, and the Bible says not to be swayed by vain philosophies."

"Oh, Marietta!" Cori's tone sharpened. "Don't tell me you're giving in to that nonsense. This is your little girl. You need to do what's best for her."

"I *am* doing what's best for her. Who knows what kind of ideas a psychiatrist would put in her head? No, thank you. I'll pray for her, and—"

"Listen to yourself. There's a great big world out here, and you're terrified of it."

Marietta's jaw tightened. "I don't live in a cave, Corinne. I know all about your great big world, about the pot parties and free love. I don't want that for Katie. She's going to have a good Christian upbringing."

"Even if it kills her."

"I have to go," Marietta snapped. "Katie will be home any minute."

"Look, I didn't mean to fight. I just wanted to tell you how sorry I am. I liked Joe."

Marietta sighed, remembering how Cori too had adored him when she was a little girl who used to come for sleepovers. "I know."

They spoke another minute, and then Marietta said good-bye. She was halfway through chopping the onion when Katie got home. Through a blur of tears, Marietta saw her daughter pass the kitchen door on the way to her room. "Hi, honey. How was your day?"

Returning to the doorway, Katie shrugged. "OK."

"Did everything go all right? Anybody say anything?"

Katie bent to pull a wet leaf off her shoe. "Mrs. Brown said welcome back."

"What about your friends?"

As Katie chewed her lower lip, Marietta wondered if she'd asked the wrong question. Finally, the child said, "They didn't say anything."

Of course not. Marietta could picture the way other children stared at Katie now, the way she had suddenly grown strange and frightening. To ease the sorrow in her daughter's eyes, Marietta said, "There's something for you on your bed."

Moments later, Katie returned carrying a figure of a Confederate officer. Her eyes questioned her mother.

"They're yours now."

"Can I put them back? On the shelf by the model?"

Marietta's stomach tightened. "Honey, your grandpa took the model away."

Katie's eyes widened. She ran across the kitchen and clattered down the stairs. A moment later, Marietta heard a howl that made her fear Katie was about to have hysterics again. Marietta went through the doorway and down the four steps to the landing where you could go either out the back door or down the basement stairs. Katie was stomping up the steps, outrage on her face.

"Why did Grandpa take it? It was mine!"

Marietta's heart began to pound. "But it wasn't done. It was just going to get dirty and fall apart. We had to get rid of it."

Katie's eyes narrowed. "Daddy promised I could work on it."

"But he isn't here to show you how to do it anymore."

"I know how!" Katie stamped her foot. "And I asked Jesus to tell Daddy I would finish it. I promised."

"I'm sorry," Marietta said, wondering why she hadn't foreseen this.

Trembling with rage, Katie drew her fists up to her chest. *Here it comes,* Marietta thought, but no tantrum erupted. Instead, Katie forced her hands down, pressed her lips together, and turned her face into an impenetrable mask. The change was utterly unchildlike and terrifying to watch.

"Maybe it's not too late," Marietta said. "Let me call Grandpa. Maybe he still has it." As desperate hope rose in Katie's eyes, Marietta hurried to the phone.

I held myself absolutely still as Mother dialed the number, but inside me, a voice screamed, "No, no, no!" Daddy was up in heaven watching, and he was going to be so sad his model was gone. Deep in my gut I knew the model was more than just a hobby like my mother thought. I didn't have words then for what I felt, but instinctively I sensed that the project had been my father's way to commemorate his family's contribution to our country's history. "We have to get it back," I whispered, "so I can finish."

"I see," Mother said into the receiver, and her tone told me the news was bad.

Without waiting to hear more, I ran down the hall and burst into my parents' room, desperate to find something that belonged to my father. My eyes filled with tears at the sight of the blue-striped bedspread, and I ran my hand over the bump made by Daddy's pillow. Then I turned to the closet. Through the open door, I saw that his side of the rod was empty. I walked closer, unable to believe everything had disappeared. Spotting something on the floor way in back, I pulled out a faded blue denim shirt. Swiftly, I rolled it into a bundle, ran to my room, and shoved it under the bed.

When Mother knocked on my door, I shouted, "Go away!"

She didn't. I watched the doorknob turn, and my mother entered. She stood there twisting her wedding ring. "Honey, I know you're angry, but don't yell at me."

Turning away, I began to take the soldiers out of their box.

"It's hard, but when someone dies, you have to get rid of their things." She came to sit on my bed. "Listen to me. You never would have finished the model. It was too big."

"Daddy said I could work on it. It wasn't yours. It was his and mine."

Although my head was lowered, I saw my mom dig her nails into her skirt. "I'm sorry. But it's gone now, and I can't get it back."

Heat rushed into my face as I realized I had upset her. The thought made me squirm. I knew she missed Daddy too, and he would want me to be nice to her, but I couldn't. I was too mad. After a moment, she rose. "I'll go finish supper. I'm making spaghetti, one of your favorites."

Mother stood there, waiting for me to say something. After a minute she left.

I lifted my head and gazed out the window at the cloudy afternoon. More than anything, I wanted to run down the road to the corner and see my father drive up like nothing had happened. He would tell me a funny story, and then after supper, we'd go downstairs and—

But the model wasn't there anymore, and my father was gone too. Sniffling, I wiped the corner of my eye and told myself not to cry. Gazing at the soldiers spread out on my bed, I picked up one with bloodstains painted on his dark blue jacket and rubbed my finger across the red spots. Daddy had used the smallest paintbrush I'd ever seen to add those details. After a minute, I put the soldiers back in the box. Putting the shoebox on the bottom shelf of my nightstand, I said, "Good night."

The day after Thanksgiving, my mother began to work as a saleswoman in the lingerie department of Feldman's Department Store in downtown Zebulun. When she told me the news, I wasn't surprised; she'd already explained that she needed to earn money.

Then I found out her plans for me. "Tomorrow morning, I'm going to take you to enroll in a new school," she said Sunday night as she set two mugs of hot cocoa on the kitchen table.

"Why? We're not moving, are we?"

I asked because when we went to my grandparents' house for the holiday, Grandpa Albert had urged my mother to move into town.

"No, honey, we're not moving."

I sighed loudly with relief, and Mother smiled at me in a rare expression of companionship. "We like it here, don't we? We have the squirrels for company and that pair of cardinals that nests here every year. And—" Her voice broke, and she twisted her neck to gaze out the window at the dark back yard. "There's all the work your father did on this place. Like planting the willow and the lilacs. This is our home." Her voice dropped to a whisper, "The only one I've ever had, really."

I waited for a minute, but she was so lost in her thoughts that she'd forgotten I was sitting there. Reaching out, I touched her arm. "Then why do I have to go to a different school?"

She turned back to me and smiled sadly. "You're too young to be home alone, so I got permission for you to transfer to the grade school I went to. That way you can walk to your grandparents' house, and I'll pick you up after work."

"Oh." Unable to meet my mother's eyes, I fished out the half-melted marshmallow from my cocoa and popped it in my mouth. After I swallowed it, I said, "I don't think Grandma Brigitte likes me very much."

"She doesn't like me either." When I jerked my head up in surprise, Mom shrugged. "I wish I could have somebody else watch you, but I won't make enough money to pay a babysitter. Do you understand?"

My throat ached and my eyes stung with tears of disappointment, but I nodded.

"It's only till you're old enough."

"When will that be?"

She sighed. "I can't decide that now. Let's just say that the better you behave, the sooner it will be."

One day after school, I waved good-bye to my new friend Nita—a thin, brown-haired, freckle-faced tomboy who liked to run as much as I did—and walked to the exit in the chain-link fence surrounding the playground. Even though it was January, there was no snow on the ground. That was lucky for me because of what I planned to do.

After looking to the left and then to the right, I debated which direction to take. My grandparents lived only four blocks away, and I was supposed to go straight there after school, but I had invented a game that required me to explore different routes to their house. I peered to the right at a stoplight a block away, a block in the wrong direction. *I bet that's Fifth Street. I could take it to Grandma's street and head back.* My heart began to pound as I set off.

The cold air nipped at my cheeks, and wind needled its way through the fabric of my tights, but I turned up my coat collar and kept walking, searching the ground on both sides of the sidewalk. That was part of the game. Someday I was going to find a special rock that was painted white with a red *K* on it for my name.

In the game, my father wasn't really dead. The government had hired him to be a spy, which was why he went away. Because his mission was dangerous, he couldn't tell me about it, but I was sure that someday he would contact me. When I found the special rock, I would lift it up and find a glass tube with a secret message inside like something on the TV show *Get Smart.*

Even though I knew the game wasn't real, I couldn't stop playing it. I had to search for that rock because I had the terrible fear that if I ever got careless and didn't look, someone else would find the message and steal it.

I stopped when I reached an unfamiliar intersection of three streets. The street that ran diagonally through the intersection was much busier than the other two. I gazed in all six directions, trying to figure out which one to take.

Then I saw something that made me gasp. Rising above the buildings and bare winter branches was a tower that looked like a castle. Wondering if it was some kind of sign, I decided to go explore. Carefully, I crossed three streets until I reached the opposite side of the intersection. After walking two more blocks, I stopped abruptly. Ahead of me was an open parklike area with buildings on three sides. The tower rose above the buildings at the far end.

I headed down a broad sidewalk. In the center of the open area was an empty fountain, its concrete basin littered with dead leaves. Circling the fountain, like the rings of a target, were a walkway, curved stone benches, and an outer hedge. Cutting through the hedge were four sidewalks that led out from the fountain.

Several people, most of them carrying books, hurried along the sidewalks. I watched a young man vault over the evergreen hedge and run across the lawn, shouting, "Bruce, wait up!"

At the end of the park, I went down a walk that ran between two buildings. On the other side, I saw the back of what I'd taken to be a castle. It was a four-story building of buff stone, covered in places with the tracery of bare vines. I frowned in disappointment when I noticed metal fire escapes bolted to the wall. Maybe it wasn't a castle after all.

Somewhere nearby, chimes began to play a hymn. Looking around, I wondered what time it was. I was supposed to be at Grandma's house by 3:30.

As I rushed down the sidewalk, I tried to figure out which way to go. I hadn't kept track of my route once I started walking toward the tower.

Two men were talking on the steps of the building ahead. One was young, but the other man had thick white hair. The young man said, "Bye, Dr. Hadley," and left.

I gazed up at the older man. Mother always said never to talk to strangers, but a doctor would be safe, wouldn't he? Before I could make up my mind, he smiled. "Can I help you?"

After glancing around to make sure I had a clear path to run away if he tried anything, I asked, "Do you know where Curtis is?"

"Curtis? I don't believe I have any students by that name."

"Curtis Avenue."

"It's on the other side of this building." He started down the sidewalk. "Come this way."

I followed at what seemed a safe distance. When we reached the end of the block, he pointed down the street. "We're on Curtis now. I suppose you should go that way since there's nothing in the other direction but the campus and the river."

"Thank you," I said and began to run.

When I finally entered my grandparents' house, Grandma Brigitte called from the front room, "Is that you, Kathleen?" Going to the doorway, I saw her watching *The 3:30 Movie.*

"I've been worried sick," Grandma said as she stared at the TV screen, where a blonde girl was hanging out on the beach with a bunch of boy surfers.

"I'm sorry."

She turned and glared at me. "I'm doing your mother a favor watching you. Another stunt like this, I'll tell her to find somebody else. It's time you learned the whole world's not going to spoil you like your father did."

"Yes, ma'am." Pulling off my coat, I saw Grandpa Albert standing at the end of the hall watching me. I held my breath and hoped he'd say something to make me feel better, the way he always did with my mother, but he just turned back into the kitchen.

"Katie!" Instead of answering my mother, I turned my back on the house. I was standing barefoot in the creek with water up to my ankles. In my hand, I held a small raft I'd made from twigs, held together by weaving thin willow stems over and under each one. I bent over to release it into the water. As it began to bob downstream, I repeated what Daddy used to say, "This will take you to the Theakia. Then you'll join the Mississippi and roll down to Mexico."

As soon as I spoke Daddy's words, the pain of missing him sliced into me like a kitchen knife, and I remained doubled over. It was always like this. Whenever I tried to stop thinking about him, I felt like a robot. But if I let myself remember, the memories hurt so much that I wanted to scream loud enough to break all our windows.

When I straightened up, I saw that Mother had reached the edge of the creek and was standing next to my Keds, which I'd put there to stay dry. She stared at me with a worried look, and I felt my face grow hard. It was bad enough to feel the way I did without her asking me what was wrong.

To my relief, she blinked and said, "We need to go. Grandpa will be waiting for us."

"I know." I stared at her a moment because she looked so strange in her blue jeans and checked shirt, like Elly May on *The Beverly Hillbillies* except with dark hair. I guessed she was dressed like that because we were going to the cemetery to plant geraniums by Daddy's grave for Decoration Day.

As I climbed out of the creek, mud streaked my legs. "Go rinse off with the hose," Mother said. I started toward the house, but then she grabbed my arm. "Are you OK?" She stared hard into my face.

I nodded and tried to pull free, but she held on. "You know you could tell me if you were sad, don't you?"

What's the point? No matter what you do, Daddy will still be dead. But I couldn't say that. If I made her cry, I would feel too awful. "I know."

Mother released my arm and picked up my shoes while I went to rinse the mud away.

As Mother drove under the stone arch at the cemetery entrance, I noticed that the heavy iron gates were pushed open. A large padlock hung on one, and I wondered why they locked the corpses in at night. Chills raced down my arms.

The feeling passed as I saw how pretty the place was. Here and there, huge old trees stood like sentinels beside the roads. The grass was emerald, and most of the graves were decorated with wreaths or pots of flowers in rainbow colors. Several graves had small flags flapping in the breeze.

Up ahead, parked at the side of the gravel road, was Grandpa Albert's big black car. I saw him standing by the open trunk, holding a shovel. In a flash, I remembered the scene in *Tom Sawyer* when Tom and a friend saw a murder in a graveyard, a scene that terrified me so much I'd stopped reading the book. Suddenly, neither the sunlight nor the green grass, the jaunty flags or the bright flowers mattered. *This was a cemetery.*

I slumped to avoid looking out the window. When that didn't work, I lay down on my side and pulled my knees up to my chest.

My mother stopped the car. After climbing out and calling *hello,* Mother turned to the open door. "Katie, we're here now. You can get out."

"I don't want to."

"But..." Ducking back inside the car, Mother knelt on the driver's seat. "Don't you want to come? We're going to plant pretty flowers by your father's stone."

Feeling sick and cold, I squeezed my eyes shut. "I hate flowers."

"You know you don't mean that."

"I do!" It felt good to yell. "I hate flowers."

Even though my eyes were still shut, I felt the car springs shift as my mother lifted her weight from the bench seat and backed out of the car. "OK." She sounded worried again. "If you change your mind, we're just over there."

As soon as I was alone, I began to hum "Oh, Susanna," a song Daddy had liked. When the sound of digging came through the open window, I hummed even louder.

Over the next few years, Marietta felt she was being strangled by the iron grip of duty. Each day she followed a routine of work, housework, childcare, sleep. Each month she fought against rising inflation to pay her bills and save whatever money was left.

She sat in her isolated country house watching television as unsettling events took place in the outside world: hippies gathered at Woodstock to celebrate drugs, sex, and rock music; the National Guard killed four college students at Kent State; terrorists murdered Israeli athletes at the Olympics; the Supreme Court legalized abortion; and President Nixon resigned in disgrace. The world seemed to be spiraling out of control while she struggled to raise her daughter.

In 1974, the same year Nixon left office, Marietta turned forty. With the passing of that milestone, she feared that the best part of her life was over. She woke each morning long before the alarm was set to ring and wandered out to the kitchen to drink coffee and stare out the window, waiting for the sun to rise above the windbreak of trees on the far side of the creek.

If Joe had lived, what would her life be like now? Would she have had another baby? They hadn't done anything to prevent conception, either before or after Katie was born, but Marietta became pregnant only once. Often she wondered why God had decreed she should have just one child when her unfit mother had so many. Had Marietta done something wrong?

Such unanswerable questions assailed her continuously, and when she found herself waking an hour before dawn, she told herself she should use the time to pray. But she was trapped in a desert where no prayers bloomed.

The last time she felt this far from God, she had been a little girl, attending the Catholic Church with her mother. Marietta hated the

Latin service and once complained, "Why doesn't God want me to understand?" Her mother slapped her for daring to question.

Not long afterward, Brigitte decided she didn't have the energy to take her entire brood of children to church by herself every week. She nagged Albert to join them, but Marietta's father refused. "I told you when we married I wasn't converting."

After weeks of arguing, Brigitte announced to Marietta that, as the oldest, she had to stay home with her two little brothers Michael and Anthony. "You don't like the mass anyway."

When Albert returned from the Baptist church that Sunday, he was shocked at what his wife had done, so he confronted Brigitte as she walked in the door. "How could you decide Marietta isn't going to go to church anymore?"

Standing in the living room, watching her parents through the archway that led to the hall, Marietta saw her mother's eyes flash. Then Brigitte took her husband's arm and wheedled, "You know what terrible headaches I get. They happen every Sunday." She leaned against his shoulder. "It's the strain of keeping five children quiet during mass. I don't like coming home from church in an aggravated state of mind. It defeats the whole purpose of going."

Marietta dug her nails into her palms. Her mother was so *manipulative*—a word she had learned in the last week. She expected her father to cave in to the whining, but he surprised her. "Marietta is not your nursemaid. She needs church as much as you do, and if you leave her behind, I'll take her and the boys with me."

Brigitte stiffened. "Those children are Catholic. I won't have it."

The look on Albert's face hardened. "If you want them to be Catholic, all the children must attend church with you every week. But if you want to enjoy a peaceful Sunday morning, Marietta can watch the boys while you go to *early* mass. Then she will come to Immanuel Baptist with me."

Brigitte sputtered, but to Marietta's astonishment, she gave in. It was one of the few times Marietta had ever seen her father triumph over her mother—and he had done it for her.

Marietta loved the Baptist church the moment she stepped foot in the building. The white walls and light woodwork of the sanctuary gave it an airy feeling compared to her mother's dark church, and the stained glass window of a red-robed Jesus carrying a lost lamb looked exactly the way she'd always imagined him. Not only were the services in English, but the pastor had a straightforward way of explaining the Bible that made it crystal clear what was right and what was wrong. He didn't try to keep things from people the way the Catholic priests did with their indecipherable Latin. Marietta thanked God that he'd rescued her from Catholicism, which she blamed for her mother's devious, theatrical nature.

Now, God had abandoned her to a life of drudgery no different from the heavy burdens she'd carried in childhood. Raising her daughter should give sufficient purpose to her life, but somehow it didn't. She wanted to grow close to Katie, but their personalities were so different that she couldn't reach the child. Maybe, she consoled herself, it was better this way. Marietta believed her daughter had inherited a dangerous combination of Brigitte's melodrama and Joe's rebellion, so what Katie needed was strict oversight, not a mother who tried to be her friend.

As Marietta felt herself stagnating, Katie changed rapidly, growing into a slim girl with long legs. At ten, she was taller than her mother, and at fourteen, she was five feet, eight inches, and still growing. She moved awkwardly, yet she had a haunting loveliness as Joe had predicted. Her nose was long, her lips just shy of fullness. Her beauty came from her eyes: a grey-blue that darkened like a storm when she was fearful, deepened to the indigo of an August midnight when she was pleased, turned frosty as a January dawn when she was angry, and grew as remote as the horizon when she was sad.

Watching her daughter mature, Marietta grew afraid. Men would be drawn to Katie soon, and beneath her sharp intelligence, she was still a vulnerable little girl who missed her father. Her need would be easy to exploit. Worried about the lax morality of the times, Marietta wished that Katie were plain.

The second week of September was warm, dry, and golden as though summer wanted to linger, but I was eager to plunge into fall. I was in high school now, counting down to a future when I would go away to college and make something exciting of my life.

As I waited for the school bus, a strange brown van with patches of grey primer parked across the road from me. The horn honked, the window rolled down, and Ritchie leaned out. "Want a ride?"

"Sure." I ran around to the passenger side and got in. "Whose van?"

"Mine. Bought it last week."

A quick inspection revealed a torn seat, cracked windshield, and wires dangling from the hole where a radio used to be. Overlooking those flaws, I said, "Cool. How'd you get the money?"

Ritchie snorted. "Worked like a dog all summer." He made a careening U-turn and headed toward the highway. "Detasseled corn, mowed grass at the country club, and still had to do chores at our place."

No wonder I hadn't seen much of him. Staring at his tanned, muscled arms, I realized with surprise that he didn't look like a kid anymore. He had changed during the last year when we were in different schools: him in high school, me in junior high.

When we arrived at the school, I saw my best friend standing outside. Although she still wore her brown hair boyishly short, Nita had changed since puberty from a scrawny tomboy to a chunky girl with womanly hips and thighs. Today, she was barefoot, her toes peeking out beneath the frayed hems of extra-wide bell-bottom jeans. Her boyfriend Todd wore faded jeans, a black KISS T-shirt, and a David Cassidy shag in his white-blond hair.

Ritchie parked in the first empty space halfway down the block, and then he and I walked back together. "Hey, Ritchie," Todd said.

Slouching, Ritchie stuck his thumbs in his pockets. "Got a cigarette?"

"Naw. Nita, give him one."

"What am I, your slave?"

Todd smirked. "You know you want to be."

Shifting uncomfortably, I became aware that I was the only one of the four holding a three-ring notebook, the only one not smoking, the only one wearing nice clothes instead of jeans.

When Ritchie invited Todd to see his van, Nita put on her sandals, flicked her cigarette onto the lawn, and said to me, "Come on."

We entered the high school and went down to the basement cafeteria. On one wall, roll-down shutters sealed off the window where students could buy cooked lunches at noon, and further down, the hot table that sold slices of pizza was cold and unattended. The wall opposite the food stations displayed a mural painted by the senior class of 1973. In it, a pastel rainbow arched across a bright blue sky, and beneath it stood three silhouettes: a boy, painted in brown, sporting a large Afro; a girl, painted in yellow, with long, flowing hair; and another boy, painted in red, with a Mick Jagger haircut. Nita and I called it the Mod Squad wall after a TV show we watched when we were kids.

As we sat at a table, Nita asked, "So, you going with Ritchie?"

"No, he's just my neighbor."

Laughing, Nita took out a pen and began to re-ink Todd's name on the back of her hand. "Cool guys don't give rides just 'cause you're a neighbor."

"Cool guys?" I blushed as I recalled the new physical awareness of Ritchie I'd felt. "He's only a friend. We used to play together when we were kids."

"I bet you did. Looks like he wants to play some more."

I shook my head in protest.

Nita leaned forward. "Look, I don't care if you decide to bang the dude. But if you want to stay straight, Ritchie's not your man."

Resenting her smugness, I said, "I think I know him better than you do."

The bell rang. Nita shrugged and stood up. "Don't say I didn't warn you."

Marietta slipped off her shoes and wiggled her toes on the cool kitchen linoleum. Then she picked up a vase of pink carnations from the table and took it to the sink. She'd bought them last week when she was depressed about the anniversary of Joe's death.

As she filled the vase with fresh water, she noticed that some of the petals were brown at the edges. *They're still not too bad. They'll keep till tomorrow.*

After she put the flowers back on the table, Marietta opened the refrigerator. The sight of the pork steaks she'd planned for supper stirred her resentment. Why should she have to stand at work all day and then at the stove each evening? *If I lived alone, I could come home and take a bath, have a soft-boiled egg on toast.*

She walked down to Katie's room and found her daughter sitting propped against pillows, chewing the cap to a BIC pen and frowning at her spiral notebook.

"Doing homework?"

"Yeah, I have to write a five-paragraph essay for English."

Marietta leaned against the door frame. "Could you finish it after supper? I'm really tired and want to take a bath. I was hoping you'd cook tonight."

"I guess so."

As Katie rose, Marietta looked closely at her form-fitting ribbed sweater and saw a distinct bulge over the outline of her bra cups. "Have your bras gotten too tight again?"

Katie hunched her shoulders. "I don't know. Maybe."

"For heaven's sake, why don't you say something?"

When Katie shrugged, Marietta forced herself to draw on the patience she used when waiting on customers. "I'll measure you later. It's important to have a proper fit."

In the tub, Marietta sighed as hot water eased the knots in her calves. Katie was changing so fast. This would be the third set of new bras in a year. *Thank God for my employee discount.*

A knock sounded on the bathroom door. "Can I throw the flowers out?"

"No."

"But they're gross."

"Don't start that again. They're my flowers, and I'll take care of them."

Katie groaned and left. Her aversion to cut flowers had been constant ever since that one trip to the cemetery, and Marietta was tired of catering to it.

Thinking again of Katie's blossoming figure, Marietta stared down at her own rounded stomach and flabby thighs. Her weight, which had remained stable during the twelve years she was married, had gone up thirty pounds since Joe's death. Suddenly, Marietta felt angry. She was only forty. It was too soon to lose her figure.

The distant trilling of the telephone interrupted her thoughts. Katie knocked on the door again a minute later. "Mom, Nita wants to know if I can sleep over Friday night."

"As long as Mrs. Benson says it's all right."

"OK. Thanks." As she heard her daughter's footsteps recede down the hall, Marietta rested her head against the back edge of the tub.

I *jumped* up from the couch and began to pick up pizza-smeared paper plates and empty beer and soda cans from around Nita's basement family room. A minute before, Nita and Todd had gone upstairs. From the way they had kissed and clutched at each other while dancing, I didn't think they'd be back any time soon.

At one end of the room was Mr. Benson's prized tiki bar, the sides lined with vertical bamboo canes and decorated with a Polynesian mask. A fishing net dotted with seashells was draped like a canopy overhead, and on the mirrored shelves behind the bar stood bottles of liquor and mugs shaped like Easter Island statues. As I went behind the bar to shove the trash in the garbage can, Ritchie crossed the room toward me. Knowing that my mother would disapprove of the boys being here while Nita's parents were out, I stayed where I was with a barrier between us. To hide my nervousness, I said, "Don't you feel bad you had to quit football to get a job?"

Ritchie shrugged and sat on a batik-upholstered barstool. "Coach worked us too hard."

"Oh." I wiped down the glossy wooden bar top with a towel. "Did I tell you I had a chance to be on girls' track? Miss Everett saw me running in gym and asked me to try out. But I had to say I couldn't stay after school for practice because my mom works."

Ritchie yawned. *You're talking too much,* I scolded myself. *And we're stuck down here while Nita and Todd—* My mind refused to name what I thought Nita and Todd were doing.

"Want to shoot some eight ball?" Ritchie asked.

"I've never done it before. Can you teach me?"

"Sure." He slouched over to the pool table, and I followed him. Ritchie racked the balls, handed me a cue, and showed me how to hold it. "You got to bend over like this."

I leaned over the table in the pose he'd demonstrated and shot the cue toward the tight triangle of colorful balls. The impact sent them rolling in different directions, and a red-striped one sank into a corner pocket. "All right!" I jumped up and down. Grinning at Ritchie, I saw him watching me intently. He moved to the side of the table opposite me as I put more chalk on the cue and aimed again.

"Lean over a little more," he said.

As I followed his instructions, I realized abruptly why he was staring so hard. Nita had loaned me a knit top of her older sister's—a tight, sparkly, purple V-neck—and when I bent over to make a shot, my cleavage showed. My cheeks burned. Deliberately, I missed my next few shots, letting Ritchie win the game.

"Want to play again?" he asked.

"No, you're too good for me."

We drifted away from the pool table. When Ritchie flopped down on the gold and avocado floral couch, I lowered myself into an orange bean bag chair.

"Man, I'm tired," he groaned. "Work is such a drag. I can't wait till I'm eighteen. I'm going to take off for California."

"Really?" My interest perked up. Daddy had spent time in California after he graduated from high school.

"Yeah, Paul says it's great. Warm all the time. I'd park by a beach somewhere and live out of my van. Get a job being a lifeguard or something cool like that."

His answer disappointed me. "My dad used to tell me about the historic places and great scenery he saw in California. Someday, I want to go there too."

"Yeah?" Ritchie patted the couch next to him. "Come sit here."

The thought of being so close to him tightened something deep inside my abdomen. As I struggled to extract myself from the bean bag's amorphous embrace, Ritchie grinned. When I finally sat on the couch, he settled his arm across the back of my shoulders. He smelled like cigarette smoke.

"Know what I heard at school?" Pushing up my sleeve, he rubbed the top of my arm. "Some people think we're going together."

"Oh?" I felt jumpy beneath his touch.

"Yeah. I hate gossip."

Certain he was warning me off, I said, "Why can't people mind their own business?"

"Yeah, what do they care if I want to go out with you?"

"You do?" I could have kicked myself for sounding so eager. "I mean, don't let gossip push you into anything."

"Huh?" Ritchie gave me a baffled look, then rubbed my arm again, raising goose bumps on my skin. "Don't you want to go together?"

I blushed again. "My mom says I can't date till I'm sixteen."

"That's OK." Ritchie stroked the base of my throat, which made me catch my breath. "Going together doesn't mean we have to date. It just means you promise not to go with anyone else. And we kiss and stuff."

"And stuff?" Looking away from him, I made myself say, "I should tell you, I think it's wrong to do certain things before marriage."

"You don't think I'd hurt you, do you?" He laid a hand on my knee. It was a big hand, and I could feel its warmth through my jeans.

"Don't."

Ritchie pulled back his arm. "So you're turning me down?"

"No." I turned and saw his scowl. "I just thought if you want a girlfriend who...you know...I don't want you to expect the wrong thing."

"Jesus Christ! We've never even kissed and you're giving me a sermon."

"I'm sorry." My face went hot again.

Ritchie bent closer. "Can't you at least give me a chance?"

Gazing downward, I nodded. When he moved to kiss me, I closed my eyes. The kiss was over so fast, I couldn't even tell whether I liked it.

When Ritchie saw my surprise, he grinned and kissed me again. Before that night, I had always wondered how couples could kiss for hours without stopping. Now I knew. There was such a variety of kisses: tentative questions and staccato teasers and hard demands that raised an answering desire in me. By the time Todd and Nita came back downstairs, my lips felt swollen, and I had started to wonder if it would really be so terrible to let Ritchie go a little further.

After the boys left, Nita said, "I guess you're going together, huh?"

"Yes. And guess what? He understands about me wanting to stay a virgin."

"Right." Nita sounded tired. "They all say that till the lights are out."

Nita's skepticism bothered me more than I wanted to admit. When I returned home the next morning, I went to my room and stared at my bookshelves. Next to my brown and pinto plastic horses stood a low, sleek model car.

After my father's funeral, when everyone had come back to the house to eat ham and chicken and pineapple upside-down cake, Ritchie found me sitting in a corner, trying to be invisible so people would stop gazing at me with their terrible pity. He stood a moment, clutching a paper lunch sack, and then held it out to me. "This is for you."

I opened the bag and pulled out a model of the car from *The Munsters* TV show. It was the first model kit Ritchie ever bought, but he was only seven or eight at the time, and he grew frustrated by all the little pieces. His father and older brother Paul laughed at him for wasting his allowance on a thing like that, but I knew it was something my father would be good at figuring out, so I told Ritchie Daddy would help him. And he did. Every evening for a month, they worked on it in our kitchen. I was allowed to watch but not participate because, as my father warned me privately, this was Ritchie's special project.

Looking up from the flashy black and red model, part dragster and part hearse, I said, "But this is yours. You worked so hard on it."

Ritchie had shifted his weight and glanced down at the beige carpeting. "Your dad did most of it. I want you to have it."

At the memory, tears pricked my eyes and I hugged myself. I *did* know Ritchie better than Nita ever could. He had a reservoir of sweetness somewhere underneath the tough exterior he liked to cultivate, and now that we were a couple, maybe I could help draw it out of him.

The next six months weren't anything like I imagined "going together" would be. Ritchie drove me to school every morning and home from school on afternoons when he didn't have to work. We would park in my mother's driveway and kiss for several minutes before I went in the house—my heart pounding the whole time for fear that one of the neighbors would see us and tell my mom, a risk that somehow fueled my arousal.

Sometimes we fought because Ritchie wanted to neck in the back of the van, which he insisted would be more comfortable with its orange shag carpeting and throw pillows scattered across the floor, but I refused because I felt sure he had more than kissing in mind. A few times he broke up with me over my "stubbornness," but usually, as soon as he cooled off, he begged me to take him back.

"I don't know what it is about you," he said once after we'd been apart two weeks, our longest breakup. "I can't get you out of my mind."

I kissed him hungrily then, desperate to think I was as special as his words implied. Yet, a voice inside me scoffed, *Of course, he's hung up on you. It's because you haven't done it yet.*

That was where things stood as my freshman year rolled into spring. Ritchie kept saying he wanted a regular relationship, but I wouldn't be sixteen for over a year, and I was too scared to ask my mom to reconsider her rule because I didn't want her to know how far things between us had gone.

To placate him, one day I agreed to stop for a hamburger on the way home from school, telling myself that since my mom knew he was giving me rides, she couldn't object to a stop on the way. Ritchie was so hungry he ate two Big Macs and an order of fries, and it was nearly 4:30 when we parked in my mom's driveway, lined with a row of daffodils on either side. I leaned over and kissed him quickly. "See you tomorrow."

He grabbed my arm. "Wait. Can't I come inside?"

"Well,..." He had never asked that before. When I realized that my mother wouldn't be home for another hour, excitement took possession of me. "You've got to leave by five."

"Yeah, sure."

As soon as we were inside, he grabbed at my jacket. I jerked away. "Wait. I have to put a casserole in the oven, or my mom will get suspicious."

When I returned, Ritchie was waiting for me on the rose, peach, and cream striped couch. He looked dark and dangerous against my mother's sleek pastel furniture, and the contrast excited me.

The moment I sat next to him, he began to kiss me urgently. As he squeezed my upper arm, the thought darted into my mind, *He's pretending it's my breast,* and I teetered on the fulcrum of temptation; sometimes when I was alone, I fondled my nipples and imagined Ritchie was doing it. Now was my first chance to experience the real thing. *But it would be wrong.*

Then Ritchie's hand moved under my skirt.

"Don't!" I swatted at him.

"Dammit, you never let me do anything."

"You said you understood." I hugged a nubby peach pillow to my chest like a shield.

"Look, you never give me anything. It hurts to want you so much. I just need something once in a while." He punched the couch back between us.

Cringing, I hugged my pillow-shield more tightly. "Like what?"

He scooted closer. "Like maybe you could let me touch your breast."

"That's not a little thing."

"See what I mean? To you, *everything* is a big deal." He punched the couch again. "What if I keep my hand outside your shirt?"

In spite of my misgivings, I wanted to try it so badly I could hardly breathe. "Just a couple of minutes."

"OK, sure."

He took the pillow and tossed it to the floor. When his hand cupped my breast, I twitched. Even through the fabric, his touch felt so much more exhilarating than when I rubbed myself. As I kissed him, I imagined his other hand stroking my thigh. My breathing quickened, and I had to tense to keep from writhing in pleasure under his caresses. My conscience whispered the word *slut,* and I pushed him away.

He groaned. "What's wrong?"

"That's enough."

"Shit. What the hell is wrong with you?"

"Nothing. You said you were only going to do it a little bit."

"You're supposed to like it." He tugged the crotch of his jeans. "Other girls do."

"What other girls?"

He ducked his head. "Nobody."

I jumped up and went to stand behind one of the twin armchairs on the other side of the room. "Go home."

Ritchie stood and held out his hands to me. "Come on, don't do this."

"I'm not doing anything. You're the one running around behind my back."

"I didn't. That was last year. Before you and me."

"I don't care." I bit my lip to hold back the tears.

He came closer. "Baby, don't be like this. There's nobody but you."

It's not fair. He can make those big brown eyes look so appealing. "Were there lots of other girls?"

"Katie, stop it. You're the only girl I want." He walked around the chair and took my hand. "Come on."

No, I thought. But the thought of losing him to someone else was so upsetting that I let him lead me back to the couch.

As she arrived home from work, Marietta frowned to see a brown van in the driveway. She knew that Ritchie had been giving Katie rides, but Marietta had warned her daughter not to invite him in the house when she was alone.

Some instinct prompted her to enter the front door quietly. She found them on the couch—Katie naked above the waist, Ritchie kissing her breasts.

When Marietta slammed the door, the boy jumped up. Thank God, his pants were still zipped. But his face was sullen. As Katie snatched her blouse off the floor, Marietta pressed her lips together to keep from erupting in rage.

She waited for a count of five and then said, "Go home, Richard." He stared at her for several seconds and then sauntered out the door as though he didn't care. He didn't even glance at Katie.

Once he was gone, Marietta turned to her daughter, who huddled in the corner of the couch with her head down. Several strands of her dark hair had been pulled loose from her braid and hung by her cheeks like tattered curtains. "Go to your room, and don't come out until I tell you to."

For an hour, Marietta walked back and forth on her patio, trying but failing to pray, imagining one argument with Katie after another, and calling silently to Joe, begging him to give her some insight into their child. Nothing helped. All she could think of was how terrible it would be if that boy got Katie pregnant. All the plans Joe had made for Katie's future and all the sacrifices Marietta had endured would incinerate in the white heat of such a disaster. Finally, when she felt more weary and heartsick than furious, she went to confront her daughter.

Marietta stopped just inside the bedroom door and fixed her gaze on Katie, who'd changed into a baggy grey sweatshirt as if to hide the body she had so recently flaunted. She sat on her lavender bedspread hugging her knees to her chest. "How long has this been going on?"

Katie bit her lower lip. "We've been going together six months. But this was the first time I let him touch me there."

Marietta folded her arms across her chest. "How could you be going together when I've forbidden you to date?"

"We didn't date. We just...promised not to go with other people."

"Doesn't that strike you as devious?"

Katie frowned but said nothing.

"You've just proved you're not old enough to handle this kind of relationship. For God's sake, Katie, you're fourteen. Your father never even kissed me till we were seventeen. How do you think he would have felt if he'd seen you tonight?"

The trembling of Katie's lips was her only response. Marietta pushed harder. "Do you know what it means when you let a boy do that to you?"

Somehow, without any visible movement, Katie shrank back against her pillows. She gave a barely perceptible shake of her head.

Marietta pulled open the drawer of the nightstand, lifted out the Bible she had taught Katie to keep there, and turned to the passage she wanted. "But I say unto you, that whosoever looketh on a woman to lust after her hath committed adultery with her already in his heart."

Setting the Bible down, Marietta said, "If you indulge in sinful thoughts, you're as guilty as if you had sex. And what kind of thoughts do you think you're putting in Ritchie's head? You led that boy on, which makes you as guilty as he is."

Katie lifted her chin. "I told him we couldn't go all the way. If he got the wrong idea, it's his fault."

"Not if your actions lie to him." When Katie blushed, Marietta crossed her arms. "After supper, you're going to call Ritchie and break up with him. And you're going back to staying at your grandmother's house after school."

Katie's eyes widened. "Please don't make me go back to Grandma's. You don't know how much I hate it there. Can't I have another chance?"

"Not until I know I can trust you." Pivoting, Marietta walked away.

For the first few weeks after my mother caught me with Ritchie, I was too angry to admit I'd been wrong. *How dare she make such a big deal! I wasn't going all the way. What does she take me for?*

When the fury died down, however, I was left with a residue of shame like silt deposited by a receding flood. The Bible verses Mother quoted haunted me in the middle of the night, and I'd turn on my bedside lamp and reread them for myself. Was I really no better than a whore? Sometimes, anger would flare briefly: *I might as well have slept with him if I'm going to be punished for it. At least I'd have had some fun.* Then oppressive guilt would tamp out the flames of rebellion. Seven months later, I still felt tainted by sin.

I had tried to find peace. In August, our church held its annual revival with a visiting evangelist named Jimmie Melvyn. He bore a facial resemblance to Charlton Heston and wore a brown plaid suit and the smile of a one-time talk-show host. Melvyn told us he'd repented of working in the entertainment industry, using his personality "to sell cornflakes," so he joined the Billy Graham Crusades to preach the word of God. That night, speaking from behind the light wood pulpit of our church, he cried out that none of us knew the hour of our death, and if we didn't repent now, tomorrow might be too late. He felt such anxiety for our souls that sweat broke out on his forehead. In response, my relentless shame drove me down the aisle to accept Jesus as my personal savior. I wanted to be new, to start over, so that my mother could look at me with love and pride. For six weeks afterward, I attended classes to prepare for baptism. Pastor Samuelson, a tall, grey-haired man, taught us that going down into the water symbolized dying in Christ and rising again. I hoped it was true and that it would make me clean.

The evening of my baptism, I wore a white robe with fishing

weights sewn inside the hem so it wouldn't billow up in the water and expose my legs. The baptistery was located in an alcove behind the choir loft. Pastor Samuelson placed one hand beneath my shoulder blades and, with the other, pinched my nostrils and lowered me into a waist-deep pool. The sudden sensation of falling backwards frightened me, and cold water closed over my face. Gasping, I swallowed a little and began to choke. Panic gripped me, and I flailed my arms. I was going to drown. God had refused me and would let me die for my sins.

Sputtering, I stood up, and the congregation clapped. My gaze went to the pew where my mother sat with Grandpa Albert. She wore a calm, pleased expression, as though the ritual had gone exactly as it should. As the pastor guided me to the cement steps leading out of the baptistery, I coughed and shivered. I walked to the back room, where I stood dripping until Mrs. Samuelson brought me a towel. Hiding my face in its rough surface, I refused to weep.

Months had passed, and I still felt rejected by God. I didn't see Ritchie except at a distance in the school hallway, yet some mornings I lay in bed, imagining kissing him as I rubbed the spot between my legs that yearned to merge with something more than myself. Then would come the hot flush of guilt. By indulging in lustful fantasies, I had surely committed fornication once again. I had no right to ask God to forgive me until I'd given up my sin.

Sophomore year dragged toward its close. In May, I sat in the cafeteria with Nita the Monday after she'd gone to the junior prom with Todd, who was a year older than we were. I assumed Ritchie had gone too—he was only a junior because he'd repeated third grade—but I didn't want to ask and have Nita fuss at me to get over him. "It was a drag," Nita said between bites of pizza. "But you should've caught Mr. Ackerman dancing with Miss Spencer. Think they're screwing behind his wife's back?"

"Who cares?" I watched Ritchie's current girlfriend saunter across the cafeteria. Leanne was wearing heavy mascara, silver earrings that dangled to the ends of her bleached hair, a blue shirt knotted around her waist and unbuttoned to her bra, and tight jeans with embroidered patches drawing attention to her butt. She sat beside Brett Simons, the senior quarterback.

Nita snorted when she saw where I was staring. "Don't let that slut get you down. If Ritchie was smart, he'd dump her."

"Oh?" I asked without hope. Whatever else Leanne might be, she was a girl who gave guys what they wanted. Ritchie was probably crazy about her.

"Didn't you hear? Prom night, Ritchie caught her in Andy Hosek's car. So he slapped her. Then Andy gets into it, and Ritchie busts his nose. They both got suspended, and the bitch got off scot-free."

I gazed at Leanne, who was playfully swiping sausage off Brett's pizza. "She doesn't seem to feel too bad about it."

"Not everybody digs a guilt trip like you do."

"Cut it out," I said. Pain shot behind my eyes.

"Hey, lighten up. Ritchie's not the only dude in the world." Nita popped a sour grape gumball in her mouth. "Ever notice that guy who stares at you like a sick puppy? Doug Hines? I bet he's dying to go out with you."

"Oh, him." Even though we had three classes together, I never paid much attention to Doug, an acne-scarred nerd who always wore dress shirts and carried a battered leather briefcase.

I shook my head. "Doug's nice, but..." My voice died away.

"God, you sure have got it bad."

One Saturday in July as I stretched out my calves before jogging, Mother came into the living room. "Would you stop at Jake's on the way back? I need some brown sugar." She held out a dollar bill. "I don't suppose you've got any place to put this."

"I do." I tucked the money in my shoe. My outfit, a hot pink tank top and striped runner's shorts, had been a birthday present from Aunt Dee. Although pretty, it was so skimpy I felt like body parts were hanging out all over.

I hurried outside and, using an easy loping pace, ran past the quarter mile of mostly single-story homes. Once the last house was behind me, I picked up speed. The trees and shrubs along the road gave way to open fields. Low soybeans grew to my left, shoulder-high corn to my right. The ditches beside the road bloomed with a colorful bouquet of frothy Queen Anne's lace, blue chicory, and black-eyed Susans.

Up ahead, a flock of starlings wheeled in a huge cloud against the white sky and then settled in a field. I lifted my braid from my neck. Sweat poured down my face, and I tasted salt on my lips. Already I was beginning to sense the almost mystical sense of rhythm that possessed me when I ran. Sometimes, I imagined my veins sucking up strength from this ancient prairie where I'd been born. I loved it here, even though the land was flat as a table.

Turning the corner, I passed a white farmhouse whose yard displayed a silver milk can surrounded by orange marigolds. Half a mile farther, I turned onto Eagle Island Road. On my left, a tangle of wild shrubbery followed the line of the Theakia River. In places, openings broke through the green wall. After running another mile, I halted by one of those clearings.

From here, I could see Eagle Island, a long sandy oval overrun with thin trees and dense undergrowth. On mornings when mist from the river curled up around the island, the view made my heart ache.

Often, people sat fishing here when I ran past. The spot where I stood was empty that day, but down near the water's edge stood a table made from a large wooden spool and two rusty metal chairs with scalloped backs.

A breeze moved across my sweaty skin, and I pulled at the tank top plastered to my chest and then turned back.

As I went up the sagging steps of Jake's Store, I wiped the sweat from my face with the back of a hand. Then I pulled open the patched screen door, which squeaked as it had for years. The interior was dim after the glare outside, but I didn't need to see to find my way around. I knew every groove in the old plank floor. Going immediately to the aisle that contained baking supplies, I picked up a yellow box of light brown sugar and brushed dust off the top.

Jake was sitting behind the cash register on a battered soda fountain stool salvaged from an old drugstore. Twisting one end of his handlebar mustache, he leaned over the counter to peer at my feet. "Got shoes on, ain't you?"

"Yes."

He punched in the price on the register. "Wouldn't be the first time you came in here barefoot. Can't have it. Health regulations, you know."

"I know." Jake had been threatening barefoot children for as long as I could remember. As I handed him the money, the screen door groaned again. Turning, I watched Ritchie, dressed in jeans and a T-shirt, walk down the center aisle. He looked much the same as the day we broke up—wavy brown hair, sleepy brown eyes, a pouty lower lip—but I thought perhaps he had more muscle in his arms.

Ritchie gave me a slow appraising stare that revived my self-consciousness about my running outfit. "Hey, Katie."

Then he said to Jake, "A pack of Marlboros." Then, smiling at me, he asked, "How you doing? You look great."

"I'm a mess." I pushed back a few straggly hairs that were stuck to my face. It felt odd to look straight in his eyes; since I'd grown the last two inches, we were the same height.

"So I guess you're sixteen now, huh?"

Clutching the box of sugar to my chest, I nodded.

Ritchie came close and said in a low voice, "I really miss you. Do you suppose you could get your old lady to change her mind about me?"

A wave of dizziness passed over me. "What about Leanne?"

He shrugged. "Hell, that's over. She's...well, she ain't like you."

I shook my head. "I don't think my mom will give in. She was pretty mad."

"Yeah, that's what I thought." To my surprise, he smiled. "Well, she can't stop me from running into you at school. Right?"

He winked and moved to the counter. As I headed for the door, he called after me, "Don't forget. I'll be looking for you come September."

Cracking open the back door of the van, I peered across the parking lot to the high school. No students or teachers were in sight. I turned to Ritchie, who sat leaning against the side wall. "I have to go. I'll be late."

Ritchie stared at me with narrowed eyes and exhaled a stream of cigarette smoke.

"Aren't you going to kiss me good-bye?" I asked.

"No."

I grabbed my purse and books, jumped down to the pavement, slammed the door, and ran to the side door of the building. Ritchie was angry because I wouldn't skip class with him. I had refused, not because I feared getting caught, but because I was afraid we might go too far if we spent another hour alone.

Entering school, I held the edges of my unzipped jacket closed as I maneuvered through the crowds scurrying to class between rows of pastel lockers. Whenever I returned from a noon interlude in the van, I wondered if the other students could guess how I had spent my lunch period. Sometimes I'd meet the eyes of a passing guy and feel certain that he knew why my face was flushed.

I despised myself for becoming entangled in this secret life. When Ritchie first suggested we meet in the van, I knew he would want to do more than kiss but thought I could hold the line. Indeed, Ritchie was relentless in trying to arouse me so completely that I would yield to his pleas for sex. For all my shame, my resolve was weakening. Taking off my bra had become routine, and lately his efforts to slip his hand inside my panties tempted me more than I dared admit.

As I hurried down the hall, I wondered yet again whether heavy petting was really as bad as fornication. If only I could ask someone besides my mother. If it *was* true, then God must expect me to marry Ritchie—which meant tying myself to a boy whose highest ambition was to be a California beach bum. I resolved to break up with him before we went all the way—until I remembered how awful it had felt seeing him with Leanne.

I slipped into American history class as the bell rang. "In your seats, people," Mr. Kwan said. "You've only got two days to finish your team projects, so make the most of this period."

Sighing, I watched Doug Hines pull up his desk beside mine and grin bashfully at me. He wore mulberry bell bottoms and a flowered polyester shirt that somehow made him look dorkier than if he'd continued his earlier habit of ignoring fashion trends. "I worked on these last night." Doug handed me a set of graphs contrasting the agricultural economy of the post-Civil War South with the industrial economy of the North.

As we discussed our project, someone knocked at the classroom door. Mr. Kwan—a young teacher with round John Lennon glasses and black hair, mustache, and goatee—answered it and then came over to where Doug and I sat. "I have a pass for you to go to the counseling office, Katie. Mr. Massey wants to see you."

"Now?"

"Apparently." Mr. Kwan wandered over to the next group of students. Gathering my books together, I blushed as I wondered if someone had reported me for necking with Ritchie in the parking lot. "See you tomorrow," I told Doug and hurried away.

Through the half-open door to Mr. Massey's office, I could see him sitting at his desk filling out a form. He was a bald man of about fifty, wearing a suit the same color as his narrow fringe of brown hair. When I knocked on the doorframe, he looked up and smiled. "I have that book you wanted to borrow."

"Oh. Great." I entered his office and perched on a chair.

Rising, Mr. Massey went to his filing cabinet, over which hung a motivational poster that featured the saying, "The secret of success is that there is no secret to success." He grabbed a book from a stack on the cabinet. *"The College Handbook.* Is there a particular school you're looking at?"

"No. I just want to check what schools my test scores qualify me for."

The man laughed. "Good God, Katie, you ranked in the ninety-ninth percentile. You could go anywhere you want." Unbuttoning his jacket, he sat down. "I'm glad you're thinking about this. You don't want to end up at a second-rate institution."

"We can't afford a really good school."

"With your family situation and your scores, I'm sure you can get aid. Why don't you have your mom come in and talk to me?"

"Sure, Mr. Massey. Thanks."

Marietta's head pounded as she drove home from the store. After nearly a year of wrangling with the personnel office, she'd managed to get transferred from the lingerie to the furniture department, hoping that the commission part of her earnings would rise because of selling bigger-ticket items. She was the only woman in that department, though, and she suspected that whenever possible, her male colleagues colluded to steer customers away from her, implying in subtle and not-so-subtle ways that she wasn't very knowledgeable.

Parking her car at the end of the driveway, Marietta got out to check the mailbox. The black metal box was jammed full of college catalogs again. After tugging them out, tearing a fingernail in the process, Marietta carried them into the house and down to Katie's room, where she found her daughter sprawled on her stomach atop the lavender bedspread with several catalogs spread open before her. "What are you doing?"

"Thinking about where to apply."

"I thought you knew I wanted you to go to the Baptist college here in Zebulun."

Katie flipped her braid back over her shoulder. "What if I find something better?"

"Like one of these?" Marietta picked up the catalog Katie had been reading and leafed through the pages until she found data on the costs. Her irritation flared when she discovered that her carefully hoarded savings would scarcely pay for two years.

Tossing the catalog on the bed, she said, "Harvard? And what else?" She looked through Katie's choices: Yale, Princeton, Columbia.

"Mr. Massey said I should check out the best."

"And did he say who's going to pay for it?"

Abruptly, Katie sat up. "He said I could apply for scholarships."

Marietta folded her arms across her chest. "So they pay your tuition. Who will pay for room and board? And the car you'll need so far from home? And fancy clothes to keep up with the rich kids?"

Uncertainty shadowed Katie's face. "I didn't think about that."

"No, you never do." A wave of resentment washed over Marietta as she remembered how little her parents had supported her and Dee's desires to go to college, with the end result being that only one of them had managed it. Katie had no idea how blessed she was to have parents who'd made education a priority. "I want you to go to college, but I'm not going into debt just to give you an overpriced education. Zebulun Baptist Bible is plenty good enough for you. Maybe they'll teach you a little Christian humility."

Wincing, Katie shut the catalogs on her bed. Marietta—torn between guilt and anger—hurried from the room. Maybe she had been unnecessarily harsh, but Katie had to be realistic. She was the daughter of a widow from a working-class family in a blue-collar town. She was lucky even to go to college.

One afternoon, a week after school let out, I sat on my old swing in the back yard, ostensibly reading a biography but really staring ahead over the soybean field and pondering the future. Mother's refusal to let me consider out-of-town colleges had upended my plans. For the last few months, excitement had been building inside me over the prospect of leaving home after only one more year. Now the possibility of moving out had been pushed back at least four more years, and I didn't know how I was going to stand it. As I tried to think of alternatives, I heard Ritchie call my name.

"Back here!" I stood and glanced over my shoulder at the upper floor of the two-story house next door. The lilac hedge prevented me from seeing if anyone was in the yard. When Ritchie appeared around the corner of the house, I said, "You want to tell the whole neighborhood you're here? My mother will have a conniption if she finds out."

"I don't give a damn. I'm leaving, so she can't do a thing."

"Leaving?"

"Yeah. Finally going to California." He lit a cigarette.

The urge to cry surprised me. Things had been rough with Ritchie lately, but the thought of losing him devastated me. "Why didn't you tell me?"

"Just decided today."

I noticed his defiant tone. "Why? What happened?"

"Nothing. Finally got my fuckin' diploma, I can leave this dump behind."

"You might at least be sorry about leaving me."

Ritchie removed his cigarette from his lips and blew a stream of smoke. "I want you to come with."

Stunned, I sat back down on the swing. "How? I'm still in school."

"Damn, is that all you care about? There's schools in California."

Shutting my eyes, I pictured a highway leading up to a mountain pass. Beyond it lay California, land of Spanish missions and the forty-niner's gold rush. I could go there with Ritchie—but as what? "I can't just live with you."

He turned away from me and was silent as he gazed at his father's field. Then he faced me again. "We could get married."

"What?"

"Yeah." He hurried to sit beside me. "I should've said right away. I want to marry you."

Warily, I noticed a glint in his brown eyes. "I'm too young. I'll only turn seventeen next week."

"Paul says there's states you can get married real young. Hillbilly states like Kentucky. Hell, girls get married at fourteen down there."

I shook my head. "I don't think that's true anymore."

"Paul said it is."

Since when did Paul care about Ritchie and me? I bit my lip, afraid to make Ritchie mad. "Maybe we could call down there and ask."

"If you don't want to go, just say so. Stop being such a bitch."

Staring at the willow at the back of the yard, I felt the tug of travel lust—but an aversion to going with Ritchie. Lately, I'd been dreaming that next year, I might meet someone else. Not somebody pathetic like Doug, but someone smart and funny who liked the same things I did.

But who would want me? Even if I was technically still a virgin, I'd already gone too far with Ritchie to be considered pure. Wasn't I already as good as married to him in God's eyes?

Then there was the promise of California. I remembered reading in a catalog that the University of California had lower tuition rates for state residents. This could be the answer I was looking for. "If I got a job and saved up money, do you think I could go to university?"

He flung away his cigarette. "Christ, is frigging school all you ever think about?"

"No." I gazed down at my book as I debated what to do. The scowl on Ritchie's face told me he was losing patience. The thought of his leaving me here with no one to love me was too terrible. "All right. Let's go."

"Great. I'll pick you up in an hour." He stood. "Don't bring every damn thing you own."

It was only after he left that I realized he hadn't even kissed me.

As I packed my clothes in the old brown suitcase that had once been Daddy's, I picked up Sacajawea, the doll that still stood on my nightstand. I rubbed the beaded fringe and thought back to a time—I think I was about six—when I was upset about a scolding and ran to my father. "Mom hates me."

Daddy pulled me onto his lap. "Your mom loves you, Katydid. Don't you know that?"

I shook my head stubbornly.

"Of course, she does. Think about all the things she does for you."

"Like what?" I asked, hurt that he was siding with her instead of me.

He sighed. "What about that Indian doll you like so much?"

"You gave me that!"

Daddy shook his head. "Mom bought it as a present for you to take to your cousin's birthday party, but you fell in love with it and thought it was for you. We didn't have much money because I was out of work, but your mom couldn't stand to disappoint you. So she stayed up all night sewing a stuffed dog you could give Bernadette instead."

The memory of that conversation brought a lump to my throat and made me wonder if I was doing the wrong thing leaving my mother here all alone. Would she think I hated her?

Going to my desk, I took out a piece of paper and wrote a note:

Dear Mom,

Ritchie asked me to go with him to California. Please don't worry. He said we'll get married. I'm not running away because I'm mad. Honest. But I really want to go to a better school. California has good universities, and tuition there is low for residents. I'll write you when we find a place to live.

I'm sorry.

Katie

I sealed the note in an envelope, wrote "Mother" on the front, and carried it out to the kitchen table. When I went back to finish packing, I gazed at Sacajawea, wondering if I should take her with me. Ritchie would probably taunt me if I did, so I decided against it, but I did find the faded blue work shirt of Daddy's that I'd hidden away after his death and placed it at the bottom of the suitcase.

After driving south for several hours, Ritchie parked at a highway rest area—the kind with scattered picnic tables and a small brick building housing bathrooms and vending machines—and, despite the sign forbidding overnight parking, announced we were stopping for the night. After using the restroom, I climbed in the back of the van, dug around in my suitcase, and pulled out Daddy's shirt to sleep in.

Ritchie climbed in after me. "You mad about not going to a motel?"

"No," I said over my shoulder. "We couldn't afford two rooms."

He laughed at that. I heard him take the lid off the cooler and pop open a can of beer. "Leave that stuff alone and come here."

Nervously, I joined him. Tomorrow would be my wedding night, and I wondered if Ritchie knew to be gentle when it was the girl's first time. He probably hadn't ever been with a virgin. Leanne sure as hell wasn't one.

After finishing the beer, Ritchie gave me a long wet kiss and pushed me to the orange shag carpet. He started to unbutton my shirt.

"Can't we kiss for a while first?"

"We been kissing for a year now." He pulled my shirt down off my shoulder, shoving the bra strap with it, and immediately took my nipple in his teeth.

"Ow!" I pushed at him, but he tightened his grip on my arms.

Still sucking my breast, he pulled me onto my side so he could squeeze my butt. Then he lifted his head and kissed my lips. I tried to lose myself in what we were doing, but his impatience frightened me.

I heard him unzip his jeans. Then he pushed his body against mine. I could feel his erection, so hard that my leg hurt where his penis jabbed me. He grabbed my hand and thrust it down between our bodies. I pulled back when I encountered a warm, firm column of flesh protruding from his open fly. Sitting up, I stared at him. *God, it's so big. How will it ever fit?*

Ritchie put my hand back on it. "Rub!" he ordered. Lightly, I touched the side of his penis. Fitting his hand over mine, he forced me to curl my fingers around the shaft. "Grow up. It's time you learned the score."

After I made a few half-hearted gestures, he let me take my hand away and lowered me to the floor. With his knee, he forced my legs apart and wedged his lower body between them.

"No." I placed my palms against his chest and shoved.

Ritchie seized my wrists and forced my arms down to the floor. Leaning heavily on me, he shoved his face close to my ear. "I'm tired of playing with you."

"I'm not playing." I turned my face away from his hot, beery breath. "You said you'd wait till we got married."

"Too bad." He tightened his grip on my wrists and licked my earlobe. "Come on, we'll be legal tomorrow. What the hell difference does a day make?"

As his heavy bulk forced my legs apart, the muscles of my inner thighs felt like they were tearing. "Why spoil it now? We waited so long already."

"Too long. I'm sick of it." Releasing my arms, he drew back into a kneeling position and unsnapped my shorts. I flung myself forward to fight him.

Ritchie punched me in the diaphragm, driving the air from my lungs. My head whiplashed back and struck the floor. Before I could regain my breath, he was slapping me—two, three, four times until I was certain he was going to rape me. "You shouldn't make me so mad."

He left me, opened the cooler, and took out another beer. Bringing it with him, he sat next to me. "Drink this."

"I don't want it." I pulled myself up to a seated position. My cheeks were on fire, my ears were ringing, and I thought I was going to vomit.

"Drink it," he said, this time with menace.

I managed to swallow a little and then watched him down the rest of the can. After wiping his mouth, he smiled at me. "You know, I'm all you got now. And it's only one night. Nobody's going to know the difference."

Beginning to shiver, I hugged myself. "You expect me to say yes after what you—"

"Dammit!" Ritchie pounded the side wall of the van, and I cringed. "Everything's got to be your way, doesn't it?"

"No." Fearfully, I stared at him. He had never looked at me with such hostility, as though I were an adversary to be conquered. I could still feel the force of his palm crashing into my cheek. "All right," I whispered.

He grinned. "It's going to be great. You'll see."

As he eagerly pulled off my clothes, I felt my spirit split away from the shell of my body and shrink within me so that Ritchie couldn't reach it, no matter what he did to my flesh.

"Hey, girl, you better pay!"

The waitress's shout jerked me to a stop. Embarrassed that everyone in the café must think I was a deadbeat, I crossed to the counter at the right, where a small woman with white dandelion-fluff hair sat behind the cash register. The waitress walked over, slapped the check on the glass countertop, and hovered behind me as I fumbled to extract my wallet from my purse.

Glancing at the mint green slip of paper, I was relieved that the total was under ten dollars. Paying the check was going to leave me short on cash.

The old woman—Nancy, according to the plastic name badge clipped to her purple pansy-print blouse—rang up my order with excruciating slowness. I didn't have the heart to rush her; she had a badly humped upper spine and trembling hands. Beneath my patient exterior, however, panic surged at the thought of how angry Ritchie would be.

When I finally burst through the café exit and turned toward where we'd parked the van, I saw nothing but an empty space. I blinked as if that could make the van reappear, but of course, it didn't.

Slowly, I walked in that direction and stopped by a spindly maple sapling planted in a circular opening in the concrete. *He went to get gas,* I told myself, but then remembered that he'd filled up right before we went to the courthouse. I searched the street in both directions and then stared at the empty pavement.

That was when I saw my suitcase standing on the curb next to the expired parking meter. My throat constricted, and I felt uncomfortable pressure in my ears as though the atmosphere had thickened. The ground seemed to tilt. Feeling faint, I sat on the suitcase, closed my eyes, pressed my abdomen, and prayed, *God help me.* Somewhere to my right, a bird lifted into the air with a loud flapping of wings.

The words *He left me* buzzed in my brain. My cheeks burned with the humiliation of being tossed out publicly like a sack of trash. Then rising up through the chaos of shame and fear was another feeling that demanded recognition—the clear certainty that Ritchie could never hurt me again. I exhaled deeply, and the world righted itself.

Where to now? I certainly didn't have enough money to get to California; I wasn't sure I even had enough to get home, nor did I have any idea how my mother would greet me.

Tears welled in my eyes as I thought of my father. He would have welcomed me back, no matter what I'd done. Of course, if Daddy were still alive, I doubted I would have run away.

"Ran out on you, did he?"

Jumping up, I turned to see the waitress from the restaurant. The name stitched on her salmon uniform was Angelene. I gazed into her light brown eyes, expecting to find scorn, but instead saw weary understanding. "You learn to size people up in my job. I could see right away that boy only cared about himself."

As I took in that brutal assessment, my shoulders slumped. "I guess that makes me a fool."

She snorted. "No more than any other woman in the world. We all seem to need at least one jackass in our life to learn what's what."

I gazed at the space where the van had been parked fifteen minutes before, still not believing Ritchie had driven away without a good-bye. Wouldn't he regret it and come back for me, just like all those times we broke up in school? *God, I hope not!* I realized and turned back to the waitress. "Is that why you came out here? To tell me that?"

"No, Nancy sent me to fetch you. You sit on the curb, the police are liable to arrest you for vagrancy." She hefted my suitcase. "You're not from around here, are you?"

"No, I'm from Illinois. About an hour from Chicago."

Angelene snorted again. "Figures. Al Capone country." Then she went down the sidewalk past the café and the jewelry store beyond it, and turned right at the corner. "No sense letting everybody gawk at you like a sideshow freak. I'm taking you around to our break room."

I followed her, surprised that the same person could be both so cutting and so kind.

We turned up an alley, walked past the rear of the jeweler's, and entered the back door of the café, finding ourselves in a small entryway with a time clock. To the left, an archway led to the kitchen where a cook was working the griddle. In front of us, a door opened onto a room with a row of lockers, a refrigerator, a dinette set, and a counter with a sink and coffee maker.

Angelene set down my suitcase and gave me the once-over. "Nancy's going to come talk to you soon as she can. You're not going to light out before then, are you?"

I shook my head.

"Good. 'Cause she's the kindest soul you could ever hope to meet, and I don't want to see that kindness thrown back in her face. You understand me?"

"Yes, ma'am," I answered automatically, an answer that earned me a grudging smile.

"Appearances to the contrary, sounds like somebody raised you up right."

With that, she walked out, closing the door behind her.

I sank into one of the orange plastic chairs and took out my wallet again. I had seventeen dollars and change. Was that enough to get me home?

Thoughts of my mother filled my mind. What I wanted more than anything was to run to her, feel her arms envelop me, and cry on her shoulder. I wanted her to pat my back and say it would be all right, that of course, she still loved me. But when I tried to picture her, all I could visualize was a face tight with anger.

Grandma Brigitte wouldn't be any better; she'd give me an even harder time than Mother would. And Daddy's parents had moved to Florida not long after he died.

I was still trying to decide what to say to Mom when Nancy entered the room, hunched over like a crone in an illustration from a German fairy tale, yet propelling herself without the use of either cane or walker. She moved slowly, carrying a piece of pie on a small plate.

Nancy set the pie in front of me and placed a fork next to it. It was chocolate, with a thick layer of whipped cream sprinkled with chocolate shavings. "Angelene said you hardly touched your lunch."

Then she moved over to the coffeepot, filled two heavy white mugs, and turned back to the table. When she saw I hadn't picked up the fork, she said, "Don't you like chocolate? I can get you something else."

"Chocolate is fine." I gazed at the plate, thinking I had never seen anything look so delicious. "But I'm low on money, and I can't afford to pay."

"Nobody asked you to." After carefully depositing the mugs, she sat next to me. "You've had a shock, so you need food in your stomach and sugar in your bloodstream. You eat that and drink the coffee too."

"Yes, ma'am." Using the side of the fork, I sliced off the pointy end of the pie, put it in my mouth, and let the piece melt over my tongue. I'd expected it to be pudding topped with Cool Whip, but the taste was richer than that and the texture fluffier. The filling tasted like the kind of chocolate used in German chocolate cake, and the topping was obviously real dairy cream. I sighed with pleasure, saw Nancy smile, and took another, bigger bite. Then I took a cautious sip of black coffee. The few times I'd tried it, I hadn't liked it, but now the dark, slightly bitter taste perfectly complemented the almost cloying sweetness.

As I ate, energy and hope trickled back into me. I hadn't realized how worn down I was until the sugar and caffeine began to work their magic. Irreverently, I thought, *This is what communion should be like. Not dry saltines and unsweetened grape juice.*

I laid my fork on the now-empty plate and looked at Nancy. She lifted her mug and smiled at me over its rim. "You don't need to tell me how you got into this fix. All I want to know is whether you have some place to go."

In that instant, I knew exactly who was most likely to give me a welcome as sweet as the pie I'd just eaten. "Yes," I answered.

The ringing of the telephone woke Marietta. She was slumped with her head on the kitchen table. Lurching from the chair, she reached for the aqua wall-mounted phone and discovered that her right hand was numb where her head had pressed down on it. She switched the receiver to her left hand. "Hello?"

"Marietta, it's Dee."

"Oh." Disappointment that the caller wasn't Katie squeezed Marietta's heart like a vise. "What's wrong?"

"Nothing. I'm calling to tell you Katie is safe."

"She called you?"

"Yes. That boy she was with ran off and left her in Kentucky."

Marietta expelled a deep breath and checked the clock. It was half-past eight in the morning. "Where in Kentucky?"

"She's not there now. She had enough money for the night bus to Indianapolis, so she took it and called us from the station. Ken drove down to get her. They should be here soon."

Safe. Ever since reading Katie's note, Marietta had prayed for such news, but now when it came, she felt more alienated from her daughter than ever. "Why didn't she call *me?"*

"I think she's afraid you might not want her back."

Marietta tightened her hold on the receiver. "Because she's been sleeping with him."

"Don't jump to conclusions. Wait until you talk to her."

"Why? Do you know something you're not saying?"

"Marietta, it's not my story to tell."

"What time do you want me to pick her up?"

"Oh,..." Dee shifted into her soothing, peacemaker's tone. "You've had so little sleep. I'll bring her home, sometime before supper."

After she hung up, Marietta stared at her right hand, still so numb that it seemed disconnected from her. Just like her daughter.

First, Marietta telephoned her pastor; two nights ago after she read Katie's note, Marietta had called him to ask for prayer. Now, after she told him the latest news, she went to shower. As hot water rained down on her, she imagined her reunion with Katie. She wanted to be like the father of the prodigal son and rush to her child, saying, "I love you. I was worried about you. I'm glad you're home," Eventually, they would need to deal with Katie's wrongdoing, but first Marietta had to make it clear that Katie's safety mattered most.

She pictured the scene a dozen times, hopeful that this reunion would bring about a new, closer relationship between them. Hours later, as she was scrubbing her stove to keep busy, she heard car doors slam in the driveway. Her heart froze. Any joy or relief vanished, driven away by the memory of the long nights she'd spent not knowing where Katie was and wondering why she had preferred to run away with a boy who would ruin her life than stay with her mother.

Marietta wiped her hands on a dish towel and walked to the kitchen doorway. Dee entered the house first. An unseen hand closed the front door, and then Katie stepped out from behind her aunt and gazed at her mother with frightened eyes. Irritated that Katie was already playing the victim, Marietta demanded, "What have you got to say for yourself?"

Katie flinched and lowered her gaze. "Nothing. I made a terrible mistake."

Marietta blinked, surprised by the swift admission. She stepped forward into the living room and tried to launch into the welcoming speech she had planned, but all that came out was, "At least, you're home."

"So, can I come back?" Katie asked in a small voice.

"Of course! I'm your mother. No matter what you do, I'll never stop loving you."

Katie nodded. With a visible effort, she looked into her mother's eyes. "Thank you."

Seeing that Katie still hadn't set down her suitcase—Joe's old brown case—Marietta softened her tone. "Put your things away, and we'll talk later."

Nodding, Katie came around the armchair, walked past her mother, and headed into the hallway. The two didn't touch.

As soon as the bedroom door closed, Dee said quietly, "Don't be so hard on her. She's been through a terrible time, and she was afraid of facing you."

Marietta's head snapped toward her sister. "Am I such an ogre?"

"Not to me, but you're awfully strict with her."

"I've had to be. She's too much like her father."

Dee raised her eyebrows. "But you loved Joe, even though he was a rebel."

Marietta folded her arms across her chest. "It's not the same. First of all, I wasn't his mother. Second, when a girl acts wild, she suffers harsher consequences than boys do."

Dee hesitated and then said, "We talked a lot on the drive here, and I can tell you Katie's beating herself up for what she did. I think what she really needs is to hear that you love her."

"I just said that! Anyway, she already knows it."

Dee shook her head. "I don't think she does."

The quiet words stabbed Marietta. She turned toward the kitchen to keep her sister from seeing the tears flooding her eyes. "You'll stay for supper, won't you?"

"Can't. I promised Ken I'd be home by dark."

Marietta swung back to face her. "It's only a ninety-minute drive, and you have to eat."

"I'd be in the way. You two need to talk."

After her sister was gone, Marietta made two mugs of tea and carried them to her daughter's room, where Katie, dressed in jeans and a faded denim shirt she didn't recognize, sat cross-legged on the bed.

Marietta lowered herself into the oak rocker in the corner and instantly regretted the choice. The chair triggered memories of singing her baby to sleep in those days of talcum-scented intimacy that were lost to her forever.

Katie sipped her tea and put the mug on her nightstand. "He lied to me. He swore we could get married in Kentucky, and I was stupid enough to believe him."

Her face was bruised, and she spoke with a dazed quality that made Marietta want to shake her. "Did you want to marry him?"

"He was leaving, and I'd never see him again. He said we could go to California, and I really wanted to attend college out of state."

That's meant to make this my fault, Marietta thought. "Do you love him?"

Surprise widened Katie's eyes. "I don't know. But I thought he loved me—" Her face crumpled. "I thought I knew him, but he was horrible. He—"

"I don't understand you at all. So much secrecy and deceit for a boy you don't even love. And you were sleeping with him too."

Katie went as pale as frost. "No. Not till...two nights ago."

Marietta gripped the arms of the chair. "You tried that story once before, remember? I know you've been carrying on with him a long time."

"I've been seeing him, yes, and kissing. But I didn't sleep with him until I thought we were about to get married and only then because—"

Marietta cut her off. "Can you give me a single reason to believe you?"

Bowing her head, Katie shielded her face with her hand. Marietta watched a tear fall onto the side of her palm and slide down to the bony knob on her wrist. After a few seconds, Katie looked up. "I know you won't believe me, but it's true."

She spoke with dignity, but her face was filled with despair. Marietta pitied her—but not enough to let her go on lying. "I'm not going to punish you for this little escapade. What matters more is to make sure you don't do it again."

"I won't. I'm never going to date anyone else."

The melodrama fueled Marietta's anger. "Don't be ridiculous. I want you to fall in love and get married—only not to someone like Ritchie. I've arranged for you to get counseling. Pastor Samuelson will meet with you once a week."

Folding her arms across her chest, Katie asked, "For how long?"

"As long as he thinks it's necessary. I realize I can't force you to go, but if you really want to convince me you've changed, you will."

After a long moment, Katie nodded.

The pastor's office was lined with ceiling-high shelves holding leather-bound volumes of theology, brightly colored books on the Christian family, and dusty tomes in Greek and Hebrew. Their towering presence reminded me of a Sunday school song: "Joshua fit the battle of Jericho,...and the walls came tumbling down." Glancing over my shoulder, I shifted my straight-back chair farther away from the nearest set of shelves.

Pastor Samuelson, a grey-haired, long-faced man with wire-rim glasses, handed a Bible across to me. "Please read verses four through six."

I skimmed them, felt my heart sink, and read quietly:

Ye have not yet resisted unto blood, striving against sin. And ye have forgotten the exhortation which speaketh unto you as unto children, My son, despise not thou the chastening of the Lord, nor faint when thou art rebuked of him: For whom the Lord loveth he chasteneth, and scourgeth every son whom he receiveth.

"What do you think that means?"

"That we have to fight sin until it hurts." *And I didn't,* I thought. *I just rolled over and opened my legs so he wouldn't beat me.*

Pastor Samuelson raised his eyebrows. "But what does it tell you about God?"

Dutifully, I scanned the verses again. "He's like a father. He does what's best for us, even if it hurts."

The minister nodded. "Tell me about your own father."

I gazed at the books behind Pastor Samuelson. It was becoming harder and harder to remember Daddy except as he appeared in photographs. "He was tall and blond and smart and funny. He taught me history, and he encouraged me to be creative."

Falling silent, I gazed at the pastor's thin-cheeked face. He seemed kind, and I wondered if he could discern the longing I felt for my father, the ache that everyone seemed to think should have gone away by now. Instead, he asked, "What's Ritchie like?"

"I don't want to talk about him."

He sighed and steepled his fingers before his face. "Isn't he older than you?"

"Yeah. Two years."

"Well, your mother thinks you're looking for a father figure."

"Ritchie?" I laughed. "He's a spoiled, overgrown baby who has temper tantrums, and nobody in their right mind would see him as a father figure."

Pastor Samuelson actually smiled. "I can see that. But I'd like to know more about your feelings about men."

"Why?"

"Because you strike me as a lonely, unhappy girl. I think that makes you vulnerable to the kind of man who'll take advantage of you."

My impulse to deny his words drowned in a rising tide of sorrow. I *was* lonely. How could Pastor know that when I'd never admitted it to anyone? If he understood that, maybe I could tell him everything. "Ritchie hit me," I whispered. "On our way to Kentucky. He—"

"Oh!" Pastor Samuelson coughed and crossed one leg tightly over the other.

My hope faded into futility. *He doesn't want to know what happened. He only wants to warn me off sex.*

After a moment, he said, "I want you to think about God's relationship to you as a father. Think about ways he can fill your loneliness."

"Yes, Pastor."

Afterward, as I walked to the car, I mused on the phrase *father figure.* So that's why my mother insisted on counseling. She was hoping I would latch onto Pastor Samuelson as a father substitute, and magically, all of my problems would be solved. *How can she be so dense?*

I watched apprehensively as Mother returned to the table with a fresh cup of coffee. Ignoring her food, she sipped from her turquoise mug and jotted a long column of numbers on a paper napkin. Then she frowned as she added the total.

For two weeks, she had been in a foul mood, tinkering with her budget daily as though bankruptcy loomed. Her actions frightened me because my applications for financial aid and early admission were due on the fifteenth. On Sunday, my desperate need to figure out what was wrong led me to eavesdrop on Mom's weekly phone call to Aunt Dee. "I'll go crazy if I don't get out of that job. But maybe it's stupid to want to go into business for myself."

Hearing that, I had told myself that my mother's irritation had nothing to do with me. Now, however, my anxiety gained new strength. "Mom, can we talk?"

"What is it?" she asked, starting a new column of numbers.

"The application for financial aid is due next week."

Sighing, my mother laid down her pen. She pushed her reading glasses up to the top of her head and rubbed the sore spots on the bridge of her nose. "You won't qualify for aid. I have too much money in the bank."

Stunned, I leaned back in my chair. "I thought we were barely getting by."

Mother shook her head. "Your father left insurance money I never spent, and I've saved some too. I have enough to pay for four years at Zebulun if you live at home." She sipped her coffee, and the hand holding the mug trembled. "But I've decided that it's time you took responsibility for your life. After graduation, I want you to get a job, and when you save enough money for half your tuition, I'll provide the rest."

"You want me to work?" For as long as I could remember, I had dreamed about attending college, carrying a stack of books, walking past ivy-covered buildings, and debating significant events of history. Now she wanted me to postpone that. I pictured myself waiting on customers as my mother did each day. And I knew. Mother had decided to use part of my college savings to escape from the store.

Fighting to stay calm, I tried to reason with her. "Won't it be harder for me to gain admission once I'm out of high school?"

Her eyes narrowed, and her voice turned bitter. "I doubt it. Not with your test scores."

She hates me. Because of what I did with Ritchie, she doesn't care about me anymore.

Pushing away from the table, I ran from the room.

Shortly before I finished high school, Mother informed me that a man she knew from the choir worked at the Zebulun Coupon Redemption Center and might be able to get me a job. She said it would be clerical work, which I thought sounded better than working in a factory or as a waitress. The man brought an application to church, and Mom helped me fill it out. The next thing I knew, I was scheduled to start a job the first Monday after graduation.

The center, housed in an old brick warehouse with frosted windows that let in light but no outside views, had two divisions; each was in its own massive open space with pipes and ductwork running overhead and rows of grey metal desks marching down the concrete floor. The coupon group dealt with grocery stores and other retail businesses that accepted consumer coupons. Once a week or once a month, depending on the volume of their business, retailers would mail all the coupons they had redeemed to the redemption center, which would tally the total face value and refund the store the money it had deducted from customer orders. The redemption center then filed for reimbursements with the manufacturers. Clerks had to sort the coupons by the various companies—General Mills, General Foods, Kraft, etc.—ring up how much each manufacturer owed, and make sure that the sum of the subtotals equaled the total amount that had been paid to the retailers.

My job wasn't that complex. I worked in the promotion group. Manufacturers such as Campbell's sometimes ran offers saying they would mail a premium like a cookbook filled with soup-based recipes to any customer who mailed in ten soup labels and a form with their name and address. One team of girls (everyone who worked there as a clerk was a young woman) opened the letters, checked that they contained the right number of labels or box tops or whatever was required, and then sent the completed forms over to typists like me. All day, every day, for over a year, I did nothing but type addresses on labels so that girls in yet another department could stick them on the packages containing cookbooks or movie tie-ins or whatever the manufacturers were giving away that month. My third day there, I realized that the constant din of typewriters at my end of the floor reminded me of the sound of machine guns in an old World War II movie, and after that, I could never escape the feeling that I was under siege. I earned the minimum wage of $2.65 an hour. Every Friday as I deposited my paycheck in the bank, I told myself I was one week closer to walking away from such mind-numbing work forever.

PART TWO

History Major

SEPTEMBER 1979–
DECEMBER 1983

As my mother drove between the stone pillars marking the entrance to the college campus, I stared ahead at Sandford Hall, the administration building. *I should have started here a year ago.* Anger soured the buoyant mood I'd woken up with.

The building, whose width ran more than half a city block, was constructed of rough-hewn yellow limestone. The center block was fronted by a bay that rose the full height of the four-story building and then narrowed into a two-story octagonal tower with lancet windows. Recalling the long-ago day when I first saw it, I could see why I'd believed it was a castle. Now I wondered if this was the magical kingdom where my dreams would come true.

"Where should I pick you up tonight?" Mom asked.

Glancing at the arched wooden door, I said, "There, by the entrance." I slid out of the car without saying good-bye. Walking around to the back of the building, I noticed how empty the campus was. Only incoming freshmen were required to attend Orientation Friday. According to the letter I'd received, I was supposed to take a tour of campus, register for classes, and buy my textbooks today. The schedule for the rest of the weekend included a cookout and a welcoming program this evening, a hymn sing and ice cream sundaes Saturday night. As a commuter student, I was going to miss those social events.

The carillon in the bell tower of the chapel sounded the half hour. My tour was supposed to start in fifteen minutes from the steps of the student union, a red-brick colonial building whose entrance was topped by a white pediment with a center acorn. The union faced the back of Sandford Hall across an expanse of lawn carved up by sidewalks running in all directions—each taking the shortest path between two campus buildings. *Might as well walk over there.*

As I sat on the wide stone banister, a young man came scurrying down the sidewalk. He stopped short when he saw me.

"You here for the tour? I'm your guide." He ran up to me, seized my hand, and pumped it once. "I'm Steve Crawford."

"Katie Thompson." I watched him shift from one foot to the other. He was slight of build but about my height, and he had curly brown hair, dark eyes, and a sharp nose in a thin face.

Steve rolled his shoulders like a prize fighter loosening up before a bout. "What dorm are you in? I'm a resident assistant in Murrow."

"I commute from a few miles outside town."

Steve nodded and cocked his head to the left, then to the right. "This is my first tour. I'm kind of nervous because I'm not good with groups."

"Then why are you doing this?"

"Oh, I'm over-responsible, I guess." He rubbed his left shoulder. "My mom says it's because my dad's gone."

"I'm sorry." My throat tightened, and I lowered my gaze. "My father's dead too."

"Mine's not dead. He left us." Steve paused. "When did...you lose yours?"

"I was eight."

"Wow, that must be rough." He stopped fidgeting. "I sort of know how you feel. I've never really accepted my dad being gone."

"No," I whispered, and Steve took the cue to be quiet.

Other students arrived, most of them wearing T-shirts and shorts or jeans. My khaki skirt and pink blouse felt as conspicuous as a parka at the beach. Jumping down from my seat and joining the others clustered on the sidewalk, I vowed, *I'll find a way to fit in even if I don't live on campus.*

Late that afternoon, I sat on one of the curved benches surrounding the fountain at the center of the quad I'd crossed on my long-ago trek to find a castle. The humanities and mathematics buildings stretched behind me, with only an arched walkway between them to provide access to the quad from the far side of campus. Colonial-style dormitories stretched along each of the long sides of the grassy rectangle, and ahead of me was the back wall of the student union where my tour had started that morning. Because the day was warm and clear,

I had chosen this place to start reading my world history textbook, the subject I was most eager to delve into.

Two girls passed me as they headed for the cookout behind the dining hall. Even from a block away, I could smell grilling hamburgers. Then two guys cut across the grass. All day I'd seen students walking around in pairs, braving the uncertainties of orientation in the company of their roommates. Across the quad, Steve exited the back of the student union and walked toward me in a jerky way that made me smile.

"Hi. Aren't you going to the cookout?"

I shook my head. "I can't. My mom is picking me up when she gets off work."

"If you want to go, I could take you home after."

I met his eyes warily. *Is he angling for a date or just being "over-responsible"?* Unsure how to read him, I said, "I really can't, but thanks for offering."

"Anytime. You don't want to get too cut off from stuff, living off campus."

"I guess not." I looked at my watch. "I've got to go."

Monday, I was the first student to arrive for my 9:15 history class, held on the third floor of Sandford Hall. The room, painted tan with forest green trim, smelled musty. At one side, three narrow arched windows overlooked the tree-dotted front lawn of the campus. I took a seat in the center of the second row and set my textbook and notebook on the tablet-shaped desk attached to the right side of the chair. A minute later, a girl with red-gold hair and stark black mascara entered and sat next to me. She wore a summery floral dress with lace edging the neckline.

"Didn't we take the same tour Friday? I'm Ann Marie Russo."

As I told her my name, the girl took out a mirror and freshened her peach lipstick. "I like to get to my classes early the first day and check out the guys."

Oh shit.

Ann Marie sighed. "I should've worn jeans like you. My roommate said I look silly, but she's a PE major, so I figured what does she know about clothes?"

Hearing her insecurity, I felt a grudging sympathy. "What do you care what she thinks?"

"I don't know. I wish we had more in common." Ann Marie glanced at the door as two guys walked in. One was short, the other heavy, so she turned back to me. "My oldest sister said girls used to have to wear skirts all the time. Then in '69, they had a big sit-in."

I raised my eyebrows. "They protested the dress code?"

"Other stuff too. Mandatory ROTC or something. Connie told me, but I forgot."

The history of the world according to Vogue, I thought. The classroom was filling quickly now, and I gazed up front where the professor was unpacking his briefcase. He was younger than I'd expected. His round face was framed by collar-length, pale blond hair, and he wore glasses with tortoiseshell frames. He looked to be over six feet tall, with a medium build and a slight stoop to his shoulders.

"My sister said this is his first year," Ann Marie said loudly enough that the professor glanced our way. "I hope he's good. I hate history, don't you?"

"No," I answered just as loudly. "I'm going to major in history."

I opened my notebook as the teacher sat on the front of his desk and said, "Good morning. My name is Peter Taylor, and as some of you know, I'm new here. I'd like to start by telling you my philosophy of history."

A low groan swept the room, but Dr. Taylor continued without acknowledging it. "Many of you may think that history is a boring list of dates and facts. Others think it's mostly about wars and kings and presidents. I don't agree. I think history is about us."

I glanced up from taking notes and saw him smile at the skeptical looks before him. "Think about it. Everything humanity has ever accomplished began in the mind. All that's happened throughout history has evolved because people thought about things and experimented.

"Because of that, history is more than the story of leaders. They're important, but people like you are important too. Think about the first woman to plant some of the grain she gathered rather than feeding it all to her children. And the neighbors who imitated her when they saw that she had more food next year, until a whole tribe turned to agriculture. That process of thinking about problems and seeking solutions still goes on today, and you're part of it. You are all part of the social forces that shape our times."

Hopping off his desk, he walked back to the chalkboard. "Historians often debate the relative influence of *great men* versus *social forces."* He wrote those phrases on the board. "For example, what caused the Protestant Reformation?"

My hand shot up, and he nodded at me. "Martin Luther nailed ninety-five theses to the door of Wittenberg Cathedral to protest corruption in the Catholic Church."

Dr. Taylor shoved his glasses up the bridge of his nose. "Yes, that was the igniting event, but consider this. In the century before Luther, several reformers made similar criticisms of the church. Some, such as Jan Hus, were martyred for doing so. Why was Luther more successful at gaining followers?"

When no one answered, Dr. Taylor underscored the phrase *social forces.*

Ann Marie whispered to me, "See, I told you history was boring."

"No." I kept my gaze on Dr. Taylor. "It's wonderful."

Six weeks into the autumn term, Peter Taylor came to the end of his lecture and said, "So as I explained today, there was no single cataclysmic event that can be cited as the fall of the Western Roman Empire. Nor was there a single cause. Any questions?"

The class remained silent. Peter looked over the rows of students and saw mostly boredom. He was so backlogged with grading that he hadn't had time to prepare the kind of lecture he wanted, sprinkled with human interest stories to make the past come alive.

The bell rang to end class. "Leave your essays as you go out."

Randy Summers approached the lectern. He was a dark-haired young man with the build of a tight end. The previous Saturday, Peter had jogged over to campus to shoot some baskets and joined a pick-up game with Randy and his friends. "That was an awesome game on Saturday, Dr. T. You handle the fast break pretty well."

Peter laughed. "You mean, for an old guy? I have a brother about your age, and he keeps me on my toes."

"You got some slick moves," Randy said, giving Peter the thumbs-up sign. "See you again sometime, huh?"

"Sure."

As Randy sauntered away, Peter saw Katie Thompson waiting for him. She was wearing navy corduroy pants and a white sweater with irregular horizontal stripes in various shades of blue and brown. Her mouth was compressed in a thin line, and her eyes looked worried.

"Dr. Taylor, may I talk to you about my paper?"

He placed the new batch of essays in his briefcase. "You need an extension?"

"No, not the new paper. The first one."

"Oh." Peter glanced at his watch. Chapel was in five minutes, but he could see they were going to be late. "What's the problem?"

"It's my grade. I shouldn't have gotten a B+."

"Katie, do you want to set up an appointment to discuss this? I think I graded you fairly, but I'll listen to what you have to say."

She raised her chin. "That's not what I meant. I should have done better and earned a higher grade. You told us to check our sources, but I used some books of my father's and didn't check how old they were."

"Don't worry too much. I deliberately graded hard this time to drive my point home. You have plenty of time to pull up your grade."

"I know, but I want to see if I figured out what I did wrong." She pulled a thin sheaf of typewritten papers from her folder. "I rewrote it."

In spite of her obvious effort to appear in control, her hand trembled as she held out the essay. Peter rubbed his left temple in the gesture he used when he needed time to think. "You're very conscientious, but a rewrite wasn't part of the assignment. It wouldn't be fair to other students if I changed your grade."

He was astonished at how red she turned. "I don't want a new grade. I just want to be a good historian." Her voice cracked, and she pulled back the papers. "I'm sorry. I guess you're too busy for this."

"No, I'm not. You should come to me with problems. I'll try to read it before Wednesday. Would that be OK?"

Katie hesitated and then said, "That would be great."

Peter smiled when he took the paper from her. As he watched her walk away, a long black braid hanging straight down her back, he felt uneasy about the conversation. Her shining intelligence, expressed in both her written work and oral contributions to class, had already caught his attention. Why would someone as smart as she was be so insecure? Maybe that father she mentioned was pushing her too hard.

I sat on my favorite bench near the fountain with my arms folded across my chest and my head down, too dispirited to attend the required chapel service, even though students were allowed only five absences a quarter before being put on disciplinary probation.

Reviewing the conversation with Dr. Taylor, I groaned. *He must think I'm a spoiled brat who complains every time she doesn't get an A.*

Then I opened my paperback copy of Dante's *Inferno*—black with a medieval painting of hell on the cover—and tried to focus on the first canto. The opening description of the gloomy forest and the three beasts encountered by Dante did little to lighten my mood. I was still struggling to get into the text when the 11:00 chimes started. People began to pass me on their way from chapel to class.

As I gathered my things, someone called my name. Steve came toward me, using the stiff-jointed gait that reminded me of the tin man in *The Wizard of Oz.*

"I didn't see you in chapel." He sat straddling the stone bench. "Is something wrong?"

His question resurrected my anxiety, and I stared down at my books. "I stayed to talk to Dr. Taylor. He thought I was complaining about a grade when I only wanted to know what I should've done differently. Now he'll think I'm a crybaby." I smoothed a bent corner of *Inferno.*

"Bet it's not as bad as you think. I'm sure he realizes you want to get off to a good start. Besides, I heard he's pretty nice."

"He is. And a great teacher. I really want to impress him."

"You will. Just be yourself."

"Thanks." I smiled at him, surprised at how much better I felt.

Steve cleared his throat. "Katie, do you know what the Harvest Banquet is?"

"I heard it mentioned but...not really."

"It's a dinner we hold every year in early November. It's a week from Saturday." He searched my face. "I bet lots of guys already asked you."

"You're kidding." Embarrassed, I laughed. "I'm not popular that way."

"But you're so beautiful." His hand flew to his mouth. "I mean, I'm not asking you because of your looks. I think you're really nice."

I stared at him, surprised that he would say I was pretty just to take my mind off my worries. He was a sweet guy. "OK. Should we meet on campus?"

He frowned. "I'll come pick you up."

"That's silly. I live ten miles from town."

Steve sat straighter. "A gentleman should always see his date home."

Over-responsible. Suddenly, I wished I'd turned him down. If he was that old-fashioned, how would he react if he learned about my past?

Foolishly, I thought the Harvest Banquet would be like Thanksgiving, intended to celebrate the bounty of autumn. That was a misconception. When we entered the hall where it was being held, I saw none of the pumpkins, gourds, or cornstalks I'd been expecting. Instead, easels spread around the perimeter of the room displayed blown-up photographs of a church-run school and clinic in Kenya. My heart sank.

Steve knew a few of the other students at our assigned table, so as we ate chicken Florentine and wild rice, I listened to them talk about a service project the student government was organizing for spring break; volunteers were going to the Dominican Republic to build small cinderblock homes for people who'd lost everything when Hurricane David hit in August.

Later, as pieces of cherry-covered cheesecake were delivered to each place, our after-dinner speaker stood at the podium. He was a missionary from Nairobi who announced he was speaking on John 4:35: "Say not ye, 'There are yet four months, and then cometh harvest'? Behold, I say unto you, 'Lift up your eyes, and look on the fields; for they are white already to harvest.' " He went on to stress that the world was filled with people who were literally dying to hear the gospel of Jesus Christ, and God wanted each of us to discern whether we were called to become "fishers of men."

I laid my fork across the dessert plate, next to the square of sweetened cream cheese topped by blood-red spheres that had looked so tempting just minutes before. What was I doing there? Probably no one on campus was less qualified to be a missionary than I was; I didn't believe God had forgiven my own sins, so how could I preach about his love to anyone else?

Afterward, Steve walked me to the coat check and handed our ticket to the attendant. He seemed every bit as subdued as I was. As we exited to the parking lot, he said, "I know we just ate, but would you mind if we stopped somewhere for a cup of coffee?"

"No, I guess not." If he was tired and needed a pick-me-up before driving me home, I certainly wasn't going to argue.

Instead of heading to the campus snack bar, Steve drove to a downtown diner that was open until 11:00. We walked to a booth in the back corner, unbuttoned our coats, and sat across from each other on bench seats upholstered in forest green vinyl. A waitress came over and took our order for one cup of coffee and one of hot tea. Then Steve said, "That message really hit me hard."

"Yeah, me too."

The waitress brought our drinks right away and set them on the fake-wood laminate tabletop. Steve added cream to his coffee as he said, "Until tonight, I thought I knew what I wanted to do with my life."

"What's that?"

He gazed into space as though formulating a reply. "I'm a math major, and I've always wanted to be an actuary."

I set down my mug. "I have no idea what that is."

"They work with statistics to calculate risk. Probably the most common career is with insurance companies to calculate premiums, but some businesses hire actuaries to analyze other kinds of risk."

The job sounded almost as boring as the label typing I did the previous year. "Why does that appeal to you?"

Excitement lit up his face. "I want to help people minimize their losses in bad situations. If you do it right, everybody benefits—both the insurance company and the policy holders."

I nodded, surprised by his enthusiasm. "You could do a lot of good. So why are you second guessing your plan?"

He hunched over the table. "Don't you think that, instead of worrying about protecting people's cars and houses and...*things,* I should be trying to protect their immortal souls?"

"Not everyone is cut out to be a missionary. You don't like public speaking, so how persuasive could you be? You like math and statistics, and you're good at taking responsibility, so maybe being an actuary is exactly what God has called you to do."

Steve blinked. "Do you really believe that?"

"Yes."

He considered it a moment. "I'll pray about it."

"Good." I sipped my tea, which had already gone cold.

As I reached for my purse, thinking we would leave, Steve asked, "What about you? You said the message hit you hard too."

Shoot, that was a mistake. I pondered for a moment and decided I could reveal part of what was bothering me. The part that didn't concern Ritchie. "When people talk about spreading the 'good news' about Jesus, I'm not even sure what they mean."

"How can you say that? You're saved, aren't you?"

My cheeks flared with shame. "I don't know."

"Haven't you ever confessed to God that you're a sinner and asked him to forgive you?"

"More times than you can possibly imagine."

"Then you're saved," he said with confidence. "You just have to believe it."

I rested my elbow on the table and my chin on my hand. Sometimes Steve made me feel old and world weary. "It's not that easy. If that's all it took, Christians would forgive each other. But they don't. They judge each other all the time."

"Some do, but that's not Christ's way."

I shook my head. "In my experience, they all do. Besides, if Christ's blood washes us clean and makes us new creatures, then why..." I fell silent, wishing I could admit the truth, that if anyone at school discovered my past, they would see me as irredeemably ruined no matter how many professions of faith I made. But I wasn't ready to chase Steve off forever. "Look at the college. It's so rule driven. Everyone always says that Judaism was legalistic and Jesus came to free us from that, but they don't act like it."

Steve's eyes grew wide. "You really feel this way?"

Just like that, I felt like the snotty kid in first grade who destroys her classmates' belief in Santa Claus. Disillusioning Steve would saddle me with more guilt than I wanted to deal with. "Sometimes," I lied, "when I'm tired or things seem especially hard. It'll pass."

Leaning forward, he touched my arm. "God loves you very much, and he'll forgive anything—not that I think you've done anything so very bad. The rules aren't about earning our salvation. They're to keep us safe."

Safe? I stared at him as though he'd just assured me the moon was made of green cheese. I hadn't felt safe since the last time I ran into my father's arms.

As I entered the history department, located in a front corner on the ground floor of Sandford Hall, I saw Dr. Taylor locking the door of the first office on the right. "Hi," I said, wondering if he'd forgotten our appointment.

"Is it one already?" Pushing up the sleeve of his olive tweed jacket, he checked his watch. "I thought I had time to run to the snack bar for a Coke."

"I'm early."

"Come on in."

"No, please. Go get your Coke. I'll wait here."

He glanced at me over his shoulder as he struggled to turn his key in what was obviously a sticky lock. "My caffeine addiction can wait half an hour."

"Please, go ahead. I don't mind."

With a jerk, he finally unlocked the door. "At least, wait in my office."

I stepped inside as he switched on the light. "Can I get you anything?"

"No, thanks."

Once I was alone, I looked around the small room. Although bookcases lined two walls, the shelves were half empty, and unopened cartons were stacked on the floor. Papers, several layers thick, littered Dr. Taylor's desk except for one place of honor that displayed a battered, rust-speckled tin cup, which looked to be from the Civil War, and an autographed baseball on a black stand. Perched atop a stack of ungraded essays was an open package of banana crème sandwich cookies.

When Dr. Taylor returned, I was crouching on the floor examining an etching of Appomattox Court House that he'd propped against the baseboard. I rose and took the chair in front of his desk. "Do you like the Civil War?"

Dr. Taylor set down his extra-large Styrofoam cup, removed his jacket, and draped it across the back of his chair. He was wearing a pale yellow shirt with a green-and-gold striped tie, and the impeccable color coordination of his clothes made me wonder if he was married. He wasn't wearing a ring. In answer to my question, he said, "I don't know that anyone *likes* the Civil War, but I did my dissertation on it. I examined the advantages the Union army gained from enlisting immigrants who'd fought in Europe."

"Oh." I covered my mouth to hide my disappointment with the boring topic. On impulse, I said, "When I was little, my father built a model of the battle of Gettysburg."

Dr. Taylor's eyebrows rose. "Gettysburg? That's quite an ambitious project."

"Not the whole battle. Just the first skirmish. My great-great-grandfather lost a leg there."

"I see." Noticing the cookies, Dr. Taylor opened his top drawer and put the package inside. "I'd love to see the model sometime if your father wouldn't mind."

I lowered my gaze. "It doesn't exist anymore. My father died when I was eight, and my mother threw it out."

After a long silence, Dr. Taylor said, "I'm sorry."

I looked up and saw him regarding me with sympathy and something else—reevaluation, perhaps. Sliding one finger under the earpiece of his glasses, Dr. Taylor rubbed his temple. "What did you want to see me about?"

"My major." Pausing, I pulled a ball of fuzz from the black wool skirt I'd worn to seem more adult. "My mom worries that it won't prepare me for anything practical. Like if I was a math major, I could become an accountant or an actuary."

Dr. Taylor stared at me. His eyes were hazel; from a distance, I'd assumed they were blue. "Your mom wants you to switch to math?"

"That was just an example. If you say math, people assume you'll get a job, but with history, you get a blank look. Who hires historians?"

He raised one eyebrow. "You mean, besides colleges? Katie, a liberal arts education isn't meant to train you for a specific job. It gives you a broad background of valuable knowledge."

Impatient at being fed what I already recognized as the standard college line, I said, "I believe that, but my mom doesn't. She didn't attend college, and since she's spending so much money, she wants my degree to pay off."

"I see." As Dr. Taylor leaned forward, pale hair fell across his forehead. "History is good preparation for several careers. Law, for example. Or a field that uses research skills, such as library science." He smiled with a hint of self-mockery. "There's even teaching."

Teaching, I thought. *I could do that.* "Wouldn't I have to be an education major?"

"Not to teach in high school. You major in your subject area and take education courses to become certified in secondary education. A lot of people get the certification just to have something to fall back on."

"You mean I could get certified just to keep my mom happy."

"I suppose." He frowned. "I'm not encouraging you to deceive her."

"Oh, I wouldn't," I said quickly.

An expression of relief crossed Dr. Taylor's face, making him look even younger. I wanted to say something to prolong the conversation, but I couldn't think what, so I rose. "Thank you for meeting with me."

"Anytime. I am your advisor, after all. Katie, I hope you don't switch your major. You have such a passion for history."

"Thank you." I allowed myself to look into his eyes once more before I left.

After parking in front of his family's Lake Forest, Illinois, home, Peter Taylor pushed hair off his forehead. *Here goes.* This was his first visit since he'd started teaching. His parents hadn't liked his choice of a Baptist college instead of a prestigious university—but then again, they had never understood his decision to become "born again" as the popular phrase went.

The house with its white-painted bricks and massive pillars resembled a Southern plantation more than the homes they'd had in Charleston and Atlanta when Peter was a child. They moved here when he was sixteen. He went back to the South for college, choosing Duke partially because of its reputation and partially because of Eileen, the girlfriend he'd left behind when they moved to Illinois. Considering how that relationship turned out, he'd have done better to stay in the North.

His head throbbed. Pushing up his glasses, Peter rubbed his temples. Dr. French, his department head, had been displeased that his end-of-quarter grades weren't in by the deadline, so Peter had worked until three AM and dropped them off on his way out of town.

Carrying a paper-wrapped flower arrangement, Peter walked to the door and rang the bell. Then he entered the foyer with its black-and-white-checked marble floor.

Peter set the flowers on the Queen Anne hall table. As he hung his overcoat in the closet, his sister bustled out from the kitchen. "You silly goose. Why'd you ring the bell? We couldn't imagine who it might be."

He kissed her forehead, smiling at her Southern accent. Marian was the only one of the family who had one; their parents were originally from Wisconsin, and Peter and Joel both sounded like Midwesterners. Peter suspected that Marian practiced her drawl when she was alone to maintain her self-image as a Southern belle.

Pulling away, Marian went to the mirror to make sure he hadn't mussed her platinum curls. "What's this?" She plucked at the florist's paper.

"Flowers for the table. Do you know if Mother has something?"

"Just that old cornucopia. I'm sure this'll be much nicer."

Their mother called from the kitchen. "Is that Peter?"

"Yes'm, he'll be right there."

As Peter picked up the arrangement, Marian grasped his sleeve. "Wait a little minute. I have something to tell you."

"What is it, sugar baby?"

She scrunched her nose at the old nickname. "I brought a boy home for Thanksgiving. Joel's been horrid about teasing him. You'll be sweet, won't you?"

"Of course. What's his name?"

"Jeffrey Adams." Her eyes flashed with pride. "He's going to be a doctor."

"Just let me say hi to Mother before you introduce us."

They walked back to a kitchen that blended old and new: classic built-in features like a huge walk-in pantry and glass-fronted cabinets contrasted with the latest, high-end appliances.

Peter's mother was peeling potatoes at the sink. A tall, thin woman with the same fair coloring as her children, Pamela Taylor wore a cranberry wool dress with a cameo at her throat.

"Here, this is for you," Peter said.

"You didn't need to do that." She dried her hands and removed the paper from a bowl containing bronze and yellow mums, white carnations, and a thick ivory candle inside a hurricane lamp. "How lovely. I'll put it on the table. We can light the candle for dinner."

"Marian said you set up the cornucopia. We can put this on the sideboard."

"Don't be silly. It's too pretty for the sideboard." As she carried the flowers to the dining room, Marian and Peter followed her.

"Let me move this." Even though Peter placed a protective hand over the fruit and gourds as he picked up the horn of plenty, an orange tumbled to the floor.

"I'll get it," Marian said.

Peter set the cornucopia on the sideboard and turned to see his mother put a mat under the flowers to protect her great-grandmother's Chippendale table. Marian pulled out one of the splat-back chairs and crawled after the orange.

"Did you find it?" Peter asked. "There's a place for it right here."

"We can't put it out now, silly. It's bruised."

Feeling betrayed by the vestiges of childhood clumsiness, Peter backed away with his hands behind his back. Pamela smiled. "This was so thoughtful."

"Glad you like it," he mumbled.

Marian tapped her foot. "Come meet Jeff."

After smiling at his mother, Peter followed his sister to the study. Their father sat in the leather armchair, Joel sprawled on the burgundy Persian carpet, and a strange young man perched on the edge of the leather couch with his hands clutching his knees.

"Look who's here." Marian made introductions and left the room.

Smiling, Peter held out his hand. Jeffrey had short brown hair, a grey Shetland pullover, and blemishes on his chin. "Do you prefer Jeffrey or Jeff?"

"Either one, sir."

"You don't have to call me sir."

Jeff grinned. "It slipped out. Marian said you're a prof."

"Assistant professor," Peter's father interjected. Patrick Taylor had a dark, heavily jowled face and coarse black hair shot with grey. "Nothing formidable about that."

"Hello, Dad."

"How was the drive?"

"Not bad." Peter glanced at the football game on TV. "Who's winning?"

"Goddam Lions. What the hell does Armstrong think he's doing, letting them get a 13–0 lead by half time?"

Sitting down, Peter loosened his tie. "Jeff, I hear you're in med school."

"First year."

"Smart move." Patrick pushed his bulk out of the chair and crossed to the bar to refill his bourbon. "Medicine, law, business. Those'll be the shrewd choices in the eighties. Joel here is going for an MBA as soon as he graduates."

Peter glanced sharply at his brother. "Is that true?"

"Yeah." Joel nodded for emphasis. His hair was a darker blond than Peter's, and he was shorter with a blocky build like their father. "Pop thinks I should go to Northwestern."

"It's a good school. But what about forestry?"

Joel shrugged. "I can support conservation groups once I'm successful."

Peter met his father's smug gaze. "You just couldn't leave him be, could you?"

Joel sat up. "Don't get mad at Pop about this. I decided on my own."

"You mean he didn't offer to pay if you switch?"

Joel frowned. "Everyone else thinks it's a good idea."

"Fine." Peter stood. "I need some aspirin."

In the kitchen, his mother was alone, rinsing a kettle of sweet potatoes.

Peter took a glass from the cupboard and a bottle of Pepsi from the refrigerator. "Why didn't you tell me Joel switched his major?"

"I thought he should tell you, dear."

He took a gulp of cola, hoping the caffeine would ease his headache. "Do you approve?"

"Whatever he wants is fine with me. You know that."

"But this isn't what he wants. Dad's bribing him."

She turned to face him. "Your father's doing his best. He only wants you to be happy."

"No, he wants us to make a lot of money so he can brag at the office."

Peter's mother gazed at him with a wounded expression he knew well. He could remember nights in early childhood when he would climb out of bed and walk to the living room and find her unable to sleep because of loneliness. They would cuddle on the sofa until they both grew drowsy—unless he complained that he wanted his father to come home. That always drew a rebuke: "You know he has to travel for his job." And she would send Peter back to bed.

"I just wish Dad cared more about our interests and less about our earning power."

Pamela laid a hand on his arm. "Your father isn't the mercenary you think he is. Can't you get along?"

Under her pleading glance, Peter grew ashamed. "Remember when I was little? You'd tuck me in and tell me where Dad was traveling and what you imagined him doing in each city."

She smiled softly. "Of course I do. Why?"

Peter thought back to those days when his father had seemed a mysterious, powerful god who visited them only on a whim. "Nothing."

During dinner, Peter forced himself to stay quiet as his father railed against the Carter administration. "We'd have the hostages back from Iran by now if a Republican was in the White House. Hell, they never would have been taken in the first place."

Glaring as though he dared someone to argue, Patrick piled more turkey on his plate. "Peter, have you thought about my advice to buy a house?"

"Yes, but I have too many school loans to pay off."

Patrick waved a forkful of turkey in his direction. "Look at the money you're throwing away on rent. You could be building equity instead."

Peter stared down at his plate, where cranberry juice swamped his mashed potatoes. "As soon as I scrape together a down payment, I'll look into it."

"Hell, if that's what's stopping you, I'll give you the down payment."

Damn, Peter thought. *Why does he always use money like a club?* "I'm not a kid. I don't think I should let you pay for it."

Patrick dropped his fork onto his plate and glowered at his son. At the other end of the table, Pamela cleared her throat. Patrick glanced at her, then back at Peter. "Consider it an early inheritance."

Peter looked to his mother, who smiled and bobbed her head encouragingly. Remembering her plea for harmony, he sighed. "That's very generous."

As Peter and Joel played basketball in the driveway, Peter faked a moment of fatigue and—when Joel lunged for the ball—ducked, pivoted, and shot over his head. The net swished as the ball sank through the basket.

"Great shot!" Joel slapped his back. "Not bad for an old guy."

Peter caught him in a headlock. "I'll show you who's an old guy."

"You are!" Joel struggled against the hold. "You're practically thirty!"

"Even when I'm fifty, I'll run you into the ground." Peter punched him lightly in the stomach. "Look at this beer gut. You're getting as big as Dad."

Wrenching free, Joel went after the ball, which had bounced onto the brown grass. "He's not always wrong, Pete."

"You're saying you really want to give up forestry?"

Joel started dribbling, producing a series of hollow thunks. "That idea of being a ranger. It's kid stuff."

At that, Peter felt as sorrowful as if he were the one giving up a dream. Joel was special to him, much more so than their self-absorbed sister. "When are you going to visit me? I'll introduce you to some cute coeds."

"No, thanks. I can do without your Baptist coeds. How about you? Are you dating?"

Peter shook his head. Then he dived in and stole the ball. "Right now, I'm too swamped to get out and meet anybody."

Joel put his hands on his hips. "Don't give me that. You're still gun shy 'cause of Eileen."

"Don't be ridiculous. That was years ago." Peter shot the basketball and watched it drop cleanly through the net. "Enough talking. Are we going to play or not?"

By winter, I was seeing Steve every weekend. I didn't love him, but he was thoughtful and kind, so I hoped something might develop if I gave him a chance. Sometimes his earnestness rubbed my nerves raw, but whenever I felt impatient, I reminded myself of the time Nita—not exactly a connoisseur of "nice guys"—had urged me to switch from Ritchie to Doug. How different life would be now if I'd listened.

Steve waited until our fifth date to kiss me. After that, he limited himself to two kisses a night as though any more would be an insult to my assumed purity. His deference shamed me.

In March, he took me to see the movie *Coal Miner's Daughter* about the singer Loretta Lynn. Half an hour into the film, I stiffened. Up on the screen, fourteen-year-old Loretta was marrying an older man against her family's wishes. The wedding took place in a bare Kentucky church. I stared at my lap, remembering Ritchie's promise that we would get married in Kentucky.

Soon the dialogue told me that the scene had changed to the wedding night. A moment later, the girl cried out in protest. In a sick daze, I watched the husband force himself on his young wife without tenderness, without preparation, without consideration for her obvious ignorance. Nausea rose in my throat, and I began to tremble so hard my teeth chattered. My mind flooded with memories of Ritchie grunting and sweating, of his heavy weight, of the tearing pain. Digging my nails into my palms, I forced myself to sit still.

A long time later, when I looked at the screen again, the girl was on stage singing. I had no idea how far into the movie we were.

The rest of the film was a blur. When the credits started to roll, I grabbed my purse and jacket and ran up the aisle. Outside, Steve caught up with me and took my hand. "I'm sorry. I didn't know there was a scene like that."

"That's OK," I said quietly. *He doesn't know,* crowed an inner voice. *He thinks you're upset because you're a virgin, like he is.*

Instantly, I felt chagrin. Deceiving someone like Steve was nothing to be proud of. During the ride home, I remained silent.

Steve parked in our driveway. When he leaned over to kiss me, I cried, "Don't!" He jerked back, and I realized I had come to a decision without even thinking about it. "I'm sorry. I can't see you anymore."

"Why? What did I do?"

I gripped the door handle. "Nothing. It just isn't working."

"But why? Is it something I said?"

"No. You're a nice guy. Much too nice for me."

Steve gulped noisily. "I'm boring. That's it, isn't it?"

I shook my head.

"Please, tell me what I did wrong. I'll try to change. I—"

"Don't." Yanking up the door handle, I got out of the car and bent down to say, "It's not you, it's me. I'm not what you think I am." Then I ran up the sidewalk without looking back.

Over the summer, I worked at Burgerland in Zebulun—a fast-food restaurant that had ivory walls with brown and orange horizontal stripes, booths with ivory molded plastic seats that had orange vinyl cushioning on the backs, and a sign outside featuring a cartoon burger with a face on the top bun and French fry legs and arms. Everyone who worked at Burgerland (except the manager) had to wear an orange uniform with a brown collar and hat—colors that made my fair skin look sickly.

One day, as I operated the drink dispenser, tucked behind the wall that framed the opening over the counter, a girl with a Southern accent whined, "I thought you were takin' me to a nice place."

The man who answered sounded like Dr. Taylor. "Sugar, I don't have time today. We'll do it next time."

Reluctant to be seen in my hideous uniform, I ducked even farther out of sight. As soon as Dr. Taylor paid for his order, I turned to the manager. "Mac, I need more ice."

On the way back to the freezer, I peered out the window in the employee door and spotted Dr. Taylor and his companion in a booth. The girl's pale hair fell in a cascade of curls, and she wore a pink and white sundress.

I didn't think he'd go for such a Barbie doll. Or call her Sugar!

The second week of autumn term, I went to the snack bar and bought coffee-flavored yogurt and a banana for lunch. I carried them through the saloon doors into the seating area, decorated with swag lamps designed like ship's lanterns, narrow smoked-glass windows, and ebony-stained pedestal tables and captain's chairs. I snagged the last empty booth. As I stirred my yogurt, Dr. Taylor walked up. "May I join you?"

"Of course." Watching him set down a bag of barbecued potato chips, a bowl of fudge-ripple ice cream, and a large Coke, I thought, *The man's a junk food addict. How does he keep from getting fat?*

"I see you're taking modern European history." He nodded toward my stack of books as he ripped open the bag of chips. "How do you like it?"

I shrugged. "I don't know. I never really got into Napoleon."

"You're not on Napoleon already!"

"No, we're on the Thirty Years' War, but I was looking ahead at the syllabus, trying to decide what to write my research paper on."

Dr. Taylor grinned. "That's the Katie I know. Always a step ahead."

Instead of pleasing me, his praise left me breathless with longing. "I'm also taking Developmental Psychology."

"That sounds interesting." He stirred his ice cream to mix the fudge throughout, which amused me. I liked it when bits of Dr. Taylor's younger self peeked out from behind the professorial demeanor. "How was your summer?" he asked.

"OK. I had to earn money, so I worked at Burgerland."

"Really? I eat there sometimes but never saw you."

"Huh," I said noncommittally. "What did you do?"

"Went on my annual camping trip with my brother. Then I taught summer school and bought a house. Oh, and my sister came to visit."

His sister, I thought with interest until I remembered "Sugar's" accent. Of course, Dr. Taylor wouldn't mention her.

He checked his watch. "I have to go. Keep me posted about Napoleon."

"Sure." I watched him leave, thinking, *God, I miss being in his class.*

That winter, I took my first course with Dr. French. The department head was a crusty old man with white hair, wild eyebrows, and a speaking voice like a pompous Spencer Tracy. He assigned seats, prescribed meticulous formats for papers, and addressed students as "Miss Thompson" or "Mr. Bennett." Despite his old-fashioned ways, he was a spirited teacher who illustrated his lectures with maps, slides, and artifacts he'd collected over his long career. I ended up with a grudging respect for him, although I never felt comfortable in his presence.

That quarter, my mother also became a student by studying interior decorating at the community college. I couldn't see the point of the class because I liked the clean lines and pastel colors of our home, not that it mattered. *Two more years, and I'm out of here.*

One evening, as I was washing dishes and listening to a tape cassette of the latest Eagles' album, the telephone rang. When I answered it, Aunt Colleen said tearfully, "Is my sister there?"

"Just a minute." I set the receiver on the counter, turned off the cassette in the middle of "Heartache Tonight," and went to knock on Mother's door. "Aunt Colleen's on the phone."

Mom came out of the bedroom, wearing a faded robe and a clear plastic cap on her hair, which was smeared with purplish foam. I stepped back when I caught an acrid odor. Amused that she was dying her hair, I followed her into the kitchen. A moment later, she exclaimed, "Oh, that poor child! This morning, you say? How's she taking it?"

My mother dabbed her eyes with the tie belt to her robe. *Bernadette* was my immediate thought. My cousin, only three months younger than me, was married and already expecting her second child.

Mother reached for the marker clipped to the plasticized message board on the wall and wrote, "Morrisey Funeral Home. Wake, Thurs. Funeral, Fri., 10:00."

Then she said, "Tell Bernadette to call if there's anything we can do. She's got to take care of herself for the new baby's sake." She hung up the phone.

"What happened?"

"Bernadette's boy, Bobby, caught spinal meningitis and died."

"No!" I thought of the lively fifteen-month-old child I'd last seen at Christmas, pushing a wooden train through Grandma's house.

"He was cranky and acted like his neck hurt, but Bernadette didn't take him to the doctor until he started vomiting. He died this morning at one."

She sighed and patted her plastic cap. "I better wash this off." Then she looked at me. "Do you have a suitable dress for the funeral?"

Panic swept over me. I leaned back against the table for support and pressed a hand against my stomach. "Do I have to go?"

My mother's sorrowful expression flared into anger "How can you be so selfish? I could understand your fear of funerals when you were eight, but you're an adult now."

I frowned. What was she talking about? I'd never been to a funeral —but the very thought of one made me feel like walls were closing in. "I just can't."

"Don't think I'm going to make excuses for you. You can explain it to Bernadette yourself." She flounced out of the room.

Peter Taylor closed his office door and laid his head upon the stack of papers on his desk. Dr. French had set two goals for him this academic year: to improve at meeting deadlines and to get published. This week, Peter had an article printed in a prestigious journal. It was a piece he was proud of—but French had hated it.

The old man hadn't quarreled with the premise: a comparative study of the post–Civil War United States and early twentieth-century Italy. Both countries had an industrial North and an agricultural South with a seemingly unbridgeable economic gap between the two. Dr. French's objection centered on Peter's conclusion that in both nations, Northern business interests actively retarded development of the South so they could exploit the region.

"I question your judgment in promoting such a leftist view."

"It's not leftist," Peter responded, resisting the urge to shrink in his chair like a chastised schoolboy. "It's sound economic analysis."

"Then why did you find it necessary to quote this man Gramsci? Don't you know he was a founder of the Italian Communist Party?"

"He was also a brilliant scholar."

Dr. French slammed the journal on the desk. "You know what this college stands for. I will not have it said that I harbor Marxist historians on my faculty."

Remembering, Peter took off his glasses and rubbed his eyes. He didn't understand Dr. French. How could a man who was so scrupulous about the teachings of their faith compromise on the standards of academic scholarship?

But maybe he, Peter, was the inconsistent one. As a Christian, he believed in absolutes: the Ten Commandments, the teachings of Christ, the Bible as revealed truth—although not the literal, word-for-word transcription the college proclaimed it to be. As a historian, however, he believed that no revelation was ever final. In research, Peter was willing to pursue any line of inquiry that might prove fruitful, even if it led to answers that challenged the status quo.

He had been naïve. Why hadn't he seen that religious conservatives had a vested interest in the status quo? Apparently, his department chair wouldn't countenance any scholarship that cast doubt on the holy trinity of God, democracy, and American capitalism.

Until recently, Peter hadn't associated Christianity with such narrow thinking. After Eileen left him during their senior year of college, Peter had felt worthless. Glen Foster, a classmate in the history department, befriended him, asked Peter to study together, invited him to join a campus fellowship group, and described how his own faith helped him deal with disappointment. Peter's growing belief in a heavenly father who loved him enough to save him from sin and despair eased his ever-present longing for his earthly father's approval. When the time came to look for a teaching position, applying to Christian colleges seemed the obvious choice.

Peter rubbed his temples, put his glasses back on, and stared bleakly at the journal he had been so excited to receive just yesterday. *What have I done to myself?*

During spring quarter, as part of my teacher training, I had to work half a day each week as a teacher's aide at Zebulun High School. Seeing the school afresh, I noticed details I'd grown blind to as a student; some of the acoustic tiles in the ceiling were warped, the pastel lockers had lighter patches where graffiti had been painted over, and the beige speckled floor looked like all the surface shine had been buffed away years before. As I walked the halls of that tired old building, I felt transported back to the period of my life I most wanted to escape. *It's over,* I told myself. *You're a grown up now.*

My assignment was with Mr. Kwan, my former history teacher. In April, he told me, "The students are doing group work. Walk around, make suggestions, that kind of thing."

I nodded and went over to the nearest group. From discussions I'd observed, I knew that these three were among the brightest students in class. Yet, Ryan was reading *Sports Illustrated,* and the girls were playing hangman. "How's it going?" I asked.

"We're done," Ryan said. He was cute, with blond hair and brown eyes that made him look like the lead singer in a bubblegum pop group.

"What's your project?"

Ryan yawned. "I'm giving a speech on Woodrow Wilson, Nan's got one on the Treaty of Versailles, and Amy's doing the League of Nations."

I pushed my braid back over my shoulder. "That's not group work. You're supposed to collaborate. Why don't you use the information in your reports to give a panel discussion on the League of Nations? Or hold a debate?"

"Why should we?" demanded Nan, a petite girl with wedge-cut red hair.

"Because it fills the requirements of your assignment better."

Ryan glowered at me. "You're not our teacher."

I started to respond, then realized he was right; I had no authority. To avoid getting embroiled in an unwinnable argument, I said, "Suit yourself," and moved to the next group.

Danny, a chubby boy with chipmunk teeth, said, "Listen, Miss Thompson. We're doing President Harding and the Teapot Dome scandal, so we decided to make a newspaper like *National Enquirer.*"

"That sounds great."

The second group member, a hulking boy named Nick, smirked. "Want to see one of our pictures?" He hunched over his paper so I couldn't see what he was doing and a minute later handed me a line drawing. Inside a rectangle, a man and a woman were embracing, with the woman's legs wrapped around the man's waist.

"What's this got to do with Teapot Dome?"

"It doesn't. It's another scandal about Harding. He used to ball his secretary in the White House closet."

"Nick, this isn't funny."

He gave me a wide-eyed look. "I'm not joking. It's in a book Mr. Kwan loaned me."

"Even if it is, you know you can't put that in a class project."

"Why not? If it's true—"

"That's enough!" I crumpled the paper and went to drop it in the trash can. As I moved to another group, I saw Ryan talking to the teacher.

After class, Mr. Kwan asked to speak to me. As I stood in front of his desk, he gazed up at me, and the fluorescent ceiling lights reflected off the round lenses of his glasses so I couldn't make out his expression. "Katie, Ryan complained that you tried to take over their project."

"I just suggested ways to improve it."

"He said they were already done, and you insisted they do extra work."

"Those kids could stand a little extra work. They're smart, but not one of them put half the effort into this project that they're able to."

Sighing, Mr. Kwan scratched his goatee. "That's their choice. If you're going to teach, you have to learn that most kids aren't as motivated as you are."

The bell rang, and the students for the next class settled down and grew quiet. Incensed that he'd used the word *if,* I said quietly, "You don't think I should be a teacher?"

He held up his hands palms out. "I didn't say that. We need bright people like you, but it's not just knowing your subject. It's knowing about people too. Let's talk more about this next week."

Mr. Kwan began to take roll, and I picked up my belongings from the table behind his desk. As I walked out, I thought, *There isn't going to be a next week.* My mother would make a stink if I quit the program, but I didn't care. This was how I made decisions, with my gut.

Wednesday as I headed toward the humanities building for my Civil War class, I saw Dr. Taylor walking ahead of me. When I called his name, he stopped to wait. A brisk spring breeze fanned his hair.

"I finished the book you loaned me," I said when I reached him. From my stack, I pulled out his copy of *Gettysburg: The Final Fury.*

He tucked it under his arm. "Did you like it?"

"Yes, it reminded me of my father's stories." Glancing sideways, I saw him smile.

"I'm glad I ran into you. There are a couple of things I want to discuss. Do you have any free time today?"

"Yes. Next hour and at 2:15."

"Fine. We can walk to my office after class."

I stood back to let Dr. Taylor unlock his office door. "Sometimes this takes a minute," he said as he struggled with the key.

"Is it sticking again?" I asked, remembering he had the same problem last year.

He gave me a sheepish glance. "I never had it fixed." He jiggled the knob until he succeeded in turning the key.

Typical. Like the broken button on his coat, the papers he was always late returning, and the junk food he ate because he didn't take time to pack a lunch. What he needed was an organized person to track details for him. Following him inside, I noticed that, even though his desk was as messy as ever, he'd finally shelved the last of his books. At least, it was progress.

"Have a seat." Dr. Taylor removed a stack of essays from one of the visitor's chairs and set them on the filing cabinet. "I read your outline and thought we should discuss it."

I immediately straightened my posture. "What's wrong?"

Removing his glasses, he held them up to the light and wiped the lenses with a handkerchief. Then he pulled my outline from a folder. "I'm concerned about the last section. The part about how Reconstruction would have worked if Lincoln had lived. Do you see any problems with that?"

Picking at a hangnail on my thumb, I muttered, "No."

"That's speculation, not history. No one knows if Lincoln's plan would have succeeded. I was surprised to see you make such an elementary mistake."

I yanked at the hangnail so hard it bled. "Sorry," I mumbled and lifted my thumb to my mouth to suck away the blood.

"I wonder if Lincoln is a good topic for you. I know he's a hero of yours, which might hamper your objectivity. Besides, I'd like to see you get away from this 'great man' theory and try social history for a change."

"I can do this topic!"

"It's your decision." Dr. Taylor leaned back in his office chair, crossed his right leg over his left, and jiggled his foot. "How's your teacher's training?"

Staring at him, I tried to guess what was coming. "I quit the program. I don't get along with teenagers very well. They goof off too much."

He smiled as though I had confirmed something. "Maybe you should go to grad school and try for college teaching. You certainly have the intellectual bent."

I blinked. "I never thought of that."

"I know a way you could explore the idea." Dr. Taylor leaned toward me. "We received a budget allocation for a department assistant next year, and I suggested you. You'll have to interview with Dr. French, but I think he'll hire you."

I glanced at the Civil War–era tin cup on his desk and then at the shelves of books, so many of which I wanted to borrow. Hadn't I just been thinking that Dr. Taylor needed someone to help organize things? It seemed like a sign. "I'd like to work here."

"Great. I'll set up the interview."

One afternoon in October, Peter's sister Marian showed up unexpectedly at his office, dressed more like someone going to a formal tea than dropping in on her older brother. She wore a burgundy beret perched on her platinum curls and a burgundy and beige plaid dress with wide shoulders and a brown leather belt cinching the waist. "What brings you to my domain?" Peter asked as he gestured her to a seat.

Marian smoothed out her skirt as she sat down and then laid her clutch purse in her lap. "Jeff refuses to get married till he finishes his residency. I wish you'd talk to him."

"I can't do that, Sugar. You two have to decide this on your own."

Marian wrinkled her nose. "Oh, Jeff's just scared. If he thought the family would approve, he'd see it my way."

Peter removed his glasses and sighed. "If you can't convince him, I don't see what you expect me to do."

Her green eyes flashed. "I expect you to take my side for once. You'd do it fast enough if it was Joel. I'm tired of waiting. I want to get married."

They heard a knock. At the open door stood Katie, her face a deep red. "Sorry to interrupt. You said not to leave these tests in your mailbox."

"Right." As Peter took the stack from Katie, he saw her shoot Marian a hostile glance. Startled, he asked, "You haven't met, have you? Marian, this is Katie Thompson, our department assistant. Katie, this is my sister."

Katie's tight expression melted into a smile, and she held out a hand. "Nice to meet you, Miss Taylor."

Ignoring the gesture, Marian spoke in a purr. "So you work for my brother."

Katie's arm fell to her side. "I work for the department," she said in a tight voice. Then she turned to face him. "Anything else, Dr. Taylor?"

"No," Peter said, wondering at the tension sparking between them.

As Katie closed the door behind her, Marian tossed back her head and laughed. "Why, Peter, I had no idea you were such a Don Juan. That little girl is in love with you."

He went to the filing cabinet in the corner and locked the tests inside. "That's absurd."

She raised her thinly plucked eyebrows. "Is it? I know jealousy when I see it, and she was fit to kill me till you said who I was."

Ignoring her cattiness, Peter returned to the reason for the visit. "You're making a mistake trying to force that boy into marriage."

Marian stood. "You're awful high and mighty. But you're not perfect, you know."

She walked out, leaving Peter shaken. At times, he had wondered if Katie had a crush on him, but she was always so intent on her studies, he let his concerns subside. Now, he wondered if he had unwittingly led her on.

Damn, why wasn't I more careful? The answer was obvious—and disturbing. He liked the girl. He had come to think of Katie as a friend. Had he caused her pain? She would certainly be hurt if he started to avoid her. Maybe if he ignored the crush, she'd outgrow it and they could both retain their dignity. At least, he hoped so.

After work, I went to the gym and changed into running clothes. The weather was in the low sixties, perfect for running outside, so I jogged onto the red synthetic outdoor track that ran in an oval around the football field, with bleachers along the outside of each straightaway. As I began my run, I found myself driven by an unaccountable sense of urgency. Although I knew it was best to start slowly, I surged to full speed after only 100 yards. *Run,* instinct told me. *Run and don't think.*

A voice in my brain started counting paces. When I forced it to stop, a new chant began: *left, right, left, right.* Anything to block thought. Some idea was chasing me, some knowledge I had to avoid.

So I ran as hard as I could. I circled the track so long that I lost count of my distance sometime after the fifth mile. My side ached. A low flame spread from my hips down my thighs. My shins felt about to crack.

"One more lap," I gasped. Rounding the curve, I stumbled and caught myself just before sprawling. My legs quivered. I staggered to the bleachers and collapsed into a seat like a marionette without strings.

As soon as I caught my breath, the thought that had chased me for the last hour ran up and pushed itself in my face. That thought was Peter.

"No," I said but hadn't the strength to fend off the memories. Peter lecturing in class. Joking with me in the campus snack bar. Surprising me with ice cream the day I oiled his sticky lock. With the images came a thought I had long harbored but refused to put into words: *If only he wasn't dating that girl.*

Well, he wasn't. She was his sister. What difference did it make? Did it wipe away the taboo against students dating professors? Did it erase my shameful past?

"I can't love him," I whispered. "I won't let myself."

After that, I rationed conversations with Peter like cups of water to see me across a desert, and I prayed each night for God to change my heart. Yet, whenever I was at work, my nerves were like radar tuned to Peter's every movement. When he called me into his office to assign a task, I focused not on his instructions but on the warmth of his voice, the spicy scent of his aftershave, the rhythm of his fingers drumming the desk.

Late one Friday in January, I came out of the workroom to find an almost deserted department. Only Peter's door was ajar, and a light shone behind the frosted-glass window. Like a beacon. Stopping in front of the door, I knocked and then pushed it open. "I finished my work. Need any help?"

He scowled at the papers scattered across his desk. "I wish you could. I have two sets of exams to grade. I'll be at it all night."

Entering the office, I asked, "Are there objective sections I can check?"

Peter looked at his watch. "Your mother will be here in twenty minutes."

I glanced from the papers to his tired face. "I'll work late."

"But how would you get home?"

"I could stay at my grandmother's. She lives six blocks away."

"Are you sure? I really don't expect this."

"It'll be good for me. To see if I want to teach in college," I answered, pleased with myself for thinking of such a persuasive argument.

To gain more space, we moved to the seminar room across the hall. Purple drapes hid the tall windows. The north wall held a green marble fireplace flanked by glass-fronted bookcases. Above the mantel hung a portrait of Jonathan Morton, an abolitionist who left the college a sizable endowment in 1883. In the center of the room, a long dark table was surrounded by twelve ornate Tudor chairs.

We sat at the table with Peter on my right. The wind rattled the wooden window frames, and I wondered if the predicted snow had started yet. Beside me, Peter chewed the end of his pen as he graded essay questions.

As I checked answers, I found myself evaluating the multiple-choice questions and thinking how I might have written them differently. I became so absorbed in the work that I lost track of time. When I heard the door to the department open, I checked my watch. Mother was twenty minutes late. "I'm in here!"

She appeared in the doorway. "Why aren't you ready?"

"I offered to work late tonight."

After pulling off her gloves, my mother brushed snow off her red knit cap and black wool coat. "You can't. The storm's heavier than expected. We have to leave now."

Peter rose, picked up his mug, and left the room.

"I can't leave," I protested. "There's work to do, and I said I'd stay."

"The storm is bad. The roads could close anytime."

I stood, drew myself to my full height, and stared down at my mother. "Go home without me. I'll stay at Grandma's house."

Carrying his mug of coffee, Peter reentered the room and stopped behind my mother. "Maybe I can drive Katie home."

She whirled on him and slapped her gloves against her other palm. "Do you know what it's like out there? What is so important that you have to keep my daughter during a blizzard?"

He blinked as though just waking up. "Blizzard?" Glancing toward the still-closed draperies, he murmured, "Nothing, I guess."

She turned back to me. "See? Now get your things."

"No." My anger felt like a ferocious Doberman straining against a leash. Even as I made my stand, I knew I was behaving irrationally, driven by a primitive urge to fight my mother over a point that could be better proved another way, but I couldn't shake the certainty that I must lay claim to adulthood now or watch it recede out of reach. "I'm not a child. I can decide for myself."

My mother glared at me as she pulled on her gloves. Then she marched out of the room.

Peter stood looking after her with the expression of someone who had witnessed a hit and run, and then he dropped into his chair, hunched over his stack of papers, and began to grade another essay.

For two hours, we worked in a silence so heavy that I feared he was angry. I didn't dare ask. When I finished the objective section of the last test, he said, "I better get you home."

After he packed his briefcase with the unfinished work, we walked out to the faculty parking spaces behind Sanford Hall. Quarter-sized snowflakes fell on a world painted in watercolor shades of blue-shadowed white. A six-inch layer covered his Toyota. As we cleaned it, Peter asked, "Do you mind if we stop for a hamburger? This promises to be a long drive, and I need to eat. I'll buy you supper too."

"You don't have to. Just take me to my grandparents' house."

"No. I told your mother I would."

"She won't really expect it."

"Katie, I promised." He used the no-nonsense tone I suspected he'd learned as an oldest brother, so I climbed in the car. The decision to brave the storm seemed foolish, but if it meant spending another hour alone with him, I'd take the risk.

The streets were deserted except for a snowplow, whose rotating yellow light cut briefly through the storm and then disappeared. When we walked into the orange-and-ivory environment of Burgerland, Mac came to the counter. "Don't be long. I'm just about to close up, send these kids home."

He glared at me, who had worked for him two years before, and guilt warmed my cheeks. I nodded, and Peter placed our order.

At the table, Peter pulled the pickles off his hamburger and dropped them on the orange plastic tray. As though continuing an ongoing conversation, he said, "Consider the pros and cons before you pursue college teaching. My friend Glen is at a big university and has much more time for writing than I do. A small school's more personal, but you have to do more committees. And there's politics, like having to choose research topics your department approves of."

"Really?"

He smiled ruefully and shoved his glasses up his nose. "Sorry to be so negative. I've been worried because my third year review comes up in March." I shot him a questioning look. "Assistant professors are expected to make tenure in six years, so they get reviewed after three to see if they're on track."

The thought of his being evaluated like a student shocked me into exclaiming, "You mean, they might fire you?"

He choked a little and wiped his mouth on a napkin. "I hope not. There are things I dislike about Zebulun, but I'd hate to start over somewhere else." He grimaced. "I'm not giving a good impression of college teaching, am I?"

"It's probably good for me to hear. I had no idea it was so hard."

"It isn't for everyone. But I'm not coping very well."

"That's not true." I shook my head emphatically. "You're a wonderful teacher."

Peter frowned. "Hardly. Anyway, it's not just teaching. It's publishing articles and playing up to administrators. And at Zebulun, it's watching every move you make so no one can accuse you of an indiscretion." He blushed and lowered his gaze.

My face grew hot again. Was he warning me? But that would mean he knew I loved him, and I'd tried so hard to hide my feelings.

Crumpling his burger wrapper into a ball and dropping it on the tray, Peter stood. "We should go. It's not getting any better out there."

The headlights illuminated little of the road ahead. Instead, they shone on a swirl of black and white that reminded me of a Jackson Pollock painting I studied in art history. When Peter leaned over the steering wheel to get closer to the windshield, my shoulders tightened in sympathy.

"Dr. Taylor, I'm sorry you got caught between my mother and me."

He grunted and nodded at the foggy window. "Could you wipe that again?" As I used a napkin to clear the glass, he asked, "Do you always fight like that?"

"No, but it's always tense. Every so often, we lash out at each other."

"Sometimes families are like that." When he leaned forward again, I looked ahead and saw that the snow seemed to be thinning. Peter pushed on the accelerator, and the car began to slide. Lifting his foot, he let the speed drop back down to twenty miles per hour.

The moment of danger exhilarated me. Here we were, alone in the enclosed space of his car, braving the storm together. The intimacy moved me to say, "I was always closer to my father. My mother doesn't care about me."

"I'm sure that's not true."

"No? I could have gone to an Ivy League college—my scores were high enough to get scholarships—but she wouldn't let me apply. She didn't trust me at a secular school and said she'd withhold the college money she saved if I went somewhere else."

"So you settled for second-rate Zebulun." His tone was dry.

"I didn't mean it that way. I just think it's unfair she limited my choice." Peter said nothing, and I feared I sounded too whiny. *Way to impress him with your maturity.* I wished I could snatch back my words.

Moments later, I saw a faint orange glow ahead that was probably the neon sign of the tavern by home. "Slow down. I think we're near the turnoff. Yes, see that break in the median?"

"Just barely." As he turned left, the car started to fishtail. He managed to stop it just before we skidded into the opposite lane. "Anything coming?"

Biting my lip, I stared down the westbound lanes but could make out only swirling snow. The flakes had grown larger again. At least, I didn't see anything that resembled oncoming lights. "I don't think so."

Accelerating cautiously, he steered toward what looked like the entrance to the unplowed frontage road. "Curve right and then turn sharp left, following the edge of that grove," I told him.

Snow had blown heavily across the pavement. When he tried to accelerate through the first drift, forward momentum drove the car up onto snow piled higher than the undercarriage. The wheels spun uselessly.

"Shit!" He turned off the ignition. "I have a shovel in back. I'll dig us out."

"I'll do it." I unlocked my door.

"No. Stay in the car. I only have one shovel, and I'm stronger than you."

"Then I'll walk to my house and get another one."

"You will not."

"It's only a quarter mile."

"No!" Grabbing my arms, he pulled me around to face him.

I sucked in my breath, intensely aware that he was close enough to kiss me. What would he do if I leaned toward him? Then he said, "You don't realize how dangerous these conditions are. If snow soaks through that cloth coat of yours, you could get hypothermia and grow disoriented and wander off in a field."

Even though he had once again reverted to oldest-brother tone, I retorted, "Isn't it just as dangerous for you to be out there shoveling? I can help."

Peter sighed and released me. After gazing out the window at the sideways-blowing flakes, he said, "We'll take turns."

He went first. I waited only five minutes before opening my door and stepping into knee-deep snow. As I forced my way through the drift, a blast of wind blew tiny needles in my face. Standing at the front of the car, Peter was staring bleakly at the shallow trench he'd started.

I took the shovel. When he didn't protest, I examined him closely. His trousers were covered with gobs of snow that reminded me of frosting scrolls on a wedding cake, and instead of boots, he was wearing dress shoes that were caked with white. "Your feet must be freezing. Go start the car and put them under the heater." He shook his head.

Planting my feet, I began to shovel. Within minutes, sweat drenched my shirt beneath my jacket, while the gusting wind scrubbed my face raw.

Peter stamped his feet. "Let me work for a while."

"Is there anything in the trunk I could use as a makeshift shovel?"

"I doubt it." He reached into his pocket. "Here are my keys. Go look."

I slogged to the rear of the car. Opening the hatchback, I saw a down sleeping bag, a gas can, jumper cables, and a coil of oily rope. Spotting an empty wiper fluid jug, I wondered if I could cut the top off and make it into a scoop. I yelled into the wind, "Do you have a pocketknife?"

"At home with my camping stuff. Why?"

"Never mind." I slammed the hatchback and struggled to the passenger door. Reaching into the back, I grabbed a large Styrofoam cup from the litter on the floor. *Thank God, you're a slob,* I thought.

Peter laughed when he saw what I held. "Planning to bail out *Titanic* with a teacup?"

"Do you have a better idea?" I asked, flinging a cup of snow at him.

"Yes." He held out the shovel. "Spell me a while."

Grinning, I handed him the cup. "Ditto."

I pushed the shovel into the drift, but before lifting it, I closed my eyes. *If I could, I'd preserve this moment forever, the two of us teasing each other and working side by side. I'd put it in one of those snow globes like Grandma has.* Then I scooped up a shovelful of snow and tossed it aside.

Twenty minutes later, Peter leaned on the shovel. "I think that does it. Can you drive a stick shift?"

"Sort of." Nita had let me practice once in Todd's pickup.

He looked unconvinced by my answer. "Depress the clutch, shift into first, and accelerate slowly. I'll push from behind. When I yell, stop. We may have to rock it out of here."

On the first try, the car strained against its snowbound inertia but didn't move. I stopped accelerating when Peter called, and I felt the car slide back. The second time, the car pulled free. I drove beyond the drift, stopped, and opened the door. Once outside, I saw Peter on his knees, struggling to rise from where he'd fallen when the car lurched away. "Are you all right?"

"I'm fine." He stood and brushed himself off.

Although we encountered several more drifts on the road, we didn't get stuck again. It was nearly 10:00 when we stopped in front of my house. "I'd better not try that driveway."

I bit my badly chapped lower lip. "You will come in for a while, won't you?"

"I don't think so. I think I'd rather face that drift again than your mother."

Turning away so he wouldn't see my fear, I saw a bundled-up figure wading through the drifts on the driveway. "Too late. Here she comes."

"Oh, Lord. Probably wants my head on a platter." He stepped out of the car and called, "Mrs. Thompson, we're all right. Sorry to have worried you."

Rolling down the window, I heard Mom call back, "Come in the house."

"I have to start back."

"There's more snow coming. They're warning people to stay off the roads."

Ducking his head inside the car, Peter said to me, "Talk to her."

I made fists inside my mittens. "No, she's right. It's too dangerous for you to drive back when you can spend the night here."

"I can't do that."

"Dr. Taylor, please. You wouldn't let me walk a quarter mile. How can you think of driving all the way back to town?"

He climbed back in the car, maneuvered it onto the lower part of the driveway to prevent it from being hit by a snowplow, and turned the ignition key with a jerk. "You know, you're not half this difficult in class."

In the house, Mother stood with her lips pressed together and her arms folded across her chest as she watched us shed our snowy coats and footwear. "Do you need supper?"

"No, we ate." Peter faced her. "Mrs. Thompson, let me say again how sorry I am."

A beat passed before she answered, "As my daughter pointed out earlier, she's an adult and can risk her life if she wants. But that doesn't alter the fact you took advantage of her sense of duty. I find that inexcusable."

"Mom!" I exclaimed, mortified that she would berate him like a child. Peter laid a restraining hand on my shoulder. I turned to him, reveling in the unexpected sensation of the two of us standing together as a team against my mother.

Although Peter was staring straight ahead, it was to me that he spoke. "Your mother's right. I used poor judgment."

I looked back at my mother, expecting to see some softening at his admission. Instead, indignation blazed on her face. She glared at Peter until he removed his hand.

Mother flicked a glance toward me. "Get some bedding and make up the couch in the basement."

"The basement?" I stepped forward. "He'll freeze down there! What's wrong with the living room couch?"

"I'm sure he'd like some privacy. The space heater will keep him warm."

"This is ridiculous. You're just doing this because—"

I stopped when I saw the glint in her eye. *Because of Ritchie,* I completed the thought in my mind. *She thinks that if Peter sleeps up here, I'll lure him into my bedroom.* The idea was absurd. I had no intention of seducing him...and if I had, one flight of stairs wouldn't stop me.

In the lengthening silence, he said, "The basement will be fine."

I jerked around to argue but felt pity at seeing the discomfort on his face. In spite of my apologies in the car, I had once again thrust him into a conflict with my mother. "All right."

The basement of the Thompson house was one of the saddest places Peter had ever seen. Against the far wall stood a sagging couch the color of pea soup and a workbench whose surface was bare. The forest green linoleum was cracked.

Katie, her arms laden with blankets and towels, nodded at the empty center of the room. "Remember I told you about the model of Gettysburg my father was building? That's where it stood before my mother tore it down." She set the bedding on the workbench. "This sofa is in terrible shape. The springs are shot, and it's going to give you a backache."

Peter shoved his hands in his pockets. He felt cold, damp, and deflated. With just one sentence, Mrs. Thompson had punctured his self-serving belief that he'd made a commendable sacrifice in bringing Katie home. He never should have let her work late in the first place. Now, all he wanted was to get under covers and hide from the humiliation that had trailed him down here. "It'll be fine. You forget, I sleep on the ground when I camp."

"That's an idea." Her face lit up with inspiration. "I could put the cushions on the floor to give you more support."

Swiftly, Katie arranged the three cushions in a line perpendicular to the couch. "This will put you in front of the space heater," she said, nodding at the squat, electrical unit nearby. She reached over and turned it on.

Then she spread a sheet on the cushions and tucked it beneath them. Watching, Peter had a jolting memory of Eileen, wearing nothing but a slip as she changed their sheets. "Don't!"

Katie cringed as though he'd slapped her and scrambled to her feet. She waved toward the corner behind him. "There's a bathroom over there."

She looked so miserable that Peter felt as though he'd kicked a puppy. "I'm sorry. I didn't mean to snap at you. It's been a long day."

Katie lifted her face, causing Peter to feel like he had plunged into a turbulent ocean. Waves of sorrowful longing rose and fell in her beautiful eyes. "It'll be all right," he murmured. "We survived the storm, didn't we?"

"I guess so," she whispered.

Peter longed to hug her. He knew it would be a foolhardy gesture, one that offered her false hope, but the pain he saw in her eyes was more compelling than any amount of reason. Leaning forward, he gently kissed her forehead. "Good night, Katie. I'll see you in the morning."

The college library was a three-story building of red brick with a castellated tower at each end. Peter sat in the college archives on the top floor of the east tower, a room with wooden cabinets and glass-fronted bookcases, all locked, and rows of carrels with old-fashioned brass gooseneck reading lamps positioning light directly over the desks. With pristinely gloved fingers, Peter turned the yellowed pages of a nineteenth-century diary. His nostrils twitched from dust as he scanned a page of bold handwriting in ink that had faded to purplish brown:

This day I wrote to President Lincoln to condole with him upon the death of his son. Many times I have sent missives exhorting him to heed our urgent call for Abolition. Alas, I fear he waited too long; now the Almighty has sent the Angel of Death to his very door. I must remind him again that God will not be mocked.

Peter closed the diary. At his review in March, Dr. French had said if he wanted to make tenure, it was imperative to improve his publication record. French then suggested that Peter go through the Jonathan Morton papers with a view to writing the abolitionist's biography.

Reading the diaries discouraged Peter. Morton had been an arrogant bastard. It would be impossible to write a sympathetic biography—and unacceptable to Dr. French to produce any other kind.

However, he had little choice but to please the department head, who had bluntly named the other problem jeopardizing Peter's career: "I'm sorry to say that people are speculating about the nature of your relationship with the Thompson girl. I am told that you and she are seen frequently together."

"We haven't done anything wrong."

"I assured the committee of that. But I have observed the girl since being alerted of the concern, and in my opinion, she is indeed infatuated with you. You must discourage the attachment."

"And embarrass her needlessly? Katie hasn't done anything wrong, any more than I have. She's been careful to keep an appropriate distance."

Dr. French scowled, bringing his unkempt white eyebrows together. "Do you mean to say you're cognizant of her feelings? And you have done nothing to put her off? Are you in love with the girl?"

"No." Peter looked down at his lap. "I don't think so."

"I had hoped for a less ambiguous answer. If you expect to receive tenure at this institution, you must get the situation under control at once."

Recalling the meeting, Peter felt his stomach churn. The ultimatum was clear: his career or his friendship with a girl nine years his junior, a girl for whom his feelings were too complex to define easily.

Staring at the green cover of the Morton diary, Peter felt ashamed of his cowardice in avoiding Katie. He typed his handouts at home, came in early to make copies, and graded papers with his office door closed. In the last six weeks, Katie's look on seeing him had changed from pleasure to uncertainty to baffled hurt.

Today he'd shunned her again. Earlier, he'd seen Katie sitting on the grass, studying in the May sunshine. Her hair hung loose, tumbling down her back in waves—caused, he assumed, by the braid she usually wore. Peter longed to cross the lawn and tell her how pretty she looked that way, but instead, he scuttled into the library like a cockroach seeking cover.

Suddenly, Peter swept up the diaries, locked them in their cabinet, and returned the key to the curator. He peeled off the white cotton gloves as he raced downstairs. Outside, Katie still sat in the same spot. He paused to catch his breath. After checking that no other faculty members were in sight, Peter strode across the grass. "Hi."

Shielding her eyes, Katie looked up at him, her expression guarded.

Peter dropped his briefcase and sat beside her. "What are you working on?"

"My independent study. Dr. French is letting me compile local history. Today I'm recording the story of how Shiver Creek got its name."

"Tell me."

Katie pushed back the cuticle of her thumbnail. "I'm not sure you'd like it."

"Please."

She sighed. "All right. A French-Canadian fur trader married a woman from Quebec and brought her here. Soon he became jealous of the other traders who visited their cabin. When they had a baby, the trapper accused his wife of being unfaithful even though it wasn't true.

"One morning, they argued out by the woodpile until he beat her and walked away. The woman dragged herself back to the cabin and discovered her baby was gone. Despite her injuries, she ran outside and followed her husband's footprints through the mud to the creek, where she found her baby underwater, its blankets caught on tree roots.

"Meanwhile, the husband ran to the trading post and confessed his crime. When the traders came, they found the wife rocking her dead baby in her arms and shivering uncontrollably before a cold hearth. They say she never spoke again, and for the rest of her life, shivered whenever she heard a man's voice."

Falling silent, Katie met Peter's eyes. Her face was as white and still as marble, and Peter wanted to touch her cheek to see if it was cool. Instead, he placed his hand over hers, which was lying on the grass. Staring at the shadows at the base of her throat, he imagined holding her. Stroking that rippling black hair. Kissing that sad mouth.

His face flamed, and his penis grew hard. Jerking back, Peter pulled his briefcase onto his lap as camouflage. "That's a moving story. I'm sure your paper will be fine."

Katie gazed at him mournfully. A burst of laughter from passing students reminded Peter that they were sitting in a public place. As his erection began to subside, he said, "I have to go," He stood, holding the case awkwardly in front of him.

He walked away, telling himself, *You're in deep trouble, Taylor.*

Two days later, Dr. French dropped into Peter's office, asking for a progress report. When Peter answered that he didn't want to write the Morton biography, French adopted a Jack Benny pose—his right arm across his chest, the fingers of his left hand resting on his cheek. "I hardly think you're in a position to be choosy, my boy. You need to publish something substantial within two years, and you don't have another idea, let alone a start on the research."

Peter bristled at the condescension. "I just don't find him a congenial personality."

French raised his eyebrows. "I thought we were discussing a work of scholarship, not a letter to a pen pal."

"Yes, but—"

"No buts. This sort of dithering is the reason you've published only one article since you joined the faculty." French shifted his weight and chopped one hand into the palm of the other. "Unless you can bring me a full outline for another project by the end of this week, I expect you to buckle down to work on the Morton book. I am trying to help you retain your position in this department, and an appropriate sign of gratitude would be your diligent cooperation."

Peter closed his eyes and said, "Yes, Dr. French."

When he opened them again, the old man was gone.

Impossible old goat. Peter got up to close the office door, wishing he had the nerve to slam it hard enough to make the whole department shake. But with his luck, he'd probably break the frosted glass window.

Frowning, he sat and reached for his Fergie Jenkins–autographed baseball.

The summer Peter was nine, his father was in a car accident and stayed at home until his concussion healed. Before then, Peter had spent his vacation playing dolls with four-year-old Marian and reading to two-year-old Joel. When Patrick saw those activities, he roared, "Stop being such a sissy. Go play ball with the other boys."

Desperate to please his father, Peter roamed the neighborhood, throwing himself into any ballgame he could find. When he went home at night with bruises and painfully jammed fingers, Patrick would look up from his paper and ask how many hits Peter had versus how many strikeouts. And always look dissatisfied by the answer. No matter how hard Peter tried, his father seemed to reject something in his very nature.

He'll say "I told you so" if I don't make tenure.

The phone rang, and he picked it up. "Dr. Taylor speaking."

"My, aren't we formal. Darlin', do you look as stuffy as you sound?"

"Who is this?" Peter demanded, but he knew. He could never forget that warm, seductive voice.

"I know it's been a long time, but I can't believe you forgot me."

"No, Eileen, it just took a minute."

"It's nice to talk to you too." She laughed.

"Just a minute." Holding his hand over the mouthpiece, he closed his eyes and exhaled. *You can do this.* Then he lifted the receiver to his ear. "How did you get my number?"

"You don't sound a bit glad. Here I am, visiting Chicago, and I go to the trouble to call you, and all you can do is growl."

"As I recall, you said everything you had to say before you walked out."

She sighed dramatically, and Peter could visualize the pout. "That was a long time ago. I was just a nasty little old girl then. I'm awful sorry about it now."

Peter was shocked by how much he wanted to believe her despite the caustic nature of their breakup. After two stormy years of living together, he'd caught her sleeping with one of his friends. Her answer to his fury had been, "Don't look so surprised. Toby's twice as good in bed as you could ever hope to be."

"Eileen, what do you want?"

Another sigh. "I want to see you. For old time's sake."

Her voice—as sweet as pecan pie—reminded him of the kittenish girl he'd once loved, a girl who developed claws only after her parents' divorce.

"I've changed," he said. "I became a Christian the year after we broke up. I gave up some of the things we used to do together."

Her laugh tinkled across the wire. "Y'mean like having carnal knowledge of your girlfriends? Marian said you'd become poky as a Southern Baptist."

Marian! Peter grabbed his letter opener and jabbed the desk blotter. So his sister had instigated this call. She still hadn't forgiven him for refusing to persuade Jeff.

"Can't we visit a while? I'm free this evening."

Peter scrambled for a lie. "I'm going to a concert here at the college."

"Why, I'd love to come along. Unless you already asked some little girl."

Little girl. The very phrase Marian had used about Katie. That clinched his suspicions. "No, you can come if you like."

After they settled the arrangements and hung up, Peter swore under his breath. Eileen was the last person he wanted to deal with, and Marian had to know that. What a bitch she was.

I *sat* in the front row of the balcony of the chapel, a 2,400-seat auditorium painted eggshell white with rows of chairs upholstered in nubby purple-black fabric. The college orchestra, arrayed across the shining wood of the vast stage, was warming up their instruments. In the back wall of the stage, an opening revealed an elaborate set of organ pipes. To my right sat Ann Marie and her roommate Liz, a tomboyish girl I didn't know very well. We each had to write a report on a live performance for music appreciation class, a task I'd put off until the last concert of the year because classical music bored me.

"Hey, look," Liz said. "Your boyfriend's down there with another woman."

"What?" I leaned forward and looked down, scanning for Steve, and saw Peter Taylor walking up the aisle with a petite woman I'd never seen before holding onto his elbow.

I pulled back hastily. "I don't know what you mean."

"Come off it. I've seen you two in the snack bar, with Dr. Taylor practically slobbering over you."

"That's not true," I protested, but Liz wasn't looking at me. She was staring at the hand Ann Marie had placed on her arm.

"Don't tease her," Ann Marie said. "She can't help the way she feels."

Liz gave Ann Marie an oddly tortured look and then slumped in her seat. Turning away from them, I bit my lip. Was my secret so obvious? No wonder Peter avoided me.

The overhead lights flickered off and on, causing a sharp increase in noise as people hurried to their places. I scanned the auditorium until I found Peter and his date sitting on the center aisle about two-thirds of the way back from the front. The woman had long, honey-colored hair, large gold hoop earrings, and a taupe calf-length skirt with a high side slit. When she leaned toward Peter and shook her tawny mane at him, I felt a surge of hatred.

The auditorium grew dark. As the conductor took his place before the college orchestra, I chided myself, *What did you expect? Of course, Peter dates. Why would he fall in love with you?*

Lifting my chin, I gazed at the musicians, who now looked blurry. *Don't you dare cry,* I commanded myself.

Peter opened a canister and took a deep whiff of coffee to clear his head of Eileen's musk perfume. She was in the living room, insisting she needed a jolt of caffeine before driving back to the city.

The concert had been agony. Always a provocative girl, Eileen had become one of those women who radiated sexuality. Sitting with her in Connor Chapel, Peter sharply recalled the unquenchable desire he'd once felt for her and the delight that he, at least, had found in their bed.

To banish the memories, he ticked off her faults. She was manipulative, shallow, and bored by intellectual topics. The sting of the old rejection was as sharp as if her words had lashed him yesterday—but the fact that she had sought him out was like a proffered salve. Knowing Eileen as he did, he understood exactly what she was offering. She would sleep with him without hesitation, and she wouldn't mind keeping the affair secret to protect his career.

But was it ever that easy? Peter was no longer the kind of man who could take her without guilt. Was he going to throw his years of careful celibacy away?

When the coffee was done, he carried a tray into the living room and set it on the mission-style coffee table. Eileen had slipped off her shoes and curled up on the black leather couch so that the slit in her skirt revealed most of her leg. Peter handed her a mug. "Level with me. Why did you call? I thought you were married."

"I was, but me and Woody just couldn't get along." She scooted close to him. "You know, you really were the sweetest boy I ever knew."

"You didn't always think so."

Eileen pushed out her lower lip. "That was on account of Daddy and the divorce. I've grown up since then. But you're not giving me half a chance."

Peter's tongue felt thick as he asked, "A chance for what?"

She took his mug, set it on the coffee table, and kissed him. As he slid his arms around her, Peter wondered how he could have forgotten the enticing smoothness of thin silk over warm skin. Eileen pulled back and began to undo her buttons.

When Peter reached to stop her, she took his hand and slipped it inside her blouse. He allowed his fingers to graze the lace edging of her bra—but then he thought of Katie. He pushed Eileen away. "No. We're not going to do this."

"Why not?" She moved close and brushed the front of his trousers. "You're not going to pretend you don't want to."

"I told you. I'm a Christian now. There are other things I want more."

"I see." Her voice changed to a cold steel blade as she rebuttoned her blouse. "How nice you found religion after you couldn't cut it with me. God, you're a pitiful excuse for a man."

He stood, finding strength in his newfound ability to refuse her. "And what kind of woman does that make you, coming to beg for my love?"

Eileen turned red. "Just call me a good Samaritan who took pity on the wrong son of a bitch." She slipped on her shoes, snatched up her purse, and left.

That summer, whenever I caught myself dreaming of Peter, I made myself remember the concert and his stunning companion. By fall, I had armored myself with resolutions: I would not enroll in Peter's classes, I wouldn't seek him out to talk, and if we chanced to meet, I'd smile politely and walk on.

Then Maggie, the department secretary, called me. "We're having an open house during homecoming. Could you give me a hand?"

"What about Brent?"

"Oh, he's worse than useless. I told them not to hire a boy for your old job."

On homecoming Saturday, I drove to Sanford Hall wearing a new midnight blue dress and navy pumps with two-inch heels. When I walked into the Morton seminar room, the memories of the January Friday I worked late here with Peter washed over me. Compared to that winter night, the room looked almost cheerful with the purple velvet drapes open and autumn sunshine pouring through the windows. Maggie looked up from the gold and purple chrysanthemums she was arranging in a low bowl at the center of the table. She tended to wear feathery Farrah Fawcett hair and flowery Laura Ashley dresses, neither of which suited her brisk personality. "The silver trays are in the workroom. And cookies from the bakery. Would you set them out?"

Crossing the hall, I saw Brent—dressed in a polo shirt, khaki chinos, and loafers with no socks—arrive and enter the seminar room.

Maggie's rebuke carried throughout the department. "Is that your idea of party attire? You're supposed to be one of the servers."

Seconds later, Brent joined me in the workroom, a utilitarian space with metal cabinets, a copy machine, a typewriter on a stand in the corner, and a work table with a paper cutter and heavy duty stapler at one end. "What should I do?"

I paused from arranging butter cookies on a paper-doily-lined tray and nodded at a cutting board and pile of lemons. "Cut those in wedges."

Brent sighed as he reached for the knife. "I thought I got along with everyone in the department, but it's different when you work here. They're all so quirky." He tossed a few wedges in a glass bowl. "Did you know that Dr. Ogilvie naps in his office? And I swear, Dr. Bunsen never smiles."

Footsteps approached, and Peter walked into the workroom. Instead of his usual tweed jacket, he was wearing a moss green wool sweater over a green-pinstriped oxford shirt. "Katie. I didn't know you were here."

"Maggie needed another server."

Peter's gaze traveled from my loose hair to my high-heeled shoes. His Adam's apple bobbed. "You look nice. I like your hair that way."

Then he turned to Brent and laid a piece of paper on the table next to the cutting board. "This worksheet you left in my box yesterday has eight typos. Will you redo it after the reception?"

"But it's homecoming. I was going to the football game."

"I told you I need this Monday." Peter pulled a gold pen from his breast pocket and circled the mistakes. "It has to be retyped."

"Will I get paid for the time?"

Laying down his pen, Peter frowned, a stern expression I imagined him using on his younger brother. "Do you think you should?"

"Dr. Taylor!" Maggie called from the other room. "Could you help me move some furniture?"

Before he left, Peter said, "I expect a clean copy by this afternoon."

As Brent snatched up the paper, Peter's pen rolled to the floor. "That's his quirk. He always assigns stuff at the last minute."

I stooped to retrieve the pen. "I never had problems with him."

"No, I guess you wouldn't."

I stiffened at the implication. "If you're done cutting lemons, take that tray to Maggie."

Alone, I gazed at the pen, engraved with the letters *PHT* beside the clip. Wondering what the *H* stood for, I slipped the pen into my in-seam pocket.

After the reception, I walked through the department picking up crumpled napkins and dirty dishes. The sound of sporadic typing came from the workroom. Peter stood by his office door, laughing with a former student. The red-headed girl's flirtatious smile made me want to claw her face. *You have to get over this,* I told myself and went into the seminar room. A minute later, Peter joined me. "Need help?"

"No." I busied myself placing white ceramic mugs in a plastic dishwasher rack.

"Where are you going to wash those?"

"Maggie will take them back to the dining hall. The dish crew will do it." Facing him, I brushed my hand against my dress where I could feel the weight of his pen in the pocket. I wondered if he'd missed it yet.

Peter licked his finger and picked up a few crumbs from one of the cookie trays. "I don't see you much anymore. How are you?"

"Fine. Senior year is busy."

"Lots of social life?"

"No, just course work."

Dr. French entered the room; he was so much shorter than Peter that he looked like a white-haired gnome. "Am I interrupting something?"

"No." Peter jammed his hands in his pockets.

"Then may I see you in my office?" They left together.

So I'm off limits. Reaching into my pocket, I stroked Peter's pen. I imagined returning to the college after I'd finished grad school. The department would hire me, and I would work by Peter's side. He'd be married by then, maybe to that honey-haired siren, and I'd never be able to confess my love. *It's better that way. Then I won't ever have to tell him about Ritchie.*

At times, Peter wondered if his career at Zebulun was worth the price he was paying. In the past, he had always looked forward to each new research project. Now, every day of the foreseeable future held the same soul-crushing task: writing the biography of a man he despised.

Even worse, he missed Katie. She seemed to know that their relationship was under a ban and treated him with a stiff formality he couldn't crack. Once he ran into her in the quad and asked her to join him for coffee. A brief glow lit her face before she shook her head. Watching Katie hoist her books and walk away, Peter felt like Tantalus, seeing the one thing he craved more than anything else recede beyond reach.

One morning, his colleague Dr. Bunsen, a fortyish woman wearing a French twist and a severely tailored suit, waylaid Peter outside his office. "You're the Thompson girl's advisor, aren't you? You know, she's considering graduate school. She can go far—if she avoids distracting entanglements."

Stunned by the woman's lack of subtlety, Peter glared after her as she moved on.

He found himself replaying the encounter all afternoon, even when he went to play basketball with his friend Wayne Krueger, a political science professor who had been at the college a year longer than Peter. Agitated by the idea of Katie becoming as sterile and pretentious as Yvonne Bunsen, Peter drove toward the basket, using sharp blows to dribble the ball as though he were slapping down Dr. Bunsen's schemes. When his layup sank successfully, he felt he'd scored a moral victory.

Wayne—a trim six-footer with dark hair and a mustache that made female students compare him dreamily to Omar Sharif—ran past him to retrieve the ball. Placing his hands on his hips, Peter walked down the court trying to catch his breath. As he tossed sweat-soaked hair out of his eyes, he glanced up at the balcony, where an indoor track circled the gym. There, as if summoned by his thoughts, ran Katie.

She wore the school colors—a purple T-shirt and purple satin shorts with a gold stripe—and she looked beautiful. As Katie made the turn, she glanced down and their eyes locked. Then Wayne ran up and punched Peter's arm. "Hey, you in this game or not?"

In the shower later, Wayne said, "What happened to you? First, you're playing like Larry Bird, then you lose it."

"I can't talk about it. Not here."

As Wayne lathered his curly, dark brown hair, an herbal smell permeated the shower stalls. "Why don't you come home with me for supper? Lena's been bugging me to ask."

The unpainted brick walls of the Krueger kitchen were hung with gleaming copper pans. Ceramic bowls and pots of ivy stood on an iron baker's rack, and a jug of red carnations enlivened the table.

Wayne heated up a kettle of pea soup and served it with homemade rye bread. He and Peter were halfway through the meal before Lena ambled into the kitchen. When they first arrived, she'd poked her head out of the room that served as her studio and announced, "I'm finishing a painting. I'll eat later."

Now she looked as satisfied as if she'd just climaxed. Stopping at the table, Lena kissed the top of Wayne's head.

"You have cadmium yellow on your nose."

"Mmm." Lena crossed to the cabinets. She had a round face, brown braids coiled around her head, a stocky figure, and baggy paint-streaked clothes.

When she took down a wine glass, Wayne exclaimed, "Lena!"

"What?" When he pointed at the glass, she laughed. "Peter won't care. Besides, I didn't sign your fusty old pledge." Disappearing into the pantry, she returned with a bottle of Cabernet.

Marveling at her boldness, Peter wondered if Wayne's marriage had caused him trouble at his last review. Lena was a scandal among faculty wives. An abstract artist, she dressed like a Bohemian, used her maiden name, Volkov, and declared openly that she didn't want children. Luckily for Wayne, his department head wasn't as puritanical as Dr. French.

Wayne sliced more bread. "So what's bothering you?"

Peter glanced at the print of a Renoir nude on the opposite wall. Wayne and Lena had built a cozy enclave seemingly untouched by college prohibitions. How could they understand his dilemma?

"It's about that girl, isn't it?"

Peter dropped his spoon in his bowl. "How did you know?"

Wayne wiped his mustache with a napkin. "Last year before your review, one of our colleagues told me of his 'concern.' He suggested I warn you to back off. I told him I trusted your judgment more than I did faculty gossip."

"Oh dear," Lena said. "Looks like we're all going to need wine."

Peter's face grew tight with anger. "You didn't need to warn me. French told me to stay away from Katie if I want to make tenure."

"What gives him the right?" Lena demanded, handing Peter a filled goblet.

He took it without protest. "Student-professor affairs are a problem at some schools—and as a Christian school, we can't afford a hint of scandal. But my friendship with Katie isn't like that."

Tilting her head, Lena gazed intently at his face. "You love her, don't you?"

"Yes." The unguarded admission surprised Peter, but he realized it was true.

Lena smiled. "And I bet you want to marry her."

Peter put down his glass. His underarms were suddenly damp. "Wait a minute. I've never even gone out with the girl."

"Nonsense. You've known her for years. What's dinner and a movie going to tell you that you don't already know?"

Thinking of the constraint that now existed between Katie and him, Peter shook his head. "I think we lost our chance. There is such a thing as bad timing."

Lena rolled her eyes. "Timing, hell. Wait till she graduates in June and then tell her how you feel."

But she wants to go to grad school. How can I ask her to give that up to stay with me? Peter rubbed his temple and said, "I'll see how things stand at the end of the year."

Lena raised her wine glass. "To June."

"To June," Peter reluctantly repeated.

As I stood on the lawn outside Connor Chapel, a red-brick building with a massive pillared portico over three double-door entrances, I wondered if I were the only miserable person at graduation. All around me stood jubilant seniors in their purple caps and gowns, surrounded by grinning relatives dressed as if for church. People laughed, took photographs, sniffed congratulatory bouquets, and made promises to keep in touch. On the wide chapel steps, Ann Marie and her fiancé posed while one of her sisters snapped a photo. Then I saw Liz glaring at them from across the lawn. *Had they argued?* Liz had been touchy ever since Ann Marie got engaged. *At least, someone else is as unhappy as I am.*

Near me, Grandma Brigitte fumbled with a new camera. "I don't think that's how the film goes in," Mom said. "Let me try."

Over my mother's shoulder, I saw Peter exit the back of Sandford Hall and walk toward us. He had shed the black tam and dark blue and black gown he'd worn to graduation and was wearing a tan summer suit.

As he drew near, he said, "I was hoping to see you. To ask you to write."

My chest squeezed painfully. "Are you leaving?"

His face scrunched in confusion. "No. Aren't you going to grad school?"

"I have to save money first. I'm starting a job here in Zebulun next week."

"Oh." He grinned. "So we'll see each other around town."

My throat tightened in frustration at his unthinking optimism. "Maybe. We never have before."

Instead of responding to my cynicism, Peter reached into his jacket pocket and handed me a small present wrapped in rosebud-patterned paper. "I thought this would be handy if you were leaving, but you can probably use it anyway."

When I removed the paper, I found a burgundy leather address book with my initials stamped in gold on the cover. "It's beautiful. Thank you."

"I hope you don't mind, but I—"

Grandma's voice broke in. "Kathleen, it's time for pictures."

Peter lifted his eyebrows. "Kathleen?"

"My grandmother doesn't believe in nicknames." We moved toward my family, and I introduced him to them.

Grandma Brigitte frowned over the top of her glasses. "Do you want your picture taken or not? That professor, or whatever he is, can work the camera."

"I'd love to," Peter said.

After he took the photographs, my mother said, "Can I take one of you and Katie?"

Panicked at the thought that Dr. French might see us together, I shook my head, but Mom was too busy advancing the film to notice. When I turned to Peter, he whispered, "Don't stand so far away. I don't bite."

Although I smiled for the photograph, my face felt tight with anxiety. Then Peter shook my hand. "Let's stay in touch. Drop by campus next fall if you can." He hurried away.

Drop by. He'll never make a move. I crumpled the wrapping paper from his gift. If Peter Taylor thought I was going to come mooning over him, he had another think coming.

I couldn't stay angry, though, not when Peter had given me a present. During the graduation party at my grandparents' house, I retreated to the bathroom, leafed through the address book, and discovered what Peter was going to say before he was interrupted. Under *T,* he'd printed his address and home phone number. Beneath that, he'd written, "I'll miss you."

Pressing the book to my chest, I cried, "Oh, Peter, if you care, why didn't you say so?"

A *week* later, I started working as an administrative assistant to one of the sales managers at Cel-Fo, a manufacturer in west Zebulun. The company fabricated adhesive-backed, cellular-foam gaskets used in everything from tractors to sewing machines to outboard motors.

At first, I wasn't sure I liked my boss, Ed Marsden. He had a cocky smile and seemed all too aware of his good looks: thick chestnut brown hair, grey eyes, and a strong face with a square jaw. He looked like he kept in shape, and on his desk, he had two ten-pound weights.

I worked in a small outer office connected to his. On the wall to my left was a row of black metal filing cabinets holding price quotes, part specifications, and copies of completed orders. I sat at a matching metal desk facing the outside door. On one corner was a white phone with buttons for several outside lines and another button for the office intercom.

My first day on the job, Ed gave me a tour of the factory—a huge open room with glass-block windows in otherwise bare cinderblock walls and row upon row of strange, dangerous-looking equipment. As soon as we entered, noise bombarded us: the kathunking of machinery, the high beeping of a passing forklift, a burst of static as the intercom blared, "Bill, line five."

Telling me to stay within the yellow safety lines painted on the concrete floor, Ed led me to a corner where massive rolls of material stood. "This is quarter-inch neoprene." He peeled back a corner of black, rubbery stuff. "I want you out here a lot. The more you learn about the operation, the more you'll help my customers."

Then he led me to a coating machine where a giant roll of paper was being unwound, spread with smelly adhesive, pressed onto tan foam material fed from a second roll, and rewound. "We coat the paper, then apply it to the cellular foam. The paper has a silicone backing, so it peels off, leaving the adhesive on the gasket."

I nodded, trying not to breathe in the fumes. The operator wasn't wearing a protective mask, but that didn't reassure me.

"This is a punch press," Ed said, referring to a machine stamping out gaskets from densely compressed grey material. He handed me one, a ring with a tab that made it look like a *Q*. "That's part 5760043 for Allied."

All the numbers and strange names tangled inside my brain. As I slipped the gasket into my skirt pocket to study it later, a balding African American man approached us. "Hey, Ed, who's this pretty lady?"

"Katie, this is Bill Flowers, one of our supervisors. This is Katie, my new assistant. I want her to get to know things out here."

"Sure thing. If you have any questions, miss, you just ask me."

As Bill walked off, Ed said, "He knows more about this place than I do."

Tuesday, the door to my office slammed open. A blonde with a large bosom and thin legs stood there. "Where's Marsden?" She strode past the filing cabinets and through the connecting door to Ed's office. "Dammit, Ed, you're not supposed to go out there and badger Bill. Leave the expediting to me."

Ed answered in an amused tone. "What's the matter, Carla? Afraid of losing your job?"

"Don't get cute. Because you went out there and pushed Allied, Martin got put on hold. We're going to lose that account."

"Isn't that too damn bad? Martin orders what, five grand a year? Allied's a two-million dollar account and growing."

Carla's voice went up a decibel. "I'm not here to debate their fucking worth. I'm telling you I'm supposed to coordinate the schedule."

"Look, when Stan tells me to do it different, I'll do it different. But you and I both know he won't do that." Ed's voice took on a teasing warmth. "Look, honey, I always told you not to take it personal."

"Can it, Ed. Your bullshit doesn't work on me anymore."

As Carla came back into my office, she paused by the side of my desk and threw me a speculative look. For an instant, I thought she was going to tell me something, but then Ed appeared in his doorway. Carla's face hardened, and she left.

"That's our expediter. She thinks she owns this office. She started out at your desk."

"You mean, she used to work for you?"

Ed grinned. "Funny, isn't it? When she sat there, she never minded going outside channels to push orders. But since her promotion, she's real sensitive."

Deciding it was wise to switch topics, I nodded at a brown accordion file that stood on my desk. "Can I ask you about the open order file?"

Ed came over and laid his arm along the back of my chair. "Shoot."

"Is it OK if I reorganize it? Right now, they're sorted by letter, but within each slot, they're jumbled. If I alphabetize them, I can find orders faster when customers call."

"Good thinking. Keep taking initiative, and I'll see that you advance." He patted my knee, his fingers lingering a beat too long. I lurched my chair closer to my desk, and Ed pulled back. "For a really good idea, I'll buy you lunch."

After he left, I tugged my skirt down. His physicality unsettled me, but I told myself it was just part of his salesman's bag of tricks.

After his sister's wedding, Peter had trouble falling asleep. It was a sticky night, his room wasn't air-conditioned, and because he was at his parents' house, he was wearing basketball shorts and a T-shirt even though he preferred sleeping naked. When he heard the grandfather clock downstairs strike three, Peter went to the kitchen to get a glass of milk.

Leaning against the edge of one of the white tile counters, he wiped sand from his eyes. Without his glasses, he could barely see across the room. He sighed. For the last two hours, he'd been wondering why people bothered to get married. His parents had never been happy, and Peter wouldn't give a nickel for Marian's chances. Wayne and Lena were the only well-matched couple he knew.

As he sipped the milk, he heard scuffling in the hall. His mother entered the kitchen, wearing a pink seersucker robe and a hairnet. "I thought I heard you get up."

"Go back to bed, Mom. I didn't mean to disturb you."

"Do you think I could sleep when something's bothering you?"

Years before, Peter had been the midnight comforter to her loneliness, back when she was younger than he was now, and the role reversal felt odd. "Nothing's bothering me. I'm just keyed up from the wedding."

Pamela came over and brushed hair back from his forehead. Without makeup her complexion was like old porcelain, slightly yellowed and scored with fine lines. "I'm worried about you. Why didn't you bring a date to the wedding?"

He sidestepped and carried his empty glass to the steel sink. "You know you're my best girl."

Frowning, Pamela twisted one end of her tie belt. "That's not funny. I'd hate to think I was one of those mothers who turn their sons off women."

He turned in surprise. "You're not."

"Then what is it? You used to talk about getting married, but you haven't mentioned it in years. Marian thinks you're still in love with Eileen."

"She's wrong." Acutely aware that he wasn't wearing anything beneath his skimpy basketball shorts, Peter moved so the butcher block table stood between them.

Pamela knotted her belt a second time. "Is there anything you're not telling me? Because I'd love you no matter what. It wouldn't matter if...I mean...your father—"

He wondered what his father was complaining about now. During Peter's childhood, Patrick had constantly admonished him, "Act like a man."

With the memory, came insight. "Oh God," Peter exclaimed. "He thinks I'm gay."

"No, darling, he doesn't." Pamela put her hands out in denial, but Peter could see the truth in her eyes. "We just want you to be happy. I worry I did something wrong. Your father says I hovered too much."

"Mom, please." Peter went to hug her.

She sniffed against his chest. Looking down, he saw her hairnet had slipped to one side. "Mom, I'm not gay. I lived with Eileen, didn't I?"

"Yes, but Phil Donahue had this program about men who didn't discover their...you know...until after they were married."

"Orientation," Peter said. She began to cry harder as though his knowing the term was a damning sign.

He sighed. "I wasn't going to say anything yet, but I have fallen in love. With a girl."

Pulling a tissue from her pocket, Pamela blew her nose. "Of course, it's a girl. You don't have to tell me twice." Her tears stopped. "So why didn't you bring her to the wedding?"

"It's a complicated situation."

Pamela frowned. "She's not married, is she?"

"Is that what you think? I'm either a closeted homosexual or a homewrecker?"

"I'm just trying to understand why you have to keep her a secret."

Feeling defenseless without his glasses, Peter squinted at his mother. "She was one of my students. She just graduated. I never told her how I feel because it wouldn't be proper. Now that she's out of school, I thought I should give her some time on her own before I call."

"Is she awfully young?"

"Twenty-two, twenty-three. But she's not some giddy kid."

"Oh?" His mother raised pale, thin-plucked eyebrows.

Peter rubbed the back of his neck. "Look, I really don't know what's going to come of it, so there's no point in discussing this."

Pamela straightened her hairnet. "OK. I'm sure you know what's best."

Right. That's why the third degree.

Exhausted as he was, Peter didn't sleep that night. As soon as it was light, he left a note on the kitchen table and drove home. A week later, UPS delivered a box containing his birthday presents: two shirts, a bottle of Old Spice aftershave, and a $200 check. Obviously an apology.

Leaving the bank after depositing the check, Peter paused in the entryway to put on prescription sunglasses against the August glare. He glanced through the outer glass door and saw Katie exit the pub across the street, followed by a trim man with the chiseled good looks of a *GQ* cover model. As they turned the corner, the man put a hand on her lower back.

"Damn!" Peter tore off his sunglasses. Who was that guy? He looked almost old enough to be Katie's father.

Must be her boss. He better not make a pass at her, or I'll—

Do what? The image of himself as Katie's defender faded. For all he knew, that man could be Katie's uncle. Or her pastor.

"I've been a fool," he said aloud just as a small elderly woman, wearing a straw sun hat and a dusty pink cotton dress printed with white flowers, exited the door leading from the bank. She leaned on her cane and stared up at him.

"I expect so. But you don't have to be one all your life." She crossed the foyer and exited through the door that led to the street.

After supper, I scrubbed the wooden table spotlessly clean before spreading out the fuchsia polyester blend I planned to make into a blouse. As I read the instructions, I wondered if I should have chosen an easier first sewing project. But I needed to build a career wardrobe, and buying clothes was expensive. I glanced at my mother, who stood at the sink peeling carrots for her lunch. *No, I'll figure it out myself.*

Thunder boomed, and rain spattered the concrete patio outside. The storm made me restless. Recently, I'd bought a red 1978 Pinto—and that bit of freedom from my mother made me long to move to my own place. But if I did, I'd never save for grad school.

Mother came to the table and fingered the fabric. "That's a nice color. I saw a photo of a blouse this color with an electric blue suit. It looked very chic." She pronounced the word *chick.*

The phone rang and she turned to grab it. "Hello. Yes, she is." Giving me a bemused look, Mom handed me the receiver and left the kitchen.

"Katie?" said the caller. "This is Peter. Peter Taylor."

"Oh, hi." I laid down the scissors and dropped into the nearest chair.

"How are you?"

"Fine. How are you?"

"Can't complain. Been doing lots of research this summer. Did I tell you I'm writing a bio of Jonathan Morton?"

"No, that must be exciting."

"Really, it's a bore. The man was a stuffed shirt. But if you want to succeed in old academe, you have to publish, publish, publish. You'll find out soon enough."

If I didn't know his voice so well, I would have sworn an imposter was making this glib small talk. "I don't know when I'll be able to afford grad school."

Peter instantly grew serious. "Why didn't you apply for financial aid?"

"I'd still have to borrow money, and I don't want to do that."

"But at least you'd be on your way. A lot of people leave school intending to go back and get so caught up earning a living, they never do."

I glanced around my mother's twenty-five-year-old kitchen: the turquoise-flowered curtains, aqua walls, birch cabinets, and aqua-and-white-checked floor. Familiar details that should have felt comforting made me yearn again for escape. "I don't think that will happen. I like my job well enough, but it's not something I want to do the rest of my life."

"How is it?"

"OK. My boss wants me to learn as much about the operation as I can."

"What's he like?" Peter's tone sharpened. "An old-fashioned big-business type, judging everything by the bottom line?"

"No, he likes to mentor people. He's not old-fashioned at all."

"I see. A young guy just out of business school."

"He's in his late thirties, I think."

Peter paused and then said, "We have so much catching up to do."

My breath caught in my throat. "Uh huh."

"I wondered if you'd like to have dinner with me."

Dinner. Like a date? Clutching the table edge and fighting to keep my voice calm, I said, "That would be nice."

"How about tomorrow? I'll pick you up at six."

"Great." After I hung up, I pressed my hand against my stomach, which was doing flip-flops. This was what I'd wanted for years. Wanted *and* dreaded. I couldn't escape the certainty that once Peter knew me better, he'd realize I wasn't good enough.

The next evening, Peter arrived promptly. As we walked out to his car, a goldfinch feeding on a roadside thistle took alarm and flew away. *I know how you feel,* I thought.

Peter backed out of the driveway and turned toward the highway.

When we passed the Pelletier farm, I saw Ritchie's mother taking down laundry. She glanced at the car, and I fought the urge to hunch down so she wouldn't recognize me. Seeing her felt like a bad omen.

Staring at my fingernails, I worried that I should have polished them. Remembering the woman at the concert, I wondered if Peter preferred the glamour type.

"I thought we'd go to Andrew's," he said.

My stomach tightened. Andrew's seemed too pricey for a platonic get-together, but I didn't want to make a fool of myself by assuming this was a date. With all my heart, I wished Peter would stop the car and say, "Let's go for a stroll. I want to talk."

I tasted something salty and discovered that I'd bitten my lip until it bled. Averting my face, I felt the damage with a finger. *When am I going to break this stupid habit? You'd think I could act grown up for one night. Peter's never going to fall in love with someone as gauche as me.*

Andrew's restaurant had semicircular booths with overstuffed dark green seats lining the mirrored walls. The table linens were pale peach. A floor-to-ceiling partition made of frosted glass etched with calla lilies separated the dining room from the bar area at the front. Brass chandeliers with clusters of frosted glass shades shaped like calla lilies hung from the ceiling.

After handing Peter two oversized, gold-tasseled menus bound in dark green leather, the hostess smiled. "Tonight we're having a summer special. Our extensive salad bar comes free with any entrée. Your waiter will be with you shortly." She left.

Katie looked overawed by their surroundings, so Peter leaned across the table. "None of the really fine restaurants in Chicago have salad bars."

"Oh?" She turned big eyes on him. "Do you go to fancy restaurants often?"

"No, but I have a theory. In the city, people look for increasingly exotic cuisine. In the country, they just want lots of food. It's the farm legacy."

She laughed.

Pleased by her reaction, Peter smiled at her. She was wearing one of those straight dresses that button down the front. *Coatdresses,* Marian called them. Peter had never liked the style, but on Katie, it looked good. The vertical periwinkle stripes accented her thinness, while her full bust strained against the mannish cut. The effect was surprisingly provocative.

The waiter approached their table. After they gave their orders, Peter winked at Katie. "On to the world-famous salad bar, shall we?"

She slid out of the booth, and he took her arm—but dropped it as they neared the buffet. Ahead was a familiar white-haired figure.

As the man turned and saw them, his bushy eyebrows shot up in surprise.

"Dr. French." Peter forced a smile. How could he have forgotten who'd recommended this place? Now he recalled that Dr. French and his wife ate here almost every Friday.

Mrs. French, a small, plump woman with white curls, came to her husband's side. Dr. French coughed and said, "Martha, you know our Dr. Taylor."

"Yes, of course." Her girlish bow-shaped mouth, coated in mauve lipstick, smiled.

"And this is a recent graduate, Katie Thompson."

"Oh." Mrs. French's eyes widened, and her smile dissolved.

"Hello," came Katie's subdued voice. Peter turned with the intention of taking Katie's arm and staring down the Frenches, but they were already moving away.

"I don't think I want any salad," Katie said. "I'll meet you back at the table."

"*Would* you like dessert?" Peter asked as Katie cut off a tiny cube of chicken Kiev, lifted it halfway to her mouth, and then returned it to her plate.

She shook her head, which didn't surprise him. She had eaten barely half her entrée. During dinner, she listened silently as he talked about the Morton biography. Now he tried a new topic. "Did I tell you my sister Marian got married?"

"That's nice."

"I guess so. I wish she hadn't rushed. She's never given a thought to a career. Since the day she met Jeff, she's wanted to get married."

Katie gazed into the flame of their candle, burning within a frosted glass cylinder. "Some girls are like that."

"But she could have both. Don't you think?"

She shrugged.

Damn, Peter thought. *This isn't going anywhere.* Leaning across the table again, he said, "I have an idea. Let's finish our coffee and go somewhere we can walk...and talk."

A smile of relief lit Katie's face, and Peter felt a fool. Here he'd been trying to impress her when what they really needed was to restore their friendship. Once that was back in place, they could figure out the rest.

When Peter asked me where I wanted to go, I suggested Riverview Park so we could walk along the river. As soon as we got out of the car, however, Peter noticed the bandstand and made a beeline toward it. The nineteenth-century, white-painted wooden structure had lattice railings on five sides and gingerbread trim along the eaves of the roof. In front of it was an open swath of lawn for concert seating, but a formal rose garden with wedge-shaped beds surrounded the other sides of the pavilion like sections of a wheel.

Trailing Peter on the paths between the beds, I clenched my teeth. The flowers' perfume made me want to gag; it called up the vision of a blanket of roses draped across a coffin, something, I supposed, I must have seen on television.

"It's beautiful," Peter called back over his shoulder. "I've never been here. What a shame that hotel your father told you about burned down."

"Let's go see the river." As I turned away from the garden, I felt relief. The Theakia was my old friend; nothing could hurt me there. "Tay-AH-kee-uh," I whispered like an incantation.

"Your father told you such wonderful stories." Peter fell in beside me. "I envy your memories of him."

The longing in his voice struck me. "What's your father like?"

We stopped at the road that ran parallel to the curve of the river. A car was coming toward us, its headlights burning like the eyes of a dragon. After it passed, Peter said, "I get along with my father about as well as you do with your mother."

We crossed to the riverbank. Standing near a huge willow, we stared down at the brown water. After a week of rain, the river was turgid and debris littered its surface. "But he must be proud of you."

Peter snorted. "He thinks teaching is for weaklings who are too afraid to fight it out in the real world."

"Oh, Peter." I reached for his hand, then afflicted by self-consciousness, changed my mind. Instead, I watched him gaze at the sky as it turned the silvery lavender of twilight.

"You know," he said, "when I was a kid, we used to go camping. Even there, we couldn't agree. He liked activity: hiking, swimming, canoeing. I preferred to observe nature. Joel's more like Dad. As soon as he was old enough to come along, he and Dad grew close and I became the outsider."

My heart swelled with pity. "But you don't resent your brother."

"Joel? I could never take it out on him." Peter turned toward me. "It's funny. The smell of the water made the camping memories come rushing back."

"The river does that. Sometimes I think it's magic."

"You love it, don't you? It must be nice, having roots in one place."

I sighed. This was what I'd missed, our ability to tell each other about our lives. If we got this back, I wouldn't ask for anything else.

Peter coughed. "So, um, did you agree with what I said in the restaurant? That my sister shouldn't put all her eggs in one basket?"

I squinted at him, perplexed by the change in subject. "I don't know. We only met once."

"But what about women in general? You, for instance. Are you still planning to teach in college?"

I tore a branch off the willow and pulled it through my fingers, ripping off leaves. "I think so."

"Is that your only goal?"

"What do you mean?"

Peter pushed his glasses up his nose. "Well, careers are important, but they're not everything. Don't you think women like Dr. Bunsen are just as short-sighted as Marian? I mean, how about you? Do you think you'll ever marry?"

Anger filled me, as sudden and intense as an allergic reaction, and I tossed the branch away. "How am I supposed to answer? It takes two people to make that particular decision."

As Peter moved toward me, the glow from the streetlight silvered his pale hair. "I know, but what if—"

"No. You're the one who taught me that historians don't deal with *what ifs.* So here are the facts. Since my father died, I've been alone. I couldn't count on anyone to give a damn. So how do I know if I'll marry? I can't even imagine hearing the man I love say he loves me back."

"Oh, Lord." Peter bowed his head, took off his glasses, and pinched the bridge of his nose. His shoulders slumped, making me feel like a bully.

"I'm sorry," I said.

Putting his glasses on, he peered at me through the gloom. "You haven't done anything to be sorry for. I'm the one who— Christ, I blew it, didn't I?"

"No." I held out my hand, but he ignored it.

"I did. I was trying to do what was right, but I let French browbeat me into hurting you." Self-reproach filled Peter's voice. "I don't even know if I'm the man you were talking about—God knows, I don't deserve to be—but I do love you."

Stunned, I pressed my stomach and exhaled slowly. The world was spinning as though we were on a carousel. What I'd said in anger was the unvarnished truth; I had never imagined a moment like this.

"Katie?" He took a step toward me. "Say something. You're scaring me."

"Peter, I..."

"What?" His voice coaxed me as he took my hands.

"I love you too. But your job. Dr. French. What are we going to do?"

"Don't worry about French. We haven't done anything wrong."

Peter caressed my cheek. His touch was full of the same wonder I felt. He put his arms around me and pulled me close. "You're so beautiful." Putting his hand beneath my chin, Peter lifted my head and kissed me lightly. "This feels strange after telling ourselves not to for so long."

I nodded, too overwhelmed to speak. Laying my head on his shoulder, I breathed in the starched cotton smell of his shirt.

He reached under my loose hair and rubbed the back of my neck. "Maybe we should take things slow. I mean, if you want to date other people, I'd understand."

I pulled away. "Is that what you want?"

"Sweetheart, no." Gently, he stroked my hair. "I just want to be fair to you. You're so much younger than I am."

"I've known how I feel about you for years. Why would that change now?"

"I hope it won't but..." Releasing me, he walked a few steps away. "I'm older and more experienced than you. You should have the chance to explore your options before—"

"Before what?"

Peter ran a hand through his hair and stared up at the sky. Then he came to me and took my hand. "Before I ask you to be my wife."

"Your wife?"

"Is that crazy? I never thought I'd propose on our first date."

He kissed me again, this time with a passion that stunned me. He had always seemed so cerebral. Fearful of the sudden hunger I sensed in him, I turned my face away. Instead of stopping, Peter kissed my neck. Against my will, I imagined his lips sucking at me, like the suction cup on an octopus.

Peter buried his face in my hair. "God, I want you so much. How long do you think we should wait?"

Wait? My stomach cramped. His eagerness felt too much like what I'd been through with Ritchie. "What do you mean?"

"How long should we wait to be married? Do you want a June wedding?"

"Oh." Relief made me light-headed. "No, I don't care about that."

"I was thinking, maybe it's too soon, but I get two weeks off at Christmas."

I had a sudden image of walking down the aisle toward the front of the church, decorated with massed poinsettias. The image was so appealing, my panic subsided. "That would be lovely."

As Peter bent to kiss me again, I went cold. *What if he finds out about Ritchie?*

The next day, I went to Peter's house for lunch. As I drove slowly, looking for his address, I discovered that he lived only a few streets from the Theakia. I felt strangely reassured knowing that even after I moved to town, I would still be close to my river.

After parking on Peter's street, I stared at his small one-story house with buff siding on the upper half and brick on the lower. I wondered what the inside was like. Considering the way his office looked, he probably left a ring around the bathtub and dirty socks on the bedroom floor. Soon, I would be living here with him. Washing our clothes together. Using the same bathroom. Sharing a bed. Until two days ago, I'd never even called him by his first name.

As I approached the porch, Peter opened the front door. He wore navy shorts and a striped T-shirt. His feet were bare, which embarrassed me for some reason. "Hi." He stepped back to let me inside. "I saw you sitting in the car. You're not having second thoughts?"

"Of course not."

"Good." He kissed me briefly. Then I stepped past him. A low bookcase separated the entry from the living room, furnished with a black leather couch and matching recliner. The leather surprised me—it seemed too macho. A glass-topped coffee table held a bust of Frederick Douglass.

"Come on," Peter said, taking my hand.

We walked into the dining room, where he handed me a cone of florist's paper. "These are for you."

Flowers. Chills cascaded over me. With trembling fingers, I removed the paper from a bouquet of crimson sweetheart roses and baby's breath.

"I don't have a vase. I'll get something to put them in."

As Peter went into the kitchen, I dropped the bouquet on the table and backed away. I heard running water.

Peter returned, carrying a filled jar. "My mother says if you trim the bottoms, they last longer." He held a paring knife toward me.

"Why don't you do it?" I moved past him to the window.

He lay down the knife. "What's wrong?"

"Nothing." I watched a neighborhood cat stalk a robin in the yard.

Peter came up and put his arms around my waist. "What is it? You're happy about our engagement, aren't you?"

"Yes." Folding my arms over his, I marveled at how good it felt to be enclosed in his embrace. "You'll think I'm crazy."

He kissed my ear. "You can tell me."

"I'm sorry. I don't like flowers. Whenever you pick them, they die."

"They die anyway."

"I know it's silly, but I can't help it. When I look at flowers, I see death."

He pulled away. As I leaned my forehead against the windowpane, I heard paper rustling. *He's going to change his mind about us.* Then Peter returned. "There. All gone."

Slowly, I faced him. "You're not mad?"

"Of course not." He tweaked my nose. "Think how much money I'll save over other husbands."

Husband. I shook my head at the strangeness of it and smiled.

Taking my hand, Peter gave me a tour of the house. The kitchen had a red tile floor and 1970s coppertone appliances. Both the dining room and master bedroom were furnished with mission-style furniture. A brown leaf-print bedspread covered Peter's queen-sized bed. The back bedroom held a desk, a black filing cabinet, and a twin-sized bed. We returned to the living room and sat on the couch. "Do you like it?"

"Sure," I lied. Everything felt so masculine that I didn't know if I'd ever feel at home. "At least, we won't have to scrounge for furniture like most newlyweds."

"*Newlyweds.* I like the sound of that." Peter took off his glasses, placed them on the end table, and moved toward me. After several slow kisses, he cupped his hand around my breast outside the fabric of my blouse.

I tensed. Even though I wanted him to touch me there, fear rippled through me. It deepened almost to panic as Peter unbuttoned my blouse. When he slipped his hand inside my bra, I cried, "Don't!"

"All right." Peter pulled back and brushed away the hair that had flopped in his face. His brow furrowed. "I know it's all happening pretty fast. But Katie, I have no intention of seducing you before the wedding."

Unable to look at him, I hung my head. "Sorry. I just—"

"Shhh." He drew me close. "I want to ask you a hard question. OK?"

I nodded, but I began to tremble. *He's going to ask if I'm a virgin. And when he finds out I'm not, the wedding will be off.*

"Do you think you're worried because I'm so much older than you?"

The question bewildered me. "Why would I be?"

Peter rubbed my arm. "There's something I should tell you. I didn't become a Christian until I was twenty-one, and...before that, I was sexually active."

I stared at him in disbelief. He always seemed so moral, I'd never suspected something like this. "Why are you telling me?"

He sighed. "Because I lived with someone in college. I'd rather you heard it from me than my family."

Feeling sick, I swallowed. "Did you love her?"

"I thought so. But it was a mistake. Does it matter very much?"

Yes, I thought. *It means you can't judge me for Ritchie.* Moving closer, I leaned my head on his shoulder. "What's past is past. Let's not talk about it again."

A week later, I was typing a price quote when Ed approached my desk from the side. "What's this?"

Keeping my hands poised on the keys, I glanced at him. "What?"

He lifted my left hand and stared pointedly at my new engagement ring: a marquise-cut diamond set on a white-gold band. "You've been holding out on me. I didn't know you were seeing anyone."

I felt a blush rising as I swiveled to face him. "The relationship was...lowkey until recently."

"It's a pretty ring. Modest but stylish. Is he anyone I know?"

Modest. That stung. I had been drawn to much smaller diamonds, but Peter insisted on at least three-quarters of a carat, which I had thought grand. "He's a professor at the college."

"I see." Ed's eyes glinted. "No wonder you kept it under wraps."

"It's not like that." I turned back to the typewriter. "I have a question about this quote."

Laying a hand on my shoulder, Ed leaned over me to see what I was pointing at. Then, as if acknowledging that I was spoken for now, he dropped his arm to his side.

When Peter took Katie to meet his parents, she curled her hair and wore a silky fuchsia blouse, a black pencil skirt, high heels, and the first makeup he'd ever seen on her. Ruefully, Peter wondered why she had chosen the night she met his father to turn up the sex appeal.

When they arrived at the French restaurant in Chicago, Peter's parents were waiting for them inside the entrance, standing next to a wall-mounted stone fountain with water trickling from a lion's head into a shell-shaped basin. Ignoring his son, Patrick took Katie's hands and inspected her from head to foot. "Peter never said he landed such a looker. I didn't know he had it in him."

Clenching his jaw, Peter put his arm around Katie's waist. Since he was fifteen, he'd known his father was habitually unfaithful, and Patrick's blatant appraisal of Katie outraged him.

The host, an impeccably suited man with a long face and basset-hound eyes, led them to their table. The restaurant was divided into several intimate dining rooms, each one containing five or six tables and its own fireplace. The décor was rustic, with items like copper roosters and vintage wine posters decorating the bare brick walls. Once they were seated, Pamela glanced at her husband to see if he was going to speak and then said, "Is Katie short for Katherine?"

"Kathleen."

"Oh, you must be Irish."

Katie looked puzzled. "Yes, and German, French, English. Maybe a little Potawatomi."

Patrick snorted. "So Peter's bringing an Indian into the family."

She stiffened. "Not Indian. Potawatomi."

"Same thing." Patrick signaled a waiter and ordered a double bourbon. Turning back to Katie, he said, "What do you do?"

"I'm an administrative assistant for a sales manager."

"A secretary. Didn't know you had to go to college for that."

Katie's eyes flashed, and Peter had to suppress a smile. He'd seen that look before when Katie fought with her mother. "I am *not* a secretary. I go into the plant to check open orders, do rough drafts of sales projections, and even draft simple price quotes."

Patrick raised his glass in a salute. "Now, that's a real job. I bet you didn't learn those skills at that pansy-ass college. On-the-job training, right?"

Katie looked to Peter in consternation. Patrick continued speaking, ignoring the waiter who stood ready to write down their order. "That's what I don't get about this liberal arts shit. It doesn't train you to do anything. What does your company make anyway?"

"Gaskets."

"See, now that's something people can use."

Peter slapped his menu shut. "Do you mind climbing down off the soapbox so we can order? The man's waiting."

Shrugging, Patrick said, "I'll have steak *maison,* medium rare, with *pomme frites.* And onion soup."

After they had all ordered, Pamela said, "Katie, have you booked the hall for your reception? I'm surprised you could find anything on such short notice."

"Oh, that's not a problem. The reception will be held at church."

Pamela's eyebrows rose. "Your church has a big enough facility to host a sit-down dinner?"

Peter intervened. "Mom, we're not having a sit-down dinner. It's going to be a morning wedding, followed by a luncheon buffet."

"Oh." Her tone cooled. "An informal wedding. What kind of dress will you wear?"

Katie licked her lip, now bare of lipstick. "A full-length gown. Isn't that proper for a morning wedding?"

Peter's mother waved the question away. "Things are much looser than they used to be. I suppose you can wear whatever you want."

On the way home, Katie chipped the polish off her thumbnail. "Your parents hate me. Especially your dad."

"No, he doesn't. He was hassling you to get at me."

"Why?"

"I told you, he disapproves of me. He thinks I'm—" Peter couldn't admit what his father really thought. "He has certain ideas about what a son should be, and I don't measure up."

"He seems to care a lot about success." Katie scraped harder at her nail. "Maybe if I had a better job or richer family, he'd respect you for marrying the right kind of girl."

"Don't say that. You're exactly the right girl for me. Besides, you impressed Dad in the only way he cares about."

She looked up. "What do you mean?"

"He thinks it's most important for women to be pretty, and he was quite taken by you."

She was silent a few moments. "You think I'm pretty?"

The question stunned him. "Katie, you're not pretty. You're beautiful."

"No, I'm not." She gathered her hair and began to braid it.

Sighing, Peter realized he didn't have the energy to argue with her.

The afternoon of the wedding rehearsal, I put on my veil and stared in the mirror. It didn't seem possible that in twenty-four hours, I would be Mrs. Peter Taylor. Closing my eyes, I pictured myself in my wedding dress.

Mother had wanted me to buy one at Feldman's to get her discount, but I hated every gown there. Half of them were cheap imitations of Princess Diana's ballooning, puff-sleeved monstrosity, while the others were hideous confections of lace overlays, sequin appliqués, and satin bows. I wanted understated elegance. On my own, I went to a bridal salon and found the perfect dress. Its princess-seamed, dropped-waist bodice was of icy white crushed velvet; the flowing A-line skirt was of heavy white satin Jacquard. Except for a half-inch band of seed pearls bordering the jewel neckline and deep V-back, the dress was devoid of ornamentation. I loved it.

The gown's price enraged my mother, but I defied her and paid for it myself.

Leaving the mirror, I picked up my bouquet of white silk roses and lilies of the valley. Using silk flowers had been Peter's idea. As I stroked the petals, I had a vivid memory of myself as a child playing with a red carnation. I shuddered and shook it off.

Laying aside the bouquet, I reviewed my preparations. Peter's ring was in a little pouch strung on the hanger of the dress. The bridesmaid's gifts I'd bought for Nita and my cousin Bernadette were tucked inside my purse. My suitcase was packed, and I'd checked twice that my birth control pills were in the zipper compartment.

I'd been on the pill since September, not that I needed to start so early. Throughout our engagement, Peter maintained rigid self-control. Although we kissed passionately, he never again put his hand inside my top or touched me below the waist. Gradually, I began to regret warning him off. I'd enjoyed necking with Ritchie, at least in the beginning, and I wanted to feel that burning excitement with Peter. Sometimes, I unfastened an extra button of my blouse or touched his thigh to tempt him to go further. His restraint in the face of those provocations both reassured and frustrated me.

My thoughts turned to the conversation I'd had with Nita the night before when she took me out for a bachelorette dinner: "What am I going to say if Peter asks me why I don't bleed on our wedding night?"

She looked up from the menu and shrugged. "Tell him it's because you used tampons."

"He's not going to believe that. Anyway, I don't want to lie to him."

Nita twisted her mouth in a wry expression. "Right. 'Cause it's so much better to let him think something that isn't true."

She was right, of course, but I'd waited too long to come clean, and I couldn't tell Peter about Ritchie now. He'd never call off the wedding just 24 hours before, so what was the point of making us both miserable?

Besides, I reminded myself, *he's not a virgin either, so he can't exactly throw stones.*

Sighing, I took off my veil and put it in its box. My mother knocked and then entered my room and sat on the bed. "We may not have a chance to talk tomorrow. I wanted to tell you I like Peter. He's a good man. I think he's good for you."

I said nothing, resenting the way she spoke as though I was being handed to a guardian.

Mother took off her glasses, pulled a tissue from her pocket, and wiped the lenses. "I know this is last minute, but there's something we should talk about." She put her glasses back on and stared at me. "Have you told Peter about Ritchie?"

"That has nothing to do with him."

"So you've let him assume you're a virgin?"

Her severe expression frightened me. Was she planning to tell Peter herself? Hugging myself, I said, "He's never asked. Maybe he doesn't care."

"Maybe he does. You should have told him."

"Why? Are you trying to ruin my wedding?"

My mother shook her head. "No, I'm trying to save your marriage. Don't you understand that you can't build a life on lies?"

"Lies! That's all you expect from me, isn't it?" My rage swelled until I thought my brain would explode. "You always think I'm lying, even when I tell you the truth. I only slept with Ritchie once, and I won't tell Peter that. If you do, I'll never forgive you."

My mother winced. Rising, she held out her hand. "I didn't mean to upset you."

"I'm not upset." Strangely, I no longer was. I saw fear on my mother's face, so I knew I held a potent weapon. "I mean it. If you say one word, you can forget you ever had a daughter."

"I'm not going to tell Peter anything. I only thought it would be better if—"

I gave her a menacing stare, and she faltered. Crossing to the dresser, I brushed my hair. "I'd like to be alone now."

Mother walked to the door and stopped. "I'm sorry. This is such a special time for you. I didn't want to fight."

Pain shot behind my eyes. I laid down the brush and began to rub my temples. After several seconds of silence, my mother went away.

It was a six-hour drive to Door County, Wisconsin, where they would be staying in the cabin owned by Peter's friend Glen. Peter had planned to ask Katie to split the driving, but once they were on the road, she acted so giddy that he didn't trust her behind the wheel. For two hours she chattered nonstop, switching from topic to topic: the reception, the new bedroom curtains she wanted, the traffic, the forecast for snow, and a big gasket order due next week. She didn't require a response from him until she asked, "Did you notice Ed's wife?"

Peter thought about all the people he'd met in the reception line. "Not really."

"She was the tired-looking woman in the beige dress."

He still couldn't picture her but said, "OK. What about her?"

"I was surprised she wasn't dressed more fashionably. The scuttlebutt at work is that she's quite wealthy."

Peter gave Katie a sideways glance, wondering why he was supposed to care. "Just because someone's rich doesn't mean they like to spend money."

"I know. It's just that Ed always notices what women wear."

Her offhand tone struck a wrong note. "Are you saying Ed comments on your appearance?"

"Well, he does notice when I wear a new outfit."

A tiny spark of jealousy flared. "I'm not sure I like that. I don't want your boss flirting with you."

"It's not flirting, exactly. He's a salesman. It's second nature for him to be charming."

Peter's hands tightened on the steering wheel. *Don't make too big a deal of this.* Striving for a lighter tone, he said, "Well, if you need someone to tell him to back off, I'm your man."

Katie turned her head away to look out the passenger window.

Then she said abruptly, "I suppose your parents will have to put us in separate rooms at Christmas."

"Of course not. There's a double bed in my old room."

"Oh." Falling silent, she pulled out the contents of the glove compartment and began to refold all the maps.

They didn't reach the cottage on the shore of Green Bay until after ten. Peter had to drive up and down the dark highway twice before he spotted the evergreen-flanked turnoff. When they reached the end of the driveway, the night was too dark to see anything but the hulking shape of a building to the right of the graveled parking area.

The front door opened onto a room paneled in knotty pine. Before them was a massive stone fireplace over which hung a wooden pendulum clock, stained green and decorated with rosemaling. Peter turned up the thermostat. From the open kitchen to their right came a dripping sound; Glen had warned Peter that he left the faucet open a little to keep the pipes from freezing in winter. Peter went to turn it off.

Returning to Katie, Peter kissed her forehead. Then he carried their suitcases into the bedroom. Logs and kindling were laid in the fireplace there, built back to back with the one in the living room. Peter lit the fire. Pushing back one of the heavy draperies, he stared out at a solid wall of darkness and wished it were light so he could show Katie the bay.

In the living room, he found her browsing through the bookcase. "It should be warm in here soon."

She nodded and continued to leaf through a book.

Peter went back into the kitchen. The cabinets were empty, but the refrigerator held a beribboned bottle of champagne with a card saying, "Congratulations!"

"Come see what Glen left us!"

Katie walked up behind him. "I thought you said he was a Christian."

"He is. Not everyone thinks it's a sin to drink. I don't."

"But you signed the school's pledge."

"I think I can make an exception for our honeymoon." He returned the bottle to the refrigerator. "Maybe it's too late tonight. Let's go unpack."

The bedroom was already warmer. Taking off his down jacket, Peter said, "Give me your coat. I'll go hang them up."

He returned to find Katie sitting on the bed and shivering. Peter draped the bedspread around her and put his arm across her shoulders. She flinched. "It's been a long day, hasn't it?" he asked.

Katie nodded.

Although he'd been fantasizing about this night for months, Peter knew what he had to do. He yawned loudly. "Boy, I'm tired. Do you mind if we don't even try to make love tonight?"

She inhaled sharply. "Are you sure?"

"I'm sure."

Relaxing, she leaned against him. They sat that way a long time before going to bed.

Waking early the next morning, I couldn't get back to sleep. I was too aware of Peter's naked body next to me and his elbow pressed against my back. I was already so close to the edge of the bed, I had no place left to go.

As the light grew stronger, I rose. I adjusted the thermostat, which Peter had turned down when we went to bed. Moving stealthily, I braided my hair, pulled on jeans and a sweater, and went to the living room. On the couch was a folded quilt. I sat and wrapped myself in it.

The quilt was pieced from velvet squares in dark colors—coffee, puce, evergreen, and deep plum flowered with mauve—and knotted with tufts of red yarn. Stroking its softness, I wondered how Peter could sleep nude in this cold. I had never suspected he was the type.

As I snuggled deeper into the velvet quilt, I heard the toilet flush. Moments later, Peter came out wearing a robe. His hair was tousled, and he wasn't wearing glasses. After bending down to kiss me, he dropped heavily on the couch. "Looks like I married an early bird."

He squinted at me, and I stared at his pale lashes. Without glasses, he looked so young. Letting the quilt fall from my shoulders, I leaned forward to kiss him. Peter put his arms around me, slipped one hand beneath my sweater, and rubbed my back. "Come back to bed."

I drew back, pulling my hands inside my sleeves and folding my arms across my chest. "Don't you want to go get breakfast?"

"Later." He led me to the bedroom and sat beside me on the bed. Tugging the end of my braid, he said, "Let me loosen your hair."

Peter went to get my brush from the bathroom. Kneeling behind me, he unbraided my hair and brushed it with long, continuous strokes. I tried to let the soothing rhythm relax me, but I felt myself growing tenser with each passing moment.

He set down the brush, reached for the hem of my sweater, and pulled it over my head.

"Peter..."

"Shhh. I know you're nervous, but trust me. It'll be all right."

He ran one finger along the edge of my bra and pulled it down just enough to see the first deepening of color around my nipple. Sighing deeply, he kissed me there. Then he unhooked my bra. As he lowered me to the bed, Peter's robe fell open. I closed my eyes.

Peter cupped his hands around my naked breasts as gingerly as if they were made of porcelain. Solemnly, he kissed the left one and began to suck. As his tugging grew more insistent, I held my breath. I wanted to become aroused, could remember the urgency I'd once known with Ritchie, but the harder I tried, the more desire eluded me.

Shifting his position, Peter unzipped my jeans, slid his hand inside them, and rubbed my buttocks. I cried out in a seemingly impossible mix of fear and pleasure and dug my fingers into his shoulders. Removing his hand, Peter said, "Take off your jeans."

I stood and stripped off the rest of my clothing. When I lay back down, Peter kissed me and, without warning, inserted his finger into my vagina.

"Stop! Please stop!"

"Relax," he murmured.

"No, stop!"

Peter moved off me. "If you can't stand that, how can you—" He clamped his mouth shut and turned away.

Oh, God. I've failed him. I touched his shoulder. "I'm sorry. I'm nervous."

"I know." Turning, he stroked my cheek. "I'm sorry if I seemed to rush. Let's try you on my lap, with your legs around my waist."

I positioned myself as he asked. During the kissing that followed, his penis grew hard and pressed up against me. I embraced him to keep from quaking with fear.

Taking that as a sign of eagerness, Peter lowered me to the bed. At the moment of penetration, I gripped the bottom sheet to keep from shoving him away. Peter lifted his head to look at me and instantly pulled out and rolled off to the side.

Reaching down, he rubbed his penis and then glanced at me with tears in his eyes. "I'm sorry. I should have taken longer. The first time is always hard."

The first time, I thought dully. *That means he can't tell I did it before. Everything was so awful, it never even occurred to him to question the lack of blood.*

Thursday Peter and Katie went hiking in Peninsula State Park. It had snowed the day before, and the fir trees were draped with thick white shawls. As they crossed a trail rutted with cross-country ski tracks, Peter noticed that the cold had painted brilliant color on Katie's cheeks. He wanted to kiss her but was afraid to ruin the moment by reminding her of sex. Although she didn't refuse to make love, he could tell that she barely tolerated intercourse. He was trying everything he could think of to get her in the mood and wondered what he was doing wrong.

She was so beautiful naked—translucent white skin, long elegant legs, full breasts that pushed aggressively forward. Peter found it one of life's ironic jokes that Katie didn't feel as sexy as she looked. His guilt about her lack of pleasure kept him from reaching a quick climax, so each time they made love, he pulled out long before he was ready in order to spare her.

Sighing, he took his 35mm camera out of its case. "Go stand in front of that birch. I'll take your picture."

Katie stood by the tree and stuck out her tongue. "Didn't your mother ever warn you your face might freeze that way?" he called as he focused the lens. When she started laughing, he snapped the photo, the last one of the roll.

Peter wound up the film and put the camera away. A snowball thumped into his chest.

He ran after Katie, who'd taken off. Within seconds, he realized he'd never catch her. Snatching up some snow, he pressed it together and threw it like a fastball; it hit Katie in the back. "Ow!" Following the curving trail, she disappeared from view.

Reaching the spot where he last saw her, Peter stared at her tracks, which led off behind a rotting log. He could see no sign of her. This section of woods was populated mostly by deciduous trees: tall, thin, and bare, with their lowest branches at least ten feet above the ground. It was like staring into a forest of telephone poles. Where could a grown woman hide?

"Katie, let's call a truce."

To his relief, she poked her head out from behind a lone evergreen.

Peter waded through ankle-deep snow and fallen leaves. When he reached her, Katie put her face up to be kissed. The moment their lips touched, however, she threw her arms around him. "Gotcha."

As they returned to the trail, Katie squeezed Peter's hand. "You know, this is the first trip I've ever taken."

"You're kidding. You've never been out of Illinois?"

"Well, I visited Aunt Dee in Indiana." She dropped his hand. "And I drove across the border into Kentucky once."

"So now that you're an experienced traveler, where should we go next?"

She halted and used the toe of her boot to dig at a half-buried rock. "Mexico, I guess. My father used to talk about the Aztec ruins."

"That would be fun. Maybe we could go in a couple of years."

"You mean it?" Her tone was so amazed, she sounded like a little girl.

Laughing, Peter tugged her braid. "Sweetheart, you have as much say in it as I do. Besides, I think Mexico would be fun."

"Good." Loping down the trail, she called back, "You can't throw snowballs there."

PART THREE

Storm Chaser

MAY 1984–
OCTOBER 1985

I answered the phone on the second ring. "Ed Marsden's office."

"Hi." The caller was Peter. "I know we said we'd meet at home and go from there, but I'm running late. Can you pick me up here?"

"What about your car?"

"We'll swing by the college and get it on the way home. Please, sweetheart."

"OK, I'll be there at six."

Maybe it was for the best, I thought. We were going to a retirement dinner for Dr. Ogilvie from the History Department, and after I got to work that morning, I decided I was wearing the wrong thing: the midnight blue dress I bought my senior year. The few times I'd stopped by the college since our marriage, Peter's colleagues had treated me more like a former student than a faculty wife. This way, I could change into something they'd never seen before without having to explain myself to Peter.

At the house after work, I plugged in my electric rollers and put on my fuchsia blouse and black pencil skirt, the outfit Peter's father liked so much. I curled my hair, freshened my makeup, switched to black pumps, and rushed out the door at five to six.

When I arrived at the History Department, it looked deserted except for the light showing through the frosted window of Peter's office door. I knocked once, turned the knob, and entered. Peter stood at the filing cabinet, putting away a stack of papers.

When he turned toward me, his eyebrows lifted. "You look nice."

"Thank you," I said, remembering that he'd used the same phrase the first time I wore the blue dress. The present fell away and I was his student again, tormented by love for a man who would be forever out of reach. Except that he wasn't. Not anymore.

I crossed to Peter. Putting my arms around his neck, I kissed him and slipped my tongue into his mouth. Desire rose within me. *Yes! I do want him. I've been complicating something that's really quite simple.*

He pushed me away. "What do you think you're doing?"

"I—" Tears flooded my eyes. "I've always wanted to kiss you here."

Peter slapped shut the briefcase on his desk. "Half the college thinks we slept together when you were a student. It's not going to help if they find us making out on my desk."

Anger surged, displacing the hurt. "It was just a hello kiss from a wife to her husband."

"Don't be naïve. Our marriage didn't exactly quell the rumors. We have to be extra careful, especially here."

He brushed past me to open the door. "Ready?"

No, I wanted to say. *I'm not going.* But that would only create more gossip, and with French breathing down his neck, Peter couldn't afford that.

As he locked the door, I gazed at the sign on the door of the Morton Seminar Room across the hall, remembering the night I stayed late to work with him. Then as now, a large part of the pull had been the prohibited nature of the action.

Instantly, self-revulsion flooded me. *What the hell is wrong with me? Can I really feel sexual desire only when the relationship—or the circumstances—are illicit?*

Peter and Katie were the last to arrive at the dinner, held in the private room at Andrew's Restaurant. Peter paused inside the doorway to get his bearings. The walls were painted a muted pine, and as in the main dining room, peach tablecloths covered the tables. Dark green ceramic vases holding peach gladioli stood on plinths at intervals around the walls. A head table stretched across the other end of the room with six round tables arranged before it. In a far corner stood what looked to be a cloth-draped plinth.

Spotting a desk with a seating plan and a large basket where people could deposit congratulatory cards, Peter steered Katie in that direction. She took a blue envelope from her purse and balanced it atop a small mountain of well wishes. They had contributed to the department collection for a present, but Peter had wanted to write something personal to Dr. Ogilvie, who encouraged him during his first year at Zebulun.

After noting their assigned table—one of two directly in front of the head table—Peter led Katie into the gathering. In addition to the history department faculty, several deans, the provost, the college president, and even an emeritus president were there. Usually, at a formal dinner like this, Peter mused, guests would cluster at the bar, but soft drinks obviously didn't have the seductive pull of alcoholic beverages. Most people were scattered around the perimeter of the room, talking in small groups. Peter spotted Dr. and Mrs. Ogilvie with Yvonne Bunsen and headed their way.

Dr. Bunsen looked to be lecturing the guest of honor. Dr. Ogilvie had silver hair with a fringe cut high across his forehead in the manner of a Roman emperor, puffy bags beneath his blue eyes, and an almost perfectly square jaw. When he saw Peter, he stepped away from Dr. Bunsen and said, "Ah, the last of our merry band."

He shook Peter's hand and beamed at Katie. "And your beautiful wife." Dr. Ogilvie leaned forward and kissed the air by Katie's cheek. Then he beckoned his own wife forward; she was a thin woman with iron-grey hair and warm brown eyes. "My dear, this is a former student, Katie Thompson, now Katie Taylor. I used to feel miffed that she hardly ever took my classes. Now I understand. She only had ears for this captivating fellow." Dr. Ogilvie slapped Peter on the back.

Wearing a pinched expression, Yvonne Bunsen backed out of their group and walked away. Dr. Ogilvie shook his head and lowered his voice. "I know you've gotten guff from Erwin and Yvonne. Now that I'm a free agent, I can say how happy I am for you both. As Pascal said, 'The heart has its reasons that reason knows nothing of.' He was a wise man."

Katie blinked rapidly as if fighting tears. "Thank you, Dr. Ogilvie. You make me wish I had taken more classes with you."

"Nonsense. I'm well aware that I ceased to be interesting several years ago."

"Bruce." Mrs. Ogilvie laid a hand on his arm. "This isn't an evening for regrets."

As Dr. Ogilvie met her eyes, the self-mockery drained from his face. "You're right."

To Peter, he said, "Thank you so much for coming," and then the Ogilvies walked off to greet other guests.

Watching Dr. Ogilvie's retreating form, Peter exhaled. "That was... unexpected."

"I didn't know he was so nice," Katie said. "I just thought he was a befuddled old guy."

After double checking that no one was near, Peter said quietly, "It can't have been easy for him. He came to the college a couple of years before Dr. French, but he wasn't selected department chair when the post became available. Some people think he gave up."

Privately, he wished the old man had expressed his approval of their marriage before tonight. Some days, Peter felt that everyone on campus was shooting him censorious looks. Maybe if he'd known pockets of sympathy existed, he might have gone easier on Katie earlier that evening—*But no,* he reproached himself. *I have only my own bad mood to blame for that.*

The stupidity of his reaction infuriated him. For the last year, he had racked his brain for ways to ease Katie's discomfort with sex; the problem was that no matter how slowly or gently he proceeded, the moment he showed any excitement or inclination to move past foreplay, she became paralyzed with dread. Normally, he prayed to see any sign of passion in her, and yet tonight he had rebuffed her because of fear someone might see them and disapprove. Did he really think his chance to make tenure was so fragile that kissing his wife could shatter it?

People were starting to sit down, so he took Katie's hand and headed toward their seats.

Once everyone at their table was settled, they introduced themselves: Lillian Harris, a professor of history emeritus; Elliott Love, vice-president of finance, and his wife, Nancy; Jolanda DeVries, head librarian; and Andrew Wolcott, a nationally prominent Baptist minister who was a trustee, and his wife, Rebecca. As the number of impressive titles mounted, Peter felt Katie shrink into herself. He was grateful that, rather than one of the "great men," the person on Katie's other side was Lillian Harris, a woman with a scholarly, no-nonsense demeanor compounded of a sensibly short haircut, wire-rim glasses, and a penchant for classic suits and low-heeled shoes. As they ate, Katie spoke quietly with the older woman, asking about her academic specialty and sharing her own interest in the Civil War.

The after-dinner speeches focused on Dr. Ogilvie's personal qualities rather than his sparse academic achievements. The college president spoke about Ogilvie's service on numerous committees, Dr. French praised him as a helpful student advisor, and Dr. Bunsen talked about the kindness he displayed toward colleagues. As Bunsen finished, Katie turned to Peter, raised her eyebrows, and cocked her head toward the stage. He shook his head to indicate that he wouldn't be speaking. Then Maggie, the department secretary, walked to the podium. Katie snapped her head toward Peter, indignation flaring in her eyes. He felt a surge of gratitude for her instinct to defend him.

"I've been asked to make a presentation on behalf of the department," Maggie said. "As the proud descendant of Scotsmen, Dr. Ogilvie naturally has developed a love for the game of golf. So the History Department has a retirement gift we hope will fuel this passion for many years." She walked to the corner and whipped off a cloth from a set of new golf clubs.

Dr. Ogilvie's hand flew up to his mouth, and then he turned to his wife, who beamed at him without a trace of surprise. Everyone rose and applauded. Under cover of the noise, Peter said to Katie, "I'm sorry I was such a jerk earlier."

She shook her head. "No, you were right." She sounded defeated. "I don't know what's wrong with me."

"Nothing's wrong with you," he began, but by then, Dr. Ogilvie had moved to the podium to express his thanks, and Peter couldn't say more.

One evening in mid-December, I arrived home to see a lamp shining in our bedroom window. Even though we were trying to save money in case Peter lost his job, he seldom remembered to turn off lights or conserve water.

I wished he would let me take over our finances. We had a budget, but I had no idea if we kept to it because Peter insisted on paying the bills. My only financial responsibility was to buy groceries with a weekly allowance. He didn't know I had saved nearly eight hundred of that in the last year. Someday, when we needed emergency funds, I would prove I was a good manager.

Among our mail was a thick manila envelope addressed in Peter's handwriting. His manuscript of Jonathan Morton's biography had come back again—no doubt killing Peter's chance to receive tenure when the Faculty Review Committee met next month.

Entering the house, I dropped the envelope on the bookcase. If Peter wasn't awarded tenure, the college would give him a contract to teach one more year. I wanted him to leave now but feared he would postpone the onerous task of job hunting as long as possible.

I dreaded the night ahead. Peter would get home from his evening class about ten. After reading the rejection letter, he'd flip through the manuscript, pausing to read passages aloud and ask, "Does this sound too biased? Too wordy? Too dull?" Then he would review our budget and propose cuts I knew would never be implemented. We had been through this twice before.

In the back bedroom, I pulled a box from under the bed and took out the burgundy plaid flannel shirt I was making as an anniversary present. As I sewed on buttons, my anger rose like floodwaters behind a dam. Peter was obsessed with trying to prove himself at Zebulun. Why couldn't he seize the chance to find a better position? French had forced Peter to show him the biography before it went to publishers and demanded that some passages be changed to portray the abolitionist more favorably. And Peter, still hoping for tenure, had caved in. He was losing his integrity.

Then there was the problem of our physical relationship. I couldn't understand why I didn't enjoy sex when I loved Peter so much. He was kind and patient, never rough. For years, I had burned for Ritchie with a lust I found difficult to resist, but I rarely felt that way about my much nicer husband. During our engagement, the thought of being seduced by Peter had titillated me until I sometimes gave in to the temptation of masturbation despite its ensuing burden of guilt. Since the wedding, however, our efforts at intimacy left me frustrated and resentful. Peter was older and more experienced than I was. Why didn't he know how to arouse me?

I sighed, snapped off my thread, and put the finished shirt in its box. After sliding that back into its hiding place, I went to the kitchen to eat.

As he pulled off his gloves, Peter saw the manila envelope on the bookcase that divided the entry from the seating area. He tore it open and extracted a letter that began, "Dear Dr. Taylor: While we read your manuscript with interest—" He didn't read further.

Peter carried the envelope as he walked through the dining room toward the kitchen. Pausing in the doorway, he saw Katie lean into the refrigerator, half disappearing behind the coppertone door. "I'm home."

"I heard you." She stood and carried a foil-covered bowl to the sink. "It's amazing how much food we waste."

"Katie, my book has been returned."

She gave him an unreadable look. "I know. I'm sorry."

As Peter moved to hug her, she ducked into the refrigerator again. When she emerged, she held two half-filled bottles of Pepsi.

"Where are you taking those?"

"To the sink. I've told you, it goes flat if you don't drink it right away."

"I don't believe this. You're yelling at me for wasting soda?"

"I didn't yell."

Peter pivoted and stalked around the dining room table and into the back bedroom. He slammed the door. *God, this is unfair.*

When Katie knocked, he called, "Leave me alone." He dropped his manuscript on the desk and began to unbutton his coat.

"Peter, please."

He opened the door but blocked her entrance.

Katie folded her arms across her chest and hunched her shoulders. "I'm sorry. I only complained about the pop because you asked what I was doing."

"So it's my fault?"

"I didn't say that." She searched his face. "Please stop looking at me like I'm the enemy. I didn't reject your manuscript."

"No, but you didn't offer much comfort."

"I said I was sorry." To Peter, it seemed that she pitied herself more than him. Whatever emotion Katie felt at any given moment dominated their lives. She'd fall into a mood, and he'd cater to it. But not tonight.

She sighed. "I really am sorry. I felt terrible, so I started cleaning to distract myself."

Her eyes darkened with shame, and Peter thought, *What's the use? It's like beating a whipped dog.*

When he took her into his arms, she said, "It'll be all right. You can still publish the book, and that will help you get another position."

Her assumption that his present job was beyond saving hurt Peter even though he knew she was probably right. He remembered how sympathetic she had been when she was his student. Where had that empathy gone?

On Sunday, I sat on a stool watching Peter clean shrimp for the Frogmore stew he was making for our anniversary. As he used a paring knife to dig out a vein, I fingered my gift from him, a bracelet dangling a silver heart engraved *Always.* He'd promised to give me a new charm every year. When I was fifty, I'd be wearing a jangly chain with twenty-seven trinkets. I already felt the weight of them.

He was wearing the flannel shirt I made, although it was tight across the stomach. Lately, he seemed to be gaining weight, which I didn't understand. The meals we ate were much healthier than the junk food he used to live on.

Wrapping up the shrimp shells in newspaper, Peter dumped them in the garbage. "I've been thinking. There's no reason not to keep submitting the manuscript. Maybe it'll get accepted before I start job hunting next year."

"Sounds like a good idea." I refrained from pointing out that I had mentioned it first. "Please give me something to do."

"Husk that." Peter nodded toward a pile of sweet corn on the table and began to slice a smoked sausage into chunks. "I'm starting to look forward to a new job. Maybe once we're settled, we can start a family."

"You mean...children?"

He paused with his knife in midair. "Sure."

Rubbing corn silk off my fingers, I faced him. "What about grad school? Did you assume I stopped wanting to go when we got married?"

Peter pushed his glasses up his nose with the back of his wrist. "You haven't mentioned it lately."

"I don't talk about having babies either."

"Are you saying you don't want children?"

I shook my head. Although I didn't particularly want a child, I wasn't ready to open that discussion. "I'm saying you shouldn't assume. Like when I was your student, you made all the decisions about what kind of relationship we could have without ever asking me."

Peter lay the knife down on the counter. "That's not fair. I hardly had a choice. I'm in enough trouble as it is because I married you."

"Then why did you bother?"

"Because I love you." He pulled me into his arms. "Sweetheart, let's not fight. I'm sorry I forgot about grad school. And I'm sorry things worked out like this. You must be frustrated I can't hang onto my job."

The shame in his voice made me feel guilty for starting an argument. I hesitated, then gave him a lingering kiss to hint I was willing to make love.

To my surprise, he didn't respond in kind. Instead, he buried his face in my hair. "It'll be all right," I murmured. "You're a good teacher. I know you'll find a place that appreciates that."

For quarterly inventory at the end of January, Ed and I were sent next door to the warehouse, a three-story building that housed drums of adhesive, rolls of cellular foam, and skids piled with cartons. Although Cel-Fo generally produced on order, one floor of the warehouse held finished parts. Some were futures, orders customers wanted in installments but which Bill produced in a more-efficient single run. Others inhabited the graveyard, a wasteland of dusty boxes holding parts that had been overrun but never ordered again. Occasionally, a service center inquired about an obsolete part, and it was cheaper to store old cartons than to run fifty gaskets.

We made our way to the finished stock area where I stood with a pencil poised over my clipboard as Ed climbed among the pallets and called out the part numbers and amounts stenciled on boxes. To protect his business clothes, he had changed into a green pinwale corduroy shirt and close-fitting tapered jeans that drew attention to his trim physique as he clambered among the stacks. Feeling self-conscious about being alone together on the top floor, I tried to keep my gaze fixed on my recordkeeping.

When we were almost done, the freight elevator groaned and disgorged Bill and Carla, who came toward us. "Need help?"

"No, we're on the last skid," Ed said. "Go on. We'll meet you at Skinny's."

Minutes later, I wrote down the contents of the final box. Jumping down, Ed wiped his dusty hands on his jeans. A wisp of a stringy white substance clung to the side of his head just above one ear, so I pointed to it and said, "Cobweb."

He ran his fingers through his chestnut hair and shot me a questioning look.

I nodded.

Ed came closer. "Let me buy you a drink. Everyone wants to know why you never go out."

"I need to go home."

He grinned. "Peter must be some husband, the way you run home every night."

I turned away. "I'm going to take this list to Stan."

"Wait." Glancing back, I saw Ed drop the taunting smile. "I'm leaving. I accepted a new job with Better Gaskets in Chicago."

"But they're competitors."

His grin returned. "Yeah, and they offered a twenty percent raise."

The stark reality of that figure silenced me. Ed was going. He'd hired me, trained me, encouraged me—and now he was leaving me in a place where I hardly knew anyone else. "Maybe I will go out."

"Katie." Ed took my arm. "I tried like hell to convince Stan to give you my job, but he doesn't think you're ready. Sorry."

Gazing at the nearest pallet, I saw the corner of one box had been chewed open, probably by rats. The gaskets should be thrown out and subtracted from the inventory, but—*Fuck it.*

"Thanks for trying. I'd probably hate the traveling anyway."

"Yeah, it would take you away from that superman you're married to. At least, I got you to go out."

"Only for a Coke," I warned as we walked toward the elevator.

Walking up to our house, I stared at the dark windows and wondered if Peter was home. Just in case, I paused on the step, cupped my hand in front of my mouth, and checked my breath. Somehow, I'd let Ed talk me into drinking wine instead of Coke.

As I opened the door, loud classical music assaulted me. It was a choral piece. Men's and women's voices wove together in mournful tones, made oppressive by the volume.

The room was lit only by the green display light on the stereo. Finally, I spotted Peter lying on the couch. "Hi!" I yelled over the music.

No answer. I switched on a light. "Are you all right?"

Peter sat up and rubbed his eyes. He was still wearing his suit. "I heard from the committee. It's official. No tenure."

"I'm sorry." After turning off the stereo, I sat beside him and took his hand. "They're fools, Peter. They don't deserve you."

"Don't." He pulled away. "I need some time to think. Give me the pep talk tomorrow." Gesturing for me to stay put, he walked toward the bedroom.

As I watched the door close, I thought, *And I hurried home for this.*

That spring, my mother quit her job, rented a store in Zebulun she named "Marietta's Attic," and stocked it with country-style furniture and housewares. For a week beforehand, she advertised the grand opening in the *Zebulun Herald.* I agreed to work there the first day in case a crowd showed up.

Most of the day, the store held several customers, but few bought anything. They wandered in, pointed out tables they liked and lamps they didn't, ate free cookies, and left. Listening to Mother describe a cabinet to a couple who were clearly just browsing, I marveled at her composure. Her smile didn't waver when the man said, "Thanks. It's really not our style."

Personally, I liked her merchandise: floral sofas, oak rockers, pedestal tables with ladder-back chairs. Gazing at a plaid armchair, I wished Peter and I could afford to replace that godawful black leather living room set.

When I went to the back office for more cookies, I scanned the notations on Mother's desk calendar: "Call delivery company" and "Place new ad." My own long-range plans were so nebulous compared to these nitty-gritty details. After seeing what Peter was going through, my interest in academia had fizzled. Before Ed left, he suggested I get an MBA. Pondering the idea anew, I thought I might enjoy a business career if it wasn't in sales. Picking up the tray of cookies, I returned to the showroom.

First thing Monday, my new boss, Alan Barnes, exited his office and approached the cabinet where I was filing. Dressed in a polyester suit and cheap tie, he was a short man with glasses and thinning hair. He stopped several feet away so he wouldn't have to tilt his head up to talk to me. Since Barnes became my boss, I'd taken to wearing flats, but I was still inches taller than he was.

"Have you finished typing the letters I gave you Friday?"

"Not quite. I always do my filing first in case you need to find a quote."

"I see." He watched me a few seconds. "Why do you sort through the whole folder before you put the quote away?"

"Because I file them by part number."

His small eyes narrowed, making him look like a possum. "Don't. It's a waste of time. I need those letters now."

"I only have one more to type."

"Then you should have done it before you left Friday." Tightening his necktie, he left.

I slammed the drawer and returned to my desk. Fifteen minutes later, when I brought Barnes his letters, he pointed at printer's boxes stacked on his credenza, "I want you to stuff envelopes with those brochures. Unless, of course, you have urgent filing."

"I was going to compile sales figures for your quarterly report."

He scowled. "I'm perfectly capable of doing my own work."

"I used to do it for Ed." I clenched my fists behind my skirt. "He said it saved him time."

With a felt-tipped pen, Barnes scrawled his signature. "Marsden isn't here anymore. From now on, you'll do your job as I define it."

As he drove home, Peter felt like a knight who'd been mauled by a dragon. That afternoon, when he defended a student who faced expulsion, both French and the dean of women treated him like a miscreant who had no right to comment on a question of morals.

His mood lifted when Katie met him at the door with a kiss. As she pulled out of Peter's arms, she smiled at him. "Come in the kitchen while I finish supper. How was your day?"

"Awful. One of my advisees was expelled." He loosened his tie. "She's a good kid. Only a month to graduation, and they threw her out for a first offense."

Katie laid out pork chops on the broiler tray. "What did she do?"

Peter grabbed a bottle of Pepsi from the refrigerator and poured himself a glass. "She was found in her boyfriend's dorm room."

"No wonder. Everyone knows that's an automatic expulsion."

"Yes, but they were having problems and needed to talk. You know how hard privacy is to find on campus. Once her boyfriend got her to his room, he pressured her to sleep with him."

Katie set the pepper mill on the counter. "Did she?"

"No, and he tried to force her. She managed to escape into the hall, right into the arms of the RA who came to investigate the shouting. I argued against the expulsion, but it didn't do any good."

"What made you think it would?"

"I think the boy deserves the stiffer penalty. He should be expelled, and she should get probation."

Katie crossed her arms. "They seem equally guilty to me."

"But he tried to rape her."

She shook her head. "That wasn't rape."

"Yes, it was," Peter answered, surprised that she didn't side with the girl. "He coerced her with a threat. He said they'd both be caught and expelled if she made any noise."

"So she had a choice."

"You call that a choice? Have sex you don't want or get expelled? I'd say if a woman has to give in or face unpleasant consequences, it's rape."

Katie gripped the back of a chair so hard her knuckles turned white. "What about this? A girl I knew— Her mother forbade her to date her boyfriend. So they eloped to Kentucky, and on the way, he wanted sex. When she asked to wait till they got married, he hit her. So she did it."

"She was raped."

"But she said yes!" Katie's voice had turned shrill.

Uneasiness stirred in Peter's gut. "If she said no, what would have happened?"

Katie instantly looked away. "He'd have beaten her. And done it anyway."

"Can't you see she didn't have a choice?"

"Then why didn't she know? Wouldn't she know if she was raped?"

Who is this? Peter wondered and felt his palms grow damp. "Didn't anyone explain it to her?"

Jerking her chin up, Katie regarded him warily. "She never told anyone...except me. He ran off and left her, so she came back to school."

Peter's misgivings gelled into a terrible suspicion. Katie's anguish made no sense unless— *That's impossible. She would have told me.*

The timer went off. "Shit!" Katie cried, pulling the pan out of the broiler and moving the pork chops to a platter. "I didn't get the potatoes mashed."

"We can eat them boiled."

She stared at the pots on the stove, and her shoulders slumped. "I'm not hungry. Would you mind eating alone?"

"What are you going to do?"

"Walk to the river. I need some air."

"Let me come with you."

When she shook her head, Peter peered into her eyes. They held a skittish look that warned him not to push her. "Be back by dark." She nodded and hurried from the room.

Peter fixed a plate and sat at the table, although he had no appetite. Katie's words came back to him: "Her mother forbade her.... Eloped to Kentucky." On their honeymoon, Katie had said she crossed the border into Kentucky once. At the time, he wondered at the strange phrasing.

He blinked back tears as certainty took root. Now he understood why she'd been so terrified on their honeymoon and why, ever since, sex seemed like a chore.

Why hadn't she told him before the wedding? He would have given her more time to adjust. But...she hadn't known it was rape. All this time, she must have blamed herself for giving in. That's why she kept it secret.

Peter rose quickly. *I have to find her. Tell her it isn't her fault.*

He halted as jealousy scalded his veins. *They eloped. Had she loved the boy?*

And what happened afterward? How did she make it home? There were so many gaps in the story. Watching the sky outside darken, Peter realized he could never ask. Katie would return with the face of a stone monument and never mention the subject again. If he told her what he guessed, she'd withdraw into a shell that God himself couldn't penetrate.

Glancing at the clock, Peter saw that she'd been gone an hour. Then he looked at his food. Butter had slid off his potatoes and congealed into a greasy white layer on the plate. Peter scraped his food into the garbage, tied up the plastic bag, and carried it outside. Katie mustn't see that he hadn't eaten. She must never suspect that he guessed the truth.

Although I didn't want to admit it, Peter's approaching birthday frightened me. On August 9, he was going to turn thirty-four, the same age Daddy was when he died. *Don't be morbid,* I scolded myself. *Plan something fun.*

"I'm taking you to dinner," I told Peter but refused to say where.

The evening of his birthday, I drove west on Main Street through the main shopping district. At the far edge of Zebulun, we passed a produce stand, a bowling alley, and an abandoned factory before heading into farm country. The corn stood tall in the bronze glow of the evening sun. Glancing back toward town, Peter asked, "Where are we going?"

I laughed and gestured toward the wide expanse of green. "Look out there. The world is flat, no matter what anyone says. I'm taking you to the western edge to dine with dragons."

After ten miles, I turned north and drove to Sawyer's Landing, a town built on both banks of the Theakia and an island in the center. I crossed the bridge to the island and parked behind a sprawling white building with black shutters.

The building, which stood on a narrow point of land, had a wide veranda on the three sides overlooking the river. At the front, baskets of red begonias hung from brackets on either side of black double doors. A gilt-lettered sign proclaimed, "The Crackerjack Inn." A brick walk led from the steps of the inn to a boat landing, where water slapped softly against pilings. The clouds above the river were tinged with the gold of approaching sunset.

I squeezed Peter's hand. "Our reservation isn't for ten minutes. Why don't you enjoy the view while I tell them we're here?"

Peter nodded. He stuffed his hands in his jacket pockets and wandered across the grass.

I walked up the steps and through the entrance. A wide staircase rose before me. To the left was a hotel desk with a highly polished counter and pigeonholes on the back wall. I didn't want Peter to know it yet, but our reservation included lodging for the night.

After registering and checking in with the dining room hostess, I went outside and found Peter at the water's edge. "They can seat us now."

Inside the dining room stood a baby grand piano on which a white-haired man played "Memory" from the musical *Cats.* On the south wall were three sets of French doors, open to the veranda. A warm breeze drifted into the room, where ceiling fans gently circulated the air.

The hostess, a petite platinum blonde dressed in royal blue, seated us in the southwest corner. Peter opened the menu and frowned. Leaning over the table, he whispered, "Sweetheart, how can we afford this? You know we're trying to save money."

"Don't worry. I've been putting aside the grocery money I don't use, and I have enough."

Just as I decided on shrimp and artichoke pasta, Peter murmured, "I'm really tempted."

"Order whatever you want."

He looked up. "I was debating whether to have a glass of wine."

"Honey, you don't owe that college a thing."

Peter shook his head. "It's all right. I can do without."

He looked so miserable that I was tempted to tell him we were spending the night—except that would ruin the scenario I'd planned. After dinner, I was going to tell him to look in the trunk of the car for his present. What he would find there was an overnight bag.

The sunset lingered as we ate, but by the time we finished dessert, it was too dark to see the water. The waitress laid our check in front of Peter. "We'll charge this to your room if you sign here."

Peter shook his head. "There's been some mistake. We're not staying at the inn."

"But the hostess said—"

Biting my lip, I reached for the check. "It's all right. I'll sign for it."

The waitress frowned suspiciously and carried the signed check away.

"What's this all about?" Peter asked.

"We are staying tonight. I was going to tell you after dinner."

The hostess came to our table. "Excuse me, but you are guests of the inn, aren't you?"

"Yes. My husband didn't know because I wanted it to be a surprise."

"Oh." The woman twisted her diamond stud earring. "I'm terribly sorry. I hope we haven't ruined your evening by letting the cat out of the bag."

Although Peter smiled, his eyes were flinty. "Of course not."

The hostess looked from him to me. "Let me make it up to you. Dessert is on the house."

"Thank you," I said.

After the woman left, the lines about Peter's mouth deepened. Speaking slowly as if to an especially dense student, he said, "You know we can't afford this."

"But—"

"I mean it. It's irresponsible given our situation."

Exasperated, I threw down my napkin. "Maybe it will cost less if you stay alone."

As I hurried from the dining room, Peter scraped back his chair. He caught up with me on the veranda and grabbed my arm. "Simmer down."

I yanked free. "You simmer down. I said I had the money."

"The future is so uncertain. We should be saving every cent."

After glancing behind me at the open doors, I gestured for him to follow me. I stepped onto the lawn and stopped in the glow of a lamppost that illuminated the path. Turning to Peter, I said in a low voice, "You think I don't know that? That's all you've talked about for months."

"You're exaggerating."

"No, I'm not. Why do you think I did this?" I swept my arm wide. "To be extravagant? No, I did it to give you a night off from worrying."

Peter went very still. Then he reached for my hand. "I appreciate that."

"You don't act like it. You act like I'm two years old."

"Sweetheart, I'm sorry. I made a mistake."

I gazed past the inn toward the parking lot and handed Peter my car keys. "Our bag is in the trunk." As he walked away, I moved to the riverbank and wished I could climb in a boat and drift off. Why did marriage have to be so hard?

I inserted yet another rolodex card into the typewriter. Mr. Barnes had asked me to retype all his customer contact information because he claimed he couldn't read Ed's handwriting. The task catapulted me back to the horrible job at the coupon redemption center. This was not the direction I wanted my life to go.

Barnes entered my office with Stan Plesniak, vice president of sales. Stan was in shirtsleeves with the cuffs rolled to the elbow, and he was eating a Granny Smith apple.

"I'll get that quote." Barnes opened the middle drawer of a filing cabinet.

Stan came over to drop his apple core in my wastebasket. "How's it going? Bill says he never sees you out in the plant anymore."

"I've been busy."

Noticing my task, Stan frowned.

A drawer slammed. "Katie, I can't find the new Jamieson quote. Everything's all mixed up. Who taught you to file?"

"You told me—" I caught myself in time. Humiliating Barnes in front of our boss would only make him hate me more. I stood. "I'll find it."

When I turned from the cabinet, quote in hand, Stan was watching me. He walked over, opened a drawer at random, and rifled through the folders. "You used to keep these files in perfect order. I remember Ed telling me how you reorganized everything. What happened?"

"I..." As I glanced at Barnes, my face flamed. "It got out of hand. I'll clean it up."

"I see." Stan's tone hinted that he saw more than he was saying. "Alan, let's step into your office. There are some things I want to discuss."

Returning from lunch, I set a shoebox on my desk, took out a pair of pumps with three-inch heels, and slipped them on. Never again would I downplay my height to placate Barnes.

When I sat down, I discovered that the rolodex was gone. I knocked on Barnes's door, crossed to his desk, and—relishing the way I towered over him—said, "I need your rolodex so I can finish those cards."

"I gave the job to Tanya so you'll have time to clean up the files. And go out to the plant more. Stan is annoyed you've been neglecting that."

"Yes, sir."

Glaring at me, Barnes took a pencil, poked it into the electric sharpener, and held it there until it was nothing but a stub. "You took fourteen extra minutes at lunch. Don't let it happen again." He threw the pencil away.

One morning in October, I walked out of the bathroom to find Peter in his robe, sitting slumped on the couch. "Why aren't you dressed?"

"I was thinking about calling in sick."

I stared at him, but in my mind, I saw Barnes clocking my return from lunch each day. "You can't stay home the rest of the year."

His chin jerked up. "I never said I wanted to. I just need a break once in a while."

"Fine. I have to get ready for work."

Peter padded after me into the bedroom. "You don't know what it's like making myself go in there day after day."

"Don't I?" I stepped out of the closet, zipping up my red dress. "Do you have any idea what my job is like? My new boss hates me and wants me fired."

Peter's mouth dropped open. "Why didn't you tell me?"

"Because you have enough to worry about." I put on my simulated pearls.

"How can you be mad at me for not knowing something you kept to yourself?"

I brushed my hair with angry strokes. "You could ask. Just once, you could say, 'How was work today?' "

In the mirror I saw him rub the back of his neck. "You're right. I'm sorry. I've been too self-absorbed."

His swift apology deflated me. I paused, debating whether to say it was OK.

"Your boss," Peter said hesitantly. "Why would he want to get you fired?"

"Because I know the customers better than he does, and he's scared. I think someone told him Ed recommended me for that job."

Peter laid a hand on my shoulder. "If it's so tense, don't you think you should quit?"

I slammed down my brush. "One of us has to stay employed."

His head snapped back. Stiffly, he walked to the closet, gathered his clothes, and carried them to the bathroom.

Going into the kitchen, I packed yogurt and an apple for lunch. Then I measured grounds into the coffee maker and filled the glass pot. Although I believed my anger was justified, Peter's hurt expression swam before me like the afterimage of a flashbulb. Over the running water, I heard the front door close.

Still holding the pot, I ran through the house and out the door as he pulled his car away. I loped down the sidewalk and into the street, waving the coffee pot at his rear window. Water sloshed over the rim. The brake lights went on. As I reached the driver's door, Peter rolled the window down. "I'm sorry I said that. Please come back inside."

Peter stared ahead, his jaw tense. "I'll be late. We can talk about it tonight." Shifting the car into first, he drove away.

After changing out of my work clothes, I started to fry Italian sausage for lasagna. The dish was one of Peter's favorites, but I rarely made it because of the high cholesterol. The smell of pork and fennel filled the kitchen. As thunder crashed outside, I glanced at the clock. It was 5:25. Peter would be home soon.

Reviewing the complicated recipe I'd started, I murmured, "Should have left work early." I could have gotten away with it; Barnes had been out on a sales call all afternoon. Now my back tightened as I rushed to get the lasagna in the oven.

By the time the noodles were cooked, Peter was definitely late. Was he too mad to come home?

Once I finished the layering, I slid the pan into the oven and set the timer. It was after 6:30. Where was Peter anyway? If I was mad, I'd run it off, but I'd never known Peter to use exercise that way. Maybe he was out driving. The image came of him speeding through the storm as lightning flashed on the horizon.

I went to the front door and opened it. A passing car made a spitting noise, and rain blew in my face. *Peter isn't going to die in an accident,* I told myself. *He's a good driver.*

But my father was a good driver. That hadn't stopped the drunk driver of a beer truck from skidding on wet pavement and smashing Daddy's car.

Shuddering, I walked into the dining room and began to set the table. Then the front door opened. I ran to Peter, crying, "Where were you? You're so late."

He hugged me. "I stayed to play basketball with Wayne. Didn't your boss tell you?"

I pulled back. "You told Barnes?"

"I called during lunch. Didn't he give you my message?"

"That bastard. I've been worrying for over an hour."

Peter touched my cheek. "It's OK. I'm here now."

Impulsively, I hugged him again. "Oh, Peter, I'm sorry for what I said."

"I'm sorry too."

Running my fingers down his tie, I said, "Let's not fight anymore."

"Not if I can help it." Peter kissed the top of my hair. Then he lifted his head and sniffed. "What's cooking?"

"Lasagna. To make up for this morning."

"Then I take it back," he said, tweaking my nose. "Let's fight every week."

Later, a nightmare woke me. The memory of it was hazy, but it had something to do with being trapped somewhere during a storm.

I walked into the bathroom and splashed cold water on my face. As I climbed back into bed, Peter rolled over. "What's wrong?"

"Just a dream. Go back to sleep."

He propped himself on his elbow. "Is something bothering you?"

Without warning, my eyes filled with tears. "I got scared tonight. You're never late, and I panicked."

He stroked my cheek, then lifted his finger to his mouth to lick my tears. "What about?"

"That I was going to lose you. That you might—"

Although I shied away from the word, he understood. "I won't die. I'm only thirty-four."

"People do die that young."

His voice grew quieter. "I wish I could promise that nothing's going to happen to me. But nobody can promise that."

When I didn't answer, he took me in his arms. His skin was warm. I clung to him, wishing he would swear to keep me safe. Then Peter's hand moved down my hip. I tensed but didn't protest when he pulled up my nightgown. As he kissed my breasts, I told myself, *It'll be over soon.*

Peter stopped. "Don't you want to?"

"If you do."

"No, here." He handed me back the nightgown.

I had blown it again. After putting my gown on, I curled up on my side, facing away from him. Peter put his arm around me and curved his body behind my back. "Go back to sleep, sweetheart. Everything's all right."

Two days later, I came home to find Peter, still wearing his dress shirt and slacks, asleep on the leather couch. His tie lay bunched on the coffee table by a half glass of orange juice. His face was pasty white, his hair clumped in damp spikes.

"Peter?" I pushed aside the bust of Frederick Douglass and sat on the corner of the table. Placing a hand on his forehead, I felt how feverish he was. "What's wrong?"

He grunted and opened his eyes. "Flu."

"Isn't it early in the year for that? What are your symptoms?"

"Chills, fever, achiness, sore throat. I think I caught it from Maggie."

"I guess that sounds like flu." Rising, I went to the back bedroom to get an afghan to spread over him. "You shouldn't get chilled."

"I know. I meant to change into pajamas and go to bed, but I was so tired."

"You have pajamas?"

Peter laughed feebly. "Mom used to give them to me because she thinks sleeping nude isn't nice." Sitting, he leaned against the arm of the couch. "Would you turn the bed down?"

"Sure." I went to pull down the covers and plump Peter's pillow. Then I searched through his dresser until I found a pair of hunter green pajamas. As he came through the door, I asked, "Do you want some chicken soup?"

He clutched at his stomach. "No. Just sleep."

After quietly shutting the bedroom door, I chewed my lip. I knew little about treating illness, but my mother, as the oldest in her family, might know. It was Thursday, the night the store stayed open until nine. I dialed the number and said, "Mom, I need help. Peter's got the flu, and I don't know what to do."

She sighed in irritation. "There's not much to do. He should rest mostly. Give him Tylenol if he needs it. No aspirin. Is he vomiting?"

"I don't know. Maybe."

"Make sure he takes in plenty of liquids. Soup, 7 Up, juice. Small amounts at a time so he keeps it down. No caffeine."

"All right. Thanks." I went into the kitchen. We had lots of Pepsi, coffee, tea, but no 7 Up or chicken soup. "Gone to the store," I wrote on a piece of paper. "Back soon."

Tiptoeing into the bedroom, I found Peter sleeping on his side facing my pillow, so I put the note there. As I gazed at him, my heart clenched like a fist around a sharp kernel of pain. I loved him so much. What if he died?

The next morning, I brought Peter a tray with herbal tea, orange juice, and 7 Up. He sat up and rubbed his neck. "I'll float away if I drink all that."

"How are you?"

"Better, I think. I don't ache as much, except my neck. It feels stiff."

"Oh?" I sat on the bed next to the bump his knees made in the covers. *A stiff neck. Why does that set off warning bells?*

As Peter sipped his tea, his face scrunched up. "What is this? It tastes like boiled twigs."

"Chamomile. It's supposed to soothe the stomach."

He set the mug down so hard that tea sloshed. "Forget it. Get me Lipton's."

"My mom said no caffeine."

Putting on his glasses, Peter looked at me. "I'll just get it myself after you go."

"I might stay home to take care of you."

He carefully moved the tray to my side of the bed and pulled me toward him. "You're upset over nothing. It's just flu."

Even though I often wished he would wear pajamas, I didn't like encountering that layer of flannel between me and his chest. I slipped my hand inside his top. "What if it's not?"

Peter sighed. "If I'm not better by tomorrow, I'll see a doctor."

During lunch, I went to a library and looked up "stiff neck" in a medical guide. One entry listed it as a symptom of spinal meningitis. Squinting in concentration, I recalled that meningitis had killed my cousin Bernadette's little boy.

The other symptoms of the disease were fever, achiness, headache, sensitivity to light, and sometimes a rash. I slammed the book shut and hurried back to work.

When I entered my office, Barnes came looking for me. "I have six price quotes to type. I promised Argyle they'd go out today."

"OK." I accepted the folder, then sat down and grabbed the phone.

"You don't have time to gossip. I need those by three."

I put the receiver down. "The mail goes out at four."

"I have to proofread your work, don't I?"

"Fine, I'll get it done. But I still have four minutes of lunch hour, and I'm going to make a call." Swiveling the chair so my back was to him, I dialed home. Peter answered, sounding as though I'd awakened him.

"Does your neck still hurt?"

"A little. Why?"

"Do you have a headache? Does light hurt your eyes?"

He was quiet a moment. Then, "Katie, what is this about?"

I bit my knuckle. "I looked up stiff neck at the library. You may have spinal meningitis. You should go to the doctor at once."

"Katie." He fell silent, and I pictured him rubbing his temple as he decided what to say. "I don't have spinal meningitis. I have the flu."

"You don't know that. You have to go to the doctor and get a spinal tap."

"What?" Peter made a strangled sound. "Look, I do *not* have meningitis."

I gripped the receiver more tightly. "All I'm asking is that you check it out. Would it hurt to call the doctor and describe your symptoms?"

"Let's wait until you come home," he said, using the studiously patient tone I hated. "If you don't agree I'm better, I'll call."

"At 5:30 on a Friday night? Fat chance you'll have of finding him in."

"Then I'll go to the emergency room. Will that satisfy you?"

No, I thought, but I could tell that Peter had made all the concessions he intended to make. "OK. We'll decide when I get home."

When I hung up, Barnes was still standing there. He had listened to the entire call. With difficulty, I held my tongue and channeled my anger into typing fast.

When I got home, Peter lay on the couch listening to the second Brandenburg Concerto. "Should you be up?"

Twisting his neck to look at me, he smiled wryly. "Hello to you too."

Sitting on the coffee table, I felt his forehead. "Your fever seems down."

"I told you I'm better. Look." Peter pushed himself up and tilted his head from side to side. "My neck is fine. I just—" A hacking cough interrupted him.

I frowned. "I thought you said you're better."

"Better, not well."

"Then you should stay in bed all weekend."

The doorbell rang. "Who could that be?"

I stood. "My mother. I was so worried, I asked her to stop by."

When I opened the door, Mother swept into the room, went to the couch, and felt Peter's forehead. "He doesn't have a fever."

"No, he's better."

"You mean, you dragged me here for nothing? I wanted to work late."

"I didn't find out myself until a minute ago." I headed toward the kitchen. "Since you're here, let me make you coffee. Or a sandwich."

Mother followed me. "Whatever gave you the crazy idea he had meningitis?"

"I told you. He had a stiff neck." Glass coffeepot in hand, I faced her. "Isn't it better to be safe than sorry?"

"Not if your melodramatics inconvenience other people."

"I wasn't being melodramatic. I had a legitimate fear for my husband's life. You of all people should understand that."

Mother stopped unbuttoning her coat. "I wouldn't bring up your father's death if I were you. Talk about melodrama. I'll never forget that scene you made at his funeral."

"What are you talking about? I didn't go to Daddy's funeral."

Her face grew as hard as a hangman's. "Yes, you did. In front of everyone, you started screaming and kicking your grandmother. You tossed such a fit we had to sedate you."

"You're lying!" The coffeepot slipped from my hand and shattered on the red tile floor. I stared at my mother and willed her to leave.

Instead, I heard Peter ask, "What's going on?"

As he entered the kitchen, I closed my eyes and tried to remember. The sound of Bach in the other room sounded like...solemn music playing from overhead speakers. I recalled putting on a black dress and standing still as Aunt Dee curled my hair, a memory that made me wonder if Mother was telling the truth. For a queasy moment, I could smell the past—a heavy, perfumed memory. Then it faded, and I opened my eyes. "No. It's not true."

"Have it your way if you'd rather live with a lie." Mother gave Peter a look of pity. "It wouldn't be the first time."

"Get out of my house." I wanted to sound firm, but my voice shook. As Mother left the kitchen, I sagged back against the counter.

Peter skirted the broken glass to take me in his arms. "What was that about?"

"She said I was at Daddy's funeral. That I made a scene to get attention."

"Why on earth would she tell you a thing like that?"

I leaned into him. "She's mad I asked her to check on you. She says I'm too hysterical."

Peter patted my back. "You were how old when your father died? Eight? You'd be inhuman not to get hysterical at his funeral."

Lifting my head from his chest, I said accusingly, "You believe her."

"It does explain some things."

I grabbed the lapels of his robe and gazed into his face, wishing I didn't see sorrowful belief stamped there. "Then why can't I remember?"

"Sweetheart, it's perfectly normal. The experience was more than a child could process, so you blocked it from your mind. It's called hysterical amnesia."

There was that word again: *hysterical.* I strained to pull up some scrap of memory. Nothing. Pulling away from Peter, I wondered if I were losing my mind.

At the store, Marietta took three extra-strength Tylenol tablets with strong coffee. She hadn't slept. Every time she closed her eyes, she saw Katie's devastated expression. For the life of her, Marietta didn't understand why she'd been so cruel.

Carrying her mug to the table at the rear of the showroom, she resumed trying to write a catchy newspaper ad. She had tried ads with coupons, ads offering discounts, and ads promising high quality, but nothing had pumped up sales to a level that could support her —and her savings were dwindling.

The bell on the door rang, and Marietta glanced down the length of the store. Near the front stood a silver-haired man with his back to her.

She approached him. "May I help you?"

He turned. Immediately, she judged from the fine grey suit and flashy diamond ring that he had money. "You are Marietta?" he asked with a slight Spanish accent.

"Yes."

"I may call you this? Or do you prefer Mrs...."

"Thompson, but Marietta is fine."

He flashed her a brilliant smile. "Dr. Ernesto Montoya at your service."

The words were spoken with such flair that she half expected him to click his heels. *Montoya?* Taking note of his dark skin and black eyes, she concluded he was Mexican. "What are you shopping for today?"

"Everything. Recently I have moved here to work in the hospital. I brought nothing with me from Mexico City except for a few treasured items, so I must furnish my entire apartment."

"I see." Marietta's heart began to pound. Furnishing a whole apartment could net her thousands of dollars. "What style are you looking for?"

He began to rub the fingers of his right hand. "I know nothing about furniture. When I went to the department store, the man there refused to advise me. Candi Martin, a nurse I work with, said you could help me."

Marietta remembered Candi, a plump woman who bought a child-sized rocker for her granddaughter. Although grateful for the reference, Marietta felt overwhelmed by the request. "I have to be honest. I'm not trained as a decorator."

"But I do not want anything fancy. I want my apartment to be comfortable like what I see here. It is a great favor, I know, but I need a woman's advice. My late wife always took care of our home."

He looked down, obviously struggling with emotion.

"I'm sorry. How long since she passed away?"

"Two years." He wiped away a tear. "After she was gone, a whole city seemed empty."

"I understand. My husband died seventeen years ago, and I still miss him."

Dr. Montoya nodded. "Then you will help me?"

"Of course. Let's sit down and discuss what you need."

Leading him toward the worktable, she gestured for him to take the single chair. Then she went to the office to get one for herself. When she returned, Marietta found him peering at her rough draft of a newspaper ad.

"You write your own advertisements?"

Marietta blushed. "They aren't very good, but my store is new. I can't afford an agency."

He nodded. "Have you tried radio? My son Roberto—Robert—works in Los Angeles. He tells me that Americans do not read anymore, so he produces commercials for the radio. He says it is the best advertising value."

Marietta thought of the Sony Walkmans she saw everyone wearing now. "That's a good idea. Thank you. Now, how many rooms do you have?"

The sound of Katie moaning woke Peter. He switched on the bedside light and shook her arm. "No!" she shouted and sat up, breathing hard.

"You were dreaming," he said as she blinked and pulled up the fallen strap of her nightgown. "Was it the same one?"

Katie ran her fingers through her tangled black hair. "Yes, I was in a cabin in a storm, but this time a child was with me." She exhaled deeply. "I don't understand why the dream keeps coming back."

"You've been upset a lot lately." Peter pulled her against his shoulder. "Probably when things calm down, the dream will go away."

"But what if I keep having it? What if it means..." She grew so tense that her muscles felt hard against his arms. "What if something's wrong with me?"

"Nothing's wrong. Your subconscious is trying to tell you something. When you figure it out, the dream will stop."

She slumped against him. "I hope so."

Peter woke at 2:13 to discover that Katie wasn't in bed. He sat up and listened. The house was as still as if he were alone. He got up to look for her.

The living room was empty and so was the bathroom. Katie wasn't in the back bedroom either. Worried, he walked into the dining room and saw what he hadn't noticed coming straight on from the front room. She was at the back window, standing behind the floor-length draperies.

"Katie?"

To his dismay, she shrank into the folds of fabric. Peter cautiously approached her and held out his hand. "What are you doing?"

"Just looking outside." She stepped out into the open.

Peter took her hand, which was cold. "You had the dream again, didn't you?"

Nodding, Katie glanced at the window. "It's so vivid. It's hard to believe it's not really raining. You think maybe there is a storm that stops when I wake up?"

The irrationality of her question frightened him. "Katie, it's just a dream."

She laid her palm flat against the glass and gazed outside again. "It's trying to tell me something. But I can't figure out what."

When Peter tried to hug her, Katie jerked away and leaned her head against the window.

"Sweetheart, maybe you need help."

"No."

"But getting up at night and hiding behind the drapes isn't normal."

"I wasn't hiding."

Peter rubbed his hand across his lower face and prayed for patience. "All right, what about the dream? Your fears for my safety? The fact you can't remember your father's funeral? I think you need counseling."

She turned on him furiously. "You think I'm crazy."

"No, but I think you have unresolved feelings about your father's death."

"Unresolved?" Her voice screeched. "I know exactly how I feel. I was a child, and I needed him. What kind of God would let him die? Can a counselor tell me that?"

She veered away and ran into the kitchen. Peter followed and switched on the light, but he stayed back as she turned on the faucet and splashed her eyes. *She's crying,* he thought with relief. After she dried her face with a paper towel, he laid a hand on her shoulder.

The features she turned to him were perfectly composed without a trace of tears. Peter's skin prickled with unease. "I really think you need a counselor. You're still grieving."

"I don't want to talk about this."

Determined not to let her walk away, Peter put his arms on either side of her, bracing his hands against the counter. "Promise me something. If you have the dream again, you'll get help."

"I'm not crazy."

"I didn't say you were. But I'm concerned about you. Just as you worried when I had the flu. Didn't you do the same thing then—make me promise to get help if I didn't get better?"

Katie shook her head.

Peter sighed. "I'm just asking you to talk to someone. Like Pastor Samuelson."

"No." Her face took on a hunted expression.

"Just once," Peter said. "Maybe he could recommend someone else."

Katie ducked her head so he couldn't see her eyes.

"Sweetheart, I really think it will help. If it doesn't, you can stop."

"Oh, all right." She pushed against his arm, and he released her. Moments later, the bedroom door slammed.

I drove past the church to the lot directly behind it and pulled into the driveway of the parsonage—a one-story home built of brick in many colors ranging from cream to rust. A bay with a large picture window pushed out from the center of the house. As I climbed the three concrete steps to the small square stoop located to the right of the bay, my stomach ached. The dream had returned twice last week, so Peter insisted I make an appointment. He had no idea—and I couldn't tell him—of the hurtful counseling I received from the minister when I was in high school.

Moments after I rang the bell, Pastor Samuelson opened the door. "Come in."

I followed him to a small study furnished with a desk, bookcases, and two armchairs by a window overlooking the back yard. Gesturing toward the chairs, Pastor Samuelson drew oatmeal-colored drapes against the darkness outside. I sat in one armchair, and he took the other. He had aged in the eight years since I'd met with him before; he had always been thin, bordering on gaunt, but there was a stoop to his shoulders now and his cheeks were sunken, giving him a shriveled look. "What seems to be the problem?"

"Stress, I think. Peter was denied tenure because he hasn't published enough. He's disorganized and puts things off until it's too late."

The pastor frowned. "I thought you were here to discuss your problems, not Peter's."

"They're connected. I don't like my job either. Peter promised when we got married that I could go to grad school, but now I have to wait till he finds a new position. Meanwhile, I'm stuck working for a tyrant."

Pastor Samuelson twisted a button on his light blue cardigan. "If you're having problems with your marriage, why isn't Peter here with you?"

"It's not a problem with our marriage," I insisted. "It's that tension is giving me nightmares, and Peter wants me to talk to someone."

"Have you prayed about the situation?"

"Yes," I said, even though I hadn't. "But God isn't going to give me a better job unless I get out and look for one."

"Are you sure it's God's will for you to change jobs?"

"Yes." Quickly, I recounted my problems with Barnes, stressing how unfair he was.

Pastor Samuelson walked to his desk, picked up a Bible, and returned. "I take it you think this man is threatened by you. Have you tried to help him? Show him you want him to succeed?"

"Turn the other cheek?" I asked, not bothering to hide my sarcasm.

He opened his Bible. "It's more than that. Listen. 'In all things obey those who are your masters on earth, not with external service, as those who merely please men, but with sincerity of heart, fearing the Lord. Whatever you do, do your work heartily, as for the Lord rather than for men.' The point is, by giving your boss cheerful service, you please God."

I twisted my engagement ring so the stone was hidden against my palm. "That seems impossible. I despise Barnes."

Pastor Samuelson leaned forward. "Then I'd say that, rather than running away, you should try to redeem the situation. Perhaps even ask Mr. Barnes to forgive you."

"For what? I haven't done anything wrong."

He cleared his throat. "I see a pattern in your attitude toward Mr. Barnes *and* Peter. Both men have been placed in authority over you."

I shifted in my chair, but he held up a hand to forestall my protest. "Hear me out. Mr. Barnes is your supervisor and Peter is the head of your marriage, yet you've indulged a spirit of resentment toward both men. I fear that changing your outward situation will not make you happy. The only way you'll be content is to develop a submissive attitude."

I clenched my fists. "You mean, because I'm a woman."

"No. Each of us is under authority, and in every case, the authority over us was placed there by God. By defying those above you, you defy God himself."

"I've tried! I never complain about my job to Peter. And whenever I go out of my way to help Mr. Barnes, he orders me to stop."

Pastor Samuelson lifted up his palms. "Don't you see it's possible to do the right actions and yet be in the wrong? Your resentful attitude conveys itself."

Lowering my gaze, I murmured, "Then what's the point? I can't win."

"Not on your own. But if you obey God faithfully and seek him in prayer, he will change your heart."

I wondered exactly what I was supposed to pray for. A personality transplant? "And if I can't?"

Pastor Samuelson's expression was grave. "Hardening your heart to God is no small matter. You risk permanent estrangement from him."

In other words, I'll be damned.

He paused before adding in a brighter tone, "Remember, you can't do anything by your own power. Read the Bible, pray every day, and God will give you the strength you lack."

"Thank you." I stood to leave, wondering at the irony of thanking a man who'd just handed me a life sentence.

I was standing in a one-room cabin. Each of the four corners of the room held piles of broken dishes, bits of yellowed lace, and musty, discolored books. One wall held a great stone fireplace, streaked with soot. Dead leaves were scattered on the hearth, and a rusty andiron lay on its side.

A storm raged outside. I moved toward the center of the room where a boy waited, a pudgy towhead with glasses. He threw his arms around my waist and squeezed like a too-tight belt.

Breaking his embrace, I hurried away, certain he wouldn't follow me, certain that he'd chosen the center of the room as the spot farthest from the storm. Reaching the window, I pulled open the drapes. The wind shifted, driving a silver curtain of water against the glass.

How cleansing it would be to stand naked in the rain and let it run down my skin. I leaned closer to the window. As I gazed outside, a great chorus called to me in the rising wind. The voices sounded familiar, and I longed to join them. Whatever spirits rode the storm, they belonged to me far more than the boy did.

Abruptly, I began to pirouette around the room. The sound of the storm grew louder, making me so dizzy I had to stop. Then the cabin door blew open. "I have to get out of here," I said and started across the room.

"No!" the boy screamed. "Bar the door!"

I continued walking, mesmerized by the tempest. The rain would save me. It would wash away the dirt and the boy's grimy fingerprints. When I was a step away from the threshold, the boy called again, "No, Katie, bar the door."

Hearing his terror, I hesitated. Instantly, the storm disappeared.

The bedroom was dark except for the luminous dial of the clock. Peter was breathing heavily, a sibilant whistling just short of snoring. Biting my lip, I reviewed the dream. Who was the chorus of voices calling in the storm, and why did I yearn to join them?

Rolling onto his side, Peter flung out one arm so that it touched me. I cringed and carefully slipped out of bed.

In the living room, I stared at the dark shapes of furniture. After nearly two years of marriage, I was still living in a home that bore few traces of me. This was Peter's furniture, Peter's house.

Going to the back bedroom, I wrapped myself in an afghan and sat cross-legged on the bed. The dream was trying to tell me something, but what? As I sat there, the ticking of the clock mocked me, as though some deity was measuring the time I took to solve a riddle. Keeping the afghan around me, I walked back into the dining room and stood at the window.

I stared out at the shadowy yard and imagined dancing in a rainstorm. Behind me, the walls of the house closed in. "I have to get out of here," I said, then froze. Those words came from the dream.

Turning, I gazed back through the rooms with new and terrible understanding. The boy was Peter, the cabin was this house, and the dream was telling me to leave.

I bent at the waist as though sucker punched, clutching my wrap more tightly. How could I leave Peter? I loved him.

But the dream was right. If I stayed, Peter's problems would prevent me from exploring my own needs. *I can leave just long enough to straighten out my career. Then come back and be submissive like Pastor said.*

As the clock in the back bedroom chimed three times, I felt as frightened as if it were proclaiming my last hour. What if I left and Peter refused to take me back?

I gazed toward our bedroom, wishing he would wake up and come looking for me. That would be my sign to stay. "Please, Peter," I whispered, but the moment passed. I returned to the back room alone.

In the morning, I told Peter I didn't feel well and wanted to stay home. After he left for work, I dressed in jeans and my father's old denim shirt. In the kitchen, I poured coffee and drank it. My empty stomach churned from the acid.

At 9:01, I called in sick. Then I phoned my friend Nita at work. "Hey, it's Katie. How've you been?"

"OK, I guess. Did you know I broke up with Jim?"

Jim? The last I heard, Nita had been living with a guy named Nick. "Sorry to hear that."

"No loss. He was a slime dog. Anyhow, what's up?"

"I'm leaving Peter for a little while, to sort stuff out. Could you put me up?"

"No problem." Nita sounded unsurprised. "You'll have to sleep on the couch. You want to stop by here at lunch and get my key?"

"Sure. I'll be there by one."

During his free period, Peter drove to a florist and bought a coleus. He hoped the bright purple leaves would cheer Katie up without triggering her aversion to flowers. He felt uneasy. Last night, he had been preoccupied because Glen wrote saying the academic job market was glutted with dozens of candidates for every position. Peter's resulting anxiety had prevented him from asking Katie about her counseling, and now he felt guilty.

Today would be different. He would give her the plant, make her lunch, and encourage her to talk about her feelings.

Entering their house, coleus in hand, he nearly tripped over two suitcases that stood in the entryway. Peter set the plant on the bookcase and stared. Why had Katie brought the cases up from the basement? Especially when she was sick?

Then he noticed a carton labeled "Daddy's things." The day Katie moved here, she had insisted on holding that box safely in her lap during the drive. If she was taking that carton somewhere, it could mean only one thing. She was going with it.

Peter felt as though the earth cracked beneath his feet, plunging him into a subterranean sea of hopelessness—a sea that had nearly drowned him once before. Eileen, too, had moved out one day while he was at class.

He grabbed the bookcase to steady himself and then hurried through the house until he found Katie in the kitchen. As he came through the doorway, she slipped something gold beneath her shirt tail and into her jeans pocket. On the counter were a package of wheat crackers, a jar of peanut butter, and half a cucumber. Katie clutched a paper.

"What are you doing?"

"Writing you a note."

"Dammit, you know that's not what I mean."

She flinched. Peter brought his fist to his mouth and forced himself to count silently to five. Then he said, "The suitcases. Where are you going?"

Katie crumpled the note. "To Nita's."

"Why? Why are you leaving me?"

"I'm not, exactly." She turned to the counter and swept the cracker crumbs into her palm. Resisting the urge to shake an answer from her, Peter waited as she brushed the crumbs into the trash. "I don't believe my dream is what you say. I think it's warning me I feel trapped, partly because of my job. So I'm going away to concentrate on finding something else."

Katie was silent a full ten seconds before Peter realized she was done. "Fine. We'll figure out something else you can do. Why do you have to leave?"

Her shoulders slumped. "I'm your wife. I'm supposed to be submissive and put your needs first and help with your career before I worry about mine."

"Who told you that?"

Her eyes flashed with sudden fire. "Pastor Samuelson. Last night."

Peter raked the hair back from his forehead. "Forget what he said. He's living in the dark ages. We'll find somebody else."

"No. I already know what I need to do."

"Then explain it to me. I don't get it."

She sighed. "Pastor's right. I should be more supportive, but..." Her voice broke. "I try, but he said my attitude's wrong. If I stay here, I'll keep building up the sin of resentment. So I'm going away to sort out my job. Then I'll come back and be the kind of wife God wants me to be."

Her reasoning was so twisted that Peter took hope. Surely, if he pointed out the illogic, she would stay. "Sweetheart, that's not what marriage is. It's not a case of your problems versus my problems. We should handle things together."

"But we don't."

"I know. We can do better." From the stubborn set of her jaw, Peter could tell that he wasn't getting through to her. Coming around the table, he grabbed her arms. "Give me a chance now that I know what's wrong. You don't have to go—"

"Yes, I do. The very last thing I say in the dream is 'I've got to get out of here.' "

Peter searched her face. He'd seen her wear distant expressions before but never as remote as this. Only twelve inches away, and she might as well be on the moon.

He pulled her close and kissed her hard, trying to break through her defenses. To his surprise, she responded eagerly as though she'd been waiting for this. Then she pulled away.

"Don't," she said as he moved toward her. She dragged a chair between them. "I love you, but I can't stay here. The dream is telling me to walk out in that storm alone. I don't know what the storm is yet, but I have to go."

"Katie—"

"No." She held up both hands. "I know I sound crazy, but I'm not. Not yet. But if I stay here, I'll go mad."

The recognition that he had to let her go tore into Peter like machine gun fire. The pain was agonizing. Ever since they met, he had hoped his friendship and later his love would ease the terrible sadness in her. Now she was saying that, not only had he failed to help, he had made things worse.

"Promise me you'll stay in touch and call me if you need help."

"Of course." Stepping around the chair, she clasped his hand.

Peter's throat ached and his eyes stung. He tried to hold back his tears, not wanting weakness to be Katie's last image of him. When he realized the effort was useless, he pulled her against his chest so she couldn't see. His tears fell and beaded on her black hair like dew.

She stirred. "I have to go. Nita expects me."

Peter released her and stood motionless, listening to the screen door slam again and again as she packed her car. It sounded like a shutter banging against a deserted house. She wasn't coming back. He was certain of it. When the house finally fell silent, he dialed the college and told Maggie to cancel his 2:00 class. Then he grabbed the yellow pages and looked up the address of the nearest liquor store. For the first time in years, he was going to get drunk.

PART FOUR

Misplaced Person

NOVEMBER 1985–
MARCH 1986

The morning light woke me. I stretched to ease my back, which was sore from sleeping on Nita's sagging couch—the avocado and gold floral that used to be in her parents' basement. Then I rose and crept into the hall. Nita lived on the second floor of what used to be a two-story single-family home, now divided into a two-flat. Her apartment consisted of a bathroom and three former bedrooms, two of them converted into a kitchen and a sitting room. Through her half-open door, I could see that Nita was alone in bed. *Thank God.* The guy she brought home must have slipped out as I slept.

The previous night, as the noise of passion emanated from her bedroom, I remembered the time Peter drove me home during the blizzard and imagined that I had sneaked down to him in the basement. The sounds of a stranger's orgasm fueled fantasies that Peter and I were the ones doing the sinning.

Now, stepping over a blouse on the hallway floor, I entered the bathroom, which looked like it hadn't been touched when the owner transformed the upstairs into an apartment. The floor was covered in hexagonal tiles forming black flowers on a white background. The tub was set within an arched recess, and the square white sink was a stand-alone pedestal model. But when I lifted the lid to the toilet, modern life intruded in the form of a used condom floating in the water. I flushed it and, finding a bottle of Lysol and a sponge in the narrow cupboard next to the tub, cleaned the toilet seat before allowing myself to pee.

In the kitchen, I reached into the sunflower yellow metal cabinet for the can of Folger's. As I scooped grounds into the basket of Nita's Mr. Coffee, I wondered what would have happened if Peter and I had slept together before marriage. Would we have a better sex life now if we'd been less inhibited then? Or would we have discovered our physical incompatibility and decided not to marry?

The yellow wall-mounted phone rang, and I grabbed it before it woke Nita.

"It's Peter."

"Oh, hi." Twining the cord through my fingers, I wondered if he had read my mind.

"How's your job search?"

I kicked shut a cabinet door that was always ajar. "It's not just a job search. It's more like career planning. I don't even know yet if I'm going to look for a new job."

The last part wasn't true. I had searched the job ads last Sunday and planned to do so again today, but I didn't want Peter pestering me for details.

"When I called Wednesday, you said—"

"That's because you keep bugging me for an answer. If you'd let me do this at my own pace, maybe I could get someplace." Grabbing a mug from the dish rack, I poured myself coffee.

"Sorry. You've been gone almost two weeks. Can't I call?"

His self-pity both irritated and shamed me. "Yes, you can call if you have something to talk about."

"I love you and want you to come home. That's what I want to talk about."

"But I already know that." I looked out the kitchen window at the brick wall of the apartment building next door. *Dead end.* "It doesn't help when you keep badgering me about how hurt you feel."

After a pause, he said, "Can't I say I love you anymore?"

"I didn't say that. Don't put words in my mouth. It's like..." Trembling with anger, I set my mug on the counter. "Like you're trying to prove what a bitch I am."

"That's not what I meant." He sighed. "Will I see you at church?"

"No." I walked to the phone mount and hung up.

"*Want* some of my breakfast?"

I looked up from the classified section of the paper as Nita flipped the sausage patties she was frying on the narrow apartment-sized stove. At 1:15, I'd hardly call it breakfast, but Nita had just gotten up. "Sure, thanks."

"How's the want ads?"

"Terrible." Laying the paper aside, I set the table. "Only three ads for administrative assistants, and they don't look promising. I checked everything else but can't find anything I'm qualified for." A shriek from the teakettle interrupted me.

Nita took a giant mug from the cabinet, dropped two teabags into it, and poured the hot water. "What'd you expect, an ad with your name on it? Last year I ran all over town looking for a new job and didn't find nothing."

"But that's different. You only finished high school."

Nita nodded at the paper folded up on the counter. "Yeah, how many of those are advertising for a history freak?"

"I've got two-and-a-half years of experience. That ought to be worth something to one of the industries in this town."

"What industries? They're all moving south for cheap wages."

"I'll find something. Even if I have to look in Chicago."

"What about Peter?" Nita asked as she dished up the fried eggs.

"What do you care? You don't even like him. You said he's boring."

Nita carried the skillet to the sink and filled it with water. "Maybe boring's not so bad. He loves you. That ain't so easy to find."

The phone rang. Nita answered it, then handed it to me. "Your mom."

"What's going on?" my mother demanded. "Peter said you left him."

"I can't talk about that."

"But it's crazy. How could you leave him when he's about to lose his job?"

"I said I don't want to talk about it."

She huffed but changed the subject. "I called to let you know your grandfather's in the hospital. In intensive care. I think you should come."

I could imagine the hospital scene: Grandma Brigitte faking hysteria to get attention and Mom grimly pacing the floor. "I can't."

"What do you mean *can't?* Won't is more like it."

"Look, I'm sorry he's sick, but there's nothing I can do. Besides, he won't care if I visit. The only person he cares about is you." I hung up.

*E*ntering the hospital chapel, Marietta sat at the back. It was a narrow room that had six pews about eight feet wide facing toward a wall where a crucifix hung. Below that, stood a table holding candlesticks. On either side of the cross were cloth banners made to look like abstract stained glass windows. Marietta had hoped the chapel would be empty, but a silver-haired man was kneeling in the second pew.

All she wanted was a quiet place to rest before driving home. Last night, she came to the hospital after work and waited outside intensive care until ten. Today, after hours of listening to her mother complain, she finally received word that Albert was out of danger and being moved to a regular room.

Sighing, she rested her elbow on the end of the pew, propped up her head, and closed her eyes. She was so tired she was afraid of falling asleep during the drive. There was the creak of a kneeler being pushed up. Footsteps came down the aisle, then someone said her name. Marietta opened her eyes and saw Dr. Montoya.

"I hope nothing is wrong."

"My father has pneumonia. It was touch and go for a while, but they've just moved him out of ICU."

"What of you? Forgive me for saying so, but you look exhausted."

She smiled, grateful for his concern. "I am."

"You must conserve your strength, or how will you help your father? As a doctor, I prescribe a good dinner in a relaxing setting."

Marietta laughed. "I think the best I can manage tonight is scrambled eggs."

He gazed at her. "Perhaps you will allow me to take you to dinner."

Marietta rubbed her worn wedding ring. "Dr. Montoya—"

"Please. Ernesto."

"Ernesto, I don't want to impose upon your kindness."

"No, it is you who have been kind. You did me a great favor by helping with my apartment. Allow me to repay you in this small way."

Drawing himself up proudly, he waited. He had a broad face, expressive eyes, an aquiline nose, and a neat mustache above full lips. Weary of looking after herself, Marietta agreed.

"*¡Estupendo!* Do you like Italian food? We could go to Capriotti's."

"That's fine." As they left the chapel, Marietta asked, "Why are you here? Do you work on Sundays?"

"No, I came to check on a patient who is, as you say, touch and go."

"Is that who you were praying for?"

He glanced down as though embarrassed. "Yes, I pray for all my patients. It is so easy for a doctor to grow proud and depend only on his own skill. At times, we learn the hard way that we are only human."

He disappeared into his thoughts as though reviewing a past failure that pained him deeply. Then he smiled at her. "Come. You need to eat."

The following Sunday, I went out early to buy the *Chicago Tribune* so I could check its large classified ads section. First, I circled several promising administrative assistant jobs. Then, I searched for other jobs my experience might qualify me for. One ad for an expediter made me suck in my breath. The employer was Better Gaskets, the company Ed moved to.

Monday, as soon as Barnes left on a sales call, I dialed the number and asked for Ed Marsden. He was on the line in thirty seconds. "Katie! Don't tell me, let me guess. You're behind on orders, so you're calling to give me some of your customers."

His irrepressible cockiness made me laugh. "No, I'm looking for a new job."

"Can't say I blame you. Barnes is an ass. Several of my old accounts followed me here because they couldn't stand him. You'd have been harder to steal from."

"Ed."

He chuckled. "So what do you need? A reference?"

"Well..." My stomach did somersaults. "I saw in the *Trib* that your company's looking for an expediter. Do you think they would consider me?"

"Of course! But why Chicago? Has Peter got a teaching position here?"

At the mention of Peter, I automatically glanced at the corner of my desk where I kept a wedding picture—except it wasn't there. I'd recently put it in a bottom drawer. Reaching toward my pencil holder, I grabbed the gold pen I'd taken from Peter in college. "No, he's not leaving Zebulun till June, but I can't wait. You don't know what it's like working for Barnes."

"I can imagine, kid. So you'll have a commuter marriage for a while."

"Something like that."

"Let me put you on hold for a sec."

While I listened to the Muzak version of Fleetwood Mac's "Dreams," I doodled on the outside margin of my desk calendar. First, I wrote "Chicago," then "Zebulun" beneath it with arrows going back and forth between the two. Then I wrote "Peter" with a question mark.

Ed returned. "Mr. Parrish would be glad to interview you. How's Wednesday?"

I laid down Peter's pen. "Sure."

"I know it's a long drive. Think you could be here at 11:00?"

"Yes. Thank you." Hanging up, I sat back in my chair and marveled at how easy that was. Maybe God was signaling that I was on the right track.

As the waitress set a small metal teapot before me and a frosty mug of beer before Ed, I said, "I can't believe the interview was such a snap."

"You come highly recommended." Ed watched the waitress walk away. She was wearing a thigh-length pink paisley sweater, black tights, and black boots.

I unwrapped my tea bag. "So a word from you is all it took?"

"Hartley Parrish would rather go on the word of a colleague than follow Personnel's guidelines. Besides, hiring you saved him a long, tedious process."

"Gee, thanks." It was true that Mr. Parrish hardly questioned me. Instead, when he learned I had studied history, he launched into a monologue on Jeffersonian democracy.

"Thanks, Jen," Ed said when the waitress set down his plate.

"You eat here a lot?"

"Yeah, it's close and has good service." He grinned.

Ignoring the innuendo, I glanced at the black marble walls enlivened by pink neon flamingoes. "It seems kind of trendy."

"I suppose." He pulled the lettuce off his avocado and turkey sandwich. "So you start December second. Any idea where you're going to live?"

"No. I'll come up this weekend to start apartment hunting."

"That doesn't give you much time. I have a better idea."

I swallowed my bite of teriyaki chicken salad. "What?"

Ed pulled at his cuffs as though performing a magic trick. "I called the management company that runs my building and found a one-bedroom to sublet on Sheridan Road across the street from me. The screenwriter who lived there got a job in Hollywood. He even left his furniture behind."

I put down my fork. Although I hated the idea of using a stranger's things, it would save me the expense of buying my own. All I had was $1,200 saved up from the grocery fund and one more check coming from Cel-Fo. "How does the place look?"

"I haven't seen it. Want to go look at it now?"

Just like that, I was tobogganing down a hill too fast to steer or see where I was going. I'd climbed on this sled myself by calling Ed, but I hadn't expected him to push me so hard. "Why are you doing this?"

"You asked for help, didn't you?" When I didn't answer, he raised his eyebrows. "Why don't you level with me? You've left Peter."

Jerking up my head, I glared at him. "That's none of your business."

Ed held up his hands. "OK, forget I asked."

I pulled back my hair and sighed. "I love him, Ed, I really do, but all he talks about is his failure to get tenure, and I can't stand it anymore. I need time to sort things out, but my mother acts like I'm betraying him."

Ed shook his head. "People are funny about marriage. If yours is the least bit different, everyone goes berserk. Marge and I have had an unconventional relationship for years, but we're still together."

"What do you mean?"

He shrugged. "She has her vices. I have mine. We don't hassle each other."

I had a fairly good idea what Ed's vices were, and I didn't want to go there. "Peter wasn't really part of this decision. I didn't give him a choice."

"He's an adult. He has a choice."

"Like what?"

"He'll either wait for you or get a divorce."

Divorce. That was the massive oak looming at the base of this hill I was rushing down. Could I avoid crashing into it?

Ed signaled for the check. "What's it to be? Do we go see the apartment?"

After hesitating a moment, I nodded.

At least the place is clean, I thought gloomily as I entered the living room. A beige vinyl couch was flanked by two tables and lamps made from green wine jugs. The carpet was a 1970s avocado-and-turquoise sculptured shag. On one wall hung a modernist painting of a nude woman, her figure fragmented into flat planes. A black abstract sculpture, shaped like a diseased toadstool, sat on the desk next to a blue glass ashtray.

In the kitchen, a pair of handcuffs was locked to the refrigerator handle, and a wall calendar showed a nude girl draped across the hood of a Mustang.

Holding a hand to my throat, I walked to the bedroom, dreading what I'd find there. That room, however, held only an oak dresser and a brass double bed with a new-looking mattress.

I returned to the front room and approached the rental agent, who wore a blue down jacket and a Chicago Bears knit hat. "Is this the only place available?"

"Yeah. It's a bad time of year to look." The agent reached into his pocket, took out a peanut, cracked the shell, and popped the nuts into his mouth. A piece of papery red membrane drifted to the floor.

Ed shrugged. "I think it's going to be the best you can find. May and October are the big moving times in Chicago."

"Tha's right," said the agent, cracking another peanut.

Out the twelfth-floor window, a sliver of Lake Michigan was visible between the high-rise buildings across Sheridan Road. "How much is rent?"

"It's $425. You have to pay the first month and a two-month deposit."

I whirled to face him. "That's $1,275!"

"Tha's right. We got to cover any damages. I always say, I don't know you from a hole in the wall, but you put a hole in the wall, you pay." He smirked at his own cleverness.

"Would you excuse us?" Ed led me into the kitchen. "You're not going to find any place cheaper, at least not anywhere you'd want to live."

"But it'll eat up all my savings."

"Then I'll loan you the deposit."

Shocked, I backed away. "I can't. It's too much."

Ed shrugged. "It's no big deal. I won't even miss it."

"How can you say that? You work for your money like everyone else."

"No, I don't. Marge is loaded. I work because I like the competition."

Remembering the rumors about his wife's wealth, I stared out the window at the back of a building across the alley. A wooden staircase with small porches branching off either side climbed up the wall. Borrowing from Ed felt wrong—but if he didn't need the money, was it so bad? This job meant a promotion, but to take it, I had to find a place quickly.

Ed came up behind me, so close that his breath stirred my hair. "You'd be near public transportation, stores, and the lake. And a friend right across the street."

I took a deep breath and then exhaled. "OK, but I'll repay you soon."

Back at Nita's, I called Peter and asked if I could see him the day after Thanksgiving.

"Of course! I'll make dinner."

His enthusiasm made me wonder if I should tell him about my job now. *No, better to break the news in person.*

Friday evening, white Christmas lights twinkled on the front windows of the house. I hadn't expected Peter to be in a holiday mood. When I came through the front door, he was setting the dining room table. "You put up lights."

"You like them?"

His question was so eager, I realized immediately why he'd decorated. "They're nice. I'm glad you picked white ones."

"I know you like them best." He walked toward me. Uncertain if I wanted to kiss him, I went to hang my coat in the closet.

"What's for dinner?"

"Red snapper."

I turned to him. "You don't usually make fish."

Peter blushed. "I... It's a recipe I got from Maggie."

Damn. Why is he trying so hard? Guiltily, I followed him into the kitchen. "Need help?"

"I don't think so." Peter squinted at the hand-written recipe. "I just need to sprinkle paprika on the fish and pop it in the broiler."

"I'll get it." I opened the basement door. Mounted on the wall beside the stairs were shelves we used as a pantry. As I sorted through the spices, I noticed a half-empty bottle of bourbon on the shelf below.

Reentering the kitchen, I handed Peter the paprika. "Since when do you drink bourbon?"

He pushed his glasses up his nose. "I bought it the day you left."

The old belief that it was my responsibility to look after him landed on me with the weight of a falling sandbag. I turned away and walked into the dining room.

Peter followed. "I'm sorry. It was a stupid thing to do."

Staring at the table, set with pink-flowered china we rarely used, I wondered if he would go on a binge after I moved. Ed would say he was an adult with his own choices to make. "You're a grown man. Drink as much as you want."

Peter stormed into the kitchen. I watched him take the bottle, pour the bourbon down the drain, and slam the empty in the trash. "Happy now?"

"I didn't ask you to do that."

He looked as though he wanted to retort but then shrugged. "It's better this way."

You may not think so when you hear my news.

After dinner as they sat on the couch drinking coffee, Katie kept falling silent. Peter noticed she was wearing the white mohair pullover he gave her last Christmas. Her loose black hair gleamed against the snowy sweater. Her face looked thinner, with hollows beneath her cheekbones. To Peter, she looked as unhappy as he felt.

Katie asked, "Did you see your parents yesterday?"

The question drove a dart of pain behind Peter's eyes. "No, Mom assumed I was with your family, and I let her think that. They don't know about us yet."

As Katie leaned forward to put her cup and saucer on the table, her hair swung down and hid her face. "I think you should tell them."

"Not until I have to."

She pushed back her hair. "I have a new job."

"Great! Is it a good one?"

"I think so. It's with a bigger company. I'll be an expediter, which pays more."

Relief flooded Peter at the thought that she would come home. "What company is it?"

"Better Gaskets." She dropped her gaze, and Peter felt a twinge of misgiving. "In Chicago."

For about five seconds, Peter struggled to convince himself she meant to commute—but the truth was in her face. "You're moving?"

"Only sixty miles away."

"You've been here in town, and I haven't seen you in three weeks. Was that too often?"

Her chin jerked up. "I'm going there for a job. There's nothing here in Zebulun."

"Just me." Peter pushed his glasses on top of his head and rubbed his eyes. His head throbbed. "When do you go?"

"Sunday."

"You cut it close, don't you?" He let his glasses fall back in place. "If you're working up to a divorce, why can't you just say so?"

"I don't want a divorce. I just need to be on my own for a while."

The hurt on her face, as though she were the one being abandoned, was too much for him. Picking up the dishes, he said, "French was right. I never should have gotten involved with you."

In the kitchen, Peter filled the dishpan. He wanted to throw the cups across the room—and would have if they weren't his grandmother's Haviland china, given to him because Marian wanted nothing to do with hand-me-downs. When he switched off the water, he heard silence and wondered if Katie had left. His last remark had been intended to gut her, the way she'd eviscerated him.

Unwillingly, he remembered the tormented expression his mother wore whenever his father taunted her. As a boy, Peter swore he would never treat his wife like that. He dried his hands and returned to the living room.

Katie sat on the couch, looking through their wedding album. Sitting beside her, Peter gazed at a full-length portrait in which Katie looked beautiful but tense. Posed next to her, he smiled broadly, to all appearances primed for the wedding night. *My last optimistic moment,* he thought glumly.

"If you really don't want me to take the job," Katie said quietly, "I won't."

"Right." Peter rubbed both his temples. "Then when you start having nightmares again, you can blame me."

"That's not what I meant."

"But it would happen." He moved the album to the table. "Why are you moving away? What did I do that was so terrible?"

"It's not you! I feel trapped in my life." She made a sweeping gesture. "I need to break out somehow. I wish I had a better explanation, but that's all there is to it."

"But—" Peter nearly choked on his frustration. "Before we got married, I asked if you wanted to wait. I offered to give you time on your own. You said no."

Katie closed her eyes. "I know. All I could think about was how much I love you and how long we'd already waited. I wasn't thinking about a career or...who I wanted to be. I know you tried to talk to me about it, but I didn't understand." She doubled over as if her stomach ached, and her voice grew strained. "I didn't know anything about careers. Daddy used to go from job to job, quitting whenever he got mad. And Mom was just earning money to survive, at least until the store. I didn't know how important work is or..." She shivered. "What it's like to be trapped day after day in a job that you hate."

She faced him again, this time with resolve in her face. "You're lucky. I know things have been rough at Zebulun, but at least you found something that you love to do and that you're good at. I haven't. Do you understand what I'm talking about?"

"I do." He took her left hand between both of his. "But I don't understand what's supposed to happen with us. You'll be in Chicago. I'll be here. Then in a year, I'll move to God knows where. Are we supposed to communicate by postcard?"

She sighed. "No. I'll keep thinking about what to study in grad school. By the time you get another job, I should have a plan and be ready to come back."

"What if you decide to get a degree that isn't offered where I teach?"

Katie pulled her hand free. "I don't have all the answers. Can't we discuss this later?"

Although he heard her growing annoyance, Peter couldn't restrain himself. "Don't you love me anymore? Don't you miss being at home?"

She frowned. "Yes, I still love you. But this house doesn't feel like home. It's your place with your furniture and nothing of mine."

"You never said that bothered you. If that's a reason you left, we could redecorate—" He stopped as he realized how he would have answered if she'd asked. "Well, we can afford it once I get another position."

"See? Everything has to wait for your job. But not this."

Peter tried to put himself in her shoes, but it hurt to know that she felt trapped. "I didn't know it was this bad. I miss you."

She touched his arm lightly. "I miss you too."

When Peter slipped his arm around her, she leaned against him. "Hold me. If you hug me tight enough, maybe I'll still feel it in Chicago."

Peter swallowed hard and took a chance. "Don't go."

"I already accepted the job and signed a lease."

There seemed nothing else to say. Holding her in his arms was like taking a single sip of water to quench a burning thirst; as soon as she left, Peter's blistering need would return, worse than before. Yet, he couldn't push her away. Peter imagined lifting Katie's sweater over her head and burying his face between her breasts. Tentatively, he kissed her hair. When she didn't object, he moved his lips to her mouth.

"No." She jerked away. "I've got to go."

He caught her hand. "Can't we spend the night together first?"

"No." Pulling free, she marched to the closet and put on her coat.

Peter followed. "Why do you keep running away? For God's sake, Katie, what did I do?"

Katie paused in the process of twisting up her hair to shove it under a cap. "You don't get it, do you? Not everything I do is about you." She brushed past him and slammed out the door.

Left alone, Peter thought, *Then why am I the one you keep trying to hurt?*

Sunday afternoon, I sat in my new apartment. Saturday, I had moved my bank account to Chicago and bought a city sticker for my car. Sunday morning, I took possession of the apartment and shopped for sheets, towels, and groceries. Ed had told me how much I would need for deposits to get the phone turned on and transfer the electricity to my name. After all that, I would have only about $300 to last until my first payday a month away.

Deciding to make a budget, I rummaged through the desk for paper. The long center drawer held three broken pencils and a ruler. The top right-hand drawer held two keys: one labeled basement storage and a tiny, unlabeled one. I stared at it, walked into the kitchen, and tried it on the handcuffs hooked to the refrigerator handle. To my relief, they fell off. I tossed them in the trash and then remembered that I was subleasing and couldn't dispose of anything. Retrieving the cuffs, I dropped them in the blue glass ashtray on the desk.

Desperate, I tore a deposit slip from my checkbook and on the back side listed food, gas, utilities, rent. I worried I was forgetting something. Running my thumb over the initials on Peter's pen, I wished the phone was hooked up so I could call him for advice.

I pictured him wearing jeans and a flannel shirt, sitting hunched over his desk as he reviewed lecture notes. On a winter Sunday like this, I'd be in the kitchen cooking navy bean soup and cornbread.

My mind veered to the strange bed in the next room. I had never spent a night alone, and the neighborhood scared me. Earlier, as I drove to the store, I saw black men in shabby coats hanging out in doorways, a white girl wheeling a biracial baby in a stroller, an Asian family leaving a laundromat with their clothes folded on a shopping cart, and a group of teenage boys walking with a swagger and roll that proclaimed they were looking for trouble.

My eyes stung. I walked into the kitchen, located a battered saucepan, and put water on for tea. Then I gazed at the wall phone.

Peter. Closing my eyes, I remembered how safe it felt to be in his arms. Again came the urge to call him. The prospect of staying in this strange apartment made me miss him desperately, but it was too late to say, "I was wrong. I do want to spend the weekend with you."

The doorbell rang. I went to the cramped entryway and stared at the panel of buttons for a second before identifying the one for the intercom. "Hello?"

"Pizza."

"You've got the wrong apartment."

"No, ma'am. Welcome wagon sent it."

The voice sounded familiar. "Ed, is that you?"

"Yeah, let me in. The pizza's getting cold."

As I pushed the button to release the security door, sweat broke out under my arms. Why was Ed here? Did he plan to collect on the loan by asking me to sleep with him? I felt stupid.

When the knock came, I opened the door. Ed stood there in jeans and a leather jacket, holding a flat pizza box and a bottle of wine. He looked me up and down as if measuring me and then smiled. "Welcome to the neighborhood."

"You shouldn't have done this."

"Why not?" He shoved the pizza at me. "You already eat?"

"No, but—"

"But what?" After setting the bottle on the desk, he took off his jacket and flung it on the couch. He was wearing a grey and navy sweater knitted in a swirling design. "Come on, Katie, what's on your mind? I hate cold food."

"Then take it home to your wife."

Ed laughed. "Is that what's bugging you? God, you should see your face. Marge is at her father's tonight. She left me to my own devices."

Pushing past him into the kitchen, I said, "And you took it for granted I was sitting around waiting to be cheered up."

"No, I thought you'd be busy settling in and would appreciate not having to cook." He leaned in the doorway. "If you want me to leave, just say so."

I glanced at him as I set the table. "I don't want you to assume anything. Just because I left Peter..." My cheeks began to burn.

Ed grinned. "Why do religious women always think they're about to get seduced?"

Embarrassed, I went to get glasses. "Sorry. It's been an exhausting weekend."

"I can imagine." He stepped back into the living room, returned with the bottle of wine, and twisted off the screw cap. "It's cheap stuff, but maybe it'll help."

"None for me." When he raised his eyebrows, I said, "You know I don't drink."

"Fine." He filled his own glass.

Feeling petty, I relented. "I guess I could try a little." I filled my glass and sipped the wine. It was sweeter than I expected with a slight fizz. *Lambrusco,* the label said.

"Do you suppose we could eat now?" Ed asked. "I'm starved."

For the Christmas season, Peter's friends Wayne and Lena had taken down the copper pots from their brick kitchen wall and hung a huge evergreen wreath twined with white lights and plaid ribbon. It reminded Peter of the lights on his front window, which had been dark since the night Katie told him she was moving.

"Another pork chop?" Lena held out the platter.

Peter waved at the half-eaten chop on his plate. "No, thanks. It's nice of you to have me over for dinner. Sorry I'm not doing it justice."

"Don't be silly." Lena began to clear off the table. Although her stocky figure bore little resemblance to Katie's, her thick braid reminded Peter of his wife. Like a chest pain, longing seized him and left him breathless.

Wayne took out his pipe—a vice he hid from the college administration—and began to pack it with tobacco. "I can't believe Katie moved to Chicago."

Peter accepted a mug of coffee from Lena and added cream and sugar. "I keep thinking she's having a delayed adolescence. Her mother is so strict, she never really got to rebel."

"But why take it out on you?"

"That's easy," Lena said. "Her decision to marry him was itself an act of rebellion. He was forbidden, remember? But now he's part of the status quo."

Annoyed to hear this smug analysis from the very woman who'd urged him to propose, Peter said, "So now what do I do?"

Lena spiked her coffee with brandy. "Leave her alone. Since you're not really the source of her problem, you can't solve it. She needs to do that herself."

"But I have to do something. I want to make sure that once she works things out, she'll come home."

Wayne and Lena looked at each other. "That's not really your lookout," Wayne said. "You can't make her do anything. She's a free adult."

Peter clenched his jaw and searched for a way to refute Wayne's logic, but the very room in which they sat defeated him. This kitchen with its homey brick, thriving houseplants, and cheerful yellow-and-blue stoneware had always symbolized for Peter the warm heart of a good marriage between individuals who gave each other freedom and respect. "So there's nothing I can do but let Katie go."

"I wouldn't say that exactly." Lena leaned forward. "Concentrate on your own stuff. Take better care of yourself. Figure out what to do about your career."

Peter frowned. Looking at Wayne and Lena, he saw only friendly concern, but his chin went up and his fists closed as though he were facing battle. "I'm not the only one at fault here."

Wayne removed his pipe from his teeth. "No one said you were. But your actions are the only ones you can control."

Glancing down at his coffee, Peter sighed. "I guess so. But I don't like it much."

Peter sat at his desk in the back bedroom rewriting a chapter of his rejected manuscript. It dealt with Jonathan Morton and his wife, Lavinia. When Morton learned after their marriage that Lavinia's second cousins owned slaves, he forbade her to stay in contact with any of her family. Lavinia obeyed until 1862 when she received word that her father was dying. She traveled back to Kentucky to be at the deathbed—even though her husband warned her that she could not return if she did. Peter reread a photocopy of one of Lavinia's letters:

Oh, please write and grant me your forgiveness. I know that I failed to obey you—but how could I refuse to see Papa when he was dying? He is gone now and will never come between us again. Sometimes I am so weary that I fear I shall not see you again in this life. I entreat you, Dearest Husband, to let me come home.

A year later, Lavinia died of tuberculosis. True to her premonition, she did not see Morton again, nor did she witness the end of the war. Sympathy for her twisted inside Peter. Both of them knew the pain of rejection, the loss of the marriage tie. *If I could do it over,* he thought, *I'd write this book about her.*

The expediters at Better Gaskets worked in a long office with grey metal desks and filing cabinets that looked like they'd been around since the 1950s. Hanging up the phone, I glanced at the two women who shared the space with me: Elena Nieves, a pretty brunette with a round face, in the front desk and Nancy Kupcikevicius, a thin forty-something with frosted hair, in the middle. A customer just asked me to trace a truck shipment, a task I'd never done. Elena was willing to explain procedures, but she was on the phone. That left Nancy, a hard-edged woman who smoked incessantly and drank a two-liter bottle of Coke each day.

Fortunately, she chose that moment to leave the room. I was at Elena's desk asking for help when Nancy returned. "Can't you go an hour without being spoon-fed?" she sniped in passing.

"Don't listen to her," Elena whispered. "You're doing fine."

As I phoned the trucking company, Ed entered our office and stopped by Nancy's desk. "Haven't you heard? Hart's going to make this a nonsmoking office. You might actually have to kick the filthy habit."

Nancy blew smoke in his face. "Look who's talking about filthy habits."

I hung up, and Ed came toward me. "I drove today. Want a ride?"

Afraid the others would get the wrong idea, I said, "No, thanks."

"Why not? We live on the same street, and it beats taking the bus."

Behind his back, Nancy snorted, which goaded me. "Sure, a ride would be great."

As Ed drove north on Lake Shore Drive, I watched white waves rush forward out of the darkness, spill onto deserted beaches lit only by streetlamps, and recede into oblivion. Ten days had passed since I left Zebulun, each one making me feel more isolated. Chicago was all sharp angles, harsh noises, and looming buildings crusted with grime. When I pictured home, I thought not of Zebulun but of my mother's house in the country: the gentle sweep of my river, the variable carol of our neighbor's wind chimes, and a soft coral sunset beyond fields where golden brown stubble poked through light snow. I sighed.

Ed asked, "Something wrong?"

I felt angry with him for encouraging me in this madness. "I never should have come up here."

"You're still adjusting. Give it time."

"Time won't help if I've made a mistake. Everything will just get worse."

After a moment, he asked, "What bothers you the most?"

"Everything. I hate the city. I don't fit in at work, and I miss Peter."

"So call him."

Ed's tone was gentle, so I admitted, "I did call. Sunday."

Peter had been cool. He didn't ask to see me or inquire about my job. Instead, he said that he'd scrapped the biography of Jonathan Morton and was writing about Lavinia instead. He hung up after five minutes.

Ed asked, "Does he still want you to come home?"

"He didn't say."

"I'm sure he does. He's just angry and licking his wounds."

Red taillights flowed in a thick river before us. "My mother's furious at me."

"So? She's trying to make you feel guilty so you'll do what she wants."

"You don't understand." I glanced at Ed, lingered over his strong profile, and immediately felt ashamed. "She really thinks what I'm doing is wrong."

Ed snorted. "You're the most straitlaced person I know. You're not divorcing the man, you're not cheating on him. Lots of couples live apart temporarily. Tell her this is the eighties."

I didn't answer. He honked at a car that cut us off, then said, "It's not really your mom. You're putting this guilt on yourself. Hasn't it occurred to you that a separation might be good for your marriage?"

"How? And don't tell me absence makes the heart grow fonder."

"I wasn't going to. I was thinking you might grow up." As I drew in breath to protest, he added, "Don't get me wrong. You're very responsible, but you're also naïve. It'll do you good to be on your own. Learn to cope with the world."

Is that what I'm doing? I hugged myself. *Maybe it is childish to want to run back home.*

As if reading my mind, Ed said, "That doesn't mean you can't call him, Katie. There's nothing wrong with keeping in touch."

Searching through the cupboard for a measuring cup, Peter came across Katie's favorite mug. It was speckled grey with a bluebird on one side. Clutching it, Peter sat on the nearest chair.

Sunday when they talked, he hadn't allowed himself to say he missed her. If Lena was right about Katie needing space, he'd give it to her. Yet his restraint had come at a price; that night, he suffered from insomnia. At three o'clock, he wandered from room to room. Although Katie claimed this house held nothing of her, Peter saw traces of her everywhere: the way their books were alphabetized by author, the half-finished shopping list still in the kitchen, the lavender-scented moisturizer in the bathroom.

I'll change. Maybe then she'll come home again.

To that end, he'd decided to follow Lena's advice about taking better care of himself. He'd asked Cherisse, this year's department assistant, how to cook vegetarian. If he found a few recipes he liked, he could eat meatless once or twice a week. Now, however, as Peter stared at the eraserlike block of white bean curd he'd bought, he suspected he'd gone overboard.

The phone rang. It was Katie. "I wondered what you're doing."

Delighted that she'd called, Peter chuckled. "I'm trying to cook tofu."

"What's that?"

"Soybean curd." He tucked the receiver under his ear so he could slice it. "Vegetarians use it as a source of protein."

"It sounds horrible. Why would you eat that?"

"I've been eating too much fatty junk. So I'm experimenting."

"That's good," she said, sounding more puzzled than approving.

"I'm thinking about losing some weight. Maybe fifteen pounds."

"Sounds like you made your New Year's resolutions early."

The amusement in her voice deflated Peter. "I guess so. You're the one who always tells me to eat better."

"Oh, I see."

Too late, he realized that he'd made it sound like a ploy to win her back. Changing the subject, he asked, "So how's work?"

"OK, I guess."

He heard the sound of a faucet. "You know, our anniversary's next Tuesday. Could we see each other?"

The running water stopped. "I don't think so."

"What about Christmas?"

She paused before saying, "I'm not coming home this year."

"Do you want me to come up?"

"No."

"Katie, please, can we talk about this?"

"No." Her voice grew agitated. "I have to go." She hung up.

Peter sat down and hid his face in his hands. "Stupid. You're a stupid, stupid man."

When I dialed Ed's extension to tell him that one of his rush orders had shipped, the call went through to the sales department assistant. "Hi, I was trying to reach Ed."

"He didn't come in today. There's been a death in the family."

"Oh, I'm sorry. Would you take a message?"

After giving the assistant the details and hanging up, I sat with my hand on the receiver. Should I call Ed at home to express my condolences? If Marge answered, that might be awkward. I wasn't sure Ed had told her about my move, and I didn't want her to think I was one of his flirtations. *I could mail a card to their condo. Or better yet, leave one on his desk for when he comes back.*

That evening, as I heated some potato soup I bought at the neighborhood deli, the phone rang. Assuming it was Peter, I ignored it. By the sixth ring, I feared an emergency and answered.

"Katie. You're home." It was Ed. "I thought so. I was watching out the window."

I twined the phone cord through my fingers. "You can see me from the twenty-fourth floor?"

"No. I'm...in the bar...first floor." His voice, although not exactly slurred, was slow and deliberate.

Picturing his building, I remembered that to the left of the lobby entrance was a bank of smoked glass windows with a blue neon sign blinking, "Big Shoulders Lounge."

"I heard you had a loss."

"My mother."

His words stirred the old ache for my father. "I'm sorry. Losing a parent is—"

"Katie, I don't want to be alone. Would you have a drink with me? Just one so I can talk to somebody?" He sounded desperate, so unlike the cocksure Ed I knew.

I glanced at the soup, which was starting to simmer, and turned off the flame. "Of course. Just give me ten or fifteen minutes."

"Sure." He paused and added, "Thank you."

Grabbing a spoon, I ate directly from the pan. Then I ran cold water on my wrists to perk myself up, grabbed my coat and purse, and left.

I felt vulnerable entering a bar by myself and paused inside the entrance to survey my surroundings. The room was wide, stretching along the front of Ed's building, but only deep enough for the bar and one row of booths along the windows. The bar stools and booth seats were upholstered in pearl grey. Because of the bar's name, I'd expected Chicago kitsch and sports memorabilia, but instead, the wall to the right of the entrance displayed an arrangement of autographed photographs of famous Chicago writers: Carl Sandburg, Studs Terkel, Gwendolyn Brooks, Saul Bellow, Sandra Cisneros. That unexpected nod to culture reassured me.

Ed was sitting in the third booth down, his tie askew, his arms hunched around a tumbler of whiskey. When he saw me, he started to stand, but I waved him back into his seat.

As I sat across from him, he pushed a glass of white wine toward me. "I ordered Chardonnay. If you want something else, let me know. I..." His voice caught as if on a protruding nail, and he shook his head to dislodge it. "I just want to say I 'ppreciate this."

"Oh, Ed." I pulled off my gloves, laid them on the table, and began to unbutton my coat. "Chardonnay is fine. You know I'm no wine expert."

A half smile appeared, then faded as he stared into his drink.

"What happened?"

He shrugged. "A stroke. They didn't find her for a couple of days until she missed her bridge game. They're not sure how long she lay there."

"I'm so sorry. How awful to know she suffered like that and they might have..." I stopped myself from saying, "might have saved her." It seemed cruel.

Ed hunched even further into himself. He lifted his glass and drained it, then gestured to the waitress, placing his empty near the table's edge.

I tentatively sipped my wine. It had a strange resinous taste I wasn't sure I liked. Glancing back at Ed, I said, "What was she like?"

He gazed over my head. "Bird bones and talcum powder, pink lipstick and old lace. Her voice was small and hesitant. She could be as sweet as cotton candy and dissolve just as fast. She..." He blinked. "Was my biggest fan. Had a special smile just for me." He fell silent as he accepted his drink from the waitress and gave her the ghost of his usual grin.

"What about your father?"

Ed squinted at me blearily. "My fa— Oh, he died about ten years ago. Lung cancer."

"No, I mean didn't your mother have a special smile for him?"

"Oh. Yeah. It was...pathetic. He got so he didn't see her most of the time except when she annoyed him. Then he'd cut her to the bone with some snide remark." Ed gulped his drink. "I used to beg her to stand up and refuse to take his shit."

He stared at me, his eyes hollowed out by sorrow. "But she wouldn't. She could never assert herself. Not even with me. She'd give me anything I asked for. Unless my dad said no and even then sometimes behind his back."

Ed shook his head. "I used to tell her to be stronger, but...now I wonder. Did I ever want that? Even as a kid, I knew I could take advantage of her."

"I don't think you can blame yourself for that," I said, unsure how to respond to this newly vulnerable Ed. "She was the one supposed to be in charge, not you."

"Yeah, I guess." He leaned back again and closed his eyes. "And now she's gone. I wonder if she was ever happy."

His words evoked my stormy relationship with my own mother. "I think parents are a mystery to most kids."

"Maybe." Ed lifted his whiskey glass as if in a toast. After taking another swallow, he said, "So did the Amalgamated order go out last night?"

To Marietta's surprise, Ernesto invited her to dinner at his apartment. "I want you to see how it looks now that everything is in place."

She walked slowly around his living room, noticing the pieces she had sold him—teal couch, oak rocker, and tables inlaid with ceramic tiles—augmented by his personal items. A guitar leaned in a corner, framed photographs covered one end table, and a Mesoamerican statue stood on the other. On the wall hung an oil painting of a Mexican peasant carrying a basket of calla lilies.

"It's very nice. Your things give the place character."

"No, it is the joining of our two tastes, don't you agree?"

Marietta blushed.

Dinner was a stew of pork, onions, raisins, and apricots in flavorful brown sauce. As they ate, he talked about his family. "During the revolution, rebels raided one of my grandfather's estates and killed his older son. Because of that, my grandfather turned against his country. He insisted that all of his children and grandchildren be educated in Europe or the United States, and he nearly disowned Papa for marrying an Indian."

"You don't seem to have inherited his bitterness."

Ernesto shrugged. "I have my mother's temperament. I love Mexico and would have stayed forever if Rosalinda had not died."

Marietta laid down her fork. "Why did you come here? Why not move to Chicago or Los Angeles to be with one of your children?"

Ernesto sighed. "I did live with Roberto for a while, but we argued. He acts like a conquistador, taking woman after woman as though they are spoils of war. When I advise him to marry, he calls me old-fashioned." He shrugged again, smiling ruefully. "If I stayed there, I feared I would become like my grandfather, trying to rule my son instead of letting him find his own path."

The phone rang, and Ernesto rose. "Excuse me. It may be the hospital."

But it wasn't. *"Patricia. ¡Que milagro! ¿Cómo estás?"*

As Ernesto listened, he smiled across the room at Marietta. Then he said, *"Muy bien, pero estoy un poco ocupado en este momento.... Si, con una amiga.... No, m'hija, no te preocupes. Es muy simpatica.... Si. Hasta luego."*

Returning to the table, he waved back at the phone and said, "My daughter calls often to tell me about my grandson."

"I didn't know you had grandchildren."

"Yes, one." He held his hand inches above the table. "He is small, but in my daughter's house, he wields the power of a giant. Do you have grandchildren?"

"No. My daughter's separated from her husband. I've tried to convince her to go back, but it's like talking to a brick wall."

Ernesto shook his head. "You sound like Roberto and me. The world is not as it was when we were young. Children do not want advice from their parents."

"Someone's got to talk sense into her."

"Yet if you push too hard, you will push her away. Yes?"

Marietta recalled holding Katie as a baby, remembered the weight of Katie's sleep-heavy head pressed against her neck. "I'm scared for her," she whispered.

On his second wedding anniversary, Peter looked through the mail for a card from Katie and then checked his answering machine. Nothing. Opening the refrigerator, he drank directly from a two-liter bottle of Pepsi, taking satisfaction in flouting one of Katie's rules.

He considered calling her but couldn't face getting a brush-off. Might as well make dinner and try to lose himself in a book.

Peter opened the refrigerator again. In the meat drawer was an orange roughy filet he'd intended to broil. "To hell with that!" He slammed the refrigerator door.

He drove to McDonald's and gave his order to a teenage girl wearing a striped burgundy tunic with a white collar. Two minutes later, she handed Peter a tray with two light brown Styrofoam clamshell boxes, a bright red and gold cardboard sleeve overflowing with French fries, and an extra-large paper cup of Coke. As Peter looked for an empty table, he passed a booth containing three young men, one of whom was a student of his. "Hey, Dr. Taylor. Eating out tonight?"

"Yes, um, my wife is working late." He gave what felt like an idiotic smile and then moved to a seating area on the other side of a half wall topped by a lattice screen.

Reassured that his student couldn't see him there, Peter sat, opened one of the sandwich boxes, and bit into a Big Mac. Flicking away a glob of special sauce that had oozed onto the corner of his mouth, he told himself it was time to face facts. Katie wasn't coming home anytime soon. He could do whatever he wanted. Maybe go camping. Katie was never interested because she considered it dirty. Peter decided to take a trip when spring came. Maybe Joel would come along—if he could be persuaded to leave his girlfriend for a weekend.

Peter's stomach growled as he started his second burger, and his bowels felt distended. Then an intestinal cramp hit. Chills swept over him, raising gooseflesh on his arms. Peter dashed to the bathroom.

As soon as he sat on the stool, scalding diarrhea gushed from his body. The men's room door opened. "Phew! It stinks in here!"

The voice belonged to Dan, his student. Peter sat quietly in the stall until long after the young man had left. As he gazed at the anonymous beige door before him, Peter muttered to himself, "Happy anniversary, dude. You really know how to have a good time."

At Better Gaskets, almost everyone congregated in the break room during the fifteen minutes leading up to our 8:30 start time. Unlike the office I shared with the other expediters, that common space had been recently redecorated. The walls, refrigerator, and laminated cabinets were ivory, while the table tops and carpet were dusty rose. Above the cabinets, a horizontal triple stripe of teal, rose, and peach circled the room ending in a downward spiral just before it reached the door.

As I stood by the microwave dunking a teabag in my mug, Ed strolled into the room and came directly to the counter where the coffee maker sat. He poured himself a cup and then looked at me. "You seem down. Want to talk?"

I shrugged. "I don't know."

"Come on." Taking my elbow, he steered me from the room, down the hallway, and into his office, which was furnished in a manner befitting a top salesman with sleek wooden office furniture, a black leather office chair for him, and two curved chairs with tweedy upholstery for visitors.

Once his door was closed and we sat facing each other across the desk, he said, "What's the problem? Nancy bitching again?"

"No." Holding my mug with both hands to take advantage of its warmth, I said, "Today's my wedding anniversary."

Ed took off his jacket, picked up the ten-pound weight he kept on his desk, and began to do biceps curls. "Peter didn't want to celebrate, huh?"

"No, I didn't."

"So what's the beef?"

"I miss him, but whenever we talk, he keeps bugging me to come back."

Ed pumped in silence a few times. "Why not tell him you'll call every week if he promises not to nag? If he doesn't, stop calling till he agrees."

"That sounds so cold."

He raised his eyebrows. "Colder than the way you're acting now?" When I didn't answer, he said, "I thought you were going to focus on your career, but you're still wasting all your energy on Peter."

I shook my head. "Ed, I love him. I can't cut him off at the knees."

"You got nothing to give the guy right now. Just draw the line."

"It's not as easy as that."

"You have to choose. If you're this miserable without Peter, go home."

I stared into my mug and wished it held future-telling tea leaves. "I can't. There's no opportunity for me there."

"Maybe you don't want a career. Maybe you'd rather be a housewife."

"That's not true."

Ed switched the weight to his left hand. "Then why can't you get serious?"

"I am. I can't do everything all at once, can I?" When he didn't answer, I asked, "What do you think I should do?"

"I'm not answering that. You're a big girl now."

Christmas morning, I stood in my kitchen eating cookies. Mom had reacted with surprising calm when I said I wouldn't be home for the holiday and even sent me a care package.

As I bit into a Christmas tree topped with green sugar, I wandered into the living room. On TV, a choir was singing carols. I changed channels until I found the movie *It's a Wonderful Life.* The scene was Jimmy Stewart and Donna Reed's wedding night, and he had just arrived at the ramshackle old house she wanted to make their home. Jimmy did a double take at the sight of his-and-hers slippers under the bed.

I changed channels only to find another showing of the same movie, this one close to the end. Holding his daughter Zuzu, Jimmy Stewart heard a bell on the Christmas tree ring, signaling that his guardian angel had just received wings.

Turning off the set, I flopped on the sofa. If people had guardian angels, why was life such a mess? The only part of the film that seemed true was Jimmy Stewart's feeling that the world would be better if he'd never been born.

When the phone rang, I hurried to answer, hoping it was Peter.

"Happy holiday," said Ed. "Marge and I are throwing a party this evening. Want to come?"

"I don't think so."

"Katie, it's not good to sit around and mope."

Looking at the molasses cookie I'd just taken, I said, "Yeah, but I won't know anybody, and I'm not good at small talk."

"Tell you what. I said I was going to introduce you to Chinese food. Let me take you down to Chinatown Friday night."

I pulled my flannel robe tight across my chest. "Ed, we can't go out."

"Why not? Marge is going on a ski trip, so I have to eat out anyway. I'd rather do it with a friend."

Friends having a casual meal. It sounded harmless when he put it like that, but I still felt uneasy. "Just so you know the ground rules."

"What is this, a ball game? Look, lovely as you are, I have no designs on your body."

"Sorry," I said, wondering if I was as paranoid as he made me sound.

"Great. We'll head for Chinatown immediately after work."

Friday was cold with temperatures falling from the teens into single digits, causing me to wonder if Ed was going to postpone our outing. But at 5:00, he showed up in my office wearing his wool overcoat, escorted me to his black BMW, and drove south on the expressway to 18th Street. After going east a short distance, he turned right onto Wentworth Avenue.

A couple of blocks south, a large gate nearly three stories high loomed over the roadway ahead of us. It was made of metal, painted red, with up-tilting corners on the roof and four large tiles holding Chinese characters in gold spaced between the cross beams. Driving under it felt like entering a foreign country. We passed a massive brick building with two towers topped by pagoda-style roofs, and all of the restaurant and store signs were in both English and Chinese. I felt a tingle of excitement that made me glad I'd agreed to this excursion despite my misgivings. Ed pulled into a parking garage, and then we walked a block back the way we had come. Far in the distance, I could see the lights of the Sears Tower beyond the pagoda roofline I'd noticed earlier. Ed led me into a restaurant, which he said was the oldest Chinese eatery in the city.

The décor was more subdued than I expected: a few red paper lanterns hung from the ceiling and giant painted fans adorned the wood-paneled walls. The dining room was furnished with chairs upholstered in dark green vinyl and white cloth-covered tables. The larger ones were round with center turntables that held Chinese condiments in addition to the usual salt, pepper, and sugar.

Ed ordered egg rolls, imperial fried rice, moo shu pork, chicken with cashews, Mongolian beef, and garlic shrimp. Although the spread was far too much for us, I enjoyed the wide array of tastes and textures: sweet plum sauce, salty soy, hot mustard, garlic and green onions, crisp vegetables, tender meat, crunchy nuts. We had so much leftover food that I insisted Ed take it home.

After dinner, we strolled down Wentworth Avenue and stopped in one of the shops. As I browsed, Ed held a low conversation with the shopkeeper. Ignoring them, I went to a glass case and stared at a display of jade bangles. They were a stunningly rich shade of green, but far too expensive for me. Moving farther into the store, I noticed a set of handleless porcelain teacups and a matching teapot, decorated with a creamy lotus flower on a celadon background. The simple design appealed to me.

Ed came up to me; he was holding the sack of takeout cartons and a new plastic shopping bag. "Ready to go, or do you want to visit another store?"

"No, I'm ready."

After Ed pulled into his parking garage, he insisted on walking me across Sheridan Road and riding up the elevator to my apartment door. There, he handed me the takeout bag.

"But it's yours. You could eat this while Marge is gone."

Laughing, he shook his head. "I don't do leftovers."

"OK. Thanks." Holding the greasy bag away from my coat, I unlocked my door. "Good-night."

"Wait." He held out the shopping bag. "Merry Christmas."

I didn't take it. "What is that?"

"A present."

"No. You spent too much money on me already."

Ed's eyes glinted with amusement. "Too late. I'm not driving all the way back to Chinatown to return it. At least open it and see if you like it."

I glanced at the door across the hall, not wanting Devin, the African American photographer who lived there, to look out his peephole and see me opening this so-called present. "Not out here. Come inside."

After putting the food in the refrigerator, I returned to Ed. Opening the bag, I pulled out a robe of peacock blue silk, embroidered with colorful birds on each breast.

"I can't accept this!"

"Why not? You didn't have much of a Christmas, did you?"

"That's beside the point. Don't you see how this looks?"

He took the robe and held it up, and his eyes swept me mockingly. "Like I want you to wear it for me, is that it?"

"I've told you. We can't be more than friends."

Ed flung the robe aside with a whiplike snap of his arm. "What have I done that friends don't do? Have I ever touched you? Have I said I want to? You don't have to keep the damn robe if it's so compromising. Burn it for all I care."

He left before I could reply.

That night, I dreamed I wore the robe while making love to a dark-haired man whose face was hidden, pressed between my breasts. "Tell me your name," I begged and woke up.

I walked into the living room and knelt on the couch to stare out at the dark bulk of Ed's building. Thinking of Peter, I bit my fist. It was four in the morning. I couldn't call him. What could I say? "Come save me from a man who wants to sleep with me?" I'd sound like a lunatic.

Switching on a lamp, I gazed at the robe, draped over the desk chair. Despite Ed's denial, I knew he was after me. I wanted to run back to Zebulun, but I couldn't until I repaid Ed the security deposit. Peter had savings, carefully hoarded to give us a cushion, but I couldn't ask him for that money. If he found out how much I'd borrowed from Ed, he'd be furious.

Worse, he'll never see me as an adult. I have to figure this out on my own.

Monday morning, I found a white rose in a bud vase on my desk. Propped against the vase was a small envelope. The card read, "Sorry. I was out of line. Still friends?"

Nancy slammed a drawer. "A little early for Valentine's Day, isn't it?"

Ignoring her, I tucked the card in my wallet and carried my mug to the break room. Half a dozen people were there, drinking coffee and gossiping in the last few minutes before eight-thirty. Ed sat reading *Crain's Chicago Business.* When I passed, he followed me to the coffee machine. "Well?" he asked in an undertone. "Am I forgiven?"

"I guess." We moved aside when one of the secretaries came for coffee. The pot clinked against the burner. I whispered, "You respect my position?"

"Sure." Ed switched on the high-beam smile he used on customers. "I admire your loyalty to Peter."

He refilled his coffee, then sidled closer to me as he reached for the nondairy creamer. "Give me another chance. Have dinner with me again."

"No."

"You said I was forgiven. I promise to behave."

Our coworkers drifted from the room. "I can't go out with you," I whispered.

"Then you don't trust me. Or maybe you don't trust yourself."

"That's not true."

Ed smirked. "Then why do you keep reading things into the relationship?"

When I tried to step around him, he blocked me. "Be honest. You're afraid of your feelings for me."

"No!" My cheeks flushed hot.

"Then have dinner with me Friday. Let me prove there's nothing to fear."

"I'm not afraid."

"Good. The only danger in our friendship is what you bring to it yourself."

He'd trapped me as neatly as an army that threatened two vital targets, only one of which could be defended. If I allowed him to believe I was attracted to him, he'd never relent. Yet, if I agreed to go out, that would give him the victory too. "I'll come, but only if I pay for myself."

Ed flashed his salesman's grin again. "Anything you say."

We went to a *tapas* bar. Entering the restaurant with its Moorish arches, glazed tiles, wrought iron grillwork, and trickling fountains, I felt that I'd been transported to Spain. Once again, I let Ed order. When the waiter began to set out the eight selections, I asked Ed, "Are you trying to turn me into a hedonist?"

"I can think of worse fates. Here, try this." He passed me a dish of baked dates, wrapped in bacon and glazed with red pepper sauce.

When I bit into one, the flavors exploded in my mouth. "Wow!"

Ed grinned. "Have a little of everything. That's what *tapas* are for."

As I spooned garlic potato salad onto my plate, I asked, "How's the big deal you were telling me about?"

"Not sure. I'm mailing another proposal Monday. And I'm trying to talk Cody Drake, the buyer, into coming up to see our operation, maybe in January. I have a feeling 1986 will be my lucky year."

Ed divided a chicken brochette between us as I sipped my sherry. It was cold and crisp and reminded me of nuts.

Setting the empty skewer aside, Ed stared at me. "Let's stop beating around the bush. You can trust me. I won't do anything to hurt your marriage."

"Oh?" Looking down, I fingered the faceted stem of my glass.

"You must have figured out that my own marriage isn't very happy. Marge is an alcoholic, but I didn't know that at first. We met when I was getting my MBA, and we were careless. She got pregnant, so I agreed to marry her. Right before the wedding, she smashed her car and miscarried. She begged me not to back out, and...well, I let myself be bought by Daddy's money." Self-loathing flitted across his face.

Surprised, I pushed my plate away. "Why are you telling me this?"

"Maybe to convince you to save your own marriage—if it's a good one."

If it's a good one. I saw it then. Every time he encouraged me to work at my relationship, he also planted a seed of doubt. "Stop playing games. You don't care about Peter and me."

He jerked up straight. "Dammit! Why are you so suspicious? Here I tell you something I've never told anyone and..." His face hardened. He pulled out his wallet and flung a twenty-dollar bill at me. "Take a cab home."

"Ed—"

"I mean it. Get the hell out of here."

Stung, I picked up my purse and walked away.

After pacing for half the night, berating myself first for going out with Ed and then for accusing him without evidence, I slept late Saturday—a heavy dreamless sleep that pinned me to the bed.

When I finally woke, I opened the folding doors of the closet, pulled off my nightgown, and put on the Chinese robe. The silk flowed over my skin like bath oil. In the full-length mirror on the bathroom door, the blue fabric clung to my breasts and hips, revealing every curve. I felt like a whore.

After dressing in jeans and a shirt, I went to the kitchen and glanced at the calendar. My mother's sister Cori, who lived four miles north in Evanston, was coming to visit that afternoon. *Damn. Why does it have to be today?*

Cori pushed the sleeves of her bulky Aran sweater up to her elbows and then twisted up her hair, securing it with a toothed hair clip. Marietta had asked her to visit Katie and see how she was really doing. Glancing from the wine jug lamps to the nude on the wall, Cori said dryly, "Interesting place."

Katie shifted her position on the desk chair, which she had pulled out to face the couch where her aunt sat. "The furnishings belong to the man I'm subleasing from. I'm stuck with them."

Cori shrugged. "It's a bit like a seedy motel, but it should do temporarily."

Katie's expression hardened. Sipping her mint tea, Cori cautioned herself, *Tread lightly.* She didn't know her niece very well. For the first twelve years of Cori's life, Marietta had practically raised her, and then when Marietta's attention shifted to her own child, it felt like rejection. Cori left home at eighteen, spent time in the Haight-Ashbury district of San Francisco, married and divorced while in California, and then in her thirties, returned to the Midwest and joined a religious commune that emphasized pacifism, social justice, and simple living. Consequently, she had never been part of Katie's life.

"I think everyone should spend time living on their own," she said, extending the sentiment as an olive branch.

Katie's shoulders lowered from their hunched position. "Aunt Cori, can I trust you?"

"I'd like to think so."

Her niece looked skeptical. "If I tell you something, will you promise not to tell my mother?"

Cori leaned forward, her elbows on her knees. "That depends. As long as it isn't a secret that will hurt either of you. At any rate, I'd ask you to tell her first."

Katie scrunched her nose. "I guess that's fair. There's a man I thought was a friend, but now he's after me to...have sex, but he won't admit it. And I can't convince him to stop."

"Men like that don't listen. Just break off contact."

"I can't. I work with him." She lowered her eyes. "And I owe him a thousand dollars."

Stunned, Cori let out a low whistle. "Does Peter know?"

Katie shook her head, still avoiding Cori's gaze.

"I think you should tell him."

"I can't. He'll get so mad that he might divorce me."

Cori set her mug down. "Let me get this straight. You're the one who left, yet you're afraid *he'll* ask for a divorce? If that's how you feel, why not go back?"

"I can't. I still haven't done what I came up here for."

Cori sighed. "You're just like your mother. When your dad first proposed, she said no because he wouldn't go to church. So Joe left town."

Katie's head jerked up. "That's why he went on the road."

"That's why. Marietta had this stubborn idea about how things had to be, and she made herself miserable because of it. Now you're doing the same thing."

"It's not the same at all."

"Sure, it is. If you'd talk to Peter and explain..." Reminding herself to dial down the pressure, Cori paused and stretched one arm along the back of the couch. "You know, it's usually simpler to be honest than to expend a lot of emotional energy hiding things."

Katie jumped up from her seat. "I'm getting more tea."

Cori followed her into the kitchen, where Katie refilled their mugs. "Have you talked to my mother lately?"

"Last week. Why?"

"I suppose she told you about this man she's seeing."

"Yes, he sounds nice." Cori stirred half a spoonful of sugar into her tea.

"They've only known each other two months."

"I don't think that matters much at their age."

"That's the whole point. She's too old for romance."

Cori's patience frayed. Putting a hand on her hip, she said, "You're acting like a child. I know most teenagers can't accept their parents' love life, but you should be past that by now."

"Love life?" Katie flung her mug into the sink. "My mother? She thinks sex is the unforgivable sin."

Cori wanted to retort but compressed her lips. She placed her mug in the sink and noticed that the handle had broken off Katie's. Folding her arms across her chest, Cori faced her niece. "You may not know this, but Marietta was far more of a mother to me than Brigitte ever was, and I won't stand here and let you put her down."

"Then go," Katie said and turned to stare out the back window until Cori complied.

Carefully inching his car past the high mounds of snow piled beside the parking lot entrance, Peter turned onto the street. The muscles along his shoulders felt as taut as bowstrings. It had been a long, tense day: three classes, an interminable committee meeting, and a conversation in which French asked, "How is Katie? Someone told me that she's stopped attending church."

Peter lied: "She's in Florida. Her paternal grandfather's ill."

At the end of the day, Peter drove to Sears to order a stationary bicycle. Recently, his doctor had diagnosed him with irritable bowel syndrome. Dr. Kapoor urged him to exercise to relieve stress and to change his eating habits. "Reduce caffeine and fat. Avoid heavy meals; several small ones are better. Drink lots of water, and make sure to get plenty of fiber."

Now the back seat of Peter's car held grocery bags containing bran cereal, frozen vegetables, tuna packed in spring water, and skinless chicken breasts. He still had to cook dinner. At the rate he was going, he wouldn't eat until nine.

Pulling away from a stoplight, he saw a Pizza Hut sign two blocks ahead. His stomach growled as he imagined the taste of pepperoni. According to the diet book he was using, pizza had sixteen grams of fat a slice. Peter tried to calculate how much fat he'd eaten so far that day, but his mind refused to tally the numbers.

Then he remembered the embarrassing incident at McDonald's. *If you want to indulge in fat, do it at home,* he told himself.

As he drove past Pizza Hut, his spirits lifted. *I can do this. I can take control of my life whether Katie comes home or not.*

A week later, Dr. French asked Peter to come by his office.

Worried that the old man had learned of his separation from Katie, Peter crossed the hall in a haze of fear. He glanced into Maggie's office to see if she were watching him with the vulture eye of a gossip, but she didn't look up.

French stood behind his desk facing the door with his hands behind his back. "I'm glad you have a free hour so we can confer. Have a seat."

Sinking into an oxblood leather chair, Peter noticed a thick manila folder that looked suspiciously like his personnel file on the gleaming desk. French sat and picked up a pen. "I thought I might be of assistance to you in your job search. Have you begun the process?"

Relieved, Peter said, "I've updated my *curriculum vitae* and sent out letters inquiring about available positions."

French opened Peter's file. "I've reviewed your strengths and weaknesses. We'll overlook for the moment your poor judgment in involving yourself with a student. At least, the affair terminated honorably."

"It wasn't an affair."

French droned on. "Let us presume that such a lapse of discretion will not happen again. However, you have other shortcomings that give me pause. Your procrastination and inability to achieve publication are liabilities to an academic career. I can't in good conscience give you a reference to teach at another college."

Peter's heart raced at a frightening pace. The sound of typing next door seemed to mock his distress. Breathlessly, he said, "You can't seriously imagine I was going to ask for one."

"My boy, a word from me could do you a great deal of good. And I would recommend you under the right circumstances."

Peter gaped at him.

French smiled. "You must know I have never questioned your teaching ability. You are a master at engaging student interest, so I am proposing that you seek a situation in which that is the prime qualification. I think you may be suited for the field of secondary education."

"High school? You think I should teach high school?" Peter's voice rose so sharply that the clacking of typewriter keys ceased.

"Don't take offense. I am convinced that you would thrive in an environment that does not have the peculiar pressures of academia."

Peculiar is right. Peter tightened the knot of his tie as he pictured Katie's scorn if he took a high school job. "I'm not certified."

"Private schools are often more lenient about requirements. I have a friend who's headmaster at such a school. He called me this morning to ask if we had any graduating seniors looking for positions to teach history. Instead, I told him about you."

"Without consulting me?"

French spread his hands wide. "I too was concerned about certification. He said he's hired former professors before. In such cases, the person usually works with the local university to gain his certification during summer sessions."

Peter wanted to storm out but instead asked, "What kind of school is it?"

"A respected academy in Wisconsin for motivationally challenged boys."

A boy's school. Figures. He said, "I don't think I'd be interested."

French pushed an index card with a name and phone number across his desk. "Since I already paved the way, you should inquire. What harm can it do to explore this avenue?"

Peter picked up the card and thought, *It could cost me my wife.*

Sunday afternoon, Marietta sat in Katie's living room, listening to her daughter move around the kitchen as she made coffee. Staring at the abstract nude, Marietta decided the apartment was even tackier than Cori described. However, she wasn't there to criticize. She had come hoping to persuade Katie to give Ernesto a chance; she'd even brought a homemade cinnamon apple coffeecake as a peace offering.

Katie called, "You want your coffee in the living room or here?"

"The kitchen's fine." Marietta entered and sat at the table. Picking up the sharp knife Katie had set out, she cut a big piece of coffeecake for herself. "How's your job?"

"Fine. I'm thinking about going for an MBA."

"Oh? What does Peter think?"

Katie slapped two mugs on the table. They were mismatched, and one of them had a broken handle that had been glued on crookedly. "Mom, you said on the phone that you weren't going to nag."

"I just asked a question."

Katie folded her arms. "I haven't told Peter. I want to make up my own mind."

Marietta swallowed the last bite of coffeecake. "Want some?"

"No, thanks."

"I think I might have another teensy sliver." As Marietta cut the piece, she asked, "Did you remember that your grandfather's eightieth birthday is this month?"

Katie shook her head.

"We're having a party at Deutsch Manor on Saturday the thirty-first." Marietta licked brown sugar from her fingers. "I'm bringing Dr. Montoya to meet the family."

"God, you're really serious, aren't you?" Turning away, Katie poured out her coffee and washed her mug.

"I especially want you to meet him."

"No." Without asking if Marietta was finished, Katie snatched her mug.

"You're not giving him a chance."

"No, and I'm not coming to your stupid party either."

Marietta snapped, "You're acting like a twelve-year-old."

Katie shrugged. "That's what you expect from me, isn't it? Here. Let me wrap that up before you go."

She pulled a roll of aluminum foil from a drawer, measured out a piece, placed it on the cake pan, and tightly crimped the edges. Handing the pan to her mother, she said, "Tell Grandpa happy birthday."

Jogging along Sheridan Road at 6:30 in the morning, I kept my eyes focused on the sidewalk. Although most of the pavement was clear of snow, I sometimes came upon patches of black ice without warning.

Half a block from my apartment, I slowed to pick my way over a slick area. Safely across, I raised my head and saw Ed at the bus stop down the street, reading a newspaper as the wind ruffled his chestnut hair.

I stopped and wondered what would happen if I were to walk up and tease him about going hatless in this frigid weather. He'd probably stare right through me as he had repeatedly in the two weeks since our argument.

A familiar drone heralded a green-and-white 147 express bus coming toward the stop. As the brakes hissed, I ducked into my building.

Driving home from the grocery store, I pressed down on the brake pedal and heard grinding. After letting the car roll a few feet, I braked again and heard the same sound. Once I was in my apartment, I called Peter and described the problem.

"Sounds like the brake lining's worn down."

I stretched the phone cord to reach the desk and grabbed a pen. "What's a brake lining?"

Peter made a strangled sound. "Didn't you take Driver's Ed? It's the cushion that keeps the brake shoe from hitting the drum."

I still wasn't sure what he meant but didn't ask him to explain. He obviously wasn't in a teaching mood. "Who should I take it to? Don't some garages cheat women?"

"Ask around. Or take your chances. You're so big on independence lately."

Wincing, I bit the plastic pen cap. "Sorry I bothered you."

"It's not the bother I mind. It's that you don't call until there's trouble."

"I called you the day after Christmas."

"Three weeks ago!"

"You could have called."

Peter sighed. "Let's not do this, OK? Call me next week and let me know if you got it fixed. Right now, I've got to go."

I paced as I waited for Lem, the mechanic my aunt had recommended, to come talk to me about my car. Cori lived in the same house as this guy—along with five other people who belonged to Cori's church, which required its members to turn over their incomes and live on an allowance only slightly above the federal poverty level.

The garage had three lifts holding up cars and a back wall lined with shop vacs, tubs of sweeping compound, tool carts, and various pieces of equipment I didn't recognize. The building reeked of oil. After showing a girl mechanic how to do something, Lem walked toward me. He was a short, thin man with hollow cheeks, solemn eyes, and unruly brown curls. With a nod, he led me into his office and gestured toward a seat. His desk was littered with boxes of parts, work tickets, a Honda manual, and an open bag of Fritos. The mix of clutter and junk food reminded me of Peter. After sitting, Lem gazed at an estimate form and spoke deliberately, "I'd say...this job...will run about $275."

I gasped. "I can't afford that right now. As soon as I have the money, I'll bring the car back. Is that OK?"

Nodding, he ate some corn chips. Another silence followed, in which Lem turned the Frito bag toward me. I shook my head. "How much should I pay you for the estimate?"

He wiped each finger on a rag. "No charge. Seeing as you're Cori's family."

I perched on the edge of my seat. "I promise I won't have anyone else do the work."

Lem rewarded me with the flicker of a smile before leading me to the car.

Sunday when the sneezing and sore throat started, I went running to sweat out the virus. Monday, even though I woke up with a head that felt like a pumpkin, I took the bus to work. At noon, the office manager sent me home.

Feeling like a kid suspended from school, I got off the bus, wrapped my scarf twice around my throat, and walked the five blocks to the grocery store. I had forgotten to ask Lem if it was safe to drive the car short distances.

I bought juice, soup, and cold medicine. Then I started home. As I passed the deli near the El station, an empty potato chip bag whipped by my legs and skidded around a car, still buried under last week's snow. Abandoned probably. I'd heard that the police never towed unless you called and said the trunk smelled like a dead body, although that may have been an urban legend.

At the apartment, I put the food away and fell into bed. I needed to drink liquids, but my limbs felt so heavy. Before I could make myself get up again, I fell asleep.

The next day, breathing through my nose was impossible. After calling in sick, I shuffled around the kitchen making tea and toast.

Carrying my breakfast on a tray, I settled on the couch and turned on the TV to a space shuttle launch. The countdown had already entered its final ten seconds. Rising from a bank of smoke like a primeval god, the *Challenger* lifted off. A minute later, a colossal orange-pink ball erupted on the sky like an inflamed blister, swelled, and quickly disappeared. Only an oddly skewed Y of white smoke lingered against the blue.

Shocked, I watched for several minutes as the announcers tried to make sense of the fact that seven people had just been obliterated. As the camera zoomed in on stunned and sobbing spectators, I rose, walked to the kitchen, and called Peter's office. After eight rings, the department secretary picked up the phone.

"Maggie, this is Katie Taylor. Is Peter around?"

"He's in chapel," Maggie said. "Did you forget?"

"Oh, right."

"Bet it's the time difference that got you. How are things in Florida?"

Hearing the murmur of the television, I said, "It's awful. Everyone's so upset."

"Oh, honey. Did your grandfather die?"

"My grandfather? No, haven't you heard? The space shuttle blew up."

"The one that schoolteacher was on?"

"Yes."

Maggie fell uncharacteristically silent. After a moment, she said, "No sense running up your grandma's long-distance bill. I'll tell Dr. Taylor you called."

Hanging up, I shook my head over Maggie's repeated references to my grandparents. Then I returned to the coverage of the disaster.

The next day, even though my symptoms were the same, I dressed for work. When I left my building, Ed stood at the bus stop. Walking up to him, I tried to keep my voice light as I said, "You're running late today."

He glanced at me over his copy of the *Sun Times.* A picture of the disaster loomed on the front page. "Am I?" He went back to reading.

Hurt by the rebuff, I moved away. A sudden coughing spasm wracked me.

"That doesn't sound good." Ed folded his paper and tucked it under his arm. "Shouldn't you be in bed?"

I shrugged. "I got bored."

He gave me a look that said he knew all about me, knew my loneliness and even my doubts about the way I'd treated him. When the bus came, we boarded and sat together. "You know," he said, "you need to take life easier."

The next day, when I walked into my office, Ed was sitting on my desk, glancing through a production report I'd received the day before. Neither Nancy nor Elena were in the room.

"I got a job for you," Ed told me. "A trial order for Janzenaire Industries, the big account I've been telling you about. I promised Cody Drake it'll get there Friday."

"Have you lost your mind? You know Dave has been insisting on a two-week lead time."

"He'll do this one fast. He knows how much this account is worth."

Ed reached behind him and picked up a die—a board embedded with sharp rule roughly in the shape of a parallelogram—and handed it to me. "I want you to oversee this personally. Make sure Dave slits the passes this morning and gets the punch press going this afternoon. Get it out two-day delivery tomorrow."

"OK." Moving around him, I set the die on my chair and leaned down to jot his instructions on a notepad I kept by the phone.

"I want you in my office with shipping info the moment this leaves the dock." He put his hand on my wrist. "A lot's riding on this. Don't let me down."

"I'll take care of it."

"That's my girl. You get this right, and I'll buy you lunch."

I faced him. In my chest, I felt heat that could have been anger or something more dangerous. I was tired of this game. Whatever was going to happen with Ed, I had to meet it head-on. "All right. It's a deal."

On Valentine's Day, a Friday, Cody Drake visited Better Gaskets. He and Ed toured the plant, and then Ed brought him to the expediters' office. Cody was an astonishingly ugly man with a receding hairline, pock-marked skin, small eyes, and a purple mole on his upper lip. When Ed invited me to join them for dinner, I said yes only so it wouldn't seem like I was scorning the man because of his looks.

Cody downed four beers during the meal. The more he drank, the longer and more excruciatingly boring his stories about breeding coonhounds grew. I was glad when the check came so I could leave. Then Ed said, "I'm taking Cody to a nightclub to hear a group I think he'll like. If you come, I'll drive you home afterwards."

I looked from one man to the other and said, "If we don't stay out too late." Ed grinned.

The nightclub wasn't far from the restaurant, so we set off walking west along Belmont Avenue. Wind gusted around a building. "Damn! It's colder up here than a witch's tit." Cody draped a heavy arm on my neck. "Come on down to Houston, sweetheart. I'll show you what a climate s'posed to be like."

"No, thanks." I ducked out from under his arm. "I like seasons."

"Hell, we have seasons. We just don't make an endurance test out of them."

Ed laughed. "Don't tell her that. Katie likes endurance tests."

Stung that he'd mock me, I scanned the street for a taxi.

"Here we are." Ed halted by a doorway that opened onto dark stairs. A sign proclaimed "The Dissident" in spidery black letters. Sprawled on the lower steps, a person of indeterminate gender, with baggy clothes and spiked green hair, collected the cover charge.

The club, which occupied the second floor, was a series of connected rooms. Ed led us to the room farthest from the entrance. The ceiling, floor, walls, painted-over windows, and small stage were all black. The only relief was a portable movie screen at the back of the stage.

A chicken-wire cage held the sound and light boards, operated by a young man with headphones over his red Mohawk. Clumps of people, most in their early twenties, stood around drinking. The air was fuzzy with smoke.

Under orange lights, a band—dressed in the obligatory black—was singing in a monotone, "Meltdown, meltdown, meltdown. Nuclear meltdown, meltdown, meltdown." On the movie screen, a film clip of a mushroom cloud dissolved into the Wicked Witch of the West shriveling and wailing, "I'm melting, melting..."

"Come on." Ed grabbed my hand. "Let's find a seat."

He backtracked to a cavernous room, illuminated by dim track lighting and furnished with worn sofas, most occupied by necking couples. The music was piped in. Near one wall was a raised platform with a plywood counter, behind which stood several empty bar stools.

"Sit over there," Ed said. "I'll get drinks."

Up on the platform, I took off my coat and surveyed the room. Life-sized pinups of Elvis, Marilyn Monroe, and Ronald Reagan adorned the walls, alternating with giant photos of bombed-out cities, the death camp at Auschwitz, and Vietnamese children fleeing napalm. Across the way was a large painting of Pat Nixon dressed like a French maid serving milk and cookies to Kissinger and Brezhnev—with Darth Vader hovering behind.

"What a bunch a' Commies." Cody scratched his scalp and checked under his fingernails. Then he stroked my hair. "You're smart not to cut it short like some dyke. Know who you remind me of? My granddad had a picture of this gal named Lady Godiva. She was—"

"I know who she was."

"Then you know why I like her." Cody giggled.

Shuddering in disgust, I swept my hair back over my shoulder. Ed approached carrying two beers and a 7 Up. "This next band's the reason we came. They do rock with a country western influence."

I moved over so he could sit between me and Cody. As Ed took his place, Cody asked, "You get much hunting around here?"

"In Wisconsin, yeah."

Over loudspeakers, a singer was lamenting, "Think I'm going to change my life. Get a pickup and a brand new wife. And I'll drink tequila three times a night."

Carrying his beer bottle, Cody walked onto the floor and approached a girl with tangled red curls and heavy black eyeliner and, after a moment of chatting, whispered in her ear. The girl shoved him and walked away.

"Damn," Ed said. "I wish he'd score so we could get the hell out of here."

Cody ambled back toward us with a wide grin, stopped before the plywood counter, and bowed clumsily to me. "How 'bout you and me having a little two step?"

"I don't dance."

"Don't worry. I'll teach you."

"I didn't say I don't know how. I don't dance."

Ed leaned forward, interposing his body between us. "She's Baptist."

"Hooey, so's my mama." Cody came up on the platform and swung up on his stool like he was mounting a horse. "So when's the next round of drinks?"

"Coming right up."

After Ed left, Cody moved next to me. "I had Baptists before. Whyn't you come back to my room, and I'll give you a private dancing lesson."

I stared at him in revulsion.

"Why not?" He squeezed my thigh. "I know you'd like it."

I dug my nails into his hand until he jerked it away. After sucking the scratch, Cody shoved his face next to mine. "Bitch, why you think you're here?"

Jumping down, I ran across the room and ducked into the woman's bathroom, where the first thing I saw was a condom dispenser.

"Shit!" I locked myself in a stall and stared at the graffiti scrawled on the inside of the door: "A hard man is good to find" and "Guitarists touch all the right chords." Sex might be just another entertainment choice to the people who frequented this club, but I had no desire to be on the program. After double checking the cash in my wallet, I left the bathroom to call a cab.

Ed was waiting outside the door. "Cody said you don't feel well."

I warded him off with an upraised hand. "I'm going home."

"I'll take you. Just let me tell Cody."

"I wouldn't get in a car with you. Not after the way you set me up."

"What?" Ed grabbed me above the elbow. "Did he try something?"

"Like you don't know."

"Katie! Whatever he did was his own idea."

Although Ed seemed outraged, I'd seen his skill at acting too many times to be convinced. "Let me go."

"Not till I show you something." He dragged me back into the room and pointed to a couch where Cody sat with a spiky-haired blonde. "He's a stray dog, sniffing any piece of tail that passes. If I'd known, I wouldn't have invited you."

"Why should I believe you when you're no better than he is?"

Ed's grip tightened. "What are you saying? That you'd rather brave the streets and risk getting raped than endure my company?"

I winced and looked at the floor. It was cruel of Ed to use the one danger every woman feared to undermine my decision. Defeated, I shook my head.

Over my protests, Ed insisted on seeing me upstairs. We rode the elevator in silence. I waited until I'd unlocked my apartment to say over my shoulder, "I knew you slept around, but I never took you for a pimp."

Ed's hand shot out and shoved the door, causing me to stumble inside. He followed and slammed the door behind him. "We're going to settle this right now. I did not set you up."

"Bullshit. You'd sell your own wife to get Cody's account."

To my surprise, he laughed. "I probably would. But not you."

"Really? Why not?"

"Because." He backed me up against the wall, blocking me on both sides with his arms. "If I was going to set you up with anyone, it'd be with me."

"You said you weren't after me."

He pushed his face in close. "Baby, there's a world of difference between desire and execution. I only sleep with women who want it, and you haven't figured out you want me yet."

"I don't."

"You do. Only you've got all those Baptist preachers screaming in your head, telling you what a bad girl you'd be to give in."

Sweat trickled down my back. "That's called conscience."

"What's conscience got to do with it? I'm talking about what you want." Ed bent down and brushed my lips with his. I tried to push him away, but he pinned my wrists to the wall and kissed me with bruising force until I began to feel faint. Finally, he let go and touched my lips with his finger. "Scare you?"

Panting, I looked down and said nothing.

"See. If you didn't want me, you wouldn't be scared. Disgusted, maybe mad, like with Cody, but not scared. You're afraid of giving in."

I pushed him again, but he was too strong. "Ed, I can't do this."

"Can't? Now that's an interesting word. You mean *won't."*

"All right, yes. Now will you go?"

"Not yet. We're finally getting ready to talk about what Katie wants."

"I want you to leave me alone."

"I don't think so. Let's experiment." He cupped a hand under my chin. "Kiss me once without fighting. You don't have to want it. Just let it happen."

Fear flapped in my stomach like a trapped bird. "I already know I don't want an affair."

"Affair. Another useless word. This isn't about your marriage."

This kiss was entirely different. Ed turned it into an intricate dance, a choreography of lips and tongue, of teasing feints and satisfying pressure. Instead of resisting, I arched my back so that my pelvis swayed toward him. When Ed's hand found my breast, I jerked back and pressed myself against the wall.

Ed smiled. "That wasn't so bad, was it? I'll leave you alone now."

"You will?" My voice came out hoarse.

"I found out what I need to know." Leaning down, he whispered in my ear. "Forget your conscience, baby. I'm offering what you want."

I don't want you, I told myself. But I did want to enjoy sex at least once in my life. I wanted it so badly that I could feel Ed's hand upon my body in places he hadn't even touched.

Ed grinned back at me from the door. "Think about it." Then he left.

I walked on trembling legs to the couch and sat down. Memories of making out with Ritchie flooded me until I felt so inflamed that I resorted to masturbation to get relief. Why did I never feel this way with Peter? Was it possible that Ed really was the answer I'd been looking for? If I learned to experience pleasure with him, mightn't that be good for my marriage?

"Get thee behind me, Satan," I whispered.

Most of Monday, Ed was on a sales trip to Wisconsin, but at five, he was waiting in the lobby of our office, holding a briefcase and a medium-sized paper bag, blocking my way like some mythic nemesis I must face again and again until I made the decision fate had decreed for me. Still, I tried to deflect the inevitable. "How was Milwaukee?"

"Fine. I had bratwurst for lunch. Want a ride?"

Not a muscle moved in his chiseled face, and yet his expression dared me. After fifteen seconds, he added, "No sales pitch this time. Just say yes or no."

Closing my eyes, I whispered, "Yes."

As we walked down my hall, we passed my neighbor Devin, with whom I sometimes exchanged small talk. He was a trim African American with short hair, a neat mustache, and a tiny diamond stud in one earlobe. He was wearing grey slacks and a forest green sweater.

"Hi, Devin."

"Hi." He flicked his eyes toward Ed and kept on walking.

I stopped to stare after him, certain he had guessed our plans. As soon as we were inside the apartment, Ed said, "Why do you care what the neighbors think? I bet he has girlfriends up here all the time."

"Not that I've seen."

Ed's eyes narrowed. "Must be fruity."

"What?"

"Never mind, my innocent beauty. Come see what I have." Taking my hand, he pulled me into the kitchen. He'd brought the paper bag upstairs, and now he set it on the table and produced a bottle of champagne. "Bet you never had this."

"Once." The memory of my honeymoon came back to me with sad irony. Back then, I'd felt immoral for merely drinking.

While Ed found glasses, I hung our coats in the closet. Returning to the kitchen, I picked up the bag to throw it away and discovered it wasn't empty. I pulled out a box of condoms. "What if I'd said no?"

He worked the cork out of the champagne. "I'd use them later."

The reminder that I was one of many conquests rankled. I dropped the box on the table. "We don't need them. I'm on the pill."

"Doesn't matter. I learned the hard way to play it safe." He handed me a half-filled tumbler, then held up his own glass. "To new experiences."

I stared at the pale gold, fizzy liquid. "I don't think I can do this."

"At least drink the champagne. Otherwise, it'll go flat."

My first sip reminded me of how surprised I'd been on our honeymoon to learn that champagne isn't sweet.

Ed led me into the living room, where we sat on the couch. My nerves tensed at his nearness, and to calm myself, I downed my champagne.

He refilled my glass. "Why don't you tell me what you're afraid of?"

"I'm not afraid. I think it's a mistake."

"So you find out afterward it's a mistake. You don't do it again."

"Ed, we're not talking about some new dance step."

"Yes, we are. That's all it is." He raised his glass in salute. "You think sex is some big holy commitment, but it's not. It's just something you do to feel good."

All the arguments I might have used to answer him floated in my brain and burst in tingling explosions like champagne bubbles. "I should be with Peter," I finally said.

"So why aren't you? It's because he doesn't do it for you, does he?"

I hung my head, too ashamed to look at him.

"Forget about Peter. Forget about me. What do you want?"

Ed's voice was so low and caressing that I felt a renewed strumming in the deep places of my body. I met his eyes.

After a moment, we kissed. I leaned back against the couch as Ed slowly ran his hand up my arm and touched the hollow of my throat. Focusing inward, I realized I hadn't felt such taut expectation in years. As Ed unbuttoned my blouse, I held my breath.

Standing, he pulled me up and kissed me again. Then he removed my blouse and let it fall. I flushed as I imagined having him inside me, pushing against the dam of pent-up emotion until it exploded.

He led me to the bedroom, unfastened my bra, and lifted my breasts in his hands. Closing my eyes, I breathed softly so I could concentrate on each new sensation. My body yearned to strain toward him, but I held still, afraid of doing something stupid.

Abruptly, he pulled away. "Dammit, are you in this or not? It's normal for two people to participate. You make me feel like a fucking rapist."

Rape. He spoke about it so easily. I folded my arms across my breasts and leaned back against the wall. "What do you want me to do?"

"Whatever the hell you feel like. Are you this stiff with Peter?"

I lowered my head until my hair hid my face. "I knew this was a mistake."

Ed sighed. "Jesus Christ, loosen up. Can't you think of a way to show you're interested?"

Interested? What had been a river of molten desire in me had congealed to the hardness of granite. "I guess I could take off your shirt."

"Then do it."

His commanding tone killed my last spark of spontaneity—and made it impossible to argue. Biting my lip, I pulled off his tie and undid his buttons. Ed took off his shirt. His chest and abdomen muscles were as defined as I'd suspected, but the sight did nothing to reignite my arousal. I stood rigidly as he removed my skirt and slid the pantyhose and panties down to my ankles. I stepped out of them. Rising, Ed said, "Well?"

Shivering, I unbuckled his belt and unzipped his trousers. As he stripped, I averted my eyes from his erection. Lowering me to the bed, he knelt beside me and placed my hand on his penis. "Go on."

As I stroked him, I clenched my teeth. Ritchie had made me do this. I gazed at the cracked ceiling, my mind far from Ed as I remembered the crushing force of Ritchie's weight on me.

Ed put on a condom and then pushed inside me. "God, you're tight. Relax." Pumping slowly, he went deeper each time until I felt skewered. "Come on!"

Somehow, I guessed what he wanted. "Yes," I moaned, but the word was an explosion of agony. "Yes. Yes."

In response, he began moving faster. *God,* I thought as Ed released and then grew still. *I sold my soul for this.*

After the sex was over, Ed brought me the last glass of champagne and sat next to me while I drank it. "You've never had an orgasm, have you?"

I shrugged. "I don't know." I placed pillows against the brass bars of the headboard and leaned back, not bothering to cover myself. What was left to hide?

Ed stroked my thigh. "Poor bitch. The Baptists really did a number on you."

"It's not them," I said, thinking of Ritchie.

"Of course, it is. You're like a long-term prisoner who gets pardoned. You're afraid to walk outside. Freedom's in your grasp, but it terrifies you."

Closing my eyes, I tried to picture myself in a place without walls, able to go in any direction I wanted. *Impossible.*

Ed gave me a lingering kiss, gentle and coaxing, and I felt a tiny spark of excitement.

"See, there's nothing wrong with you. Your only problem is all those voices in your head: mothers and preachers and Sunday school teachers."

I shivered. "You make it sound like I'm crazy."

"Not crazy, baby. Confused. But I can help you." He slid one hand between my legs.

I didn't protest when Ed began to stimulate me manually. As my sexual desire came back to life, I slid onto my back and waited for him to enter me a second time. Instead, he patted my hip. "I knew you really wanted it."

"Aren't you going to—"

He laughed and began to dress. "Greedy girl. I have to go. Marge is waiting supper for me. But I'll be back tomorrow night."

I sat up. "Then why did you..."

The amusement never left his face. "Anticipation is good for you."

After he was gone, I cursed myself for letting Ed manipulate me into agreeing to see him again. Rising, I slipped on a shirt and walked to the kitchen, where I picked up the champagne cork. "You might as well shove this inside you for all the good your resolutions do."

I dug a thumbnail into the cork, but its tough cellular structure didn't yield. Digging deeper, I gouged out a small chunk, then another. Fine brown flecks drifted to the table. I clawed the cork until my nails were broken.

Again, I heard Ed's voice: "They really did a number on you." Tears welled in my eyes as I thought of Peter. Poor man. For two years, I had blamed him for our frustrations in the bedroom when my own damage had blocked us.

I crossed to the phone and dialed Peter's number. When I heard his familiar voice, a sharp pain squeezed my chest. Without speaking, I hung up.

After waking in the night, I went to the front window to stare at Ed's building. In the two weeks since I first slept with him, we had been together nearly every evening. Each day I resolved to end the relationship, yet somehow, he always convinced me that the problem wasn't the affair. The problem was inside me.

He gave me articles saying that women should take responsibility for their own orgasms. Our first Saturday together, he showed me pornographic videos to demonstrate how I should perform. The images burned into my mind so that every time we had sex, I compared myself to what I'd seen and felt defeated by my own inadequacy.

Ed demanded I try new positions. Some felt degrading, but I didn't complain for fear he'd suggest something worse. Often, he insisted that I strip and dance naked for him. When I told him I felt awkward, he said, "Then do it till the shame is gone."

Instead of easing, my humiliation intensified. Being with Ed was like exploring an uncharted cavern. The paths and dimensions, even the existence of a floor ahead, were uncertain. I crept forward into an inky void—relying on groping toes, outstretched arms, straining ears, and prickling skin to detect lurking hazards. If I moved too cautiously, Ed pushed me. I stumbled, fell, sometimes hurtled into cold, utterly dark passages of the human soul inhabited by unrecognizable emotions, monsters evolved in a world without sun.

Finally, I understood why both Carla and Nancy hated Ed so much.

"Can't we slow down?" I begged. "Let me get comfortable with what we're doing before we try something new."

"It doesn't work that way. You've got to be willing to do anything."

"But I'm not."

He smiled. "Don't worry. By the time I'm done, you will be."

This isn't working, I'd think when I was alone. *Ed doesn't care about me, but if I say that it's over, he'll twist my words to make me doubt my-*

self. He might even tell Peter, and then I won't have a marriage to go back to. I have to figure out how to make Ed lose interest.

As I showered Sunday morning, I devised a survival plan. I would pretend to be what Ed wanted. I'd cultivate a sexy appearance, take initiative, feign pleasure. With luck, once Ed lost the challenge of corrupting me, he'd grow bored and move on. He was going to bring Chinese takeout that day, so I decided to wear the Chinese robe with nothing beneath it.

Just before two, I surveyed the living room. Two candles burned on the coffee table, and a chilled bottle of Chardonnay stood beside them. I knelt on the couch, gazed at Ed's building, and wondered how long before he walked in.

When the doorbell rang, I turned in surprise. *Play it light,* I told myself. Pressing the intercom button, I said, "Forget your keys?"

The speaker crackled. "Katie? This is your mother."

For one panicky instant, I considered disguising my voice and saying she had the wrong apartment. Instead, I said, "Mom. Come up!"

Scurrying around the room, I blew out the candles and put the wine in the refrigerator. I raced to the bedroom, snatched up the box of condoms, and hid it in the medicine cabinet.

Back in my bedroom, I opened the closet and grabbed a pair of jeans but was paralyzed by the next decision: sweater? sweatshirt? blouse? A knock sounded at the door.

Dropping the jeans, I hurried to the hall. As I passed the full-length mirror on the bathroom door, I saw that my robe was agape. I retied the belt and smoothed back my hair before opening the front door. "Hi."

My mother looked me up and down. "Am I interrupting something?"

"Sort of. A coworker is coming by to work on reports, and as you see, I'm not dressed."

"Oh," Pulling off her gloves, Mother said, "Is that a new robe?"

"Yes. Look, I have to change. Hang your coat in the closet."

Retreating to the bedroom, I left the door ajar so I'd hear if Ed walked in. Maybe he was running late. If I could call him before he left,...but the phone was in the kitchen, and here I was in the bedroom, trying to button a shirt with fingers that felt like sausages. Finally dressed, I grabbed a rubber band and braided my hair as I returned to my mother.

"Why does a coworker have keys to your apartment?"

So she *had* heard what I said over the intercom. "I loaned them to him. He went to get lunch, and I thought it would be easier."

"You mean, he was here earlier, and you were dressed like that?"

"No! I took a shower while he was out."

The front door opened, and Ed called, "Hungry, baby?" He walked in but stopped short at the sight of the two of us.

I shot him a warning look. "Ed, you know my mother. She didn't realize we had to work today and just dropped in."

"Hello, Mrs. Thompson." He smirked at me. "Why doesn't she join us for lunch? I ordered too much as usual."

"No!" Mother's refusal was loud. "Your plans don't include me."

Ed set down the takeout bags. "But we were going to eat first. You won't be delaying our *work.*" He emphasized the last word as if to highlight its falsity.

My mother's mouth tensed. "I should go. May I use your bathroom first?"

"Of course."

As soon as the door closed, I turned on Ed. "Are you trying to spell it out for her?"

"Why not tell her? It'd be the best way to declare your independence from the Baptist mafia." Laughing, he undid the top two buttons of my shirt.

"Stop that!" I swatted at his hand.

He laughed again. Grabbing my braid, he pulled it to the front and tugged at the rubber band. "You know I don't like your hair like this."

"Ed, please."

He blew an air kiss. "You beg so pretty." He released my hair when the toilet flushed.

When my mother rejoined us, I said, "Is there something you wanted to tell me? We could go in the kitchen."

"No, I should leave." She looked at me bitterly, and I felt sure she had guessed the truth. *Screw you,* I thought in defiance. *Who I sleep with is my business.*

"Next time call." I walked her to the door. After she was gone, I crossed the room, unbuttoning my shirt. For once, I felt entirely in charge. "Forget lunch. Let's go to bed."

Ed grinned. "Sounds good."

Entering the bedroom, I said, "The condoms are in the medicine cabinet."

I was slipping off my jeans when Ed called, "I can't find them."

"Jeez, Ed." Dressed only in my underwear, I walked to the bathroom and pointed into the cabinet—at an empty space where I'd put the condoms half an hour before. Now there was only a rust spot in the chipped paint of the shelf. "I put them right there."

"Did you check the nightstand?"

"They're not there. I put them here so my mother— Oh, God!" Frantically, I searched the trash can for the missing red box. Not finding it, I sank onto the rim of the tub. "She took them."

"That's crazy. What would your mother want with condoms?"

"Evidence. She took them to use for evidence."

Peter pedaled steadily on his stationary bike as he reread his first chapter on Lavinia. From the beginning, he'd been intrigued by her similarity to Katie: her fragile psyche, her conservative upbringing, her devotion to her father. Peter had decided to open the book with Morton's refusal to let Lavinia return after her father's death and tell the rest in flashback.

The phone rang. Grabbing the towel draped over the handlebars, Peter wiped his face and hurried to the kitchen.

The caller was his brother, Joel. "Pete, I'm sorry. I can't go camping next month."

"Why not? Yolanda upset about being left alone?"

"No, it's work. Ever since the merger, the honchos have been threatening staff reductions. Everybody's pulling overtime to prove they're indispensable."

"Makes you really glad you went into business, doesn't it?"

"That's a low blow."

"Sorry." Peter filled a glass of water. "Are you really in danger?"

"Who knows? First, we heard they'll go by seniority. Then someone said they'll axe redundant positions. Shit, if I could live off rumors, I'd have it made."

"You're a sharp guy. You'll be OK."

"You think so?" Joel's voice rose. "Sometimes, I think they're deliberately creating a pressure cooker to see who'll melt."

Peter hadn't heard his brother this upset since his best friend beat him out for the last spot on the high school basketball team. "Think it through. What's the worst thing that could happen?"

"I could lose my job."

"So what would you do?" Peter asked and then drank down some water.

"Look for another one, what do you think? But jobs aren't so easy to find."

"And if you ran out of money?"

"Shit! Move home, I guess. What's your point?"

Relieved to hear anger replace the hopelessness, Peter said, "To prove you can cope. Nothing you mentioned is impossible, is it?"

Joel laughed. "It would be hell to live at Mom and Dad's again."

"So don't let that happen."

After rescheduling for May, they hung up. Peter stood, remembering their camping trips when Joel was in high school and he was in grad school. Late at night, beside the dying fire, Joel would talk about dreams that seemed to change every year: basketball player, rock star, disk jockey, forest ranger. Peter had enjoyed listening and posing questions Joel hadn't considered. The memory reminded him how much he liked being a mentor.

Draping the towel around his neck, Peter went to the back room and searched his desk for the headmaster's card French gave him. Teaching in a boys' school might not be so bad.

He was writing late Sunday afternoon when the doorbell rang. Frowning, Peter ignored it. He was picking apart a tangled knot of events in Lavinia's life and didn't want to be interrupted.

When the bell rang again, he tossed down his pen and went to the door. To his surprise, his mother-in-law stood there.

"Come in." As Marietta passed Peter, she gave him a narrow-eyed, pinched-mouth look he knew meant trouble. She unbuttoned her coat and perched on the edge of the couch.

Uneasy, Peter took the chair opposite, crossed his legs, and jiggled his foot in the air.

Without prelude, she said, "Katie is having an affair."

"What?" Peter slammed his foot on the floor and sat forward.

"I was just there. She came to the door dressed like a whore, and five minutes later, Ed Marsden walked in. He has his own key."

"I don't believe it."

Hugging her purse to her chest, Marietta said, "It's not the first time."

"What?"

"In high school, there was a delinquent I wouldn't let her date. She met him secretly for over a year and then ran away with him. He dumped her."

"In Kentucky," Peter said hoarsely.

Marietta's head jerked up. "How did you know?"

"Katie told me." Peter felt no guilt for stretching the truth.

"And I bet she said she only slept with him once. It's a lie."

"No, it's not," he said, his voice firm. "And she only did it because he beat her. Marietta, your daughter was raped."

She shook her head. "Claiming rape is the oldest dodge in the book."

"With Katie, it happens to be true. You forget, I've lived with the resulting trauma."

Marietta crossed her arms. "Maybe so, but that doesn't change what's going on now."

"There could be a perfectly innocent explanation for what you saw."

She opened her purse and tossed a small red box on the table. "And for those?"

Squinting, Peter made out the words *latex condoms.* "Where did you—"

"In Katie's bathroom cabinet."

Peter fought down a wave of nausea. "They could have been left by the former tenant."

"There was a used foil wrapper in the waste can."

"What else did you do, hide under the bed? I don't want to hear this."

"You think I like saying it?" Marietta glared at him. "It kills me to have my only child turn out like this."

"She's not doing anything to you. If Katie is having an affair, it's between her and me."

"And God."

He stood swiftly. "With you as his self-appointed messenger? Maybe if you'd raised her with a little more love and a lot less judgment, she wouldn't be so messed up."

The color drained from Marietta's face. She hurried around the corner of the coffee table and, in doing so, stumbled. Peter reached out to steady her, but she twisted away and ran out of the house.

Stunned, Peter sank into his chair. Despite his denials, he knew that Katie would never behave as Marietta described unless she was sleeping with Ed. But why? She had once told Peter that Ed viewed women the way he viewed sales, as numbers to add to his tally. Why choose a man like that unless she'd slept with him before? Had she gone to Chicago to be with him?

Stop it! But like a tongue probing a sore cavity, his mind returned to the image of Katie, her hair down, her body arched in passion as her lover entered her. He rushed to the back room, climbed on his stationary bike, and pedaled as hard as he could. Tears ran down his face.

Riding the bus home Monday, I stared at Lake Michigan and fantasized about sailing across the choppy grey water to a new place. I had to escape this destructive affair. Maybe Peter would forgive me if I confessed and begged him to take me back. Admitting my guilt would be better than waiting for Mother to tell him. *I will call Peter. Tonight.*

As I entered my apartment, I heard music playing in the bedroom. Ed sat on the couch. "What are you doing here?"

"Waiting for you." He patted the cushion next to him. "We need to talk."

I took off my coat. "Doesn't it occur to you I might have plans?"

"What plans? You have no friends. Come here."

Crossing my arms, I said. "I want you to leave."

Ed narrowed his eyes. "I told you. We need to talk."

"I'm tired. Can't we do this some other time?"

Admitting weakness was a mistake. Ed smiled and threw his arm across the back of the couch. "This won't take long."

He said no more. It was clear that he expected me to give in. *Why not?* I thought. *Once I do what he wants, he'll leave and I can call Peter.*

Even so, dread made it hard to cross the room. I hesitated after each step, waiting for a miraculous intervention: a phone call, a doorbell, a fire alarm. In the window behind Ed, my face was a pale frightened mask etched on black glass.

When I sat down, he rubbed my neck. "You're so tense tonight. Your mother really upset you, didn't she? Scared she's going to tell Peter?" His fingers worked at a knot. "Maybe you should get it over with. Tell him yourself."

Stunned that he'd read my mind, I jerked away and faced him.

He smiled and began to unbutton my blouse. "That's what I'd do. Confession's a great way to seem more noble than you really are."

Rubbing my shoulders from the front, he said, "Except he'll never forgive you. No man can stand thinking his wife found a better lover."

The words stung like wasps. Of course, Peter would think that. My hope for reconciliation seeped away like air from an old balloon.

Ed's fingers, strong as tree roots, probed my muscles as if to take anchor there. "Stop. You're hurting me."

"It's not me." He pressed even harder. "It's the tension in your body. An orgasm would help, but you're such a frigid bitch. What a pair you are, you with your hang-ups and your pansy husband. It's a wonder you ever screwed at all."

A few renegade tears escaped. "It's not his fault. It's mine."

"At least you've learned that much." Ed tilted up my chin. "I'll tell you something else. Peter's too nice for you. And nice isn't what you're looking for, or you'd have never chosen me."

"I didn't choose you."

"The hell you didn't. No matter what you tell yourself, you walked into this on your own. Know why?" Taking several strands of my hair, he pulled them tight across my throat. "Because you want a man who'll hurt you."

I shrank away from him. "That's sick."

He let go of my hair. "Doesn't mean it isn't true. Religious women want to be forced so the man's the one to blame."

"Why do you always mention rape? I think you get off on frightening me."

He shook his head. "See how you twist everything? I'm not threatening you. I'm trying to help you understand your problem so you can conquer it."

His tone was reasonable, but the thought of sleeping with him made my gut spasm. *Too bad. Do whatever it takes to get him out of here.*

When I didn't argue further, Ed smiled. "I bought you a new outfit. It's on the bed. Change in the bathroom, then meet me in the bedroom."

I rose, fortifying myself with the promise that this was the last time. Laid out on the bed were a black lace push-up bra, a see-through blouse, spike heels, and a black leather miniskirt that zipped down the front from waist to hem. On the floor near the partially open folding door of the closet sat a large boombox playing rock music.

After I changed, I put on my reddest lipstick and walked out to the bedroom, where Ed stood looking out the window.

He pulled the blind down and turned to stare at me. Taking my hands, Ed led me to stand at the foot of the bed and whispered, "Pretend you're Linda Lovelace and put on a good show."

The reference to the porn star made me cringe and pull against his grip. Again, Ed whispered, "It's for your own good, remember?" He crushed my fingers until I nodded. Then he released me and leaned against the closed part of the closet door so he could watch.

Slowly, unfastening button by button, unzipping inch by agonizing inch, I removed my clothing, feeling awkward and ugly as I lifted my breasts, gyrated my pelvis, and turned to wiggle my ass at Ed. Whenever a new song started, I tried to lose myself in the music—but I couldn't escape the painful truth that I was betraying both Peter and myself.

Once I was naked, Ed pointed to the bed and mouthed the word *masturbate.*

I shook my head. The thought of demonstrating for Ed what to me had always been a private act of shame was unthinkable.

His face hardened. Slowly, he pantomimed dialing the phone.

Defeated, I lay on the bed and did as he wanted. Humiliation gnawed my soul, yet I forced myself to emit moans of simulated pleasure—knowing that the shame I felt now would increase tenfold if Ed ever did call Peter.

Ed shed his clothes and gestured for me to sit up. He approached the bed, standing slightly off to my side. "Beg me," he said in a barely audible voice.

I kissed and caressed his erect penis as I made myself say, "Fuck me. Please, fuck me."

"You want me?" he asked, in a whisper as soft as breath. "More than Peter?"

I froze. Ed watched me with the hard, hungry eyes of a shark. "I want you...more than Peter." The words hurt my throat as though they had jagged edges.

Ed pushed me onto the bed and shoved inside me. Shutting my eyes, I tried to retreat to the secret recesses of my mind, but it was no use. By compelling me to deny myself so totally, Ed had left me no place to hide. He possessed me body and soul, and I myself was the traitor who had opened the gate for him.

Afterward, I ran to the bathroom and scrubbed myself, knowing even as I did so that it would take more than water to make me clean again.

Then I remembered the razor blades in the cabinet, and my tears stopped. I could kill myself. Not even Ed could block that escape route. But I would never see Peter again, not in this world or the next. And Ed would delight in knowing he'd had the power to destroy me.

No. At least not till I find out if Peter will take me back. Calmer, I washed my face and returned to the bedroom, where Ed was already dressed. He zipped shut a black case that was on the bed.

"What's that?"

"Surprise!" Moving to the closet, he pulled out a tripod. "Have you heard of this great new invention called a camcorder? I videotaped your performance tonight."

His declaration slammed into me harder than any fist. "You what?"

He collapsed the tripod. "You weren't very convincing, but it shows progress. Like a report card. After you finish my little course, I'll mail it to Peter so he can see what you learned."

"No!" I lunged for the case.

Catching me by the arms, Ed held me tight as I struggled. "What are you saying? You want to end our little seminar tonight?"

I froze.

"Just say the word, and I'll send the tape home."

As I replayed the things I'd said and done before the camera, my breathing almost stopped. "No."

"Good girl." Ed patted my head as though I were a dog. "I know it's rude to fuck and run, but I really have to go."

After he left, I sank to the floor. Peter wouldn't believe I had been coerced into saying the treacherous words on that tape; Ed had kept his voice too faint and his threatening gestures out of sight. I could never cross him now.

Peter received a call at work from Dr. Wenger, headmaster of the boys' school in Wisconsin. They set up an interview for late Thursday afternoon when Peter had no classes.

As he hung up, Peter noticed Cherisse, the department assistant, leaning in his doorway. She wore a long royal blue sweater, skintight blue and green paisley leggings, and blue suede ankle boots. "Dr. T., could you like help me out? I'm having a totally gnarly time with my senior paper for Dr. French."

Peter packed his briefcase. "Why don't you ask him?"

"I can't talk to him." She twirled a strand of her permed and massively teased brown hair. "We're totally on different wavelengths. I ask him a question and he goes, 'Weren't you in attendance the day I discussed that in class?' I mean, like really."

Peter smiled at her impersonation. "But I'm not in his class. How could I help?"

"You could look at my outline and tell me, you know, if anything's majorly wrong."

"Sure. Bring it in tomorrow."

"Thanks, Dr. T. I know it's asking a lot, so..." She chewed the end of her hair. "I could return the favor. Like make you dinner?"

"Dinner?" He stiffened. "Cherisse, I'm married."

"I know. But I heard your wife's in Florida, and that's got to suck, and I remembered you asked about being vegetarian, so I thought I'd cook."

Although she wore an innocent, saucer-eyed expression, Cherisse jutted out her hip provocatively. Peter wondered exactly what she'd heard about him and Katie. Did she believe he'd had an affair with the department assistant, and was she offering the chance to do it again?

For an instant, God help him, he was tempted. Cherisse was pretty

—or would be if she washed off the rainbow eyeshadow and heavy plum blusher. Katie had taken up with another man, so why shouldn't he find comfort with a student? The symmetry between the events would make it the perfect revenge. But he had no interest in this girl, and the thought of spending more than five minutes listening to her vacuous conversation made him want to barf, as she herself might say.

"Leave your outline in my mailbox. I'll read it and get back to you."

"OK, Dr. T." With an exaggerated sigh, she left.

Wiping his sweaty palms on his trousers, Peter muttered, "Wake up, Taylor. You need to resolve things with Katie before you do something stupid."

As I carried two glasses of wine into the living room, Ed lifted the handcuffs from the ashtray. "I think it's about time to use these."

I cursed myself for not having hidden them away. "No. I won't do that."

"You will if I say you will."

"Not this time."

"But you know you want someone to dominate you."

Seeing the predator's gleam in his eyes, I shuddered. If he got me cuffed, he could do anything—use ropes, cigarettes, razors. "No, I don't care what you threaten."

He moved toward me, dangling the cuffs from his outstretched hand. Then he tossed them on the desk. "You know I'll have them on you eventually."

The phone rang. I hurried into the kitchen and grabbed it. "Hello?"

"It's Peter." His grim tone told me everything. "We need to talk. Can I see you?"

I lowered my voice. "When?"

"Tomorrow night."

The timing was so perfect, it might have been orchestrated by God. Ed played racquetball on Thursdays, so I had the evening free. "What time?"

"I can be there around seven."

"OK." I hung up and turned to find Ed watching me from the doorway.

"Who was that?"

"My mother. She wanted to tell me about a family get-together."

"Isn't that sweet." He grabbed my arm. "Come on. I haven't got all night."

Thursday night, after Peter rang the buzzer, I waited for him in the hallway. To send a conciliatory signal, I'd put on a dress he liked; it had a black skirt, a black belt, and a white bodice with black soutache braid scrolled on the collar. I'd lost so much weight that it no longer fit well, but that was true of all my clothes.

Silently, I waved him into the apartment. As Peter surveyed the room, revulsion twisted his face. "Do we have to talk here? Is there someplace else we can go?"

"There's a diner about three blocks away."

The restaurant was one of those ubiquitous Greek-owned places with predictable fare: omelets, burgers, club sandwiches, lemon chicken soup, and staples like meatloaf, fried chicken, and spaghetti with meatballs. This one was located on a corner, so it had windows on two sides of the square dining room. A U-shaped luncheon counter extended from the back wall, which had an open window to the kitchen. Booths lined the other three walls. When we entered, I chose one by the window that overlooked north Broadway. As I laid my purse on the cracked brown vinyl seat, Peter picked up a dirty ashtray and moved it to another table. I opened the menu. When the waitress came, I ordered cheesecake. Peter ordered coffee.

"How's your job?" he asked.

I could tell from his strained expression that he was as scared of this meeting as I was, so I delayed our inevitable confrontation by describing my coworkers. Whenever I paused, Peter murmured, but I knew he wasn't listening.

The cheesecake, when it came, was dry and tasteless. I shoved it aside. Peter reached into his pocket and frowned. "Are you going to get a divorce?"

The question shocked me. Surely, by now, he knew that he was the one with grounds. "Why would I divorce you?"

He flashed me a furious look, pulled a box of condoms from his pocket, and threw it on the table. "Your mother borrowed these. Need them back?"

"Peter, please." Glancing in embarrassment at the two policemen eating pie at the counter, I slid the box off the table and shoved it in my purse. "I'm sorry."

"Sorry. Is that all you can say?"

I shook my head. "I didn't want you to find out like this. I meant to tell you myself, but I wanted to end it first. I just haven't figured out how."

"How? Walk out on him, the way you did me."

His anger radiated like heat from a furnace. I flinched but said nothing.

Peter drummed his fingers on the table. "Did you sleep with him before and discover you missed him too much? Is that why you moved out?"

"It's not like that. I told you why I left. Because of the job."

His jaw hardened. "What about Marsden?"

"I don't know." I slid out of the booth and hurried to the cash register. Signaling to the waitress, I left money on the counter, rushed outside, and halted. Before me was a stream of moving headlights on Broadway.

Peter joined me. "You can't run away from this. We have to talk."

Slowly, I faced him. "I know. But there are things I can't explain right now. I know what I'm doing is wrong, but there are reasons I can't just end it."

Peter jammed his fists in his overcoat pockets. "You love him, don't you?"

"Love him?" I laughed once at the absurdity—but then couldn't stop. I leaned against a lamppost and cackled until I ran out of breath. Panting, I forced out, "I hate him. I'd kill him if I could."

"Then leave, for God's sake."

"I can't. Don't ask me to explain. I just can't."

Stepping more directly into the light, Peter stared into my face. "God damn you for being a lying bitch."

He turned and stalked down Thorndale without looking back.

Ernesto led Marietta into his dining room, where a pudgy man with sandy hair and brown eyes was putting a corkscrew into a bottle of wine. He looked up as Ernesto said, "Marietta, this is my son-in-law. Bill, this is my friend, Mrs. Thompson."

"Please, call me Marietta," she said as Bill pulled out the cork.

He set the corkscrew on the table, wiped his palms on the back of his jeans, and came to shake Marietta's hand. "Nice to meet you."

"I'm glad to meet you too."

A shrill voice overrode her words. "Bill, how many times do I have to tell you not to put a wine cork on the good tablecloth? It might stain Mama's linen."

A woman Marietta assumed to be Patricia entered the room, carrying a large wooden salad bowl. She wore a surprisingly showy outfit for a family dinner: a form-fitting black dress with a two-tiered ruffled peplum in royal blue and teal. Her curly black hair was piled high, and she wore heavy mascara and green eyeshadow shading into purple. A little boy, about two, walked at her side, holding onto one of her ruffles.

She set the salad bowl on the table, swept the child onto her hip, and turned to Marietta. "Welcome." Patricia then thrust her son into her husband's arms. "Put Jaime in the high chair and give him raisins. The rest of you take a seat." She headed back into the kitchen.

The high chair stood next to Ernesto's place at the head of the table. After Bill strapped the child in place, he put a yellow Matchbox car and a handful of dried fruit on the tray before retreating to the far end of the table.

Jaime stuffed his mouth full of raisins, then pushed his toy car over the edge of the high-chair tray and giggled as it fell to the floor.

"¿Jaime, que tal?" Bending down, Ernesto scooped up the car and then looked toward Bill. "Shall I give it back to him?"

Bill sighed. "I don't know. You'll have to ask Pati."

Staring intently at the toy, Jaime pounded his tray. "Mine! Give it to me!"

Patricia rushed into the room, set down a platter of steak with peppers, and said, "Jaime, no! You mustn't scream at *abuelo.* Tell him you're sorry."

"No!"

"Con permiso," Patricia said to her father. She lifted Jaime out of the chair and carried him to the other room. He responded with an angry wail, causing Marietta to tense. Katie had been just such a willful child—and look how she'd turned out.

When they moved to the living room after dinner, Patricia picked up the guitar leaning in the corner. "Please, Papa, you haven't played in so long."

"No, Pati." Ernesto rubbed his fingers. "You know I must rest my hands."

"That's not why you stopped playing. It's because it reminds you of Mama. She wouldn't want you to give it up."

"Neither would she want me to risk my skill as a surgeon. You do not know how my fingers ache at night, how they go numb after long operations. Playing the guitar makes it worse. Medicine must take priority."

Patricia put the guitar back in place. "Then why didn't you return to Mexico City after the earthquake? You always said you want to use your gifts to help your people, but when they needed you most, you stayed here."

"*¡Basta ya!* I am your father." He rose and disappeared into his bedroom.

Jaime began to cry again, and Bill flopped on the couch. "Why did you do that? The guitar's not that important."

Pati sat down and pulled Jaime onto her lap. "My father is a great musician. He used to tell Mama that doctoring the poor was his service to God and playing the guitar was his prayer. I don't think he should give up either one."

Marietta realized that Patricia, like Katie, didn't want her childhood image of her family to change. Her resistance would have to be addressed but not tonight. Leaving the others, Marietta knocked on Ernesto's door and entered his room. He was sitting on the bed crying.

"*Querida,* I failed. I was so busy with my patients that I did not notice when Rosalinda grew sick. If I had paid attention... By the time the oncologist saw her, the cancer had spread too much." He clenched his fists. "Then the earthquake last year. Pati is right. I should have gone back."

Sitting next to him, Marietta put her arm around his shoulders. "You were still grieving. You had the right to take care of yourself."

He bowed his head. "I've been so afraid to tell you how I failed Rosalinda."

"You think I never failed Joe? Or Katie?" Marietta paused at the name, stricken by a guilty conscience, and then went on, "We're bound to fail each other too sometimes."

"I can accept that if you love me."

"I do." She leaned forward and kissed him. They hugged for a moment and then, taking a deep breath, she said, "There's something I've put off telling you. I'm having a serious problem with my daughter."

A frown creased his forehead. "Because of me?"

"No, this is something else. Something worse." In broken sentences, she told him of finding Katie with Ed and of telling Peter her conclusions.

Ernesto gently took her hand. "You had no right to interfere in their marriage."

"I know."

"Why don't you tell her that?"

Dressed in a baggy sweat suit, I stood by the front window and stared at the hulk of Ed's building. He wasn't coming tonight because he'd gone to a customer's wake in River Forest. Even so, I felt his menace.

Running my fingers through my hair, I frowned at its oiliness. When had I washed it last? The days of the week no longer meant anything other than days Ed forced me to have sex and days he didn't. *You should have known what he was like. Whatever made you think he could help you?*

I turned away from the window, telling myself to eat. In the last month, I'd lost so much weight that my rings kept slipping off my finger. At lunch, all I'd had was a bowl of tomato soup, which I threw up as soon as I got back to the office. Opening the refrigerator, I pulled out the pan of macaroni and cheese I'd made the night before but didn't eat. The sight of it, impossibly orange, made me gag.

Opening the cupboard, I took out a bottle of bourbon, purchased because it reminded me of Peter. I dropped two ice cubes in a glass and then poured the liquor. *Only one,* I vowed.

The first sip made me grimace. Bourbon reminded me of the way my high school biology room smelled the day the class dissected a frog. After a couple of swallows, however, warmth slid down my throat and into my veins, and the taste improved.

I tinkled the ice and thought of a girl I saw that morning soliciting on the corner opposite Better Gaskets. She wore only a short fake-fur jacket, a mini-skirt, and stiletto heels.

I'm no better.

The glass was empty, and it was only nine o'clock. Too early to go to bed when I knew I wouldn't sleep. Breaking my resolution, I poured a second drink.

As I sipped it, my mother called. "What do you want?" I demanded.

"I'm calling to apologize. I was wrong to tell Peter."

Setting my glass on the counter, I put a hand to my forehead. I felt dizzy, tired, and alone, and I wished I could confide in my mother without suffering her condemnation. "You never 'pologized before."

"Will you forgive me?"

So she just wanted to ease her conscience. Disappointment, intensified by the alcohol, darkened my mood. "Why should I? You're the one keeps telling me go back to Peter. Now, 'cause of you, I can't."

"Why not? Did he say he wouldn't have you?"

I snorted. "No, he's not like you. But Ed'll never let me go."

"What do you mean?"

"Never mind," I said and hung up.

I stood in the living room of the Marsdens' condominium. The décor was cold: white carpet, white sofas, black marble tables, and abstract chrome sculptures on glass shelves. Before the fireplace lay a zebra-skin rug. Revolted by that trophy of some man's bloody hunt, I stared out the window down at the roof of my own building.

Did Marge ever stand here waiting for Ed? She had to realize there was another woman, although maybe not who. Why was she so tolerant when she was the one with the money? Did Ed have a hold over her too?

He came up behind me and slipped his arms around my waist. "Enjoying the view? Or using the window as a mirror?"

"I already know what I look like," I said, but his words made me focus on the dark glass where our image floated.

"Do you? Take a good look. You're too skinny. I don't like it."

"Then why don't you find someone else?"

He pressed close behind me. "Because I'm not done with you yet."

As he unbuttoned my shirt, I again became aware of the world beyond the glass. "Don't. People will see."

"So?" He flipped my shirt open and unhooked the front clasp of my bra.

When I tried to shield myself, Ed pushed my arms back down to my side. He squeezed my breasts and pushed his erection against me. "Make up your mind. Who's your audience, the people out there or Peter?"

This doesn't matter, I told myself. The buildings across the street didn't rise this high. I could take the small risk of exposure to strangers as long as the tape didn't go to Peter.

Ed pushed me close to the window. "I'd sell tickets except you're too scrawny to attract an audience." He pinched one nipple viciously. Then he unzipped my jeans and ordered, "Strip."

"Ed—"

"Do it."

Stepping out of my underwear, I began to shiver. He turned me around to face him, then opened his fly and pulled out his penis. "Suck it."

The command came as a relief. Down on my knees before him, I'd be out of sight of the window—and even though I hated giving oral sex, it never lasted long.

This time, just as I expected him to climax and withdraw, Ed grabbed the back of my head and pushed in as deep as he could. I clawed at him. The pressure against the back of my throat triggered my gag reflex. Clutching my hair close to my scalp, Ed held me immobile and ejaculated. Semen clogged my throat. Vomit rose to meet it. As Ed released me, I threw up on the white carpet.

Before I had finished retching, he pulled me up by the hair and slapped me. "Stupid bitch. Clean it up."

Tears spilled down my face as I ran to the kitchen. There, I switched on the light and saw in yet another window that I was naked. After closing the blinds, I rinsed my mouth at the sink. Then I searched the cabinets until I found paper towels and a bucket, which I filled with water.

Back in the living room, Ed stood at the bar pouring himself a beer. "Marge better not see a trace of that shit."

Or else what? I thought but knew the answer. Someday, when Ed got good and tired of me, he was going to destroy my marriage. All I could do was delay it.

As I crossed Sheridan Road after jogging the next morning, I imagined flinging myself before an oncoming bus. The only drawback was I couldn't guarantee that it would kill me.

Upstairs, as I walked down the hall, a tall, blond man who reminded me of David Bowie left Devin's apartment. He locked the door, put the key in his pocket, and walked toward the elevator. His face was expressionless as we passed.

Inside my apartment, the meaning of what I'd seen clicked as I snapped the deadbolt lock. Devin was gay. Why hadn't I realized it before?

God, I want out of this city. Everyone's a pervert. The instant I had the thought, shame flooded me. Who was I to judge anyone? Devin had only ever been polite to me. And chances were, his lover was a damn sight kinder than mine.

Going into the bathroom, I turned on the shower. Then I opened the medicine cabinet, picked up my disposable razor, and stared at it, unable to see a way to pry the blade free of its pink plastic casing. I laid the razor on my arm and wondered how deep I could make it bite. Not deep enough to release the pain that had formed a hard abscess inside me.

I dropped the razor and sat on the edge of the tub. My hands shook as I listened to the shower running. The image of bloody water swirling down the bathtub drain was so real that I was afraid to look behind me, even to turn off the faucet. Rushing from the room, I went to get a drink.

Coming out of the shower on Saturday, Peter heard his phone ring. He wrapped himself in a towel and hurried to answer it.

Dr. Wenger was calling to offer the position at the boys' academy. "You'll want to discuss it with your wife, but could you let us know next week?"

"Yes," Peter said, his eyes tearing at the reference to Katie.

After saying good-bye, he considered the offer. The school was undeniably impressive. While there, he had seen a German class typesetting a foreign-language newspaper, a biology class creating hybrid vegetables, and a drama group rehearsing Gilbert and Sullivan. Why on earth should he hesitate?

The simple answer was pride. His dream had been to teach in college and to become a respected authority on some aspect of the Civil War. The fact that he'd failed to realize his dream at Zebulun didn't mean it was dead.

And how would Katie view his teaching at a boys' academy, however prestigious? On the one hand, she might be more willing to give their marriage a chance if his employment crisis was over. On the other hand, she might lose respect for him if he gave up his academic career.

Peter was haunted by the memory of the way Katie looked the last time he saw her. She'd lost so much weight that her dress hung on her as though on a scarecrow. The hollows beneath her cheekbones were shadowed, and her eyes looked bruised. In all the years he'd known her, he'd never seen her so despondent. Despair clung to her as pungent as the scent of an unwashed body, as acrid as the odor of smoke lingering over a burnt-out house.

She claimed to hate Ed but refused to leave him. Why? The only answer Peter could think of was guilt. This was a woman who, instead of realizing she'd been raped, had blamed herself. Peter couldn't imagine the torturous self-recriminations she must be feeling now.

But why not end a relationship that was making her miserable? No matter how hard Peter tried, he couldn't guess her motives. And he was sick of trying. *If she wants my help, she can damn well ask for it.*

He was in the kitchen making coffee and oatmeal when the phone rang a second time.

"It's Marietta. We have to talk about Katie."

"What now?"

"I called her the other day to apologize for interfering. She said something that worried me, but I couldn't get her to explain."

He sighed. "Don't ask me. I have no idea what's going on."

"Peter, will you listen?"

The edge to her voice got through to him. "All right."

"She said Ed will never let her go. What can that mean? It doesn't sound right."

"No, it doesn't." Pushing his damp hair off his forehead, Peter remembered Katie saying she needed to find a way to end the affair. As though it were a matter of negotiation.

"Will you call her and find out what's going on?"

"You think I haven't tried?"

"She doesn't trust me." Marietta's voice cracked. "I know it's my own fault, but I'm scared for her. If you don't reach out to her, who will?"

Peter tightened his grip on the phone. "She won't talk to me either. But I'll try."

Katie's phone rang ten times before he hung up. Slowly, Peter walked toward the bedroom, replaying the conversation with Marietta. What would make Katie say that Ed would never let her go? The more Peter thought about it, the more ominous it sounded. He returned to the kitchen and dialed again.

This time a woman answered. "Lo?" The voice was thick and gravelly, not young and fluid, yet something prompted Peter to say Katie's name.

"Yeah?"

"It's Peter."

"Peter." Her voice changed at once from that of a sick old woman to that of a frightened child. "What time is it?"

"A little after nine. Maybe now's not a good time to talk."

"Don't hang up. Please."

"I won't."

She coughed, faintly as though she'd turned her face away. Then she said, "Tell me something...honestly. Do you hate me?"

Lying sleepless the last few nights, he'd felt enough hatred to strangle her. Now her tremulous tone reminded him of the wounded young woman he'd fallen in love with. "I'm angry, but also worried. Why won't you leave Ed?"

"I can't talk about that."

"What else is there to talk about?"

"Remember how I used to stop by your office before either of us dreamed of love or marriage?" Her voice broke. "I miss those days. It's been so long since I had someone to talk to."

"Katie, I'm still your friend."

"How can you be? After all I've done. You'd hate me if you knew."

Now he was the one who said, "Don't hang up." He listened impotently as she wept.

"I should...should let you go," she finally stammered.

"I'm not doing anything right now."

"That's not what I mean." Noisily, she blew her nose. "You deserve someone better. Why don't you find someone else?"

"I don't want anyone else." Peter caressed the mouthpiece of the phone. "Sweetheart, can't we work this out?"

She sighed. "I don't know. I'm in over my head."

What does that mean? Thinking of her haggard appearance, hoarse voice, and odd hints, Peter formed a terrible suspicion. "Has he hooked you on drugs?"

"No!"

"Then what's—"

"Peter, please. Don't ask."

"I have to ask. I love you. Why won't you let me help you, or your mother, or—" The dial tone cut him off.

Peter stared at the receiver, unwilling to believe she'd hung up. He couldn't stop hearing the raw terror in her voice. Swearing, Peter dialed her number again. She didn't answer.

Only after I arrived at the office Monday and saw people wearing a dozen shades of green did I remember it was St. Patrick's Day. There I sat, dressed all in black with my eyes as bloodshot as a banshee. Certainly, I'd cried enough lately to rival the wailing spirit, although I couldn't say whose death my weeping foretold—except perhaps my own.

Late that morning, a burst of laughter in the hall signaled the end of the weekly sales meeting. Elena, returning from the break room with an emerald-iced donut, reported that a group of salesman were going downtown to watch the parade. "They dye the river green. It's gross."

Ed entered the expediters' office, approached me, and dropped a message slip on my desk. He leaned close and whispered, "Cody called."

Reluctantly, I met his eyes.

"Yeah, for a while, I thought you'd lost me the account. Luckily, Cody knows a frigid little bitch isn't worth a dollar. He's sending new specs and blueprints next week. If my quote's competitive, I might still land him."

"Congratulations," I said softly, gripping a pen with both hands.

"Don't congratulate me yet. Save it till the account's won."

Then he raised his voice. "You look like hell. Why don't you go out tonight and drink some green beer? Maybe get laid by a nice, rough construction worker." Laughing, he left the room.

"Pendejo," Elena muttered. "You shouldn't let him talk to you like that."

"It doesn't matter. He's just in a bad mood."

"Yeah, but Mr. Parrish wouldn't like for him to say those things."

Avoiding Elena's gaze, I picked up the phone. "I have to make a call."

Lying on the couch, I sipped wine and watched *Wheel of Fortune.* I was wearing the Chinese robe, even though it was stained with mustard and tea. When Ed came through the door, I didn't bother to take my eyes off the TV, not even when he stood over me.

"God, you're a mess."

"So?"

"You bore me. I think it's time we called it quits."

He moved away, and I heard something clatter on the desk. Glancing that way, I saw a videotape and sat up. "Do you mean it?"

Ed shrugged. "We both know this is going nowhere. I'm letting you go."

"And giving me the tape?"

"If you want it." He held it out invitingly but then slipped it back in his briefcase. "Only there's something I want in return."

"What?"

"One last fuck...with these." With his index finger, Ed hooked the handcuffs from the ashtray. "What do you say? Fair trade?"

My stomach knotted with fear, even as I told myself this was my best chance to get that tape. I tried to rise, but my legs buckled. Staring at the cuffs as though they were a noose, I said, "Why do you want this so much?"

"I want one good fuck out of you before we call it quits."

"How do I know you won't hurt me?"

"You'd like that. You've been asking for it for weeks. And honey, you could provoke a saint to violence." He twirled the cuffs around his finger. "But we both know I'm no saint."

"Ed, that's no answer."

"It's all the answer you're going to get. You've got two choices. You get out scot-free and Peter gets the souvenir, or you give me what I want."

I pulled my robe even tighter across my chest. "But why handcuffs?"

"Why not? Sex is rough. That's the way I like it."

Pushing against the arm of the couch, I stood. "It's more than that. It's a contest with you. You're always trying to score points, and if I let you use those things, you win."

He laughed. "You think you're pretty damn smart. Tell you what. We'll both wear them: one cuff on your hand, one on mine,"

My palms began to sweat. Fear was an iron band, constricting my chest, but I reminded myself of the end goal: going back to Peter. "OK."

In the bedroom, Ed untied my belt and peeled off the robe. "On the bed."

Cold with dread, I lay down and watched him remove his clothes. Then he stood next to me. "Give me your hand."

As I held out my right arm, Ed snapped the cuff around my wrist and gave me a look of pity. "So weak. So stupid. And I thought you might be different." He pulled my hand up toward the brass bars of the headboard.

"No!" I rolled sideways, scrambling to rise to my hands and knees, but Ed knocked me down with a back-handed blow.

He stretched my arm higher. When my knuckles grazed cold metal, I braced myself to wrench free and screamed as Ed forced my hand through the bars and held it there in a strong one-handed grip. Climbing on the bed, he straddled me and grabbed my other wrist.

Still screaming, I bucked like a wild horse to throw him off. Releasing my left wrist, he tried to slap me, but my flailing arm deflected the blow. Ed grabbed it again and drew it upward.

"No!" His weight had settled on my pelvis, and my legs were going numb. I lifted my head to bite him.

"You've got this coming." Just then, Ed froze and looked toward the door.

When I struggled to free my right arm, he hit me in the face. Pain reverberated through my skull. Ed clamped his hand over my mouth. Forced into silence, I heard what had captured his attention. Someone was pounding on the door and shouting, "Katie, are you all right?"

"Don't yell, or I swear you'll regret it." Slowly, Ed removed his hand. Then he stood and threw my robe at me. "Answer it. And don't say anything stupid."

When I swung my legs to the floor, the restored circulation made my legs tingle. I staggered out of the bedroom. The voice was familiar, but I couldn't place it. "Who's there?"

"Devin, from across the hall. Open the door."

I pulled my robe tight, cracked the door, and peered out. Devin's face creased in a frown. Acutely aware of the handcuff on my wrist, I kept my right hand out of sight. "What is it?"

"That's what I want to know." He was visibly agitated, totally unlike the cool neighbor I was used to. "I heard screaming. You all right?"

Behind me, Ed walked out of the bedroom and stood out of view. He had pulled on trousers. "I'm fine," I said. "We were arguing, and I didn't realize it got so loud. I'm sorry."

Devin narrowed his eyes. "You sounded awful scared. Is he hurting you?"

"No."

"Look, I know you're afraid of him," Devin whispered. "Come over to my place, and we'll call the police."

"That's not necessary."

He gripped the edge of the door. "Girl, don't go back in there. It's going to get worse."

Ed came up where Devin could see him. "What's that black faggot want?"

Devin's face hardened. "Look, man, I'm onto you. Any more screaming from this apartment, and I'll call the cops."

"Go ahead." Stunned, I swiveled my head and saw Ed push his chest out defiantly. "If it comes down to your word against mine, who do you think the cops would believe?"

"Ed!" I shook my head at Devin, trying to convey that I wouldn't be a party to such a threat, but he wasn't looking at me. He stared at Ed with fear flickering deep in his eyes. After a moment, he turned on his heel and went back across the hall.

Ed slammed the door, grabbed my wrist, and snapped the cuff around the spindle of the doorknob. He pushed his face close to mine. "Been playing house with your little neighbor? You like faggots, don't you?"

I lunged to scratch him, but Ed seized my free hand and twisted my arm behind my back. I cried out in pain. "Forget it," he said. "You're not strong enough to fight me. You've never been strong enough." Releasing me, he returned to the bedroom.

I tried to work the cuff free but couldn't get it past the knob. *Stay calm. Any moment now, he'll unlock you.*

After a few minutes, Ed returned completely dressed and picked up the key from the ashtray. "What'll you give me for this?"

Clutching my robe shut, I shrank against the door. "What do you want?"

He held the key under the desk lamp and turned it so it flashed in the light. Then he dropped it in the ashtray, "Nothing. I like the way things are just fine."

"You can't leave me like this."

He laughed. "Why not? I'll be back."

"When?"

"Maybe tomorrow. Maybe Thursday. You'll keep." He put on his coat and turned to go.

Frantically, I pulled at the handcuff, ignoring the way it chafed my skin. As Ed walked away, I screamed, "No!"

He halted and gave me a quelling look. "Do that again, and I'll gag you," he said and disappeared into the kitchen. The back door opened, then closed.

In a burst of panic, I yanked at the cuff until my wrist was raw and blood welled up through the broken skin. When I ceased struggling, I felt hot pain. Tears filled my eyes as I glanced around desperately for something like an umbrella to knock the ashtray off the desk and pull it toward me. There was nothing.

Think. There has to be a way out of this.

The only answer that came to me was Devin. I could call for him —except that when he saw my ugly situation, he'd think I deserved it. No, it was better to wait for Ed. He wouldn't really leave me here all night.

Leaning my head against the door, I felt the urge to go to the bathroom. I'd drunk two glasses of wine before Ed arrived.

Opening the door, I stared at Devin's knocker. Out of reach. What if I called him and the woman down the hall came out and found me instead? Within hours, the story would be all over the building. Yet, I couldn't wait until Devin came out on his own. My bladder would give out.

When I called his name, my voice echoed down the hall, but nothing happened. I called again more loudly. To my relief, he came out within a few seconds.

"What is it?"

"I'm sorry to bother you. I need help."

His eyes narrowed. "Is he still there?"

"No. Look, can you come over for just a minute?"

Devin slowly shook his head. "Your man over there plays nasty games. I'm not walking into his trap." He turned to go back inside.

"Wait! Please!" My voice cracked, and he halted.

"Ed really is gone...went out the back. He left me like this." I stepped away from the door and stretched out my arm so he could see the shackle.

Devin's wariness fell away, replaced by concern, and he crossed the hallway. As he entered the apartment, he hissed when he saw my bloody wrist.

"The key's in the ashtray on the desk. I can't reach it."

Silently, he freed me. After handing me the key, he crossed his arms and stared at me. "You're playing with fire. Why don't you end it?"

Gingerly, I smoothed back a flap of torn skin. My wrist stung, and I was anxious to soak it in cool water. "There's stuff I have to work out."

Shaking his head, Devin muttered to himself. Then he said, "Let me tell you something. I had a sister like you. She stayed with her husband till he beat her blind in one eye. You want that to happen?"

"He doesn't beat me."

"Right. What's that bruise coming up on your cheek?"

I glanced down.

"Yeah, well, I guess I can't tell you what to do." He shook his head. "You need help again, you come knock on my door. Day or night."

As I walked the three blocks to where my still-unrepaired car was parked, I shifted my suitcase from hand to hand. All night, I'd lain awake, and as morning dawned, I made a decision. I couldn't stay here and fight Ed anymore, not even to protect Peter. So I'd called in sick, planning to run away. Once Ed found me missing, he would mail the tape, but he was going to do it eventually anyway. At least, if I was gone, I wouldn't have to watch it devastate my husband.

My plan was to drive carefully to the bank, withdraw the $214 I had in checking, go to a used car dealer, sell the Pinto for whatever I could get, take a cab to the bus station, and keeping some money in reserve, buy a ticket for the farthest destination possible.

Walking down Winthrop Avenue, I didn't see my car. The space where I'd left it was occupied by the skeletal remains of...a red subcompact with a distinctively curved shape. I set down the suitcase and walked closer. The windows were smashed, the hood was up, holes gaped where the headlights used to be, and the metal wheels rested directly on the pavement.

Backing away, I sat on my suitcase. Why had God let this happen? Now I had no way out. My $200 wouldn't take me very far—and once it was gone, I might have to do something even worse than sleeping with Ed to survive. Defeated, I trudged back to my apartment.

When I returned to work the next day, more than a dozen pink message slips littered my desk. Nancy had been out too—and was still sick—so Elena hadn't kept up with the calls.

For the next several hours, I was too busy to worry about Ed. A little after two, I received a call from Tom Kosmicki at Waukegan Marine Corporation. "Where are my gaskets? You said they were shipping Friday."

"Let me check." Just then, Ed entered the room and came toward me.

"Don't put me on hold," Tom said. "All I want is the name of the carrier and the weight of the shipment so I can trace it."

"I'm checking." I felt Ed's gaze on me as I glanced at the calendar and saw the reminder for Waukegan—for this coming Friday. "Are you sure that was promised for last week?"

"Fuck! Didn't they ship? My line'll go down at 3:30 without those gaskets. Put me through to Ed Marsden."

"Please, let me check on it first."

"No. Get Marsden. Now."

Putting Tom on hold, I looked at Ed. "It's Tom Kosmicki, having one of his fits. He expected a shipment to go out last Friday, but I have it marked for tomorrow. He insists on talking to you." I held out the receiver.

"Shit, can't you do anything right?" As Ed took the phone, he noticed the bandage on my wrist. His eyebrows twitched. Then he jabbed down the flashing button on the phone console. "Tom, what can I do for you?"

Moving to Nancy's desk, I called the production manager, who said that five hundred pieces were ready. I passed a note to Ed.

"Tom, how many you need a day? Super. I'll drive up and have them there in an hour."

As soon as he hung up, Ed grabbed my bandaged wrist so tightly that I cried out. "I'll deal with you later." He stalked out.

A wave of terror swamped me, and a whimper escaped my lips.

Elena turned in her swivel chair to look at me. "Are you all right?"

"I don't know." Grabbing the letter opener on the desk, I ran my finger down its too-dull blade and dropped it. "I'll be in the bathroom."

Hurrying down the hall, I passed Ed's open office door. The sight of his filing cabinets halted me. What if he kept the videotape here, instead of at home where Marge might find it? After glancing both ways, I ducked into the office and closed the door. The first two cabinets held only customer files. The third was locked, so I searched the desk for the key. Nothing.

Frustrated, I brought my fist down on the desktop, littered with layers of blueprints and spec sheets. The papers, bearing the stylized *J* of the Janzenaire logo, were stamped with the red word *confidential.* Ed must have been really angry. Ordinarily, he was meticulous about the security of his files.

Off to one side, I spotted a letter from Cody. At the bottom was a Post-It note with a handwritten P.S.: "Glad to hear you got the halter on K. I look forward to riding that little filly."

My stomach lurched. Now that Ed was tired of me, he was going to force me to submit to Cody. Why had I thought he'd ever let me go? Putting a hand to my abdomen, I again saw the word *confidential* on the blueprints. I folded them up, carried them to my office, stuffed them in a manila envelope, and after telling Elena I was sick, left with the envelope under my arm.

All the way home, I prayed that Devin would be in his apartment, not out on one of his photography assignments. To my relief, when I reached my hallway, I heard jazz seeping through his door. I knocked.

After a moment, Devin opened the door. The music grew louder. He cocked one eyebrow at me.

"Sorry to bother you, but I wondered if you'd help me."

"How?"

"I'd like to stay here for a couple of hours." Remembering the blond boyfriend, I blushed. "That is, if you don't have company."

His face remained noncommittal. "Sounds serious."

"I'm trying to break up with that guy. I want him to return my key and...something else he took. But I'm scared to be there when he comes."

"I get that. But what makes you think he'll cooperate?"

Gesturing with the envelope, I said, "Because I've got something he wants more."

"I see. Wait a minute." Devin disappeared into his apartment.

As the wail of a saxophone rose in a mournful solo, I checked my watch. Unless Ed got bogged down in traffic, he'd return from Waukegan soon.

The music ceased, and Devin returned with an overnight case. "The place is yours for the night. I'll stay with a friend."

"That's not necessary. I just need a couple of hours."

He shook his head. "What if it doesn't go down the way you plan? You'll be safe here as long as you don't tell him where you're hiding. And..." He searched my face and then shrugged. "What he said about the cops was the truth. I can't afford to be here if there's trouble."

Heat suffused my cheeks. Devin must despise me for my presumption that he was here to rescue me. "I'm sorry you got sucked into this. I'll figure something else—"

"No!" He punctuated the exclamation with a karate chop to his palm. "Just stay here out of sight, and make sure he's out of that apartment before you go in. Call the police and say you suspect a break-in if you have any doubts. Got it?"

I nodded my head. "Thanks."

As soon as I was alone, I verified that I could see my apartment door through the peephole. Reassured on that count, I gazed at my surroundings. Devin had painted his living room walls a deep burnt orange. The couch was upholstered in cream suede, and a blanket woven in a red, green, and gold African pattern was draped across the back. The coffee table, made of a highly varnished, irregularly shaped slab of light yellow wood, held a stack of art and photography books that I would have enjoyed looking through if I weren't so tense.

I called the office just before closing. Faking a Southern accent, I said, "Ed Marsden, please. Tell him Mr. Drake is calling."

Ed was on the phone in seconds. "Cody, how's the weather down there?"

After a beat, I said in my normal voice, "Nice blueprints, Ed."

Something crashed in the background. "Fuck, Katie, have you lost your mind?"

"No, have you?" Tucking the phone under my ear, I gazed at a painting of black children playing in a yard. "Leaving confidential plans out like that."

"Don't mess with me. You're jeopardizing a million-dollar account. Do you realize how many jobs are riding on this?"

I laughed. "You mean yours?"

"I want those papers. I'll tear your place apart, and you with it, if I have to."

"I'm not there and neither are the papers. Why don't you call Cody and ask for copies? Tell him the little filly ate them."

That silenced him a moment. "That's what this is about? It's just locker room talk. I wouldn't let him—"

"Stop. You know what I want. Bring the tape and my key, and leave them on the desk in my apartment. Then get the hell out of my life."

"Will the blueprints be waiting there?"

I laughed again. "You think I'm that stupid? If you leave the stuff by 6:30, I'll bring the papers to work tomorrow. Cody'll never know."

"And if I don't? If I send the tape to Peter instead?"

Even though I was expecting that threat, my heart skipped a beat. I gave the reply I'd prepared. "If you think petty revenge is worth your shot at a vice-presidency, go right ahead."

"Don't play hardball with me, Katie. You're not tough enough."

"Sure I am. I've been training with a master." I hung up.

For an hour, I stood staring out the peephole, afraid that if I moved away, I would miss his arrival. When Ed finally came, my physical reaction shocked me. My hands balled into fists, my wrist started to throb with my pulse, and the muscles around my vagina tightened defensively.

Ed let himself into the apartment and came out again seconds later. Turning up his overcoat collar, he walked away.

I put an ear by the door and listened for the elevator ding. Moving to the window, I pressed my face against the glass and stared down at the front of Ed's building until he disappeared under the awning overhanging the entrance. Only then, did I return to my apartment.

The tape and key were on the desk. To be certain, I put the tape in the VCR and started it. The first couple of minutes showed only the empty bed. Finally, I entered the scene. I cringed when I saw myself in the sleazy, revealing clothes.

Sickened by the memory of what was to come, I ejected the cassette, broke open the plastic case, unwound the tape from its spool, cut it into pieces, and threw it all away.

Friday morning, I put the papers into a folder and carried it down to Ed's office. There, I found him seated at his desk with Hart Parrish across from him. "Sorry to interrupt. I've got the reports you asked for."

"Cut the bullshit. Give me back the blueprints you stole."

Stunned, I turned to Mr. Parrish, an obese man with curly steel-grey hair and eyeglasses. "I didn't steal them."

"Do you have them?" Ed demanded.

I dropped the folder on the desk. After flipping through it, Ed said, "Everything seems to be here. You can call the police now, Hart."

Mr. Parrish grimaced. "Let's not be hasty. I'm sure she can explain."

"She had no authorization to take these. For all we know, she's copied them and sent them to a competitor."

"I didn't. Mr. Parrish, listen." Knowing I had nothing to lose, I stepped toward him. "Yes, I took the papers, but only to make Ed stop blackmailing me."

Hart Parrish's eyes grew wide. "Blackmail?"

"Oh, Christ, she's crazy. Are you going to listen to this?"

I held out my hands, palms up. "Mr. Parrish, please."

He looked from me to Ed. "It can't hurt to listen to her before we do something rash."

Relief made me wobbly at the knees. Taking the chair next to Mr. Parrish, I said in a rush, "We've been having an affair, and I wanted out. Ed videotaped us without my consent and threatened to send it to my husband. So I took the papers to make him give me the tape."

Falling silent, I waited, expecting to feel shame so overwhelming it would be impossible to look at Mr. Parrish directly, but the sense of worthlessness didn't come. Instead I felt relief.

Mr. Parrish shook his head skeptically.

"It happened. Look." Holding up my arm, I tore away the bandage to reveal the dark red welt and bruising around my wrist. "Ed did this to me with handcuffs just a few days ago. My neighbor can verify that."

After examining the damage with obvious distaste, Parrish turned to Ed. He shrugged. "OK, we had an affair. But it's over, and she's trying to get back at me."

Fury propelled me out of the chair. "You liar! If that were true, I'd never return the blueprints. I only took them to get that tape!"

"Katie, sit down!" For the first time, Mr. Parrish sounded decisive. "Tell me. Did he ever say that your job depended on, uh, giving him favors?"

"My job? No—" I fell silent as I realized what he was asking. Swiftly, I grabbed the folder on Ed's blotter, sorted through the papers until I located Cody's letter, and handed it to Parrish. "Read the Post-It note. He was going to force me to accommodate his customer."

His face grave, Mr. Parrish stared at the note about three times longer than necessary. Beads of sweat appeared near his hairline. Finally, he looked at Ed. "Can you explain this?"

Ed shook his head and smiled with bravado. "A lover's quarrel. I told her it was a bad idea to sleep with customers, but she begged me to tell Cody she was sorry for their spat."

"This note indicates you were more than a messenger." Mr. Parrish rubbed his chin. "Katie, please wait in your office. I'll meet with you soon to discuss your status with the company. But first I have to talk to Ed."

"Hart—"

Mr. Parrish held up his hand. "Ed, I'd wait till we're alone if I were you."

Folding my arms across my chest, I remained where I was. "I'm sorry, but I'm not budging till I know if you're going to have me arrested."

"Arrested?" Mr. Parrish looked surprised. "No, of course not."

"Then you don't need to worry about my status with the company. I quit."

Nodding, Mr. Parrish stroked his chin. "That sounds like a wise decision. However, I would still like a word with you before you go."

Three hours later, I was back in the apartment. Before I left the office, Mr. Parrish gave me two weeks' severance pay and promised he wouldn't contest an unemployment claim. When I asked about Ed, Parrish said they were working out a settlement. "He's agreed to resign rather than face dismissal."

Now, I dialed Peter's house; the college held no classes on Good Friday. After four rings, the answering machine clicked on.

"Hi, it's Katie. It's Friday afternoon. Could you call me at the apartment as soon as you come in? It's important."

Hanging up, I went to the bedroom to sort out the laundry I needed to wash before I could pack my clothes. The phone rang.

"Peter?"

It was Ed. "You stupid bitch. What makes you think I didn't make copies?"

I stood by a mound of grainy snow on the beach just south of Ed's building. The water of Lake Michigan was the color of rain-soaked concrete. The sky, only a shade lighter, was low and heavy, domed like a cast aluminum lid. A chill breeze blew from the east into my face.

Turning up my collar, I gazed at the lake, a vast, impersonal giant, its incarnations ranging from a smiling goddess robed in sun-drenched sapphire to a winter warrior flinging missiles of ice. I longed for my familiar brown river. To plunge into the Theakia, to allow it to fill my lungs, to know that it would eventually carry me to Mexico where I had long wanted to travel, that was the death I wished for. But I'd never see the Theakia again.

Reaching into the pocket of my coat, I checked that my keys and driver's license were there. I hoped my body would be found and identified promptly. On the desk in the apartment was a note that said simply, "Peter, forgive me." Next to it was his gold pen.

Taking my first step into the lake, I recoiled as frigid water seeped through my slacks and burned my skin. Folding my arms tightly across my chest, I forced myself forward.

Waves surged around my knees. My toes curled under and my calves cramped. When something nudged my leg, I looked down to see a chunk of floating ice. Going forward was as difficult as slogging through wet cement. Then an unexpected warmth touched my cheek like a kiss. Raising a hand, I discovered tears on my face.

When the water was almost to my throat, I halted and hunched into myself, too frozen to move either forward or back. I hadn't known it was possible to be this cold. After a moment, I took another step, discovered that my foot had gone numb, and lost my footing. As I tumbled headfirst, an icy fist of water rammed into my nose and open mouth. I tried to suck in air but inhaled only liquid. Thrashing desperately, I attempted to right myself. By the time my head finally broke the surface, I had propelled myself too far from shore to touch bottom.

Frantically, I tried to tread water, but my legs were half paralyzed from the cold. I thought of Peter as I sank. My mind sped forward and saw him reading my note and crying because he thought I'd killed myself over Ed.

"No!" Beating the water with my hands, I forced my way to the surface. This time, my toes grazed the lake bed. I craned my neck to keep my face above water. Twisting in what I hoped was the direction of the shore, I thrust myself forward. The lake floor dropped away, and I sank again.

I was weaker than before. The freezing water was leaching away my strength along with my body heat. *Dear God, please. Don't let me die!*

As I hit the bottom, I crouched and pushed off, but my upward motion was slow, so slow. My lungs tightened, and my mind went blank. When I broke the surface, I instinctively tried to go into a survival float, but my sodden coat dragged me down.

Once again, I tried to tread water but kept slipping beneath the waves. As mercilessly as a shark, the cold bit through my body. My side started to cramp. If I didn't find the shore within seconds, I would drown. Already, the idea of yielding—of curling up and sinking like a stone—was as attractive as sleep.

Then something grabbed me. Adrenaline surged through my body, and I brought up my hands to fight the creature off. A human arm encircled my waist. The man (I assumed rather than saw that it was a man) pulled me to his side and began to stroke. A deep voice said, "Keep your head above water."

We swam jerkily. I was too numb to kick or try to keep afloat, so I surrendered to the man's hold. Our forward motion submerged my head so often I could hardly breathe. As I fought to remain conscious, I noticed that the stranger's skin seemed to radiate heat.

There was a thud as his feet slammed down on the lake floor. It was a moment before I was able to stand—the man was that much taller than me—but suddenly, I was up, leaning against him and coughing violently. I staggered onto the beach, fell to my knees, and vomited. Then I crawled a few feet away and collapsed on the pebbly sand. My eyes refused to stay open. My rescuer tapped my shoulder and pulled me to my feet. "Go home now."

There was a rhythm of footfalls as the stranger ran down the beach, followed by the wing-flapping of startled gulls. I opened my eyes to call thanks after him, but the man had disappeared.

By the time I dragged myself off the beach, my skin felt glazed with ice. My lips and fingernails were blue, and my teeth chattered as I waited for a break in traffic so I could run across Sheridan Road and into my building.

Back in my apartment, I ran a tub of lukewarm water and stripped. My clothes were as stiff as if they'd been dipped in plaster, and it was a struggle to peel them off, a struggle that reminded me of how close I'd come to drowning. If that man hadn't come along—I halted my train of thought. Some detail nagged at me, some odd fact I feared to examine too closely.

When I lowered myself into the tub, the tepid water felt scalding, and my skin rose in angry red gooseflesh. Staring at my bumpy thighs, I remembered the detail I'd been suppressing. The man who pulled me from the lake had been naked. But that was preposterous. No one swam naked in Lake Michigan in March. No one swam in March at all.

I sat bolt upright. Could I have imagined that impossible rescuer? But if I had, then how had I reached shore safely?

As I sat transfixed by the riddle, the air chilled my skin, and instinctively, I slid back down in the water. The action reminded me of my recent battle with the lake. The memory of the man's strong arm around me and his bass voice in my ear was too powerful to deny. Although it seemed impossible, someone *had* carried me from the lake. I certainly hadn't possessed the strength to save myself.

Uneasily, I shifted my thoughts to the night ahead. In the lonely hours, the voices of doubt and shame would return. Despair would cause me to ponder various ways to kill myself, to debate the comparative effectiveness of razors and gas and poison.

I climbed out of the tub and, wrapping myself in a towel, gazed into the mirror. These last weeks, pain had consumed me until all I could think of was ending it. The desire was there still. For a minute, I teetered on the brink of death as surely as if I had climbed out on a ledge. Then I pulled back. Walking into the kitchen, I called my aunt Cori, the one person close enough to reach me before I did something desperate. "It's Katie. I need help."

"What's wrong?"

The concern in Cori's voice broke something inside me, and I began to cry. "I just tried to kill myself. And I'm afraid if I stay here alone, I'll do it again."

PART FIVE

Truth Seeker

MARCH 1986–
AUGUST 1986

Saturday morning, Cori went down to the basement apartment where she'd installed Katie. It was a long room kept in readiness for guests and people who needed emergency housing. The furnishings consisted of cast-off pieces donated by church members, so the décor was eclectic at best. A twin bed and single oak dresser formed a sleeping area at the back, with a set of drapes in a yellow-and-orange medallion pattern that could be pulled across the room for privacy. The middle section of the room held a brown tweed love seat, a wicker armchair, and a portable TV on a cart. In the area closest to the door stood a round table with a fake white marble top and three chairs upholstered in gold-on-white flowered vinyl.

After quietly knocking, she opened the door and saw that Katie was asleep. The night before, Cori had driven to Chicago only to find her niece surrounded by piles of dirty clothes and crying because she thought she had to wash them before she packed.

"Nonsense." Cori stuffed the clothes into trash bags, except a blue silk robe and a leather skirt that Katie snatched up and carried to the trash chute.

During the fifteen-minute drive to Evanston, Katie kept her face averted in an attempt to hide her tears. Cori judged it best not to question her until she was settled, but when they reached the house, Katie staggered from exhaustion and Cori had put her straight to bed.

Sighing, Cori closed the door and went up to the kitchen, where she mixed a batch of cinnamon-oatmeal muffins. Last night, after her housemates returned from Good Friday service, they held a meeting to discuss the situation. Then Cori called Marietta to tell her where Katie was. Despite her sister's demands for information, Cori said only that Katie needed somewhere to stay. Half an hour later, Peter called and she told him the same thing.

As Cori slid the muffin tray in the oven, Ellen entered the kitchen.

A short woman with a thick shelf of a bosom, she wore a blue oxford shirt, a khaki skirt, navy argyle knee socks, and moccasins. Reaching for the coffee canister, she said, "You look tired."

"I'm worried about my niece. I didn't get a chance to find out what happened."

Ellen turned on the coffee maker and faced Cori. "I understand your concern, but you know what we decided."

Cori nodded. "I'll talk to her."

An hour later, Cori returned to the basement bearing a basket of muffins, a pot of tea, and two heavy white mugs. Once again, she knocked at the entrance to Katie's room.

"Who is it?" Katie cracked the door and, seeing her aunt, opened it all the way.

Cori followed her into the room and set her tray on the table. "I brought breakfast."

"Thanks." Despite her long sleep, Katie's face was white, and a bruiselike shadow lurked beneath each of her eyes. She stood with the table between them and refused to meet Cori's gaze.

Recognizing the sullenness as a defense, Cori gestured for her to sit down. Cori took the second chair and poured tea. "Do you want to tell me what happened?"

Katie whispered, "I tried to drown myself."

"In the lake? It's still icy!" Cori stared at Katie with new fear. If she was depressed enough to walk into that frigid water, she was closer to the edge than Cori had suspected. "Why? Does it have something to do with that man at work?"

Katie's head jerked up. "Did my mother tell you about him?"

"You did, remember? You said he was after you."

At that, Katie's defenses collapsed. "I was so stupid. He videotaped us. I didn't know...and he..." Her words dissolved into sobs.

Cori went to put an arm around Katie's shoulder. "It's all right. You can tell me."

Although Katie shrank from the touch, her sobs grew softer. "He made me do things. And now he's threatened to send a copy of the tape to Peter."

Kneeling in front of her, Cori said, "You should warn him."

"You don't understand. He'll never forgive me."

"Do you still love him?"

"Yes."

Cori weighed the dangers of what she was about to say, then decided to risk it. "Peter called here last night, crazy with worry. He loves you too."

Katie shook her head. "He won't after Ed gets through with him."

"You don't know that."

Katie lowered her gaze. "Peter's better off without me."

Sensing that her niece was feeling the lure of suicide again, Cori shook her arm to break her train of thought. "What are your plans?"

She shrugged. "I don't know. I lost my job."

"Then why not stay here?"

"But your housemates—"

"I talked to them last night. You can stay here till you're back on your feet, but on one condition. You need to get help."

Instantly, Katie drew back. "What do you mean?"

"Counseling."

"I'm not crazy. I just..." Tears filled her eyes.

"You just want to die," Cori said bluntly. "And we don't want to find a corpse in our basement some morning. If you stay here, you must see a counselor. If not, in two weeks, you'll have to find another place to go."

"There isn't anywhere else! And counseling is so expensive. Mr. Parrish said I could apply for unemployment, but—"

"The church counselors have graduated fees. I'm sure you can afford it."

Katie's eyes narrowed. "I've got two weeks to decide?"

Cori sighed. She'd met people like this before. Katie wasn't ready to change. She wanted to hang onto her secrets, use people for what she could, and move on. "Two weeks. Don't expect an extension, even if you have some emergency."

Resentment flickered across Katie's face. Ignoring it, Cori said, "You should call your mother and Peter, and tell them you're all right."

"I can't call Peter. And I don't have a mother anymore."

Cori stood. "I've told you before. Complaining about my sister won't earn you any points with me."

"Do you know what she did when she suspected about Ed? She ran to Peter that same day and told him—without even asking me if it was true."

Cori felt knee-jerk disbelief but forced herself to suspend judgment. Until now, she'd heard only Marietta's claim that Katie was a moody girl who fought restrictions. She should have known there was another side. "I won't defend her on that. And I'm afraid you're going to be mad at me. I called her last night to tell her you were here."

For an instant, Katie was visibly angry, but then her expression turned triumphant. "So there's no reason for me to call her, is there?"

The smell of Easter ham permeated the Taylor house as Peter entered his old bedroom. He stared at the walls, redecorated long since with floral wallpaper, and recalled the posters that used to hang there: Wilt Chamberlain, a Vicksburg battle map, the Great Smoky Mountains.

His desk still stood by the window. Peter remembered sitting there doing schoolwork, thrilled to discover he had the ability to form his own theories about history. He'd been sure that as a professor he would inspire young adults with a love of the past and write brilliant books that would garner praise.

Now his dreams lay scattered at his feet like the petals of a shriveled rose. Even his marriage was dead. Yesterday, when he called the house where Katie had gone, she refused to talk to him. "She needs time," Cori said.

"Time for what?" he'd asked in frustration, but Cori wouldn't explain.

So here he was, back where he'd started, hiding from a family who felt little sympathy for his broken marriage or failed career. He didn't want to face them. The only reason he'd come today was to support his brother.

Joel had brought his girlfriend to meet the family and neglected, despite Peter's urging, to tell them in advance that Yolanda was biracial. The reactions had been predictable: Patrick's disgust, Pamela's hurt, and Yolanda's own quiet fury when she realized Joel's cowardice.

Trying to smooth things over, Peter had gone to the kitchen to help with the meal, but Pamela turned on him. "Why didn't you tell me?"

"It wasn't my place. Anyway, Mom, what difference does skin color make?"

"You're a historian. You should know the answer to that."

Leaving his room, Peter went downstairs to get a shot of his father's bourbon. Holding the drink, he stared out at the yard where Joel and Yolanda were walking. She had a pugnacious tilt to her chin, and Joel was talking and gesturing desperately.

"How did I get such fuck-ups for sons?"

Peter wheeled about to find Patrick in the doorway. "Joel is no fuck-up. Just because—"

"And you?" Patrick smirked at the drink in Peter's hand. "Katie sure as hell pegged you for a loser. Is that why she left you for another guy?"

"She didn't—"

"The hell she didn't. I had her followed."

Feeling as if his last piece of clothing had been ripped away, Peter stood mutely. His father walked to the bar and poured himself a drink. "Refill? You look like you could use one."

"No." Aware of his rising anger, Peter set his glass on the window sill behind him. "You hired a detective?"

"I got a right to know who my daughter-in-law is fucking. Don't forget, I put the down payment on your house. I'll fight the bitch if she tries to take it in the divorce."

"I haven't filed for divorce."

Patrick shook his head. "You always were a dope. I don't blame Katie for dumping you. You ever find another job?"

"As a matter of fact, yes. In a boys' academy in Wisconsin."

Patrick snorted. "High school. Even I didn't think you'd sink that low." He moved close to Peter and sneered, "From what I hear, Katie landed a real go-getter. Smart girl. If I was younger, I'd go after her myself."

It took a moment to take in the full import of Patrick's words, but when Peter finally understood their ugly meaning, he shoved his father. Patrick came back at him swinging. One blow landed, but because Peter slipped to the right, it glanced off his jaw. Sidestepping, he held up both hands. "I'm not going to fight you, Dad."

His father's face twisted with fury. "Don't call me that. You're not man enough to be my son. You're just some bastard your mother passed off on me."

"Patrick!" The horrified cry came from the doorway where Pamela stood.

"Mom, he didn't mean it. He's just mad at me."

"I fucking well did mean it. And I'll get blood tests to prove it." Patrick pushed his wife aside and stormed from the room.

Feeling her way like a blind woman, Pamela made her way to the couch. "It's not true. I never betrayed him, not even—" She caught herself and raised her face, lit with a fierce pride. It was the first time she'd ever hinted that she knew of Patrick's affairs, and Peter could see it would be the last. "What did you say to make him so angry?"

"Me? You heard what he said about you. What makes you think he was any fairer to me?"

"You shouldn't pick a quarrel with him. You know he's upset about Joel."

"Mom!" He sat beside her. "He hired a detective to follow Katie. Can't you see how wrong that is?"

Pamela touched his cheek. "He did it for your own good. Why do you always think the worst of him? Please go apologize."

Peter stood and stared down at her. "No. Can't you see what a bully he is?"

"He may have his faults, but he's still your father, and he's made sacrifices for you."

It was like watching the front of a cutaway drop off to reveal the inner workings of a machine. Peter saw for the first time that his mother's sweet but suffocating pressure was the vise that pinned him under his father's hammer blows. "I can't stay here."

As he turned to go, his mother caught her breath, but she didn't call to him. Orphaned by the silence, Peter went to say good-bye to Joel.

Saturday morning, I sat on the window seat overlooking the front porch. I positioned myself half behind the wine-colored draperies so I wouldn't be noticed by anyone passing the archway to the living room as they walked down the front hall.

Seven other people lived in the Victorian house. On the second floor slept Cori, Ellen and her husband Jack, Ellen's sister Vicki, and Vicki's daughter Juliana. Lem, Cori's mechanic friend, slept in the attic, and Jack's arthritic mother Ruby had a room on the first floor. Ellen, the household manager, ran things with regimented efficiency. She had assigned me a regular set of chores: Monday, mop the kitchen; Tuesday and Friday, clean the basement bathroom; Thursday, cook dinner; and Saturday, dust all the woodwork. Everyone but Ruby had an equal workload.

The household also had rules, whose purpose I understood but still resented. I had to use yellow sheets and towels (everyone was assigned a color) and not too many of them because I was limited to two loads of laundry a week. As I discovered the first time I went running, we were forbidden to take more than one shower a day.

At dinner each night, so many conversations focused on church doings that I felt like an outsider—especially since I couldn't possibly discuss the questions that obsessed me: *Would Peter call again? Had Ed sent him the videotape? Would God ever forgive me for the mess I'd made of my life?*

In spite of Cori's urging, I didn't dare phone Peter. My emotions were too frayed. Watching television devastated me; I wept when Hallmark commercials came on, when game show contestants won prizes, when lovers in movies kissed. At night, I took double doses of Sominex. Even then, I woke to nightmares of a man (sometimes Peter, sometimes Ed) shoving my head under water. During the day, I huddled in my room and wept.

Now feeling the onset of tears, I looked down at the notepad on which I'd begun a resumé. Vicki, an office manager for an accounting firm, had suggested I use action verbs to emphasize my accomplishments. "Fucked my boss," I wrote and crumpled the paper.

As someone clomped down the stairs, I drew my legs up completely behind the draperies. Vicki called, "Juliana, come back here!"

"I'm going to the movie with Heather. You promised!"

"I said only after you cleaned the bathroom." The words were followed by the measured sound of Vicki's descent. "You have to do your chores first."

"Chores, chores, chores. I hate it here. I want to go live with my father."

"Sweetie, you know that's impossible. His work—"

"You're just saying that. You hate it that he still loves *me.*" The front door slammed.

The quarrel left me as tense as a coiled snake. Of all the people in the house, Juliana made me the most uncomfortable. I hated being reminded of the blast-furnace rage and deep-freezer pain I had felt over losing my father, and I hated that, in this case, the mother was right. I had overheard Vicki pleading on the phone, "Just a visit, Skip. She needs you."

Grief for Daddy, still as sharp as a butcher's knife, sliced into me. As I stood, I dissolved into tears. My notepad slid to the floor. Clinging to the drape with both hands, I sobbed until I could hardly breathe.

Vicki rushed into the room. Unable to face her, I flung myself onto the seat and wept into the velvet cushion. Rising from the maelstrom inside me was the need to cut myself, a craving for an external pain to match my inward agony.

"Katie!" Aunt Cori pulled me into a tight embrace. "Shhh, you're all right."

Vicki asked, "What's wrong?"

"Nothing," Cori said. "Let me be alone with her."

"But—"

"We agreed not to pry into her business."

Those words told me that Cori had kept my secrets. She at least must care for me, not that I deserved it. Peter had loved me too and received nothing in return but heartache.

After Vicki left, Cori pulled back to look into my eyes. "Listen to me. You need help."

I turned away and gazed out the window. Spring had come. Daffodils waved in the yard across the street, but I didn't care. "It's too late."

"At least, give it a try. What have you got to lose?"

My life. But I've lost that anyway. "All right," I said at last, but only to prevent an argument.

The counselor's office was aqua. Two oil paintings, one of an adobe courtyard hung with strings of chilies and the other of red desert hills dotted with juniper, graced the walls. A cactus stood on the desk. The counselor, Peg, was in her fifties with short grey hair and a lean face. She wore loden chinos and Timberland boots. She surveyed me over the top of a clipboard. "So why are you here?"

"I thought Cori explained." Whether Cori had explained or not, Peg's silence forced me to say it myself. "I tried to kill myself."

"Why?"

"I don't know." I slid off my rings and cleaned the diamond on the hem of my skirt. "I just ended a bad relationship, but I think it's more than that. I've been crying a lot lately but not about Ed. About old things that happened years ago and don't matter anymore."

"They matter if you still have tears for them."

I blinked. Nothing in Peg's matter-of-fact demeanor had prepared me for the swift support, nor did I expect to hear her add, "I'd say you're right. Whatever's wrong probably does predate this relationship. Why don't you tell me about your life, just the basic outline? We'll fill in details later."

"You don't know what you're asking."

She smiled. "Is your life such a dark secret then?"

Staring into my memories, I answered, "Yes." Then I met her eyes. "Is everything I tell you confidential?"

"Absolutely."

How much did I dare reveal? My story wouldn't show me to advantage, and yet—I wasn't asking for the woman's love. What I wanted was a release from pretense. For once in my life not to hide. If Peg couldn't allow that, then counseling was useless.

"When I was a child, I loved my father more than my mother." From that simple beginning, the story tumbled out as though I had rehearsed it.

After I finished, Peg said, "You've been through a lot, haven't you?"

"Thanks to my own stupidity."

She raised an eyebrow. "Is that what you think? I see we have our work cut out for us. And you've never told anyone all this, not even Peter?"

I shook my head.

"Why not?"

"Because he'd hate me."

"I see. Your father died, your boyfriend raped you, your mother rejected you, your church failed you, your husband lost his job, your lover blackmailed you. And it's all your fault."

"No, but...some of it was. I knew I shouldn't be with Ritchie or Ed."

"So why did you do it?"

Staring at the Navajo rug on the floor, I swallowed. Obviously, Peg didn't get the point. "I like men who hurt me."

"Who told you that?"

I jerked up my head. "Ed. How did you know?"

"The way you said it. And I noticed during your story how quickly you accept the labels other people put on you."

"Now I'm supposed to accept your labels instead."

Peg shook her head. "Just my guidance. You've had some rough experiences and haven't dealt with them particularly well. You need to explore your emotions, examine your behavior, and change the harmful patterns. My job is to lead you through that process. It'll be a lot of work, and it'll hurt. Are you ready for that?"

I blinked again. It took me a moment to speak, and when I did, the words came out in a whisper. "Then you don't think I'm crazy?"

"No, I think you've been terribly wounded, and you're tired of hurting. That's what your suicide attempt was, wasn't it, a bid to end the pain?"

Tears welled in my eyes as I nodded.

"To start, I'd like to see you three times a week."

I gasped.

"I know you're out of work, so I'll charge my minimum. Twenty dollars an hour. Can you handle that?"

After doing a quick bit of math, I nodded.

The lawyer, Stan Bombagetti, was built like a truck driver—broad shoulders, brawny limbs, overhanging gut. His expensive grey suit was as incongruous on him as gift wrapping on a brick. Folding his hands over his paunch, he said, "So, you want to divorce your wife."

"No." Pain throbbed behind Peter's eyes. "I already explained to your secretary, I am *not* seeking a divorce. I simply want advice."

Making notes on a yellow legal pad, Bombagetti said, "Go on."

"My wife and I are separated. She left me last November and has since had a relationship with another man. She's much younger than I and—"

"Excuse me. You say this *relationship"*—he twisted the word as if to make it squeal—"was subsequent to her departure. You're certain?"

"It doesn't matter. I told you, this isn't about a divorce."

"Go on."

"I'm about to move to Wisconsin for a job. I want to sell my house and use the entire profit as a down payment on a new place. Legally, can I do that?"

"If the title is held jointly, you'll need to obtain your wife's consent. She would be within her rights to demand a share of the proceeds."

Peter shook his head. "The title's in my name. I bought the house before we married, and we never changed it."

The lawyer scowled. "Sloppy. Still, it's convenient for you now. She could contest the sale, but Illinois is not a community property state. I think we could defeat her in court."

It sounded so cold-blooded. Peter scooted forward to the edge of his chair. "But she worked during the two years we were together. Doesn't she deserve a share?"

The lawyer shrugged. "That's a moral question, not a legal one.

However, let me caution you that if you offer her a small share of the proceeds, she might demand a full half."

"Katie would never do that."

Bombagetti tapped the eraser end of his pencil on the pad. "You sound very certain."

"I know my wife."

"Indeed. And did you know she was going to leave you for another man?"

"She didn't. She—"

The lawyer held up his hand. "We'll leave that point for the moment. Tell me, have you attempted a reconciliation?"

"I've asked her to come home, but she won't."

"The other man."

"No, that's over." Bombagetti's expression didn't flicker, but Peter could almost hear his thoughts: *Broke it off but doesn't want you. Pathetic bastard.* Peter lifted his chin. "Katie's a troubled young woman and not always rational."

"Perhaps you're better off without her."

"I love my wife and want her back," Peter said automatically. Then he broke eye contact as he wondered if that were still true. It was the "Christian" thing to say, but it wasn't really his first reaction anymore. He cleared his throat. "I've told her I want her back, but I think she feels too guilty. She tends to punish herself."

"And you as well."

Peter's head snapped up at that.

"Dr. Taylor, let me be blunt. You have given your wife complete say as to whether the marriage will continue, and she by your own admission is not entirely rational. I submit that this makes you irrational as well. A person in control of his life doesn't allow an unstable woman to dictate his decisions."

"But I don't want a divorce."

Bombagetti folded his hands on top of his belly. "So you say. You have children?"

Peter shook his head.

"Then you have only yourself to consider. How long are you willing to wait for your wife to make up her mind?"

Peter crossed his arms over his chest. "As long as I have to."

Bombagetti shot him a hard look. "Are you prepared to face the possibility that she may start another affair?"

"You don't know that she'll do that."

"No, I don't." His voice remained calm. "My question is based on your description of her: troubled, irrational, perhaps self-destructive. The chances of reconciling with such a person are slim. I'm merely advising you to look after your own interests."

Peter gazed at a sepia-tone etching of the Roman forum that hung behind Bombagetti's chair. "What I'm most interested in is getting her back."

"Yes, Dr. Taylor, but we don't always get what we want."

I *fidgeted* to get more comfortable on Peg's couch. "I should call Peter."

Peg stopped writing. "Why do you say that?"

"Isn't it obvious? It's the right thing to do. Everyone thinks so."

"Who's everyone?"

Propping my chin on my fist, I said, "Cori. And the others in the house. I can tell."

"Don't indulge in mind reading. It's a dangerous habit, and you haven't demonstrated a talent for it."

I crossed my leg and bounced my foot.

"How do you feel about calling Peter?"

"I've told you, I feel terrified. If he cuts me off, I won't have anything left."

"Then maybe you shouldn't do it."

Her words confirmed my fears. "You think he'll reject me."

"I don't know. It's possible, and I don't want you getting suicidal again."

Slouching down, I stared at the bright red chilies in the painting to my left and wondered if I'd be happier if I ran away.

Peg tapped her pen on her clipboard. "I think it's time I introduced you to the concept of your shadow."

Sudden chills raced down my arms. "My what?"

"The personality has a couple of aspects that might be helpful for you to think about. One is the persona. In simple terms, this is everything you think you're supposed to be, the mask you wear to be accepted. The other is the shadow, everything about yourself you were taught was unacceptable. The parts you think you have to hide before anyone will love you. In your case, your shadow is enormous. The way you were raised created a huge rift between it and your persona."

Sensing a dark presence looming over me, I shuddered and whispered as though it could overhear, "And I have to destroy my shadow to be healthy."

"That's the worst thing you can do. You need your shadow. It's part of you."

"But it's evil."

"No, this isn't the old nature mentioned in the Bible. This is different." Peg pointed her pen at me. "Take anger. Many people, especially women, are taught it's bad to be angry. So they repress it and act forgiving all the time. But the anger is still there, so it comes out sideways. Like they 'accidentally' embarrass their husband in public or 'forget' their sister's birthday."

I frowned as she continued, "Anger isn't bad. It's a defense mechanism, like fear. But some of the ways we express anger are harmful. For example, a toddler may hit his mother. If she tells him he's bad, he learns to stuff his anger."

"What he did *is* bad."

Peg held up her hand. "Yes, but his anger isn't. If his mother says, 'Don't hit. Tell me when you're angry,' he'll learn to deal with it constructively and not repress it."

I crossed my arms. "What does this have to do with me?"

"I'm coming to that. Tell me something you're ashamed of."

I groaned. I hated stating the obvious, especially things I'd already told her a million times. "Ed. I'm ashamed of what I did with Ed."

"Then why did you do it?"

"Because I'm stupid."

"No, that's not what this is about. What did you want from him?"

Hugging myself, I rocked back and forth. I didn't want to answer, but Peg wouldn't let me get away with ignoring a question. "He said he could make me like it."

"Sex. He promised to make you like sex. And you wanted that."

"Yes! I slept with him because I thought he'd be a better lover than Peter." Covering my face, I began to cry.

She spoke soothingly, "Your desire for sexual pleasure is not bad."

"How can you say that?"

"You made a bad choice. That doesn't mean the motivating feeling was wrong."

"Look, my hour's up." I grabbed my purse. "We can discuss this later."

"Hear me out. There's no one waiting."

As I perched on the sofa's edge, a calm voice detached itself from the rage in my mind and asked, *Why are you so mad? Peg hasn't said anything new.* But that was precisely the problem. Ed had used the same arguments.

"Please answer one question before you go. Do you think all sexual desire is evil?"

Looking for the trap in the question, I said slowly, "No. It's good to want your husband."

"Then why didn't you?"

"I don't know! Either he's clumsy or I'm frigid. Or both."

Peg shook her head. "It's your shadow. You grew up in an environment that taught you to be ashamed of those feelings. It taught you they were evil."

"You sound just like Ed. He always blamed the Baptists."

To my surprise, she smiled. "You're a smart woman. He couldn't have ensnared you with a total lie. But I think you'll find our conclusions differ."

Peg leaned forward and held out her hands, palms up. "Sexual desire is a healthy emotion. But you were taught it was evil, so you hid your feelings." She clenched her fists. "You repressed them, but they remained part of you. So what do you do? If you want something you believe is wrong, where do you look for it?"

I shook my head. "I don't understand what you're asking."

She cocked her eyebrows as if to say, *Yes, you do.* "When you reached adolescence, how did your mother react to your sexuality?"

The question catapulted me back to the time Mother caught me necking with Ritchie. "She said it was my fault if I made a boy get aroused. It was the same as adultery."

"Good lord! Don't you see the lie?"

What lie? Frowning, I tried to figure it out. Then realization hit me. "She taught me that sex equals adultery."

"So you took your sexual feelings and shoved them down into your shadow. But they didn't stay there, did they?"

The same excitement I used to feel about piecing together historical evidence swept over me. "It's a vicious circle. I thought sex was bad, so I avoided it. Then when my desire became too strong, I made the lie come true: sex equals adultery. My mother set me up."

"Yes. She didn't mean to. But she did."

I bit the knuckle of my thumb, remembering all the lunch periods I sneaked out to be with Ritchie. Hard kisses. His hand squeezing my breast. The tantalizing ache between my legs that was only partially assuaged by pressing our bodies together. "Ritchie," I whispered. "I wanted him...before the rape. If he hadn't hit me, I might have given in anyway."

"You might have. Those feelings are perfectly normal."

"But they were wrong." An Old Testament phrase came to me: *an abomination.* That's what I was. In ancient times, they would have stoned me.

Peg's voice made me jump. "Your desire for that boy wasn't evil. Neither was your desire for Ed."

"How can you say that?"

"Listen carefully. A desire for love is normal; it's how we act on it that's right or wrong. Somehow we need to teach you that sexual desire is healthy so you can express it with the right man."

"It's too late. Peter must hate me. I'm...defiled."

Peg sighed deeply. "I really wish you wouldn't label yourself that way. The problem with your old church is not that they teach sexual morality. It's the implication that it's all or nothing, that if you lose your virginity outside marriage, you're a whore. Katie, you *can* start over, and you can do it with joy because you know that your sexuality is something to treasure."

Shaking my head, I said, "I keep trying to tell you, Peter won't see it that way. He'll see me as ruined."

"Then that's his problem. Maybe he won't want you back, but

that doesn't mean you've committed the unforgivable sin. You can start over."

I began to cry again. Screwing my eyes shut, I took a deep breath. After three tries, I finally got the words out, "But I don't want anybody else."

"I know. And you will have to face Peter soon. You're just not ready yet."

In early May, Cori invited me to her church. As I tried to think of a tactful way to refuse, she said, "No pressure. If you don't like it, I won't ask you again. But I think you might enjoy it. It's very different from your mother's church."

Different didn't begin to describe my experience there. The service was held in a large room with a semicircle of risers facing an open space. Instead of a satin-robed choir, a group of denim-clad musicians on folding chairs led us in forty minutes of singing. Anyone in the congregation could call out a request, and everyone sang enthusiastically, some waving their hands in the air while others clapped in rhythm. At one point, half the congregation, Cori included, filed down to do a line dance. I had never seen a service like it, and while it appealed to my emotions, it also unsettled me.

After the singing, one of the church elders—Cori said there was no minister—preached about the woman at the well, who was surprised when Jesus asked her for water because Jews didn't associate with Samaritans. In response, Jesus offered her the "living water" of eternal life.

The elder emphasized that to Christ, no one is outcast. His love and grace are given freely to all—even a woman society scorned because she'd been married five times and was now living in adultery. I stiffened, wondering if my aunt had invited me deliberately to hear this message. Cori, however, cast no sidelong glances to see my reaction, and I told myself she probably hadn't even known the topic beforehand.

"God is spirit," the elder concluded, "and his worshipers must worship him in spirit and in truth."

I'd heard that verse proclaimed dozens of times over the course of my life, but now it sounded new. It reminded me of the process I was doing in counseling, reviewing the things that had happened to me and learning to interpret them in more healthful ways so I could live by my own truth, not a set of external rules.

I'd always believed the rules in the Bible were instituted by God. What did it mean that Jesus himself waved away those regulations in favor of a more intuitive, authentic worship? Was there another path to God besides the one my mother had drilled into me all those years?

"You're like a long-term prisoner who gets pardoned," Ed once told me. "You're afraid to walk outside. Freedom's in your grasp, but it terrifies you."

As much as I hated to admit it, sometimes he had told me the truth.

When Katie didn't come to the table for Sunday lunch, Cori feared that she had pushed her too far by asking her to church. After the meal, Cori found her niece on the front porch, sitting cross-legged on the swing with a Bible on her lap.

"Are you all right?" Cori asked. "You missed lunch."

"I wasn't hungry. I wanted to think."

Moving to face Katie, Cori leaned back against the porch railing. "Because of church?"

She nodded.

"Did something bother you?"

Katie shook her head. "Not exactly. But it surprised me that anybody could call out a song, and everyone would join in. Is it always like that?"

"Pretty much. I've worshiped this way so long I forget it must seem odd to outsiders."

As Katie smoothed the page of the Bible, Cori noticed it was open to the book of First Corinthians. Katie said, "I wondered what happens if someone asks for a song that doesn't fit the rest of the service. Like if it's a really happy song, but the preacher is going to denounce sin. Doesn't it get weird sometimes?"

Cori blinked, uncertain how to answer. "What do you mean?"

"Well..." Katie pulled the rubber band off her braid and untwisted the plait. Then she began to rebraid it. "I know you don't have a minister, so maybe nobody's in charge. I'm used to services where the pastor picks a theme and everything—" She twisted the rubber band back on. "Sort of goes together."

"But we do have someone in charge."

Katie's eyebrows shot up. "Who?"

Hesitating, Cori wondered if her answer would make sense. As she did, she heard a bird take flight in the yard behind her, causing

Katie to glance over Cori's shoulder. Her gaze returned to her aunt as Cori said, "We believe everyone has the capacity to be led by the Holy Spirit, so if the service flows in a different direction than originally intended, we're inclined to think the Spirit led that way."

Katie stared at the Bible on her lap and then looked up. "So, you think anyone can be inspired." Her brow furrowed. "Everyone at Mom's church follows a set of rules for the service, but nobody talks about it. They think..." She rubbed the side seam of her jeans. "They think only Catholics have formal rules about church, but they do too. The rules are just unspoken. But at your church, it seems like the singing bubbles out of people as an expression of who they are."

Pleased by the insight, Cori nodded. "That's right. We're not a pyramid with a leader at the top. We're more like..." As she searched for an analogy, she curled her hands as if they held a ball and rotated the invisible sphere back and forth. "I don't know. Something organic and interconnected."

"Like a body?" Katie asked quietly.

"Yes, something like that."

Katie lifted the Bible from her lap. "That's what I've been reading. The passage about how we're all different members of the body of Christ and how each of us is necessary."

Cori sat on the swing next to her. Taking the Bible, she scanned the passage. "What made you choose this?"

"The sermon...the part about worshiping God in spirit and truth. It seemed to fit with my counseling. About learning to be more authentic." She rubbed her forehead. "I know you don't like it when I complain about Mom, but I have to in order to explain. She always makes me feel like my personality is bad. Too emotional, too wild. This morning, I started thinking maybe God doesn't see me that way. Maybe to him I'm just a different part of the body than my mother is, but she never understood where I was supposed to fit, so she kept trying to force me into the wrong place."

"Her place," Cori said quietly.

Tears glittered in Katie's eyes. "Yes."

After setting the Bible back on Katie's lap, Cori gave her a one-armed embrace. "I believe you were visited by the Spirit today. What you've realized is profound."

Shaking her head, Katie said, "I'm not sure I believe that. I've never had any reason to think God cares about me at all."

Cori rose. "Ah, but whether you believe it or not doesn't negate the fact that he does." She kissed her niece on top of her head and walked to the front door. Just before going inside, she looked back and saw Katie with her head bowed as if in prayer.

Returning from a counseling session, I found Ellen in the kitchen putting away groceries. "Can I help?"

"Yes, thanks." She carried a ten-pound bag of brown rice into the pantry.

We worked in silence for about fifteen minutes. As I put away a dozen cans of generic frozen orange juice, Ellen asked, "Did you see your package?"

"What?" I turned to stare at her. Cold air from the open freezer fell on the back of my neck like a premonition.

"UPS delivered a package for you. It's in the front hall."

My stomach twisted like a wrung washcloth as I hurried through the dining room and into the hall, where a package sat at the foot of the stairs. It was from Peter. Lifting the carton, I was surprised at its heaviness.

I took it down to my room and opened it. The enclosed note said only, "These things are yours. I left your wedding dress with your mother. If I find anything else, I'll forward it." No signature. I turned that half sheet of typing over, thinking there had to be more. There wasn't.

What did it mean? Was Peter ridding himself of my things because he had decided to divorce me? Swiftly, I rummaged through the box, pulling out books, a newspaper-wrapped mug, and some lavender-scented powder, looking for the videotape. It wasn't there. Had Peter received it? Destroyed it? Was he keeping it for evidence?

Flopping on the tweed love seat, I leaned my head against the back. Our marriage must be over. But I couldn't let it end without a word passing between us. *I have to see him. Even if it destroys whatever progress I've made.*

First things first. I walked out to the phone in the basement hallway, dialed the counseling office, and asked if Peg was available.

When she came on the line, I explained about the package and the conclusion I'd reached.

"Tell me as clearly as you can why you want to see him."

Although I feared the answer would sound childish, I said, "I'm tired of running from the bogeyman. Since the day we met, I've been afraid Peter will find out what I'm really like. Well, now he knows. We should get together and have an adult conversation about our marriage."

"What if he refuses to try to work things out?"

I sighed. "I think I'm past expecting that. I just want...what's that word you use? *Closure.* If our marriage has to end, I want it to be face to face."

"I don't know. I'm worried that if he's hard on you—"

"Peg, I'm not going to kill myself." I twisted the phone cord around my hand. "You and Cori know every dark, ugly thing there is to know about me, and you both still care. You want me to live. I've started to want that myself."

"Good." She sounded relieved. "But don't see him until after our next session. I think we should prepare for the encounter."

After I hung up, I leaned my forehead against the wall. *I'll call him at school. He won't yell at me in the office where Maggie can hear.*

He picked up on the third ring. "Dr. Taylor."

"Hi. It's Katie."

"Yes, I still recognize your voice. Even though it's been a while."

I winced at the sarcasm. "Sorry I didn't call before. I couldn't."

"Oh? Were your fingers broken?"

"I know what you must think, but I can explain. My therapist—"

"Your what?"

I gazed up at the windows in the outer wall; they were small, horizontal windows—the kind that were positioned up by the basement ceiling and showed just above ground on the outside. "I've gone into counseling. I see a therapist three times a week."

Peter's voice softened. "I'm glad. What changed your mind?"

Tempted to lie, I hesitated before saying, "I tried to kill myself."

"I see." He sounded stunned—then bitter. "Did you miss Marsden that much?"

"I don't miss him at all. I did it for the same reason I stayed with him so long. I was afraid of what he'd do to you."

"To me? What could he do to me that's worse than sleeping with my wife?"

My grip on the phone tightened. Had I assumed incorrectly about the videotape? "Didn't he— Peter, why did you send me that box?"

"Don't change the subject. What was Marsden supposed to do to me?"

Automatically, I said, "I can't tell you."

"You never can, can you? Well, I don't care. Keep your secrets."

"Peter, wait." My stomach clenched. "I want to tell you but not on the phone."

He was silent a moment, and my hopes soared. Then he said, "If you want to drive down here, I can't stop you."

Here was something else he wouldn't like. "I don't have a car anymore. I couldn't afford to fix the brakes, so I left it on the street. Vandals stripped it."

"What did the police say?"

"I didn't report it. I didn't think it mattered."

Switching to professor mode, he said, "Someone's probably out there using your plates on a stolen vehicle. You have to... Oh, forget it. We'll discuss it when I come up."

"You're coming?"

"It's either that or have you take Greyhound, isn't it?"

Peter halted just inside my room. He wore jeans and a short sleeve shirt I didn't recognize. His eyes swept from corner to corner before he sat at the dinette table and rubbed vaguely at an old circular stain on the fake marble Formica top.

"Would you like some tea?"

"No. Just say what you have to say."

His harsh tone stung, but I reminded myself, *You're doing this for yourself, not him.* But that wasn't entirely true. The scent of Old Spice stirred memories of lying beside him in the dark, and I bitterly regretted the way I'd damaged our relationship. I began my prepared speech, "Being with Ed was a horrible mistake. I knew right away I wanted out, but he blackmailed me. He threatened to tell you."

Peter made an angry sound, but I raised a hand to silence him. "I know I should have told you myself, but I was scared that you'd hate me."

The hazel in Peter's eyes darkened almost to brown. "And after I found out? I begged you to come home."

I twisted my rings. "By then, it was too late. Ed videotaped us without my knowledge. He said if I didn't do everything he wanted, he would send you the tape. I couldn't bear to let you see it."

The skin around Peter's lips went white. His jaw moved back and forth as though he were worrying a raspberry seed caught between his teeth.

"You don't believe me."

"I don't know." He removed his glasses and rubbed the bridge of his nose. "I never got a tape."

"The day I ended things, I stole some important blueprints and kept them till he turned over the tape and my key. I was trying to break free. Then he called and said he had a copy. I guess he lied, but I didn't know that then and..."

Comprehension lit Peter's face. "You called me and then disappeared."

I nodded. Staring over his shoulder, I saw again the heavy, dark water of the lake and shivered. "I couldn't take it anymore. I tried to drown myself."

When I forced myself to look into Peter's face, his expression was unreadable. The hurt I'd inflicted had hardened him.

Suddenly, he slapped the table. "Shit! Why did you get mixed up with a man like that?"

"He lied to me. I was lonely." I held my breath, then eased it out. "And I was wrong about our marriage. Our problems were far more my fault than I realized."

Peter jerked his head back and forth as if he didn't want to hear it.

My next question stuck in my throat, blocked by a primitive superstition that warned me not to name the thing I feared. Still, I had to ask, "Are you going to divorce me?"

"I don't know. You tell me this story and...I don't know, all right?"

My eyes filled with tears.

Peter leaned toward me, then sat back in his chair. He flicked hair from his face. "I don't even know you anymore."

"I know I've wronged you. But I'm in counseling now, and I'm trying to change. If you want me back, I'd like to start over."

"It's not that easy." Peter rose from his chair and turned to go.

"Can't we talk?"

He wheeled around to face me. "My God, after the story I just heard, I need time."

My chest hurt as though he'd clamped it in a vise. "I still love you. What I did wasn't because of you. It's because I was messed up."

Peter made a violent sweeping motion. "I am sick to death of talking about you. I have to think of myself." Turning on his heel, he left.

His departure plunged me into despair. Peter no longer wanted me. Even though I'd told myself this might happen, I hadn't really believed it was possible. Gripping the table edge, I curled my body forward until my forehead rested on the surface. Pain bubbled through my chest.

Our marriage was finally over. Peter had said he didn't know if he was going to divorce me, but he couldn't hide his disgust. How would he react if he heard the whole truth, the handcuffs and other things Ed did? Even if I persuaded Peter to take me back, I'd have to keep those things hidden forever. I couldn't do it. Such a life of secrecy would kill me.

And...I didn't want to die. The knowledge switched on like a motion-sensing night-light that made it possible to walk through a dark room without banging your toe. I wanted to live. The determination came from a deep recess, the same place that had decided to pull back from drowning, a vital inner core that was part of me long before Peter entered my life.

A sweet calm, like the repose that followed running, settled on me. I had neither husband, home, nor job—but I did have a fierce desire to go on breathing. It wasn't much, but at least, it was something to build on.

Too agitated to drive, Peter shoved his hands in his pockets and hurried down the street. He walked without plan, past large wooden homes and brick six-flats, past a Mexican restaurant, across a busy street, past a bike shop, a resale store, a laundromat, then along a stretch of fine old apartment buildings from the 1920s and 1930s.

Katie's story appalled him. She'd blithely skipped over the fact that her own decision to sleep with Ed made her vulnerable to his blackmail. Why hadn't she seen that Marsden was too slick to be trusted? Was there part of her that sought degradation?

Peter shuddered. Now, when it suited Katie, when she was beaten with no place to turn, she wanted to start over. Just like Eileen. Emotional black holes, the pair of them. Why did God keep saddling him with such needy women?

Striding through a neighborhood of three-story Victorian houses, Peter looked up and saw a patch of turquoise shimmering through the trees. The lake. He stopped. Katie had said that she tried to *drown* herself.

Slowly, he walked onward until the houses gave way to a park, a block of lawn dotted with trees and picnic tables. Huge grey boulders were piled along the shoreline. Standing close to them, Peter stared at the gleaming water. From deep within, like mud churned from the lakebed itself, came an instinctive horror of drowning: the bloating, the decay, the desecration of the body by scavengers. He could see Katie's loose black hair trailing through the water behind a swollen, green monstrosity.

Peter dug his fingernails into his palms. He couldn't stop her if she was bent on destroying herself, but the thought of a midnight call announcing her death weakened him. He sank onto the nearest boulder. Despite the bright May sunshine, the stone felt cold through the fabric of his jeans.

He had married the girl, had vowed to stand by her even if love failed him. Did he love her still? The thought of touching her repulsed him as much as if she were already the corpse he'd imagined.

At least, she was in counseling. But even that news didn't give Peter much hope for their marriage. Desire, affection, protectiveness—all the complex emotions he once felt for her—had shriveled into a dreary bond of duty. Burying his face in his hands, Peter recalled her as a student, sitting in the second row in class, gazing at him in unconscious adoration. They never should have married. However, they *were* married now, and like it or not, he had a responsibility to her. He just didn't know how much more he could give.

The second Saturday of May, Peter waited for his mother in the lobby of a downtown Chicago hotel. He was taking her to tea to celebrate Mother's Day, and they'd agreed to meet there rather than have him pick her up at the house where he might run into his father.

The hotel, which he'd chosen because of its reputation for high tea, was too ornate for his taste—huge chandeliers hung from a coffered ceiling bordered by elaborately carved crown molding. Red-and-gold damask draperies hung at windows and archways; the vaguely Chinese carpet was in brilliant shades of red, gold, and indigo; and a huge bouquet of red lilies stood on a marble table at the center of the room. Scattered around the lobby were brass lamps shaped like women raising torches aloft, huge majolica pots holding palms, and European mantel clocks with enameled faces. The overall effect was one of excess for its own sake.

Just before three, Peter saw his mother coming up the half flight of stairs that led from the street-level entrance. She wore a knee-length pink sheath, and her silver-blond hair was styled in soft waves. As Peter bent to kiss her, she lifted her cheek with an air of reluctance.

They walked in silence to the restaurant where a hostess led them to a small table draped with cream damask, flanked by chintz arm chairs. A bowl of pink carnations and yellow roses sat on one side of the table before a window overlooking Lake Michigan.

"Would you like sherry or champagne before tea?" the hostess asked.

"No." Pamela stared stonily out the window as the woman walked away.

Peter examined the menu card. "Should we order extra sandwiches?"

"No."

"Mother." She didn't respond. When their waiter arrived, Peter said, "We'll have the regular assortment of cakes and sandwiches."

"And what kind of tea would madam like?"

Pamela stared at the waiter as if he were a homeless person who had accosted her for money. Peter said, "You like Darjeeling. How about that?"

She didn't answer. Struggling to hide his irritation, Peter said, "My mother will have Darjeeling, and I'll have Earl Grey."

As the waiter left, Pamela laid a hand on her chest. "I've been having pains and shortness of breath. I thought it was my heart, but the doctor says it's stress."

"I'm sorry." Peter wondered if the argument at Easter was to blame —until he caught an accusatory glint in her eyes.

During his childhood, she had often awakened him at night when Patrick was away. "I have a headache," she'd say, then sit on his bed and insist that he kneel behind her and brush her hair, never mind that he was a child who ached for sleep. When he was done, she'd crawl into bed beside him. "Just for a few minutes." As she lay next to him, Peter sensed the deep need that consumed her, a need he felt inadequate to meet.

Their tea came. Peter's hand trembled as he lifted his pot. Why had he never seen that his childhood was an obscene mockery in which his mother used him as a surrogate husband? His stomach churned, making him glad he hadn't ordered extra food.

Pamela cleared her throat. "Is something wrong?"

"No." Avoiding her gaze, Peter poured milk into his tea. He couldn't confront her, not yet. His insight was still too fragile to withstand her inevitable denial. Yet he had to say something. "Have you tried exercise to reduce stress?"

Now what? he asked himself as he sat in his darkened living room. *I don't need this mother shit right now. I have enough hassles with my wife.*

He hadn't called Katie since walking out on her a week earlier. Whenever he tried to decide what to do, the conflict between his Christian duty to forgive and his horror at her affair scrambled his brain like a radio tuned so badly it picked up competing stations. A pattern formed in Peter's mind: his mother and Eileen and Katie. Not only had his mother used him for her own ends, she had trained him to fall in love with women as desperately needy as she was.

Shame washed over him. So the disaster of his marriage wasn't all Katie's fault. He had chosen her precisely because she was—what was the phrase he'd used?—*an emotional black hole.* He'd fed on her woundedness, defining his very manhood by his ability to rescue her.

What did this mean for their future? Was it possible for them to learn a new way to be together? Or was unhealthy dependence the only basis their love had?

Peter turned on the stereo to drown out the unanswerable questions.

In late May, Peter called me and suggested we meet for dinner someplace and talk. Still unfamiliar with Evanston's restaurants, I suggested Carmen's Pizza because Lem had ordered from there a few times.

Located in a drab concrete-and-glass trapezoidal building, the restaurant overlooked Fountain Square. Peter and I sat on the second floor at a table with a view of the small plaza and its three water sprays. On the wall behind us hung Botera prints of grotesquely fat people.

"The stuffed spinach pizza is really good," I suggested.

Peter slapped his menu shut. "Still trying to reform my eating habits?"

"No," I said, stung by the hostility in his voice.

"I'll have you know," he said, jabbing my place mat, "I cut down on red meat and caffeine. I exercise four times a week. And I did it because I wanted to, not because you said so. I'm perfectly able to choose my own pizza."

I flushed hot. "Fine. Get whatever you want."

"Spinach is fine. We can order a medium."

"Then why... What are you so mad about?"

Peter folded his arms across his chest. "Everything. Including the way you used to nag me about my diet."

"I only did it because I cared."

"Bullshit. You were afraid if you didn't lead me around by the hand, I'd up and die on you like your father did." His words speared me as if I were a marlin, but he wasn't done. "I watched that idea make you crazier and crazier until you couldn't take it anymore. So you left."

My anger sparked. "I'm not crazy. You're the crazy one if you think I left because of Daddy."

"That's not entirely it. I still haven't figured out what sent you running to Ed."

You did, I thought, longing to hurt him. Only the approach of our waitress stopped me from saying it.

Peter ordered the pizza and a Sprite. The waitress looked at me. "A glass of Chianti."

Peter's eyes widened. He changed his order to a Heineken and, after the waitress left, said, "So Marsden taught you to drink."

"I guess so."

His face contorted with anger. "What other bad habits did he teach you?"

"You really want to know? You get a kick out of hearing the details?"

As I had known he would, Peter blanched. "Forget I asked."

"Why? You have a right to know if you want to take back damaged goods." Leaning closer, I lowered my voice. "He taught me to be a whore. It's not doing it for money like they say, Peter. It's trading it for survival. I went along with Ed because if I didn't, he'd tell you the truth and you'd dump me. And if that happened, I wasn't sure I'd want to live."

"Jesus, that's a hell of a threat. You get to tell me any shit you want, and if I don't like it, you kill yourself."

I shook my head. "Not anymore. I've decided I want to live and to do it by being honest."

Peter gaped at me as though I'd spoken Hungarian. "What's that supposed to mean?"

Our drinks arrived. I sipped my wine and found the sharp bite of Chianti was exactly the prod I needed. "There are things I never told you for fear you'd hate me. I've decided I have to be able to share that stuff if we get back together, or what's the point?"

Peter briefly shielded his eyes with one hand. Then he looked directly at me. "You mean like the rape."

His words exposed my secret like a searchlight. I opened my mouth, but no words came.

Peter gazed at me with pity. "The night you told me about your friend, it was so obvious you meant yourself."

My stomach threatened to heave. I pressed both hands against my abdomen and asked, "Why didn't you say anything?"

"How could I? You ran out." He hesitated and then exclaimed, "You might have trusted me. I'm not your mother."

I bowed my head. All the energy I had wasted trying to conceal the past, and I hadn't hidden a thing. "You're right. I'm sorry. So where does this leave us?"

"I don't know." He sounded exhausted. "I wanted to tell you I'm not filing for divorce, at least not now, but there's too much hurt to move back in together. We need to start over."

"What do you mean?"

"Think about it." Peter's tone became patient, the voice of my old professor. "We went into marriage knowing only one thing, how to be teacher and student. We married so quickly, we never got to know each other any other way."

"That's not true. We were friends."

Behind his glasses, his eyes shone with tears. "Friends don't treat each other the way we have the last six months."

His words sounded so final. "So it's too late."

"I don't know." He smiled shakily. "That's why I said start over. I think we should date."

Slowly, I let out my breath. The suggestion was better than I had any right to expect. "All right, Peter. That sounds good."

A *week* later, as we headed north on Chicago Avenue toward the Northwestern University campus, I told Peter about the part-time job I'd taken as a page at the public library. "The work is boring, mostly shelving books and straightening magazines, but it earns me a little money and gets me out of the house. And leaves me time for counseling."

"You can live on part-time pay?"

I felt myself blush. "Cori's church is supporting me."

"I see." Peter's tone was carefully neutral.

A stoplight halted us at the corner across from the official entrance to campus, a gothic-style iron arch set in two stone pillars. When the light changed, we crossed the street, but instead of walking under the arch, we continued north along the sidewalk, which was lined with trees and shrubbery to our right. Before long, the greenery gave way to a wide meadow that stretched east to an ivy-covered stone building with eleven tall arched windows. It reminded me of photographs I'd seen of the old universities of England.

On the other side of Sheridan Road were grand old Evanston houses—half-timbered Tudor, turreted Queen Anne, and stolid Midwestern brick—converted to student centers and academic departments. Wondering if the university setting reminded Peter of how we met, I glanced at him. He wore jeans and an apricot polo, and he looked trimmer than I'd ever seen him. With his boyish face, he could almost pass for a student.

Tearing my gaze away, I looked forward as a young man using in-line skates rounded a group of girls and headed straight for me. I swerved into Peter as the skater zoomed past. A tight pain made me look down to where Peter had grabbed my arm above the elbow.

Instantly, he released me. Walking beside him, I rubbed my arm to massage in the memory of his touch.

A block north, we passed a sign for Garrett Theological Seminary, and I checked Cori's handwritten directions to the Shakespeare Garden. There, across a driveway, was the tiny chapel we were supposed to look for.

"This way." We walked past the chapel and down a short path that cut through overgrown bushes. At the end stood a large monument with a weathered bas-relief of Shakespeare's head. Peter stopped to read a plaque that listed several of the playwright's quotations about flowers.

I gazed to my left into the garden: a formal rectangular design cut by two paths that crossed in the center where a sundial stood. Enclosing the garden was a high double hedge with a hidden path running between the walls of shrubbery.

Peter joined me, and we strolled past beds of daisies, roses, pansies, and heliotrope. The pungent scent of herbs filled the air. We halted when we saw an old couple sitting together on a bench in an arched recess in the hedge. The man had folded his hands on the head of a cane; his wife read from a dog-eared paperback of Shakespeare's sonnets: "Mine eye and heart are at a mortal war."

I heard a quick intake of breath from Peter. Pivoting sharply, he hurried down the path to a large, curved concrete bench at the far end. He placed one foot on the seat, leaned his forearm on his bent knee, and stared into the greenery ahead of him.

I came up and took his free hand. "No!" He jerked away. "Not like that."

"Like what?"

"We're not going to try to patch things up by falling into bed together."

Shock waves rolled through me. "All I did was touch your hand."

Peter sat down heavily and gestured for me to join him. Wary, I sat about a yard away.

"Do you have any idea how much you hurt me?"

An unlooked-for grace gave me the words to say. "I think so. All I can say is I'm sorry, and I'm trying to change."

For several seconds, Peter sat with his head bowed. Then he reached over to squeeze my hand and got up to leave.

Back at the house, I sorted through the mail in the front hall and found a letter from my mother. I stuck it in my pocket and said to Peter, "I thought we'd eat lunch in my room."

We stopped in the kitchen, where I filled a tray with dishes, the bowl of tuna pasta salad I'd made that morning, a plate of sliced cantaloupe, and a foil-wrapped loaf of banana bread. I asked Peter to carry a pitcher of iced tea.

In the basement, I put the tray on the table and went to lay the letter on the dresser. Pulling it from my pocket, I stared at the tight writing.

"Who's it from?"

The tension in Peter's voice made me turn. "My mother."

Relief flooded his face as he dropped onto the love seat. "Go ahead and read it if you're curious. I can wait."

I hesitated and then opened the letter.

Katie,

I am writing to ask your forgiveness. I know I haven't been the kind of mother you needed. Maybe it would have been easier if your father had lived. He understood you better and might have been a link between us. Your father had a wild streak when he was young and often got into trouble. And you are so much like him. That's why I was strict. I was afraid you'd rebel like he did, and the world is so much harder on girls who step out of line. But now I see I was too harsh. When you came back from Kentucky, I should have hugged you and said how grateful I was you were safe. But I was too angry. So I will tell you now. I love you. You're my child, and nothing you do can alter my love for you.

Tears flooded my cheeks, forcing me to lay the letter aside so it wouldn't get splotched. *She's like me, asking Peter for another chance.* I glanced at him, half-reclined on the love seat, his eyes closed. Swallowing hard, I picked up the letter again.

I have something else to tell you. I'm marrying Dr. Montoya in October. He's a good man, and I love him—not the way I loved your father but enough to think we'll be happy. We'd like you to be at the wedding. Can you find it in your heart to accept my marriage?

The part of me that had begun to open to her slammed shut again. "Damn!"

Peter sat up straight. "What's she done now?"

"She's getting married again. And she wrote this phony-baloney apology to butter me up before breaking the news." I held out the letter to him.

Peter scanned the pages and then laid them on the dinette table. "It's a very nice note. What are you mad about? That he's Mexican or that she's marrying again after twenty years of widowhood?"

"I don't care that he's Mexican. That's not the point!"

"Then what is?"

Standing with clenched fists, I stared at him. *How can he not understand? I thought he knew me better than that.* My frustration threatened to choke me, but then I remembered a technique Peg had taught me. Holding up one hand, I said, "Give me a minute to sort through what I'm feeling before I answer."

Peter's eyebrows came together in puzzlement, and he shrugged. "OK."

I closed my eyes and let the emotions wash over me, forcing myself to observe them as a spectator. After a moment, I better understood where that surge of hurt came from. Looking at Peter again, I said, "You know what my relationship with her is like. I've never felt like she accepts me. I want her to see me as who I am, to care about what I'm going through."

"But she does, at least as much as she's able." Peter waved a hand over the letter. "She's admitting she made mistakes. I thought you'd be glad about that."

"When I read the first part of the letter, I *was* glad. But—" Tears sprang into my eyes, and I had to take a couple of deep breaths. "That last paragraph says it all, doesn't it? The apology was just a setup so I'd accept her boyfriend."

"Oh, Katie." Peter ran a hand through his hair. "Your reaction to this is so out of proportion. I think you're missing what's really going on."

I remained silent, refusing to ask what he meant. After a few seconds, Peter crossed his arms. "When are you going to get over your father's death?"

"Get over it?" My voice grew shrill, and I clenched my fists trying to hang on to the calm I'd achieved moments before. "First of all, that's not why I'm upset. And second, it's not something you get over. I think about him every day."

Peter shook his head. "No, Katie, you think about your perfect fantasy father. I'll bet you don't even remember what he looks like anymore."

"Of course, I do." Choking on a new wave of tears, I turned away.

His voice softened. "It's not your mother's fault that she's alive and he's dead. I think it's wonderful that she's going to marry again."

Bowing my head, I searched my feelings once more. "You still don't understand."

"Then help me." His voice was pleading, but I wouldn't look at him.

"How can I be happy for her? It's not that I think she's betrayed Daddy. It's that—" I fell silent, stunned by the discovery I'd just made.

Peter understood without my explaining. "She's betraying you."

I nodded. "Why hasn't she ever learned to love me?"

Peter moved close behind me. "Hasn't it ever occurred to you that she wonders the same thing about you?"

I whirled around to face him. "But she's my mother."

He nodded. "She's also a person. And she's had to live with the knowledge all these years that she's your second-choice parent."

It was an accusation I couldn't deny. A maelstrom of emotions swirled inside me, and I felt nauseated. Clutching my stomach, I sat on the love seat. "I don't know what to say. This is...too much to deal with right now."

"Do you want me to leave? I can grab lunch in town and then drive back home."

I raised my eyes to look at his face and realized my frustration with him had subsided. For the first time, I understood that he offered his insights, not to tell me how wrong I was, but to be my partner in healing. Like Peg, only not as objective.

"And let that delicious lunch go to waste?" I said with a feeble attempt at a laugh. "Just give me a minute to gather myself, then we can eat."

Even though our time together had ended amicably, the memory of the way Peter pulled away from me at the Shakespeare Garden returned when I was alone. At my next counseling session, I complained, "Peter can't stand to touch me. He acts like I have AIDS."

Peg picked up her clipboard and pen. "How does that make you feel?"

"How do you think? Dirty, just the way he wants."

The counselor sighed. "Don't make assumptions." Then she gave a slight shake of her head and leaned forward. "I'm sure Peter has his own reasons for his behavior, reasons that are rooted in his feelings, not yours."

"Like what?"

"I don't know without asking him. Self-protection, maybe. Maybe he's afraid if you get close, you might leave him again."

"Oh." I crossed my leg and bounced my foot. "But I do want him now."

Peg gazed at me over the top of her reading glasses. "What do you mean by that?"

"Come on, Peg."

"No, I'm not going to try to read your mind. What do you mean?"

Blushing, I said, "I want to go to bed with him."

"Yes, but is it because you think you *should* sleep with him. Or does he arouse you?"

I jiggled my foot some more. "What difference does it make?"

"A lot. If you push him into sex because you think you're supposed to, don't you think he'll sense that you're doing it out of duty?"

Remembering the way I used to lie rigid and unresponsive when Peter made love to me, I nodded slowly. "I *want* to want him. But I don't know how."

"Give it time. The more you're honest and vulnerable with Peter, the more a feeling of trust will grow between you."

"What does trust have to do with it?"

Peg looked at me appraisingly. "Let me ask you this. You told me Ed was more attractive than Peter, but you had trouble being aroused by him. Why?"

"Because I was afraid he'd hurt me." I blinked and put it together. "I see. I didn't trust him."

She nodded. "Exactly. Katie, think of arousal as the signal your mind sends when it welcomes the idea of another person entering your body."

"Oh." I'd begun to fear I was frigid because I equated penetration with danger, but what Peg said made sense. "Then why do I have trouble trusting Peter? He's so gentle—or he was before I made him mad."

"That's more complicated." Peg leaned forward. "Remember what you told me about your honeymoon?"

I nodded. "I was terrified Peter would discover I wasn't a virgin."

"And?"

"I wasn't able to relax because I feared exposure." Something clicked. "It's trust again. I didn't trust him enough to be honest."

"Exactly."

I frowned. Was that why the most intense arousal I'd ever known had come in the early days with Ritchie, when sex was something to anticipate, not to regret? "So what do I do? Now I have more secrets hidden from Peter than ever. How do we build trust?"

"Improve your communication, and see where it leads."

Closing my eyes, I hugged myself and said hoarsely, "Tell me it's not hopeless."

"If it were, you wouldn't be here. As long as you keep trying, there's hope."

Peter woke to find moonlight pouring through the window and across the bed. The light was silver-white, heavy as rich cream, yet translucent as sheer silk. The image came to him, from when in his marriage he didn't know, of moonlight falling across Katie's naked body, highlighting her round breasts, casting shadows on her flat stomach. A black waterfall of hair rippled down her back. He remembered tracing the ridge of her spine and cupping the boyish curve of her buttocks. His penis hardened. Reaching down, he squeezed himself.

Instantly, the picture changed as if a camera had dollied back to give a wide-angle view, and the man Peter saw caressing Katie was not himself; it was Ed. Even Peter's fantasies betrayed him. His arousal vanished. He jammed his fist in his mouth and wept.

Reaching up, Peter rolled off-white paint on the top part of his living room walls. He was having his first open house in a week, and the real estate agent had suggested sprucing up the place. As he got into the rhythm of painting, he recalled his last conversation with Katie. She had called the day after they argued about her mother's letter. "I want to say that I know you're trying to help, but my problems with my mother are something I have to work on in counseling."

"Not just your mother. If you don't deal with your father's death—"

"Peter," she interrupted, "I know you mean well, but I don't want to talk about that. I'd rather work on it with Peg."

"All right." He struggled to keep from sounding offended.

"I didn't get a chance to ask. How's your job search?"

"Fine," he answered, embarrassed that he still hadn't told her about his new job. "Dr. French suggested I apply to private high schools."

"That bastard. You belong in a college classroom. You're the best professor I ever had."

Great, now what do I say? "He didn't mean it as an insult. He thought I'd like a position where I could focus on teaching without the pressure to publish. But...you think I'd be lowering myself."

"Of course not!" Her indignation sounded genuine. "I just want you to be happy."

Remembering that conversation as he applied his roller to the walls, Peter felt like a coward for keeping his secret.

For my twenty-sixth birthday, Peter took me to the same French restaurant where I'd met his parents. We were careful with each other during the meal, discussing only neutral topics like the Cubs. As Peter paid the check, I sighed. *That's one fight-free date under our belts.*

After parking at the house, Peter walked me to the porch. Lavender twilight suffused the sky, and the smell of fresh-mown grass rose from the yard. I leaned against a wooden pillar and pushed out my breasts, hoping Peter would kiss me.

He glanced at his watch. "I should go. I have a busy day tomorrow."

"On Sunday?" I abandoned the seductive pose.

"I have things to do around the house."

"But school's out. Why can't you do it Monday?"

Peter unbuttoned his collar and rubbed his neck. "I'm having visitors."

He didn't want to tell me that. Panic swelled in my chest. *Who's coming over that he doesn't want me to know about?*

Shaken, I dug through my purse for the key. "I hoped you'd come in for a cup of coffee."

Peter sighed. "I don't want coffee. But I'll come in for a few minutes."

I shook my head. "I don't want to pressure you into it. Not if you've got more important things to do."

"Katie, I didn't mean to hurt your feelings. It's just that I have plans." His tone grew defensive. "You don't tell me every single thing you do."

"What do you think I'm doing? I go to counseling, I work twenty hours a week, I wait for you to call. I'm not seeing anyone behind your back if that's what you mean."

"Neither am I. I never have."

Stung, I turned away. "Go ahead and leave."

"No. I don't know why we always fight like this. Maybe it's normal under the circumstances, but I'm sick of it. We can talk right here, or I can come inside."

Glancing at the open front windows, I wondered how much my housemates had already heard. "Let's go around back."

We walked around the side of the house, through the back door, and down the basement steps. Once inside my room, Peter said, "OK, what is it?"

"What?"

He leaned against the wall next to the door. "Look, I know you. You were leading up to something. Why can't you just tell me what it is?"

Earlier in the day, I had planned something to tell him, but I hadn't been thinking of that on the porch. All I'd cared about was being with him. Obviously, he didn't feel the same way.

I crossed the room to the dresser and lifted Peter's gold pen out of the top drawer, shielding it with my hand. Then I went back to where Peter stood near the entrance. "Remember my senior year of college? We avoided each other the whole year. I had an idea French told you to stay away from me."

"He did."

Nodding, I went on. "I was convinced we were never going to be together, so I...I took something to remember you by." Stepping forward, I laid the pen in the center of the table.

Peter looked at it without recognition, then his eyes widened. He snatched it up and checked the engraved initials. "Where did you find this?"

"You left it in the workroom the day of the homecoming tea, and I kept it."

"You stole it?"

"Not exactly. I meant to give it back, but then I began to think it was the only part of you I'd ever have. It seemed romantic to have a memento that no one knew about."

"Do you know what this pen meant to me? My mother gave it to me when I earned my doctorate. It was the only sign that anyone in my family cared. And you stole it. Dammit, Katie, why give it back now?"

I gazed directly into his face. "Because I'm trying to start over, and I don't want secrets between us. I love you."

"Bullshit. When have you *ever* tried to see things from my point of view?" Peter opened his fist, finger by finger, and let the pen fall to the tabletop. "Maybe you were right. Maybe this is the only part of me you'll keep."

"What do you mean?"

The look he gave me was pure ice. "I can't trust you, and I don't think we should see each other anymore. You'd better get a lawyer."

He turned to go. As I hurried after him, I caught my foot on a chair leg and fell to the floor, landing hard on my hands and knees. Peter shut the door behind him without looking back to see if I were hurt. That more than anything convinced me we were finished.

I started to push myself up, then collapsed back onto the linoleum. *What's the use? I don't deserve Peter—or anyone.*

Peter exited the house and paused in the dark yard to take a deep breath. The air smelled faintly of roses. His body shuddered as his taut nerves tried to shake off the tension constricting his muscles.

It didn't work. His hands clenched in rage. The pen itself was nothing—a loss he'd accepted long ago—but Katie had stolen more from him than that. He'd given her love, patience, trust, fidelity, and she had thrown them all away. First thing Monday, he would call Bombagetti and ask him to file the papers.

Coming around the side of the house, Peter saw the light streaming from the horizontal windows of the basement apartment. Katie had left them open to let in fresh air. As he looked through the screen, he saw her grab the back of a chair and pull herself off the floor.

Walk away now, he told himself. *She's not your concern anymore.*

Yet, he couldn't leave. He crouched down to watch as she went to the dresser and picked up a brush and a small silver box he remembered from her nightstand at home. She sat at the table. After brushing her hair, she braided it in a tight plait, twisted it into a coil, and fastened it with hairpins from the box. Tears ran down her face. "Oh, Peter!" she cried out. "What have I done to you?"

The bitterness inside him crumbled, freeing a wave of tenderness like sun-warmed water breaking from behind a dam. Despite everything, he still loved her. He and Katie knew things about each other that could never be understood by any outsider. Leaving her would be like hacking off half of his soul.

Damn. And she thinks I'm getting a divorce.

After I put up my hair, I bent forward until my forehead rested on the table. Until that moment, I'd been in a holding pattern, waiting for the day I could go back to Peter. Now that hope was dead. I had to start over, but how?

Help me, God, I prayed, desperate enough to send up a plea even though I didn't deserve to be heard. *Show me a path forward, and I'll try to be the person you created me to be.*

Footsteps sounded outside my room, and I jerked up my head. The door opened to reveal Peter. Rising, I wiped away my tears. "Did you forget something?"

He nodded toward the wall at my right. "When I passed by, I saw you crying. And couldn't leave."

I had to glance at the open window before I understood. Searching Peter's face, I whispered, "You came back...for me?"

He nodded.

Sobs overtook me as I ran into his arms. "It's OK," he murmured. "I'm here."

I hiccupped as I burrowed deeper into his embrace. What a luxury it was, the feeling of being sheltered by his body. How had I ever taken it for granted? "I'm so sorry."

"Shhh." Peter stroked my hair. He led me to the love seat, where we sat with his arms around me. I caught a whiff of his cologne, a new scent, sharp with the tang of lime. As I turned to gaze into his face, my body tingled with the first signal of arousal. Parting my lips, I sat without moving, monitoring each breath that passed into and out of my lungs. Peter met my eyes. He hesitated before kissing me once lightly. Placing my hand at the back of his neck, I drew him to me a second time.

He pulled away. "No, I can't." Taking off his glasses, he pinched the bridge of his nose.

"That's all right," I said swiftly, although in truth I felt as though he'd slapped me.

Peter kept his head down as he rubbed his temple. "I need time."

"I know," I said, wishing my throat didn't ache so much. "I understand."

I *looked* at Peg's painting of the New Mexico hills and, once again, pondered running away. After Peter left Saturday night, I'd had a second bout of weeping, caused by terror that eventually he'd give up on me.

Shifting my gaze to Peg, I said, "He's so angry all the time. Sometimes he seems like a stranger. He's sarcastic and secretive, and he was never like that before."

"You're going through a difficult transition. Don't forget, you've changed too."

I've changed for the better, I wanted to say, but Peg never let me get away with that sort of one-upmanship. Instead, I clasped my hands around one knee and said, "I'm sick of the turmoil. I understand why he's angry, but maybe he should see a counselor too."

Peg fixed her gaze on me. "And how long did it take *you* to come around to the idea of counseling?"

"A couple of weeks. Cori said I had to start getting help within two weeks." Peg lifted her eyebrows, and I felt my face go red. "Oh. You mean—" I sighed. "Peter suggested it a long time ago, but I wasn't ready. You're saying I should cut him some slack."

She smiled and shook her head. "No. I was just asking you to put your impatience into context. You made that realization yourself."

Peg jotted something down on her clipboard and then said, "I think it's time you told me a little more about your relationship."

I groaned, not in the mood for doing past history. "Like what?"

"Start with what first attracted you to him."

I slumped into my seat. "At first, I thought he was an amazing teacher. And then, I felt like he understood me. He didn't think I was weird for studying history."

"Why would he?" Peg asked, amused.

"No, I mean more than the obvious. My mother wanted me to do something practical, like be a teacher, and Peter was my ally in resisting her." I squinted at the ceiling, then sat up.

"I think I just figured something out. It used to make me mad when anyone called Peter a father figure. I thought they meant because he was older and liked history, which was really lame. But my father was always a buffer between me and my mother, and when I met Peter, I think I wanted him to pick up where Daddy left off."

Peg cocked her head. "That makes sense. We all carry unfinished business from our family of origin into our marriages."

"But that's terrible." Pulling back my hair, I twisted it into a thick rope. "That means I married him for the wrong reason."

The counselor smiled. "Lots of people marry for what you'd call the wrong reasons, but I believe God allows that. I think he lets us marry the very person who triggers our unresolved conflicts. Unfortunately, some people keep reenacting the same destructive patterns until their marriages founder. But others use the conflict as a catalyst for growth. You have a choice."

"So how do I choose not to make Peter a father figure?"

"Don't you know?"

With a shiver of fear, as though I knew what was behind the locked door and had every reason to dread it, I shook my head.

Peg simply stared at me.

After a moment, I said, "You're talking about my father, aren't you? You're saying that somehow I've got them mixed up in my mind."

"Not exactly." Peg paused and then seemed to decide to be forthright. "You need to work through your grief."

I sighed in exasperation. "I've been grieving my whole life."

"Is that what you think your father would want for you?"

My head jerked up. "What do you mean?"

"Most people go through stages of grief. How—"

"You mean, why haven't I gotten over it by now?"

Peg shook her head. "I didn't say that. I'm just wondering if—what's it been, eighteen years?—if the pain has eased at all."

Tears flooded my eyes as I shook my head. "You think I'm stuck, don't you?"

"You know I don't like labels. But this is what I see." Peg ticked off the evidence on her fingers. "You've blocked out the memory of the funeral. You call him Daddy as though you were still eight years old. And you're more loyal to his memory than you are to the living. The problem with all this is that you no longer have a father."

Heat rose in my face. "I do have a father. He's dead, but he—"

"What?"

Staring at my hands, I whispered, "He watches me. I know he does. He loved me too much to abandon me."

"Katie, he was killed. He didn't have a choice."

"Then what's the use of Christianity? I thought it teaches life after death."

"Not the way you've defined it. You've made your father into some poor tormented ghost, hovering over the earth to make sure his baby's all right."

"But he loves me."

"Loved. He's dead, remember?"

Closing my eyes, I asked, "What makes you think I could ever forget?"

*W*ednesday night, a newlywed couple came for a second viewing of Peter's house. The husband, a young man with short brown hair and very straight posture, was a recent Zebulun graduate who had taken his required history classes with Peter. He thought the boy's name was Rob but wasn't entirely sure. The wife wasn't anyone he recognized, but she wore the same generic makeup—pretty but not too sexy—that so many of the girls at Zebulun favored, as though it were part of their Christian duty to please the male eye. Not wanting to intimidate the boy, Peter went to work in the back bedroom as they toured with the real estate agent.

He could hear them now in the dining room. The girl (the wife, Peter had to remind himself) was saying, "I like it, but I thought you didn't want to spend this much. Maybe we should start out with a condo the way my father said."

"Honey, if you really like this place, I want to get it for you. We'll manage."

"Well, I could keep my job, at least till the baby comes."

This boy was taking on a new job, marriage, fatherhood, and a mortgage all in one year? Peter wanted to run out and say, "Don't do it!"

The phone rang. As he crossed the dining room to answer it, the couple fell silent until he disappeared into the kitchen.

The caller was Katie. "Hi, got a minute? There's something I want to talk about."

"Um, can I call you back? I'm in the middle of something."

After a long pause, she said, "Will you call tonight?"

"Sure." He heard the young couple walk into the living room. "Maybe we could talk now if it won't take long."

"I don't want to interrupt whatever you're doing."

"It's OK, Katie. What is it?"

"Remember you said I never see things from your point of view?

Well, you're right. I got used to casting you in certain roles that were convenient for me: a Civil War expert or a sympathetic teacher or—" Her voice broke. "An ally against my mother. But that wasn't fair."

Peter massaged his temple. "Did your counselor tell you to say this?"

"No." She sounded hurt. "I figured it out on my own."

"I see." Turning to the window, Peter stared at the blue siding of the house next door. Here he'd been thinking of those newlyweds as children, but they were the same age Katie had been when he married her. "Go on."

"Well, I want to learn more about your interests. So I wondered if you'd like to go camping on your birthday."

Before Peter could frame an answer, he heard the front door close. The real estate agent, a bleached blonde wearing a red power suit with wide shoulder pads, hurried into the kitchen. "I think they're going to— Oh, sorry."

Waving her off, Peter listened as Katie spoke again. "I'm not just trying to get you to spend the night with me. I'll borrow a second tent."

She really is making an effort, he thought. "We can talk about that later. Listen, I have to go now. Someone's here on business."

The following week, I invited Peter to dinner on Thursday, my night to cook. When I got home from work, he was waiting in the front room. We walked to the kitchen where I poured two glasses of lemonade, then sat across from him with newspaper spread on the table and a bunch of carrots picked from the garden.

"Why are you doing that?" he asked as I carefully dropped peelings onto the paper.

His question reminded me how little he knew of my life there. "Ellen has a compost heap, so we save all our vegetable scraps."

Peter rubbed his temple and then cleared his throat. "Remember I told you about French's suggestion for my job search? Well, I didn't tell you that I'd already found a job."

"At a high school? Why didn't you say so?"

He shrugged. "I was afraid you'd think I was a failure."

My abdomen clenched with anger, and I exhaled carefully to release it. "Peter, I love you. All I want is for you to find a job that makes you happy."

"Then you don't mind."

"I guess not," I said, feeling pushed into a corner. "You haven't told me about it yet."

"It's a boys' academy in Jaegerton, near Janesville, Wisconsin."

I lay down the peeler. "You're moving to Wisconsin?"

"Yes." His voice took on an edge. "I told you I'd have to leave Zebulun."

"I forgot. When I picture us getting back together, I see it at home."

"I'm sorry. I have to move in August, and I already found a buyer."

"You sold our house without telling me?" Stunned, I sat back. So that explained the mysterious chores and visitors.

"You said you never liked that house. Besides, time was running out."

"You're right. It's just a shock." Even though my hands were trembling, I picked up the peeler and another carrot. "Is it a good job?"

"Yes, it's a boys' school, did I say that? It's geared toward turning around bright but unmotivated students. I really like the headmaster."

As the tempo of his speech picked up, I tried to look pleased.

Peter finished his lemonade and put the glass aside. "There's something else. I'm worried that if you ever join me in Wisconsin, you won't feel at home if I pick out the place by myself like before. But I don't want to go house hunting as a couple. Too much pressure."

"I guess so." I stared at the growing mound of carrot peels, trying not to feel betrayed by the phrase *if you ever join me.*

"Here's my suggestion. I'll look on my own. When I find a place I want to view a second time, I'd like you to come with me. Do you think that might work?"

Peeling in silence, I wondered how badly we'd fight if I answered frankly. *Here goes.* "I thought we were trying to develop more of an equal relationship, not teacher and student. But with this, you're still in charge and I come in at the tag end of the decision."

He crossed his arms and adopted a mulish expression. "I can't help that. Who knows when we'll live together again?"

"We probably won't if you keep acting like you're a bachelor."

"You're a fine one to talk. You're the one who said, 'I can't worry about your problems, Peter, they're stifling me.' "

"So now you're paying me back." Gathering up the carrots, I moved them to the cutting board and began to slice them. "I was wrong. How many times, how many ways, do I have to say it? But what will it accomplish if we keep shutting each other out?"

I broke off as Juliana sauntered into the room. The lanky, heavily made-up teenager crossed to the refrigerator, took out a Diet Pepsi, and perched on the edge of the table. Glancing at the carrot peelings, she said, "Gross." Then she took a long swallow of soda while eyeing Peter over the rim of the can. "So you're Katie's husband."

"Yes," I said, not giving Peter a chance to speak. "Peter, this is Juliana."

"Peter, huh?" Juliana flipped her long blonde hair over her shoulder and leaned toward him. "I suppose she told you my parents are divorced."

"No." He gazed at her and said warmly, "I'm sorry to hear that."

With a jolt, I recognized the role of empathetic listener he'd played so well when we first met. He nodded in sympathy as Juliana launched into her latest complaint about her mother.

I slammed my knife on the table. "Juliana, you know the house rule. Stay out of the kitchen unless you intend to help cook."

"Oh, rules." Juliana hopped down and brushed Peter's arm on her way out. "See you at dinner."

Gazing at the girl's retreating back, Peter asked, "What was that all about?"

"As if you didn't know. She's looking for someone to play daddy, and you obliged the way you always do."

"Now, wait a minute."

"No, you wait a minute. You're the one who said we need to learn a new way to be together. But you like being the father figure, don't you? You decide where we move and what house we'll buy. I made mistakes, Peter, but that doesn't mean I'm not an adult. I—"

To my chagrin, I started to cry. I jumped up, grabbed a paper towel off the rack, and blew my nose on the scratchy sheet. "You never say you're glad I'm in therapy or that you think I've made progress. Maybe I don't want to live with you again if all you can do is be mad."

He rose. "You don't think I have a right to be angry?"

"I didn't say that. Of course you do, but at least give me credit for trying to make amends." I took a deep breath. "You're not doing very much to invite me back into this marriage. Sometimes, I think we'd be better off apart."

"No!" Peter sat back down heavily. "Don't say that."

The little-boy fear was naked on his face. *Finally,* I thought. *The real Peter emerges.* Sitting next to him, I said softly, "I don't want to give up on our relationship. But I need a little encouragement. I'm trying so hard."

His head drooped. "I know. But it's difficult for me to trust you, especially because you're so different now. I can never predict what you're going to do."

"I've been changing, and we're getting reacquainted. That's to be expected, isn't it?"

He toyed with the soggy newspaper. "It's jarring. I love you, but you're like a stranger."

"You love me?" Besieged by tears again, I swallowed hard.

"Yes, Katie, I love you."

For a long moment, we gazed at each other. Then I rose, touched his shoulder, and went back to making dinner.

For the Fourth of July, Marietta invited her family and Ernesto to a cookout. Early that morning, however, Ernesto was called into emergency surgery. "Sorry, *querida,"* he said on the phone. "I will come as soon as I can."

Because Albert's poor vision precluded driving, Marietta's parents rode with Colleen and her husband Phil. By the time they arrived, Marietta had charcoal glowing in the old brick grill Joe had built. "Ernesto's been called to an emergency."

"Oh, well," Colleen said. "Independence Day can't mean much to him."

Marietta counted to ten under her breath as she crossed the patio to the house. The only reason she'd planned this party was so Ernesto could experience an old-fashioned American picnic.

Phil, a greying, bespectacled accountant uncharacteristically dressed in a Bruce Springsteen T-shirt and faded jeans, followed her. "Want me to do the grilling?"

Marietta pulled open the screen door and smiled back at her brother-in-law. "That would be great. The hamburger patties are on a cookie sheet in the fridge."

As Marietta set out the rest of the food on the picnic table, Albert approached, limping from arthritis. His doctor wanted to do knee replacement surgery, but he was trying to lower Albert's soaring blood pressure first. Gazing into the yard, Albert asked, "Where's Joe?"

"Joe?" Marietta felt a chill despite the heat. "Don't you mean Ernesto, Papa? Joe's dead."

"Yeah, I remember," he said gruffly, but he stared in puzzlement at the willow tree. Then he asked, "Katie going to finish that model he was building? I could help."

Frightened now, Marietta replied simply, "No, she decided not to."

Phil called, "Got a platter? The first batch of burgers is done."

Eager to get her father's mind off the past, Marietta handed him the dish. "Would you get the cooked hamburgers from Phil and bring them here?"

"Sure." He took the platter and made his halting way across the patio.

Wondering when he'd grown so forgetful, Marietta pulled the plastic wrap off the relish tray. Colleen came over and took a carrot stick. She had recently put platinum highlights in her dark hair, a harsh look that Marietta thought aged her rather than making her seem younger.

"Did I tell you that Bernadette's pregnant again?" Colleen asked. "When's Katie going to start a family?"

Marietta scrunched the plastic into a tight ball. "You know perfectly well that she and Peter are separated."

"Oh, I forgot. So how does Katie like Ernesto?"

Marietta didn't answer, distracted by the sight of her father heading toward them with the dish of hamburgers tilted at a dangerous angle. Before she could call out a warning, he halted. One side of his face crumpled, his right arm jerked, the platter fell to the concrete, and Albert collapsed.

"Papa!" Marietta was the first at his side, followed by Phil.

Albert looked up at her. Saliva dribbled from his mouth. After a moment, he tried to sit up. "Tripped," he mumbled.

"No, Papa, I think you had a seizure."

"No!" He flushed. "Tripped!"

"Let's move him to that lounge chair," Phil said. Together he and Marietta lifted Albert beneath his armpits and guided him to the chair. Brigitte hovered behind them.

"I'll go call the paramedics," Marietta said.

"No!" Albert struggled to stand.

"Papa, calm down." Marietta shot a beseeching glance at her mother. "Please, tell him. He needs to see a doctor."

"No." Brigitte's face was white, and her eyes were wide. "He just tripped on a crack in this old concrete. I'm not going to upset him more by calling an ambulance."

Colleen pushed into the group. "All he needs is rest."

Still on the chaise, Albert reached for Brigitte's hand. "I...go home."

A few feet away, Marietta paced. If she could get her father alone, she was sure she could convince him to go to the hospital. As Phil helped him to stand, Marietta rushed to them. "At least, wait for Ernesto."

Brigitte shook her head. "Your father will be upset if we don't leave."

Weighed down by dread, Marietta followed them to the front of the house and watched them drive away.

When Ernesto arrived half an hour later, she told him what had happened. He frowned. "They are being foolish. He should be in the hospital. He may have suffered a stroke."

"I begged them to call the paramedics, but they refused. They were too afraid to admit what was happening."

"I know." He drew her into a comforting embrace. "Talk to your mama tomorrow when she is alone. Maybe then she will listen."

In July, Peter asked me to the Ravinia music festival. "It's an outdoor music pavilion where the Chicago Symphony Orchestra appears in summer. They play the music over loudspeakers into a surrounding park where people have picnics."

My heart sank because I'd never told him I disliked classical music. Now that I'd committed myself to learning about his interests, I'd have to go. "You want me to fix the food?"

"No, I want your first experience of Ravinia to be a complete surprise."

And surprised I was. After we parked in the Ravinia lot, I watched Peter take a luggage cart from the trunk and load it with a cooler, a picnic basket, and a collapsible table. He handed me two lawn chairs.

"Are we camping out?"

He grinned. "You'll see."

Peter bought tickets at the window. After handing them to an attendant, we entered the park through a brown-painted wooden gateway built in a style that reminded me of the picnic shelters at the state park near Zebulun.

Ahead of us was an ivy-covered stucco theater with an arched, forest green entrance and a red tile roof. Just as I was about to protest that I thought it was supposed to be an outdoor concert, Peter turned toward the left. Following him, I noticed other people hauling in even more stuff than we were. When we turned the corner of the building and headed toward the lawn, I understood why. Elaborate picnics were the norm. On the grass near the walkway, an older couple sat at a candlelit table drinking champagne from crystal flutes. To their left, several women in sequined tops and silk rompers were selecting hors d'oeuvres from an antipasto tray. Peter passed a bronze statue of two cocker spaniels and then stopped by a tree to spread his plaid blanket. Moving close to him, I whispered, "These people are all rich."

"Not all." Peter nodded to a family behind me whose dinner was a bucket of Kentucky Fried Chicken. Then he put a glass hurricane lamp on the table and lit the candle. From the cooler, he unpacked a bottle of Riesling, containers of German potato salad and three-bean salad, a roasted chicken, a loaf of pumpernickel, and a bowl of peaches.

Lifting a peach to my nose, I sniffed. The aroma was the distilled essence of a hot summer morning. Delighted, I put it back in the bowl. I wasn't sure what moved me more deeply, that Peter had gone to all this work or that he seemed more relaxed with me.

He smiled. "Did I ever show you this?" Grabbing three peaches, he began to juggle them. I bit back a protest—fearing he would drop that luscious fruit and bruise it. Instead, Peter tossed them in a complicated arc five or six times before catching them deftly.

"You never told me you could juggle. Where'd you learn to do that?"

Looking embarrassed, Peter sat down. "It's a long story."

"Tell me."

He sighed. "Some Saturdays when Dad had to work, Mom would drag me to the tennis club in his place. I hated it. With my big feet, I felt like a clumsy ox. Anyway, there was a cute girl from school who showed up one day, and I tripped flat on my face right in front of her. So I taught myself to juggle to prove I wasn't a total klutz."

"What happened? Did you ever ask her out?"

"Yes." The pain in his voice warned me what was coming. "Her name was Eileen. She's the girl I lived with in college."

"Oh." I hesitated but felt compelled to ask, "Why did you break up with her?"

He shook his head. "It doesn't matter."

"Please, tell me."

Peter slumped in his lawn chair. "I came home one day and found out she'd left me for a friend. She'd been sleeping with him for a while."

"Oh, Peter." I pressed a hand to my throat. "I'm sorry. You deserved better than that."

"It was a long time ago." He turned slightly away. "We should eat before the concert starts. Do you want me to open the wine?"

"Sure." Watching his shuttered face, I ached with remorse for having repeated Eileen's treachery, but this was much too public a place to say so.

Just before the concert, two young women settled in the space next to our blanket. The heavyset girl was on crutches and had one leg in a cast. She wore spiked hair, a baggy black shorts outfit, and a studded black leather cuff. The thin girl wore black spandex bicycle shorts and a hot pink tank top that clashed with her carroty hair. Each ankle was tattooed with a Native American medallion.

The concert began. The orchestra was in a glass-fronted pavilion about a football field away from us; I couldn't see the musicians from where we sat, but people stood at the windows to watch. The first piece was a Mozart overture I recognized from the movie *Amadeus.* Bored, I glanced at the two women and saw that with the coming of dusk, they had started to hold hands. I looked away.

Hot shame settled on me as I forced myself to confront the knee-jerk revulsion I felt toward homosexuals. It was based on what I'd been taught, not my personal experience. Devin had rescued me—and I'd never even thanked him. The realization of my own ingratitude deepened my sense of chagrin. *I should send him a card, let him know how much he helped me. He deserves that much.*

After the Mozart, Dvořák's romance for violin began. To my surprise, the music grabbed me right away; I visualized peasants dancing in a deep forest, near streams that trickled over mossy stones. Sliding down, I rested my head on the back of the lawn chair and gazed at the tree branches arching overhead. A small spotlight shone upward, highlighting some leaves in bright silver green and casting others into green-black shadow. The texture of the bark was thrown into sharp relief: silver ridges and black canyons. Beyond the leaves, the sky was indigo satin.

Then a plane flew overhead, winking its red light through the leaves and breaking the enchanted, timeless spell of the place. I smelled melted wax from Peter's candle.

The music ended. All around us, people began to talk and to stroll the path to the concession stands and bathrooms. The sudden buzz was disorienting.

"Like the concert?" Peter asked.

"Yes," I said and meant it.

The young woman on crutches struggled to her feet. Her friend helped her and then asked, "Want me to come?"

"No." The heavyset girl hobbled off.

Staring after her companion, the redhead lit a cigarette. The flare from the match illuminated her expression, a mixture of fierce protectiveness and longing.

Seeing one woman gaze that way at another was unsettling yet familiar. Suddenly, I remembered my college friend Liz watching Ann Marie with similar yearning. "Oh, my God!"

"What's wrong?" Peter asked.

"Nothing, I just figured out something from watching a couple over there."

"Which one?"

Scooting closer to him, I lowered my voice. "Those women. Watching them made me realize one of my college friends was a lesbian."

"Katie!" His whisper was shocked. "You shouldn't make such assumptions."

"Oh, Peter, they were holding hands. And I know I'm right about Liz too. I never understood why she was so possessive of her roommate till now. If you'd seen her face when Ann Marie got engaged, you'd know I was right."

"You sound awfully sympathetic."

His sharp tone jolted me. "You forget, I know what it's like to be at Zebulun, loving someone who's forbidden."

Peter's face softened. "Yes, I guess you do."

I didn't respond. *Forbidden.* The word sent my thoughts scurrying down a new path. Being forbidden was a trait shared by Ritchie, Ed,...*and Peter*.

Frowning, I pushed the thought away, but it refused to leave. I'd fallen in love with Peter in part *because* he was off limits; it was just dumb luck that he turned out to be such a good man. When we married, I quickly became bored. No, not bored so much as disbelieving that anyone would love me, let alone treat me well. What I expected from men was hurt and...

Abandonment. Just like that, I was a child standing on a dark country road, waiting for a father who was never coming home to me again.

No! My entire body tensed in an effort to reject the association. Lowering my head, I breathed deeply and tried to force the anger—the up-till-now denied rage at my father—back into its dark closet. The effort left me shaken.

"Are you all right?"

I looked up, so lost in a maze of emotion that I wondered who was speaking. Peter smiled, and I felt a rush of relief at finding an exit from the labyrinth. "I love you," I said.

He smiled. "I love you too. You know, I've been thinking. It might be fun to go camping."

Reaching for his hand, I said, "Great. I'm looking forward to it."

"*What* do you think?" Peter asked as I toured the house he wanted to buy.

"It's nice." It was a brick-and-stone, ranch-style house, larger than Peter's current place. The house had a combined living room and dining room, with a field-stone fireplace at the living room end. It had three bedrooms and two bathrooms, one *en suite* with the master bedroom. The kitchen had been recently remodeled. The only major flaw was that the roof needed replacing.

"Wait," Peter said. "I haven't shown you the best part."

A patio door led from the kitchen to a deck. Flower boxes on the railing held yellow marigolds and red geraniums. Taking my hand, Peter led me into the yard, down a winding path bordered with hostas, and through a hedge to where a huge weeping willow stood. About fifteen feet away flowed a creek crossed by an arched footbridge. A bench, angled to face the bridge, stood near the willow.

Sitting on the bench, I gazed around me. Obviously, Peter chose this place with my childhood home in mind—but this land was more rolling than the glacier-shaved fields I was used to, and the creek, although similar to the one bordering my mother's yard, was no replacement for my beloved river.

"I know it will be hard," he said, "with me living here before you do. Whenever you do move in, you'll probably feel it's my house just like you did before. But when that day comes, we can decorate together."

I looked him in the eye. "You think it'll be a long time, don't you?"

He turned pink. "I don't know."

Glancing back at the creek, I chewed my lower lip—a habit I was trying to break but still resorted to when I felt stressed. "Once you move, you're going to be busy with your new job. We'll never see each other."

"You can come for weekend visits." Before I could read anything into that, he added, "There are plenty of bedrooms."

"Sure," I said but inwardly told myself, *Don't cry. Not till you're alone.*

Peter checked his watch. "We should go."

"Will you be able to handle the payments on just your salary?"

"I think so. I had some equity built up, so I can make a good down payment."

Standing, I took one last look at the willow. "Then go ahead with the offer."

Two days later, I borrowed Cori's car and drove down to the Theakia River, parking on Eagle Island Road where I used to jog. The riverbank was deserted except for one elderly African American holding a fishing rod and sitting in a lawn chair close to the water. He was thin, with wrinkled skin dark as ebony, and he wore a black cowboy hat. Next to him was a large cooler with a beer can sitting on top of it.

I nodded to him as I got out of the car. "Hello," he said.

The smells of mud and alcohol were in the air, and a bee buzzed near the beer can. Feeling like an intruder, I walked to a river birch at the edge of the bank and touched its peeling bark. About five feet out, a half-rotted piling created eddies in the current.

The old man spoke, "You're the girl who used to jog hereabouts, ain't you?"

Startled, I turned. "Yes, I've been away."

"The old Theakia." He drew out the syllables—Tay-AH-kee-uh—and chuckled. "She sure is a pretty river. Looks like you've been missing her."

I nodded and turned back to the water, storing up images for the future. "I might relocate to Wisconsin soon."

"Mm, mm," the old man murmured. "The way folks move around now."

"I don't want to," I said and, in that moment, realized something. I wasn't like my father in this. Wandering held little allure for my soul. I was a homebody at heart—like my mother. "I love this place. I grew up here. But my husband has a new job."

"And your place is with him. Glad to see a young woman what knows her wifely duty." His voice was approving now, as warm and thick as gravy. "You know, the old Theakia, she won't change. She's been watering the land since long before the people came. You come back and see her sometime. She'll be here just like always."

"Yes," I answered, picturing the waves of people who had inhabited this land: Potawatomi, French trappers, German and Irish railroad workers, African Americans who'd migrated from the South for factory work. The river would always be here, but I wouldn't. My home was with Peter.

"Well, good-bye." I extended my arm to the old man.

When he took my hand, his palm was rough and dry. "God bless."

On the last Monday of July, Peter took me to the Chicago Historical Society, housed in a wide Federal-style brick building with pedimented windows and a massive central portico that faced east, overlooking Lincoln Park. We started in the Chicago history wing where I was disappointed to find that the display on the great fire took up only a corner of a room instead of a whole gallery. In a glass case were artifacts from the fire: melted coins, nails, and marbles; a stack of warped and scorched plates; a fancy doll saved from the inferno in the arms of a little girl. On the wall was a black and white map of the city with the burnt area highlighted in faded red. After examining the exhibits, we entered a tiny theater to see a slideshow about the fire.

Later, moving through the American history galleries, we came to the Civil War room. In addition to the expected letters, battle flags, pictures, and weapons were two items that commanded my attention: the table on which Abraham Lincoln had drafted the Emancipation Proclamation and the bed in which he died. "Imagine, the actual furniture," I murmured.

"You haven't lost your awe of him, have you?"

I bristled at Peter's amusement. "Why should I? He was a great man."

"But hardly a saint whose relics need veneration. The Emancipation Proclamation was part of military strategy, not a moral edict."

"I know that." I stared at the short bed, envisioning how they'd had to lay Lincoln across it diagonally. "Peter, I believe God intended the war to be about abolition all along, but the North didn't have the will to fight for it. So God allowed the first half of the war to go well for the South. Then after Lincoln issued the proclamation, the tide turned. That can't be coincidence. God turned the great evil of that war to good, and Lincoln was his instrument."

He turned to stare at me. "I've never heard you talk about God like that. Usually, you make him sound like a wrathful judge."

"I guess my sense of him has changed. The relationship with Ed was so terrible, I wanted to kill myself, but something stopped me." I paused, afraid to mention the uncanny man who had rescued me, the man I had come to think of as my guardian angel. He was still my secret. "I think God used my despair to send me running to a place of healing. The worst experience of my life led to the most good. Only God could accomplish that."

Peter put an arm around me. "You sound like you've had a conversion experience."

The observation made me laugh with pleasure. "Maybe I have."

After the museum, we drove a few blocks north to Lincoln Park Zoo and entered through the east gate. Peter led me down a wide walkway to a green, octagonal café with a bright red metal roof topped by a green cupola. We ordered hot dogs, potato chips, and Pepsis. At the condiments table, I stopped Peter from putting ketchup on his hot dog; my Chicago coworkers had taught me that doing so was anathema. Once we'd dutifully lathered on mustard, onions, and relish, he carried our tray to a green marble table facing the seal and sea lion pool on the other side of the walkway, although the crowds gathered around the iron railing to watch a feeding kept us from seeing the animals.

"I'm glad you liked the historical society," he said.

"I did, but I don't think they're making the best use of their assets."

"What do you mean?"

Noise bubbled all around us: the applause of spectators at the seal pool, the shrieks of a baby being strolled past us, the rapid Spanish of the family at the next table. I leaned forward so Peter could hear. "Take the exhibit on the Chicago Fire. The slide show was good, but the rest of the display was pitiful. There must have been millions of artifacts from the fire, and they had hardly anything. And the map was so dull. Did you see how bored kids were going through that room?"

Peter tore open his potato chip bag. "What would you do differently?"

"For one thing, I'd give a better representation of the damage caused by the fire. I'd make a big model of the city—"

"Like the battle scene your father was building."

"Sort of." I suddenly had an image of how it could be. "Wait. I've got a better idea." I moved my lunch off the green tray.

"I don't even know if this is possible, but suppose the model is made in sections, each one on a rotating plate." I held up the tray and put my hand inside the raised rim. "On this side you glue models of the buildings before the fire." Flipping the tray over, I laid my hand flat on the bottom. "On this side, you glue models of the same buildings burning, maybe lit from inside. First, you see the city before the fire. As the fire spreads, plates start flipping over so the burning buildings are up. It'd be mechanical animation like in the fancy Christmas windows downtown."

Peter stared at the tray a few seconds before comprehension hit. "Like a deck of cards spread face down, their edges barely overlapping." He swept his hand over the table. "When you flip the first card, you start a chain reaction, and they all flip so they're face up."

"Sort of. Only it might not work in a linear sequence. You'd have to program it to replicate the course of the fire."

Gazing into space as though he could actually see the model, Peter nodded. "It'd cost a lot, but it would be pretty exciting."

I smiled at the praise and then caught my breath as a new vista opened up before me. "Peter, how do people get jobs working in museums?"

"I suppose they get a degree in museum studies." He looked at me curiously. "Why? Are you interested?"

"I might be," I hedged, afraid he might scoff.

"You'd be perfect for a job like that."

My mind raced ahead to the future—going to grad school, finding work in a museum—but where in those plans was Peter? Stricken, I stared at him. "What will happen to us if I go away to grad school?"

Peter blinked and, for an instant, looked as worried as I felt. Then he said, "Maybe they offer that degree at one of the UW campuses. We won't be far from Madison. Or Milwaukee."

"Maybe." Relieved, I sat back. "And if not, we'll think of something else. Won't we?"

The question came out more plaintively than I intended, and Peter reached over to squeeze my hand. "Of course."

I smiled at him and bit into my hot dog.

After lunch, we strolled down a winding path past a small pond built for swans and then around a larger waterfowl lagoon. I paused to admire a flock of Chilean flamingos, which were not solid pink as I'd always imagined but variegated from the softest blush to the deepest coral. The next area we passed was an outdoor habitat with a herd of zebras and their young.

As the afternoon wore on, the temperature rose to ninety-five, and the heat pressed down on us like a flat iron. We fled the burning sun by ducking into the lion house, a tall building with a high arched entrance ornamented with an impressive mosaic of lions that reminded me of the Ishtar Gate even though these mosaics were not as colorful as the Babylonian art had been. I was looking forward to seeing the big cats, but within minutes of entering, the rank urine smell drove us back outside.

A little girl strolled by with a rocket-shaped popsicle: blue on the bottom, white in the middle, red on top. I tugged Peter's arm. "Look! Bomb pops. When I was a kid, we used to buy those at Jake's. Can we get some?"

Peter grinned. "Why not?"

He walked to a nearby vendor's cart and bought two. Tearing the paper off his, Peter took a large bite. I licked mine slowly as we passed the giraffe yard. The tall stately creatures stood by a tree, munching leaves from the top branches. I hesitated before confessing, "I've always liked giraffes. They made me feel better about being so tall and gawky."

"You're not gawky. You're elegant." Peter shook his head. "That's something I've never understood. Why don't you know how beautiful you are?"

Feeling a rush of heat that had nothing to do with the weather, I shrugged. "I was too different. The other kids teased me."

Peter stroked my cheek and said, "Come on. I'll show you my favorite animal."

My heart pounded wildly as I followed him. When he touched me, I'd ached for him to kiss me in spite of the crowds around us. Sometimes it felt like God was punishing me for my earlier sexual coldness toward Peter by making him the reluctant one now.

We went down a ramp to a concrete wall with a large window giving an underwater view of a turquoise pool in which a polar bear was swimming. The bear kicked off a side wall, glided past the window, rose to the surface, took a breath, swam to the wall, and kicked off again.

Noticing his cramped quarters, I exclaimed, "Oh, Peter. All these animals cooped up for our amusement. It makes me feel helpless." I moved to the window and pressed my hands against the glass. "Like their confinement traps us somehow."

"I know." We gazed at each other in one of those strained silences that assailed us so easily now. Then he glanced at his hands. "I'm sticky from the popsicle. I need to go rinse off."

"OK." I followed him back up the ramp and onto the main path. As he walked over to the nearest water fountain, I gazed into the crowd and felt my heart lurch.

There was a man, slim and a bit taller than average, dressed in jeans and a light denim work shirt. He was walking away, so I couldn't see his face, but his hair was dark gold, and he moved with an unusual rolling gait that I hadn't seen in eighteen years. "Daddy," I whispered.

The childhood conviction that my father wasn't really dead seized me. For this to be my father was impossible, I knew that, but the man was moving out of sight into the crowd, and I felt compelled to follow. Releasing the railing, I broke into a run.

"Katie!" Peter called from behind me.

"I'll be back," I answered without turning to look at him. The man was alone, and he walked so fast that even with my long legs, I had trouble catching up. He headed past the elephant yard toward the west exit.

I burst through the exit about thirty seconds after him. Dozens of people milled about the bright formal gardens to the left but not the man I sought. Before me stood the glass-domed Lincoln Park Conservatory. I glimpsed blue denim disappearing through its doors.

After running through the entrance, I halted on a red concrete path, scored to look like flagstones. In here it was as hot as outside and more humid. The room was filled with palms and tropical plants whose big glossy leaves blocked the glass roof overhead. Rushing around a curve in the path, I came upon a set of doors.

The next room was filled with ferns. Here the cement floor was wet, and water trickled. The man seemed to have vanished. The heat and the oppressive air made it difficult to breathe. Putting a hand to my breastbone, I inhaled and felt as though a sopping washrag was wrapped around my lungs. Although I felt queasy, I hurried through a door in the opposite wall.

In the next room, the man I'd been following was examining a cactus garden. He looked nothing like my father. He had a shaggy mustache, bulging dark brown eyes, and a fleshy nose.

My spirit crashed. Still breathing hard, I walked past him through yet another door. Directly before me was a kidney-shaped pond surrounded by flowering plants. I reeled back and turned left, sinking onto a bench. Around me were geraniums, begonias, and other plants I didn't recognize. Sudden chills made me shudder. Sensing something behind me, I glanced over my shoulder and saw several tall spikes of ruffled blooms. Then they vanished.

My mind filled with images of flowers: a blanket of red roses, a basket of purple mums, a white pot of pastel gladioli. I forced myself to stare at a real pink geranium, trying to banish the visions or memories or whatever they were. That was when the voices began.

"Where's my daddy?"

"He's in that box, Kathleen."

Shutting my eyes, I saw a closed casket with a dull grey finish and a covering of roses as my grandmother went on, "The minister's going to talk, and then we'll drive out to the cemetery."

"But Mommy said I could tell him good-bye. Why can't I see Daddy?"

"Hush." The memory was so vivid that my adult self could hear what the child had been unable to discern: my grandmother's urgency in trying to quiet me. "You can't see him. The coffin is already closed."

"Why? I'm going to ask Mommy to make them open it."

"No." Grandma Brigitte grabbed my arm so tightly that it hurt. "Your father was in a bad accident. His face...doesn't look right."

The horror that those words had evoked swept over me once more. I saw again the vision my vivid imagination had conjured: my father's adored face suddenly become a Frankenstein's monster. Covering my face with my hands, I began to rock back and forth on the bench. I heard footsteps on the concrete and doubled over so I wouldn't have to face whoever stood there. Through my fingers, I glimpsed a pair of cowboy boots.

"Miss, are you all right?"

Afraid that if I spoke I'd lose control, I nodded. As he left, I was sucked back into the vortex of the past. I heard the murmur of voices, whether visitors to the conservatory or mourners at a long-ago funeral, I didn't know. The scent of flowers nearly gagged me.

Then a familiar voice said my name, and I flung myself into Peter's arms.

"Sweetheart, what is it?"

"My father." My voice thickened with tears. "I saw someone who reminded me of him and followed him here. Then...I remembered the funeral. I *was* there, and something happened that frightened me."

His embrace tightened as if to protect me. "Do you want to talk about it?"

"Not here. When we're back in my room, I'll tell you then."

"All right, sweetheart." Peter released me from his hug but kept one arm around my waist. "Let's get you out of here."

Carrying two sweating glasses of iced tea, I entered my basement room. Although a heat wave had stifled the area for two weeks and the upper stories of the house felt like an oven, it was relatively cool down here. "I hope the weather is nicer in Wisconsin." I handed a glass to Peter, who sat at the table listing things to take on our camping trip.

As I rested an arm on the back of his chair, I could smell his faintly musky scent and see his blond end-of-day stubble. Resisting the urge to kiss his neck, I asked, "Where's the campground?"

He reached for a map of Door County and pointed with his pen. "On the lake side, about halfway up the peninsula."

"Lem said I can borrow his tent."

Peter laid down his pen. "Katie, why don't you sit down?"

I went to sit at the opposite side of the table. "What's wrong?"

"Nothing. I was thinking maybe we wouldn't need two tents." He stared down at his papers. "Mine's pretty big. There's plenty of room for two sleeping bags. As long as we both understand that nothing's changed."

"You mean, don't get my hopes up." Sarcasm barbed my tone.

He flushed. "You said you understood."

Staring at my hands, I muttered, "I'm tired of feeling like a leper."

"I don't think I treat you like a leper. But maybe this trip isn't a good idea."

"Why not? What are you afraid of?"

Peter pushed back from the table and walked a few steps away. "Nothing."

"Only touching me."

He turned to face me. "I touch you. Haven't we had more physical contact lately?"

"Physical contact? You make it sound like a football game. Don't you think I can tell you're just going through the motions?"

"Yeah? Well, now you know how it feels."

I reared back, then caught myself and sighed to expel my anger. "I guess I deserve that. It's just that my whole life I've been brainwashed that sex is bad, and now that I'm starting to get over it, you don't want me."

"Shit." Peter came closer and grabbed his chair back. "It's not that simple."

His expression was odd, something other than the repugnance I expected. "If you told me what you were feeling..."

At once, he shook his head. "There's nothing to tell."

I felt like pounding him to break through his defenses. If he didn't intend to have sex, why not sleep in separate tents? Then, with a lightning bolt of intuition, I understood. He was scared. It was written all over him, in the tense angle of his head and the way he avoided my eyes. He *did* want to sleep with me but was afraid, and sharing a tent was as far as he could go.

"All right, Peter. We'll take one tent."

The first night of the trip, Peter lay staring at the indigo triangle of night visible through the netting that covered the tent opening. They'd arrived in Door County about 3:00 PM and set up camp at a site located on a rocky margin of shore, next to a short pier extending into Lake Michigan. About a hundred yards north, just beyond a stand of trees, stretched a smooth, sandy beach. As soon as they put up the tent, they had gone for a swim.

The memory keeping Peter awake now was of Katie in her swimsuit. Made of a shimmery purple fabric, it had high-cut leg openings, a plunging back, and a low-cut sweetheart neckline. She looked like a model in *Sports Illustrated's* swimsuit edition.

Turning restlessly, Peter peered to see if Katie were still awake. When she didn't stir, he eased out of his sleeping bag, quietly unzipped the mosquito netting, and slipped out of the tent.

Memories of that afternoon pursued him into the dark clearing. When Katie had taken off her robe and revealed the suit, Peter felt an erection coming on. He rushed into the lake before she could notice.

At first, they kept to themselves, each acclimating to the still-cold water by swimming short distances. After a few minutes, Katie glided underwater close to Peter. Breaking the surface, she splashed him and swam away.

After traveling about twenty feet, Katie stopped and stood in waist-deep water. She was laughing as Peter reached her. "Doesn't this make you feel like a kid?"

"Uh, sure." He finger-combed his dripping hair. *A kid* was the last thing he felt like. Standing so close to Katie, Peter couldn't help but notice her breasts rising and falling with each breath, looking as though they would burst free of the suit at any moment.

He rubbed his arms as if cold. "I'm going back to camp."

Wordlessly, she returned with him. They spent a quiet evening eating smoky hamburgers cooked over an open fire, listening to the crackle of burning logs, and avoiding the one topic on both of their minds. Katie had been the first to go to bed.

Now, pacing in the dark clearing, Peter was besieged by fantasies of what might have happened. He should have led her onto the beach to make love like Burt Lancaster and Deborah Kerr in *From Here to Eternity.* He should have— But who was he kidding?

Stopping by the bush where their damp bathing suits hung, Peter stroked Katie's and tried to remember how it felt to caress her skin. Recall was impossible. With an aching heart, he took down the suit, scrunched it between his hands, and buried his face in it.

Saturday I woke at dawn with a desperate longing to be in my own bed. I felt horribly lonely, waking in a strange tent, listening to Peter breathe, and wondering if he would act as aloof as he had the day before.

As I walked to the bathrooms a quarter mile down the road, I reminded myself that Peg had warned this might happen: "Spending a weekend together raises the stakes considerably. Don't be surprised if Peter puts up defenses."

Don't overreact, I told myself. *Show Peter that you're in this for the long haul.*

By the time I finished showering, I'd persuaded myself that holding my temper would be an exercise in love. On the walk back, I focused on the beauty of the morning: the cloudless azure sky, the shining beads of dew on the foliage, the plaintive coo of a mourning dove.

I turned off the road into our campsite and halted. A fox was nosing around the picnic table. It froze and glanced at me sideways, not daring to face me directly. The creature's narrow face was alert; its fur was the burnished auburn of just-turned oak leaves; its slender feet wore white socks. After a suspended moment, it darted into the brush.

As Peter and I ate breakfast, I described the encounter. "I've never been so close to a fox. It felt magical."

Peter stood and scraped half his oatmeal into the garbage bag. "Glad this trip could offer you some kind of *wild life.* I know you got used to that."

I stared at him open mouthed as he stalked away. Even though I tried to shrug off his remark, its malice ate inexorably through my defenses. A voice inside me cried, *You're not being fair.* But, of course, he was. What had he said but the acid truth?

When Peter came back, he was withdrawn, and he remained so throughout the day, no matter how persistently I tried to engage him in conversation. Finally, I could stand it no longer. When he drove into town to buy bratwurst for supper, I stayed behind to walk on the beach.

By the time I returned, Peter was standing at the Coleman stove, checking a pot in which he was simmering the bratwurst in beer before grilling them. "Would you bring me another bottle?" he asked.

I opened the cooler and discovered two six-packs with four bottles already gone. "Why so much? You said you need only a little beer for the brats."

Peter wiped off his forehead with the back of his hand, grabbed the bottle I offered, flipped off the cap, and took a swig. "The rest is to drink."

"But I don't drink beer. I can't stand the taste."

As Peter turned back to his pot of bratwurst, he muttered, "Yeah, and I know just who developed your taste."

My patience snapped. "You have something you want to say to me?"

"No."

"You've been mad all day. Don't you think we should talk about it?"

He turned and pointed his tongs at me. "Here it comes, another lecture on honesty and openness. Sweetheart, I don't need it. Not from you." His face was scornful. "When it comes to your fling with Marsden, you haven't told me diddly. But he's there between us all the time. And I'll be damned if I let you turn me into his clone."

"Have you gone crazy? What makes you think I want you to be like him?"

"You're different, that's why. You want things from me you never wanted before."

Stunned, I sank onto the picnic table bench. Peter stood by the stove with his face angled away from me, avoiding my eyes as the fox had that morning. I'd never suspected that he thought I was measuring him against Ed's "prowess." No wonder he was scared to touch me. "It wasn't the way you think."

"Yeah? So tell me about it."

I covered my mouth with my hand and wondered, *Now what?* I could walk away, I could stonewall, I could lie, but Peter's suspicion would always be there.

"OK," I said at last, "but you won't like it." Despite the shame that threatened to press me into the dirt, I took a deep breath and told him everything—the night in Ed's apartment, the handcuffs, the plan to share me with Cody—everything but the words of betrayal I'd spoken on the videotape.

As I spoke, Peter's expression changed from anger to disbelief to horror. His reaction showed me how far from him I'd traveled and how irrevocably Ed had marked me. On his own, Peter would never think up the depravity I had described—described, hell, I'd lived through.

Peter laid down his tongs, turned the flame off under the bratwurst, walked over to a tree, and leaned his forehead against the trunk. "God damn it!" He pounded the bark and whirled to face me. "I'll kill him. I'll—" He clenched both fists, and then his whole body sagged. Tearing off his glasses, he put one forearm over his eyes and began to cry. "I didn't know," he choked out. "I thought he...tired of you... turned verbally abusive. Nothing like this."

A minute must have passed before he took his arm down from his face and said in a hoarse voice, "How could you let him do those things?"

I sighed. "It's hard to explain. He's good at controlling people. He's very persuasive, and he knows how to probe for weakness. Once I let him set the stakes—'Do what I say, or I'll destroy your marriage' —I was trapped."

"I don't buy that. You had a choice."

"Of course, I had lots of choices. But I was vulnerable and confused, and I looked to the wrong person for friendship." I shook my head. "I don't expect you to understand. You'd never think of using people like that. Ed does it all the time. He knows exactly what kind of woman to go after and how to get her to do what he wants, little by little."

"You make him sound so evil."

"Evil." I wondered what the word really meant. "Maybe. He's certainly a sadist."

Peter sat on the picnic table bench next to me. "It's incredible. You read about people like that, but you never expect them to seduce your wife."

"It wasn't about seduction. It was power and control. It was seeing how far he could push me. If I *had* killed myself, I think it would have been just another achievement for him."

The more I talked, the more I felt the impossibility of conveying what a master manipulator Ed was. Then I noticed Peter staring at my hands. Reaching out, he stroked the still-pink scar on my inner wrist. "Did he do that?"

"The handcuffs did."

Peter jerked back. "My God. He really hurt you."

I took his arm. "It's over. I broke free."

He shook his head. "I don't get it. If it was as bad as you say, I'd expect you to hate the very idea of having sex again. But you seem..."

"Like I want it." How could I explain something I didn't fully understand myself? "I know I didn't respond before. That doesn't mean I didn't want sex. I was screwed up from the way I was raised and from the rape, and I thought I had to hide my sexual feelings. Ed sensed that and promised to help me get over my inhibitions. He didn't, of course, but he did force me to admit my desires and frustrations." I twisted my rings. "I've been trying to imagine what a healthy sexual relationship might be like, but...maybe it's too late for us."

"Because of the way I've been acting?"

"No, because of what I just told you. Doesn't it change things?"

Tilting up my chin, Peter gazed solemnly into my eyes. "I don't like what I heard, but it doesn't make me love you any less."

Ducking my head, I began to cry.

"Sweetheart, don't." The old endearment made me cry harder. "Katie, please. Of course, I wish it hadn't happened, but I'm glad you finally told me."

A tightening of my throat made it hard to speak. I squeezed his hand and managed to say, "I thought you'd hate me."

He sighed. "Right now, it's hard to know exactly what I feel, but I don't hate you. To be honest, I think you hurt yourself more than you hurt me."

Humbled by his compassion, I began to tremble. Peter pulled me into his arms and stroked my hair. "I'll never betray you again," I whispered fervently. "I swear it."

Peter woke as the first light brought color to the nylon tent walls, slowly brightening them from grey to teal. Katie was curled up beside him. Last night, they'd pushed their sleeping bags together and hugged, clinging to each other like abandoned children. This morning, however, Peter found no comfort in her nearness. Instead, she sucked all the oxygen from the air.

Crawling out of the tent, he went to sit on the pier, dangling his feet over the water and watching the sky paint its face with cosmetics of rose and gold. *Like a whore,* he thought.

Peter hugged himself. What should he do? He'd been surprised to wake to a feeling of revulsion, to a sense that Katie was irreparably soiled like a beach polluted by an oil spill. As he wondered if he could ever bear to make love to his wife again, a lake breeze blew cool in his face. At the same moment, a quiet voice in the back of his mind said, "Though your sins be as scarlet..." With it came a presence: old and wise, infinitely loving.

Instantly, Peter's heart calmed. "Though your sins be as scarlet," he whispered, "they shall be white as snow." *Forgiveness.* That was the heart of the matter. God had forgiven Katie; in his eyes, she was as pure as if she had never known Ed. And God was offering to forgive Peter too for his hardness of heart and unwillingness to start over.

But how could he ever forget what had happened or want to sleep with her again? Again Peter sensed that hovering presence, recognized the gentle understanding and amused patience of a loving father toward a timid child.

I don't have to figure everything out. Just believe that reconciliation is possible. He resolved to ask Katie to move to Wisconsin with him, even if it meant having separate bedrooms. They would know when the time was right to reconsummate their marriage. Standing, he decided to shower, to take Katie out to breakfast, and to ask her formally like a second proposal.

Cautiously, he unzipped the mosquito netting and reached into the tent for his toiletry kit and towel. Katie still slept soundly, whistling a little as she exhaled. Peter smiled and backed out of the tent.

As he walked down the road, he found himself humming. Peter turned down the path to the showers, housed in a cinderblock building with a tin roof. There he discovered that he wasn't the only early bird. Eight men stood in line, all of them with military-short haircuts. A few were reading the Bible as they waited. Oddly, no one was using the women's shower. Peter joined the end of the line. "Busy place."

"We're a men's church group on retreat," said the person ahead of him, a grey-haired man with skinny shanks below the hem of his robe.

"Yeah," said the balding, chinless man who was next in line. "We want to get to Al Johnson's restaurant for Swedish pancakes before we go to church."

"Oh," Peter said. "Well, I guess I'll come back later."

As he walked back to camp, he crossed Al Johnson's off his list of places for breakfast. It was a shame. The place was a Door County tradition: a Swedish log house with live goats grazing on a sod roof. Well, they could go to White Gull Inn for Door County French toast, stuffed with cherry cream cheese and topped with locally grown cherries. The thought made him hungry. In the meantime, he was going to clean up far away from that group of fundamentalists.

I *woke,* yawned, glanced at Peter's empty sleeping bag, and was surprised to see he was already up. As I wondered where he was, I heard humming. I crawled to the door of the tent and peered outside. Peter lifted a kettle off the Coleman stove and poured water into a basin on the picnic table. Intrigued, I settled onto my stomach and rested my chin on folded hands. Peter removed his faded purple T-shirt and sponged off his torso.

He was thinner than he used to be, and his belly had lost its flabby softness. Standing half naked in the golden morning light, he looked like a heroic figure in a painting.

Peter picked up a can of shaving cream, squirted a blob into his hand, and spread it on his face. Then he walked to the car, bent to look in the rearview mirror, and scraped a razor down his cheek. When I imagined the lubricated smoothness of his skin, I felt an answering moistness in my vagina. Was he planning a morning rendezvous as he had on our honeymoon?

Wriggling my pelvis deeper into the down sleeping bag, I warned myself, *Don't get your hopes up.* Then Peter waltzed over to the picnic table and swished his razor in the basin of water with a flourish.

He rubbed his jaw and drew the razor over one section a second time. "Damn," I whispered. He once told me that he never shaved when camping. Why was he being so fastidious if not for me?

Pulling back, I glanced down at my T-shirt, which smelled of smoke from last night's campfire. I scooted to the back of the tent and rummaged in my duffel bag until I found clean underwear, khaki shorts, and a light blue shirt. Quickly, I stripped off the clothes I'd slept in and slipped on the clean underpants. I was shaking the wrinkles from the shirt when I heard the tent zipper behind me. Holding the shirt before my naked breasts, I turned.

With his head tucked down to enter the tent, Peter didn't see me until he was completely inside, kneeling on his sleeping bag. His face turned bright red. "Sorry, I didn't know you were up." He started to back out.

"Wait. Was there something you wanted?"

"Just clean clothes. I was going to suggest that we go out for breakfast."

"Oh." My shoulders sagged under the weight of my disappointment. Then I noticed that Peter was having difficulty not staring at my chest.

Deliberately, I lowered my shirt. After I was sure he'd had a good look, I pulled on the garment but left it unbuttoned.

Peter swallowed hard. "Katie..." Still staring, he rubbed his mouth.

Something told me it was time to push. "Now that you barged in here," I teased, "aren't you going to kiss me good morning?"

He looked at me with fearful eyes. Then leaning forward, he touched his lips to mine.

As my arms went around him, Peter kissed me a second time and placed a hand on my breast. I moaned. I could feel him in his caress, not just his physical body, but Peter himself, his very essence, communicating itself through the mystery of skin-to-skin contact. I was parched ground, eagerly soaking up the water of his attention. Every place he touched me—with his lips, with his hands—I experienced a fresh blossoming of desire.

When Peter entered me and we were moving together, I felt a rhythm and a driving force unlike anything I'd ever known. I reveled in the feeling of him inside me, knowing that his excitement was building to a climax even as mine was. The tension increased until I thought it would send me flying in all directions. I dug my fingers into Peter's back. At that moment, he thrust deep inside me. I shouted as I rocked with tremors, then grew absolutely still. Tears coursed down my face.

"Sweetheart." Peter withdrew and took me in his arms. "Did I hurt you?"

"No." I clung to him. How could I explain that he'd cracked me open like a walnut and entered a secret, lonely place where no one had been before?

"I went too fast. Forgive me."

"No," I said again. "Don't you know what just happened?"

He shook his head.

"I think I had an orgasm."

Peter sat back on his heels. "But you were crying."

"Because it's never happened before. Ever."

A look of wonder spread over his face. Then he met my eyes. "Will you move with me to Wisconsin?"

Throwing my arms around his neck, I cried, "Yes! Oh, Peter, yes!"

His embrace tightened. "You know, it's not suddenly going to be perfect."

"I know." Peg had told me about this too, that once we got back together, there would be ups and downs, even days when it seemed like we weren't going to make it. "Love never is perfect, is it? Anyway, all I want is you."

It was mid-Monday afternoon when Peter parked in front of the Evanston house. I jumped out of the car and reached into the back seat for my duffel bag and borrowed sleeping bag. "I can't wait to tell Cori the news."

Peter, who was walking to the rear of the car, turned to look at me. "What news?"

"Not about *that*. Just that I'm moving."

"Oh." He grinned. Opening the hatchback, he took out the Coleman lantern I had borrowed from Lem.

As we went up the walk, I said, "She doesn't work on Mondays, so maybe she'll be home. Oh, Peter, I'm so happy I want to tell the world."

He tugged my braid. "I know. Me too."

We entered the house, and I dropped my gear at the base of the stairway. Running up two steps at a time, I yelled, "Cori, are you here?"

There was no answer, so I came back down. "Damn. I'll go ask Ellen."

I was halfway down the hall when Ellen came through the kitchen door. She stopped and fidgeted with the tie to her wrap-around skirt. "Cori isn't here. She's down at your grandmother's and asked you to call."

"What's wrong? Has something happened to my mother?" The thought of losing her before we made things right between us terrified me.

"No." Ellen came close and laid a hand on my arm. "I'm sorry. Your grandfather died."

After talking to Cori on the phone, Katie asked Peter in a dazed voice, "The funeral's tomorrow. Can I spend the night at your house?"

"Of course." He reached out to hug her, but she shrugged his arm away. Pushing past him, she grabbed her camping gear and went down to her basement room, where she packed clean clothes, including a black dress. Then they left for Zebulun.

Whenever he started a conversation during the drive, Katie responded with monosyllables. Peter felt growing alarm. He hadn't realized how much he'd come to value her new openness until now, when she reverted to the stone-faced sphinx he'd lived with before.

At the house, she again ducked away when he approached her. "I need a bath. I feel grimy from the trip."

Discouraged, Peter sat on their bed, flipping through a back issue of *The Atlantic* but not seeing the pages. He told himself that Katie's emotional retreat was understandable. Maybe if he helped her feel safe...

After lingering in the tub for an hour, Katie walked into the bedroom. She wore a long white nightgown that clung to her body, making Peter catch his breath. "Feel better?"

"I guess so. I'm awfully tired." Getting into bed next to him, she pushed the magazine to the floor and snuggled by his side. "It's good to be home with you. If I had to face tomorrow alone..."

Peter slid down beside Katie. When she responded by moving closer, he took her in his arms. "I was starting to worry. You were so quiet."

"I'm sorry. I just needed to think for a while."

"About the funeral?"

She shook her head. "No, my grandfather. This probably sounds terrible, but I don't feel much of anything. We weren't close. There was a time after my father died when I wanted Grandpa to pay attention to me. But he didn't."

"Maybe he just didn't see enough of you."

Katie snorted. "Are you kidding? I saw him after school every day but can't remember a single thing he ever said to me. He loved my grandmother and my mother, but the rest of us were like strangers camped out on his lawn."

The jealousy in her voice surprised Peter. "It wasn't your fault he didn't love you."

Pulling half out of his arms, Katie stared at him wide-eyed. "I guess I did blame myself. But I'm angry at him, too. My life might have been so different if he'd reached out to me after my father died. Maybe I wouldn't have gone around looking for love from the wrong men."

Her words knifed open the barely closed scabs of Peter's self-doubt. "Does that include me?"

"Of course not." She sounded annoyed. "Do we have to talk about us right now?"

"I'm sorry. Go back to what you were saying."

Katie didn't answer. Crossing her arms over her chest, she lay back and stared up at the ceiling. *Shit,* Peter thought. *I made her angry.*

After a moment, she asked, "Is it wrong to be mad at the dead?"

"No, sweetheart. I think it's part of the process."

"That's what Peg says. It's easy to be angry at Grandpa, but I don't like feeling that way about my father. I get scared that he can see me, wherever he is, and he'll be hurt that I'm mad at him for leaving me. Because he couldn't help dying, you know?"

"Katie, he loved you. I think he'd be more upset that you were hurting yourself by holding it all in."

She exhaled loudly. "I suppose."

As we drove to the funeral home, I glanced at the clock on the dashboard and felt a rising panic. Earlier while dressing, I had put a run in my stockings so I went out to buy a new pair, taking a half hour I hadn't counted on. "We're late."

"We're fine. We may get there right at ten, but we won't be late. There's the funeral home a block ahead."

As Peter pulled into the parking lot, I bit my lip and stared at the one-story, white stucco building with arched recesses holding classical statues. As I climbed out of the car, I had to check an impulse to run.

Inside the front door, we found ourselves in a hall with gold-flocked wallpaper and red carpeting. A black sign with white letters listed the Walther service in parlor two. Peter took my hand and led me toward the right. Entering the room, we heard soft music.

A grey-haired man in a dark navy suit and gleaming white shirt approached us. Behind him, rows of chairs were filled with mourners. "We're family members. Where should we sit?"

The man clasped his hands at his waist. "But Mrs. Denault said the family was all here."

"Aunt Colleen," I whispered to Peter, not surprised that she had discounted me. To the funeral director, I said, "My aunt made a mistake."

"Yes, well, the service is about to start. There are still seats in the last row."

Feeling chastened, I moved that way, but Peter halted me. "My wife is the eldest grandchild," he said in his sternest voice. "Do you really think she should sit in the back?"

"Oh." The funeral director rubbed his hands together. "Give me a moment."

He went to the second row and, after much whispering, asked a couple I recognized as Colleen's in-laws to move. As Peter and I eased our way to our seats, Aunt Colleen glared at us from the front row. Two seats to her right, my mother sat with her head down. A silver-haired man with a hawk-nosed profile sat beside her, his arm stretched across her shoulders.

My cousin Bernadette sat next to me and held a printed program of the service. Half rising, I felt to see if I'd sat on mine. As I did, my purse slid off my lap and fell to the floor. The noise caused Mother to look around. She smiled weakly at me.

Then she whispered in her companion's ear. He turned to me and nodded. Self-consciously, I returned the acknowledgment.

As Dr. Montoya faced the front again, I gazed at the back of his head and realized I wasn't angry at my mother anymore. In the months since I'd last talked to her, I had torn apart my life piece by piece and, in the process, had stopped caring about her opinion. Or her choices.

People around us began to sing:

I come to the garden alone
while the dew is still on the roses.

I looked toward the casket. The lid was open, but the body didn't look like anyone I'd ever seen. The hair was parted too perfectly, and the freckles were hidden by makeup. There was no sense of the man, none of the vague perplexity that had always seemed the hallmark of my grandfather's personality. This lifeless thing was no more like Albert Walther than a statue in a wax museum would have been. Even though I hadn't been close to him, I felt desolate.

I sat quietly through the reading of a psalm and a poem written by my cousin Rachel, Aunt Dee's only child: "Grandpa Albert, we miss you so. All our hearts are filled with woe." Grandma Brigitte and Aunt Colleen wept so loudly that the rest of the banal poem was mercifully drowned out. My mother sat silent.

Then the pastor rose to speak. He was a total stranger to me, a young man about thirty with wavy brown hair, light blue eyes, and a crooked nose. Leaning close to Peter, I whispered, "Who's that?"

"Didn't I tell you? Pastor Samuelson retired, and we've had a new minister since Easter. His name is Andrew MacDougall."

The young man said, "I stand before you as one who didn't know Albert long. Yet, as I look out at his wife and children and grandchildren, at the coworkers and church members who knew him for so many years, I can see that he led a full life. We are gathered here to mourn the passing of that life.

"Our culture has difficulty responding to death. Some will tell you to rejoice because Albert has gone home to be with our heavenly father. And so he has. Yet we still feel pain at his passing. We believe in eternal life and in Christ's victory over the grave, but that victory doesn't render death any less horrible. Death robs us of the people we love. Didn't Jesus himself weep at Lazarus's tomb?" The pastor paused to sweep his gaze over the mourners and for an instant stared directly into my eyes.

"So we mourn. We cry and grieve because deep in our hearts, we know this is not how God meant the world to be. We were created for life and instinctively believe that life should go on forever. And so it does through faith in our Lord. But first we must weather this difficult separation."

As I listened, something within me loosened, as though the hand that had been squeezing my heart suddenly released it. The war I had been fighting with the world, with the people who told me to cease mourning for my father, was over. At last, someone—if only an earnest stranger—understood. I had been right to hang onto my grief until it ran its course. But now that I had reclaimed the memory of the funeral and wept for my father, now that I had been given public permission for those tears, and most of all, now that I had come to believe that other people loved me, perhaps I no longer needed my self-appointed task of perpetual bereavement.

I turned to Peter, who watched me anxiously. "It's all right," I whispered. "I'm fine."

At the graveside, the family sat on folding chairs and watched in silence as the pall bearers removed first the floral arrangements from the hearse and then the closed casket. The day was blindingly hot. The sun had bleached the August sky as white as paper. I used my last tissue to blot my slick forehead. Sweat drenched the back of my dress. *Maybe I should have gone bare legged,* I thought irreverently.

The cemetery grass was burned as brown as the unirrigated prairie it had once been, except for the emerald sod on a recent grave. My gaze returned to the green rectangle again and again. *Who was laid there? Had they died young?*

Pastor MacDougall stood before the casket. As he opened his Bible, Grandma Brigitte wailed loudly. I pressed my lips together and stared at her without bothering to hide my distaste. Around me, people murmured sympathetically. Why couldn't they see through her manufactured hysterics?

With a jolt, I realized that my thoughts echoed the very things my mother used to say about me. Glancing at Mother, I saw her sitting with a rigid spine and hands clasped tightly in her lap. To one who didn't know her well, she might seem indifferent, but I knew otherwise. I knew how completely my mom had adored her father, and I also knew the exhausting effort it took to push pain deep inside and maintain an impassive mask.

All at once, I felt utterly drained. I tuned out the service and tried to imagine living with Peter in the new house. Instead, I found myself grieving for past memories: Daddy at his workbench, sanding a piece of wood; my grandfather reading *Reader's Digest* in his chair, oblivious to those around him; Ritchie and the innocence of being children, wading in the creek.

The brief service ended, halting my reverie. Aunt Colleen rose, helped Grandma to her feet, and began to lead her to the car. After only a few steps, Grandma jerked free and fell to her knees sobbing.

"Mama!" Colleen shrieked. She turned wildly and called, "Dr. Montoya!"

He looked at my mother, who nodded. As he hurried to assist in calming my grandmother, Mother remained seated, staring straight ahead at the casket.

Standing in the second row, I couldn't take my eyes off her. With

Dr. Montoya attending Grandma, there was no one to comfort her. *No one but me.*

I touched Peter's arm. "Wait here."

After working my way past some cousins, I sat in the chair next to her. "Mom."

She looked at me blankly.

"I'm sorry about Grandpa. I know how much you loved him."

Pain flooded my mother's eyes. "I could have saved him. He had a stroke in July. I begged Mother to take him to the doctor, but she wouldn't listen. If I'd talked to him myself—"

"No!" It came out more emphatically than I intended. I gentled my voice. "It's not your fault."

"I could have tried harder. I could have made him go to a doctor."

"You couldn't make him do anything. He was a grown man."

My mother's sorrow flared into anger. "I don't need your platitudes. You don't know what it's like, wondering if you're to blame."

"Don't I? Don't you think I've lain awake nights, wondering if maybe Daddy was driving too fast because he thought I'd be waiting in the rain?"

Her eyes narrowed. "You always think it revolves around you. Your feelings, your pain. I lost Joe too. He was my husband."

"I know," I said, surprised that I could receive her hostility without retaliating. "I don't think I ever understood how hard it was for you. And now this. You were Grandpa's favorite."

Suspicion darkened my mother's face. "Why are you saying these things? I thought you weren't speaking to me."

"I'm sorry. I was going through a bad time, but I shouldn't have taken it out on you." I touched her arm, but the gesture wasn't enough to bridge the chasm between us. I thought of walking away but decided to try again. "I'm here because I wanted to see if I could help."

"No one can." Mother stared at the casket. "I can't believe he's gone."

"It takes time. Don't you remember?"

As my mother began to weep, I put an arm around her. She leaned heavily against my shoulder while I silently patted her arm. After a few minutes, she wiped her eyes. "I'm glad you're here."

"So am I."

"Are you—" She sniffed and looked at me warily. "Are you back with Peter?"

"Yes." I couldn't keep from smiling. "He wants me to move with him to Wisconsin."

"Oh." Mother's lip trembled, and I wondered if she'd even known about the move.

Glancing to where Dr. Montoya and Peter stood side by side, my mother said, "We should go. It looks like the men already introduced themselves."

"They can wait another minute, Mom. I truly don't want to make today harder than it already is, but there's something I have to know before I move away."

"What?"

I took a deep breath. The question on my mind was more difficult to ask than I'd anticipated. "Would you tell me where Daddy is buried? I'd like to see his grave."

Mother tore at a hangnail on her thumb. After a moment, she said, "I'll take you."

"Are you sure?"

"Yes." She stood and nodded to the left. "This way."

As she began to walk in that direction, I said, "Wait." I went to my grandfather's closed casket, which wouldn't be buried until after the mourners were gone.

Several floral arrangements had been brought to the cemetery from the funeral home. Instead of my usual horror at flowers, I felt only wonder at their fragile loveliness. They no longer symbolized death to me, but rather the extraordinary beauty contained in even the briefest life. Focusing on one perfect, pale pink rose, I gently pulled it from its basket, intending to leave it on my father's grave as a farewell offering. It was time to tell him good-bye.

Acknowledgments

I want to thank everyone who served as a beta reader for this novel in its latest incarnation: Barbara Crowe, Susan Eisenhammer, Pennie Magee, Jana Redlich Neff, and Nina Romano. Each of you added a valuable perspective that helped shape the final product.

My husband, Michael Chatlien, deserves special praise for reading the story more times than either of us can enumerate. We met in a writers' critique group thirty-six years ago, and his insights and encouragement have been essential to keeping me on track with this and every other writing project I have attempted since then.

My deep gratitude goes to two people at my publisher, Amika Press. Jay Amberg read and edited the manuscript with great care and sensitivity, and Sarah Koz understood this story at a deep visceral level that informed her glorious design. I thank them both.

About the Author

Ruth Hull Chatlien has been a writer and editor of educational materials for more than thirty years, specializing in U.S. and world history. She is the author of *Modern American Indian Leaders* for middle-grade readers. Her award-winning first novel, *The Ambitious Madame Bonaparte,* portrays the tumultuous life of Elizabeth "Betsy" Patterson Bonaparte. Her second novel, *Blood Moon: A Captive's Tale,* retells Sarah Wakefield's ordeal as a captive during the Dakota War of 1862. Her most recent novel, *Katie, Bar the Door,* explores a young woman's emotional journey from loss and abuse toward healing.

She lives in northeastern Illinois with her husband, Michael. When she's not writing, she can usually be found gardening, knitting, or spoiling her dog Coco.

Made in the USA
Middletown, DE
01 October 2021